DON'T ASK
DONT TELL

MONTE DUTTON

DON'T ASK DONT TELL

Copyright © 2022 by Monte Dutton

CITIOFBOOKS, INC.
3736 Eubank NE Suite A1
Albuquerque, NM 87111-3579
www.citiofbooks.com
Hotline: 1 (877) 389-2759
Fax: 1 (505) 930-7244

Ordering Information:
Quantity sales. Special discounts are available on quantity purchases by corporations, associations, and others. For details, contact the publisher at the address above.

Printed in the United States of America.

ISBN-13:   Softcover   978-1-959682-15-8
           eBook   978-1-959682-16-5

Library of Congress Control Number: 2022919509

Table of Contents

To all the refugees of newspapers, driven from a respectable living by the alleged Information Age ...

PART ONE
LIVES OF CRIME

CHAPTER 1

Before the Deluge

Mickey Statler started driving in the general direction of *The News-Free Press,* whose Press had been merely free, not news-free, when he had gone to work there twenty years earlier.

He was an award-winning columnist. They put cartoons of him on cardboard squares that were inserted in the machines where papers were circulated at Waffle Houses when football and basketball seasons were about to begin. They gave away tee shirts bearing those same cartoons to lucky subscribers who outpicked him in weekly football contests. *The News-Free Press* had an investment in Mickey Statler. The News-Free Press and Mickey were one and inseparable, now and forever, till death did them part, like bacon and eggs, or politics and corruption, but times were changing, and Mickey had started to fret. If *The News-Free Press's* new owner kept lessening its news, Mickey might be out of a job and going door to door, simulating Halloween 365 days a year, along with the other dozen of his onetime colleagues now trick-or-treating for a living in one way or another.

He carried the morning paper with him to the Starbucks, located inside the Barnes & Noble between his condo and the office. He put *The News-Free Press* on a table, ordered a large Blonde and a cinnamon muffin, and walked around the corner to peruse the magazine rack. There he noticed that Playboy magazine no longer ran photos of women who were fully nude. As he walked back over to the counter to receive his order from the barista, it occurred to him that if nudes weren't available in the pages of *Playboy,* Mickey Statler in *The News-Free Press* might not be too far behind.

As he sat at his table, sipping coffee, scanning idly the events of the previous day, and thumbing his cell for the events of the current one, Mickey's mood improved. After all, he had outlasted nudes in *Playboy.* Stanley Lanier was living in a small house on Lake Lure, trying to make a living with a website that had a stupid name because all the good ones had been taken and copyrighted. Suzie La Fontaine wanted to be a player's agent, and so far she had masterminded the signing of two to Canadian Football League contracts. Ronnie Leggett, once the best racing writer in the Carolinas, had moved off to somewhere in Kentucky, where he might not be growing weed but had texted Mickey that he knew where he could get some. Mickey didn't have anything against it, but the off chance that *The News-Free Press* would be willing to spend the amount of money it would take to drug-test all employees was enough to keep Mickey content with the occasional beer, or six if it was Dollar Draught Night. He had an ex-wife living at the beach, a daughter in college, and not enough of a financial reserve to take any chances.

CHAPTER 2

Mischief

She'd gone off to college on a soccer scholarship but grown tired of soccer about the time she started fancying herself a writer. She'd shown more talent in the classroom than she'd been able to muster on a field of grass, and her perspective on life had begun to change. Where once the team had invaded Tirello's Pizza Buffet after eking out a one-nil conquest of Francis Marion, now her friends gathered at a coffeehouse, arriving there high, playing alt-something on their guitars, reading their poetry to one another, and slipping out for cigarettes on the sidewalk.

When she felt her talents had exceeded her academic opportunities, she had managed to win a grant at a private school, where she longed to swim with larger fish in a smaller pond and champion a new Beat Generation to shake up the staid predictability of an ignorant society. Now she was getting prepared for her first class. What she hadn't divulged yet to her parents was that the extent of her grant was one session of summer school, and it would start draining momentarily. She was unworried. Mom and Dad would find a way. They always did.

Sitting amid the greenery on a concrete bench that would have seemed normal in a cemetery, she lit a Marlboro Light, tilted her head back, and exhaled. The heat of the day was still brewing. A breeze caused the branches on the maple trees to sway and crackle. Four or five others were languishing similarly, all but one as carelessly as she.

She became aware of an ungainly boy, black hair tousled awkwardly, wearing an ill-fitting, white dress shirt and khaki pants. He leaned against one of the trees and kept stealing glances her way. She knew that game. Pretty girls learned that certain boys were aroused by smoking. They watched the way the girl lit her cigarette, what kind of lighter she used, what brand she smoked, how she inhaled and exhaled, studying as if she were somehow their assignment, holding their cells because they wanted to snap her photo if they could do so without her noticing. She kept him at bay by occasionally turning her gaze to him just so he would avert his eyes. She didn't feel insulted. She didn't feel harassed. She thought it hilarious.

He picked up his canvas pack but slung it over only one shoulder and walked toward her. She thought he might be heading to a class in a building behind her.

"Do, do, you, you, mind if I sit d-down?"

A stutter. How charming.

She switched the cigarette to her left hand and extended cheerfully her right. Charming him.

"How do you do? I'm Marcia."

He shook her hand. "Peter."

Marcia took a draw. She left the cigarette hanging as she inhaled and took it back with her right hand. Then she obligingly turned away to exhale a thin stream. He became nervous as he looked mostly at the ground, his head bouncing a little.

"Do you mind if I-I a-ask you a question?" Peter asked.

"Obviously not," she replied, knowing he wouldn't catch the humor

"Do-do you th-think it's coo-ool to …?

"Smoke?"

"Yeah, yeah."

Marcia could see him asking her for one. She looked directly into his eyes, drew hard on the cigarette, inhaled deeply, held it a bit, and attempted to emit rings of smoke, a couple of which remained briefly defined before the breeze dispersed it. The venue wasn't the best.

Then she held what remained of the smoke in front of her, wafts of it clouding the field of vision between them, and said, with mock *gravitas*, "Yes. I do."

She ground out the cigarette with her jogging shoes, picked up her own book bag, said, brightly, "Nice to meet you," and went off to class. Peter was late for his. He was masturbating in a bathroom stall.

Her first lesson came from a pretty girl, shorter than she, who tapped her on the shoulder as she entered the entrance of the classroom building.

"Excuse me."

Marcia stopped and turned around.

"Uh, I just thought I ought to tell you that Triborough is a smoke-free campus."

"Oh," Marcia said.

"I'd die for one. I'm Lana."

"I'm Marcia. And I'm new."

CHAPTER 3

Just the Usual Brand of Absurdity

Mickey Statler walked straight to his mailbox at *The News-Free Press*, and many were the days when all he ever did there was peruse the mail, or, in most cases, throw it away. Mail was already obsolete. The standard mode of interactions – arranging credentials, interviews, photo shoots, etc. – was now electronic. No one even listened to voice messages. Hooking up with a contact required a text message. Actually speaking to another human being was a last resort. Pro athletes, in the unlikely event that they gave a friendly scribe a number, wouldn't actually answer their phones unless they noticed the incoming number was from their agent, drug dealer, or girlfriend, and it wasn't too unusual for two of the three to be the same person.

Nosy types filled newsrooms. Mickey remembered his years of desk duty as the most miserable of his life. He hated the office. He hated to be conducting an interview, knowing full well that others were eavesdropping, listening to what questions he asked and taking them wildly out of context.

Hey, did you hear that question Mickey asked?

Yeah, how lame-ass can that guy be?

Some of the backstabbers merely wanted his job. Mickey could respect that. Ambition was a good thing. A writer needed to aspire to greatness. More often, though, the detractors were the self-important wretches who thought of the rag's writers as undisciplined riffraff, out gallivanting around on expense accounts, running up frequent-flyer miles, and booking expensive hotel rooms. Mickey saw the newsroom, designed as a place to sift through and prioritize, as a humdrum collection of ass-kissers who sat around in meetings half of each day, rubber-stamping stupid ideas so that when, predictably, they failed miserably, it wasn't anyone's individual fault. Survival in the newsroom was learning how to spot what the bosses were going to do anyway and then jockeying for the most-favored brown-nose slot.

The News-Free Press was a miserable place with a miserable excuse of a sports editor. Mickey hadn't let it bother him for a long time. The position changed frequently, and, to Mickey's way of thinking, the reason was never quality.

Mickey had once been a sports editor, back in the days when the position entailed writing. Writing had gone out of style. Now sports editors were clerks, selected for their utter lack of guile and willingness to jump when upper management said so. They went to budget meetings and nodded a lot. They delivered bad news in low-key style. They never raised their voices. Their souls had been broken and testicles figuratively removed. The process had started twenty years earlier. Mickey, known then as now for his columns, had been retitled as News Sports Editor. The most ingratiating desk man, now undoubtedly selling insurance somewhere, had been dubbed Sports News Editor.

The News Sports Editor and the Sports News Editor, together, as a team, created a *News-Free Press* seven nights a week. In time, Mickey had evolved into a Senior Columnist.

Jon David McMahan was the prototype of what management wanted. The job had been conferred him not because of his innovative ideas but because he didn't have the guts to do anything but nod and take orders. He'd been on the job for almost a year, which was about average. Eventually he would be farmed off to a smaller newspaper in the chain, there to be Executive Editor or Publisher because he had demonstrated that he could be counted upon to enforce the harsh edicts from corporate headquarters without balking or offering even mild dissent.

"Hey, Mickey. Good to see you," the mound of Jell-O said.

"J.D. … I just dropped by to go through the mail and get ready for the Legion game tonight," Mickey said.

It was the summertime. Mickey had just gotten back from the Atlantic Coast Conference's preseason football showcase. The next trip out of the county he was scheduled to make wasn't until a football game on Labor Day weekend. He'd taken vacation. All he really had for column fodder was the girl who had apparently proven she could play shortstop at the American Legion level. She didn't get to hit. The pitcher did, and the designated hitter subbed for her. All Mickey had seen was her photograph. As best he could tell, she was cute, though he couldn't vouch for her figure below the neck. He didn't mind. It would be different. He wondered if male chauvinists would boo her. Women were in combat. He wondered if Korean War veterans would mind if the hot little shortstop – good field, no hit – was not only hot and little but also a little hottie. Fans rooted for teams. Writers rooted for stories. Mickey had his hopes up.

"Are you going to be a while?" J.D. asked.

"I got an hour to spare," Mickey said.

"Got your laptop?"

"Yep."

"I need to set you up with I.T."

Mickey got a sinking feeling, the kind that comes with the realization that an hour could not possibly be enough to deal with I.T. Information Technology. If the different departments of The News-Free Press had been castles, I.T. would have had a moat around it. Security was tight, ostensibly because expensive equipment resided there. One had to call before stopping by. The entrance had a speaker and a buzzer that had to be activated from the inside in order to have the door remotely unlocked. The unkempt gamers who worked there could kill two days programming a laptop to respond to a new password. The director couldn't even get in. He had a nice, sun-drenched office in the front of the building, conveniently next door to the publisher, whom he was widely believed to be fucking. Hunter Quilici was his name. Cynthia Boland was hers. Both were married. He was a triathlete with a degree in marketing who had apparently gotten his job because he could create multi-media, power-point presentations on creating effective social-media posts, attention-grabbing video blogs, and, of course, that glory of the modern scribe, slide shows. The seminars were breathtaking. A room full of employees tried not to nod off, while everything on the screen was read aloud in the off chance that anyone who worked at a newspaper might not be able to read.

In the cave, meanwhile, twenty-three-year-olds, most of whom had gotten associates' degrees in the maintenance of electronic devices, having taken four years of work to get two years of education, sat around and played video games, or that was Mickey's suspicion. On those rare occasions when he had been granted access to information central, he had noticed an abundance of action figures and Playstation cartridges for games that apparently involved rescuing princesses with antiquated weapons or prisoners of war with modern ones. The place had a lot of turnover. The cast of nerds was always changing, but a dress code never appeared. He remembered the I.T. experts by their slovenliness. He vividly remembered the one kid who always wore old-fashioned, cloth Chuck Taylors that were caked in mud. For at least a month, they had been caked in mud.

J.D. spent a lot of time in the I.T. cave, especially when he first arrived at work. He often seemed quite relaxed. His eyes were often glassy. Being the crack journalist that he was, Mickey surmised that the first of J.D.'s daily duties was to go back to I.T. and smoke cannabis through vaporizers, and the second was to offset the resulting stupor with a nice mug of free coffee. Coffee in the canteen was the last vestige of things employees of *The News-Free Press* got free. While J.D. went back to I.T., undoubtedly for another nice hit on the vape, Mickey strolled off the other way to pour himself a nice, refreshing cup of generic coffee. He didn't care what they were doing back in I.T. J.D. and the boys in the back might be having wild gay sex – they actually had their own restroom and shower – and Mickey didn't want to know. Dealing with J.D. was much smoother when J.D. was stoned, and that was probably the way J.D. saw it, too.

Mickey was reading a Dick Francis mystery on his phone when J.D. reappeared.

"You've got one of the new Dells, right?" J.D. asked.

"Nope," Mickey said and looked up. "You all right, J.D? Your eyes are red."

Mickey did not smirk. He kept a perfectly naïve look on his face.

"Damn contact lenses," J.D. said. "And allergies."

"Um. My dad had hay fever. Me, I guess I'm lucky. About the laptop. I own mine. Remember? I write stuff on the side. I got tired about five years ago of company laptops going dead, so I've been using my own ever since."

J.D. looked really stupid *and* stoned, and Mickey thought that figured because they were close to one and the same. No wonder no one ever left the building anymore.

The Sports Editor of *The News-Free Press* became almost disoriented, sifting through conflicting information that his brain had difficulty processing. He should've been writing a short story, not weighing issues of office politics and standard Machiavellian procedure. J.D. had been told to get Mickey Statler's laptop. Mickey Statler's laptop belonged to Mickey Statler. That made it more difficult to obtain. And J.D. couldn't imagine a reason for the company to want it or a justifiable defense of seizing it.

"Oh, okay," he said. "Never mind. I forget."

Then he headed back in the direction of the Information Technology citadel.

Having a zombie boss wasn't entirely a bad thing. Mickey reckoned that he had a certain freedom other columnists lacked. Of the past three sports editors at *The News-Free Press*, Mickey didn't know of another who was an apparent stoner. All three had been as stupid as mudholes, though.

The local American Legion baseball team had built a regional renown and was thus hosting the state finals on its home field. It was why Mickey was there. He just had to write a column, albeit on deadline. The high school editor, Rashawn Ling, was an executive editor's dream come true because his father was of Chinese lineage and his mother African American. Mickey couldn't imagine why Rashawn hadn't been hired out of college by the *New York Times*. If Rashawn had been R'Aquel, and thus a she, it would have happened. That bit of slightly bigoted half-humor notwithstanding, Mickey liked Rashawn and found him perceptive and possessing of an admirable cynicism for a young man. Rashawn *should* have been at the *New York Times*. All he really needed was a higher assignment so that he could experience the requisite disillusionment of every journalist who discovers that men of great athletic gifts do not necessarily share accompanying quantities of character. Once that was discovered, journalists could match up nicely.

The shortstop's name was L'Jonna Lyles, and it had been easy for Mickey to chat with her during batting practice since her participation in it wasn't needed. She was personable and enthusiastic, as women athletes were wont to be, and Mickey liked her. He wished she'd get to bat, but he knew it was unlikely in a state tournament.

As the night fell over the local diamond, Mickey strolled out on the open-air veranda that stood at one side of the "press box," which was really the place where one scorekeeper, one scoreboard operator, three boosters, and two coaches' wives made themselves comfortable so that sportswriters could stand behind them and scrawl on notepads. Fortunately, the local nine was facing a squad from nearly two hundred miles away, so the place was uncluttered, and both he and Rashawn had an air-conditioned place to sit. Mickey just felt bored and wanted to see if the summer breeze would make him feel fine. It was a mistake.

Mickey had his column angle in mind and was just watching for a while, and hoping that nothing either team in front of him would do would be sufficient to make his column idea obsolete. He was prepared for a win or a loss, but hell had no fury like a triple play or a no-hitter. He'd write around it if a kid hit for the cycle. It seemed like the more set a column was, the more likely lightning to strike.

Maybe L'Jonna could *turn* a triple play. That would work nicely.

Had Mickey been asked to draw a picture of the last person on earth with whom he wanted to chat, he would have sketched a five-foot-six, muscle-bound policeman in uniform, wearing a shiny badge and a protruding Adam's apple. A model copied exactly from this would-be sketch walked alongside and was in a mood to talk.

Within minutes, Mickey was idly trying to figure a way he could somehow craft a sports column dealing with the subject of coddled cops. It was a stretch. A colleague had once suggested in a crowd of people that Mickey Statler could write a column about taking a shit. He was resourceful, but not *that* resourceful. Good taste was quite the trick with such parameters.

The name tag said Graig Bartlesby. Sergeant Graig Bartlesby. Mickey tried to get himself occupied. He didn't know Bartlesby. Bartlesby seemed to be of the opinion that they were best friends.

"Hey, Sergeant … Bartlesby."

"You know better than to call me by my last name, Mickey. Graig."

"Hang on just a minute, Graig," Mickey said. "I gotta catch up on my Twitter feed. Damn tweeting is part of the job these days."

Mickey ran his index figure across his screen carefully. The body count was rising in Brussels. A body count was always rising somewhere. That and a death toll. Body counts rose when terrorists attacked. Death tolls rose when a river, quite often the Ganges, overran its banks, or a stray typhoon struck Osaka, or something involving Mother Nature, who had gotten just about as angry as everyone else.

Then Mickey tweeted. *Still scoreless, bottom 3rd. Avett South lefty looks sharp.* All Mickey had noticed about the Avett South pitcher was that he did, in fact, rely on his left arm. He hadn't given up a run. Surely that qualified as sharp.

Bartlesby was not dissuaded. He apparently had a bone to pick. Policemen often had bones to pick with writers of all persuasions. They were not, by nature, a trusting lot. They were also men with exceptional memories. A perceived slight might lead them to stop a motorist for driving a mile an hour over the speed limit.

"What you think about that shooting?" Bartlesby asked, folding his arms and mildly flexing his imposing biceps.

"What? Down near Columbia?"

"Uh, huh."

"Well, you know, Graig, when a law officer shoots a black kid in the back, from ten yards away, it looks right bad," Mickey said.

God. He should've just nodded and mumbled.

"You don't know what that little shit had on him," Bartlesby said, pulse quickening and sweat popping out.

"Do you?"

"Well, no, but it's dangerous out there."

"You don't reckon it might be that a white police officer might feel any black kid was more threatening than any white kid."

"No way," Bartlesby said. "No fucking way."

Profanity in a police officer suggested anger that was quickly ripening. Weightlifters so often had hair-trigger tempers. Wonder why that was?

"I don't figure it's intentional," Mickey said. "What I just said, though, is what the statistics reflect."

"They're just more inclined to being crooks," Bartlesby said. Mickey had a pretty good idea that was off the record.

"Graig, I appreciate what you do," Mickey said. "I'm glad you're here to protect the community. It's not an easy job, and you don't get paid enough. It's a stressful job. It's dangerous. But a man's got to follow the rules, no matter what job he's got."

"Are you saying I'm on the take?" Bartlesby asked, rather irrationally.

"Not unless something came out of my mouth that I didn't notice."

"Well, let me tell you something, Mickey. I've been working with this public safety department for twelve years now, and not once, not once, have I ever seen a fellow officer take part in any activity that wasn't honest and by the book."

"I congratulate you for that, Graig. Look, I've enjoyed our conversation, but I've got to pay attention to this ballgame so's I can write about it."

Bartlesby smirked, his look suggesting that he thought he had won a great debate, and that the sniveling writer was making up excuses because he was losing the argument.

Mickey thought to himself that Sergeant Graig Bartlesby sure did fit the description of a man with something to hide. One of Statler's Rules of Journalism was, *The truth is never more obvious than when being vehemently denied.* The crooks were always the belligerent ones, the ones who turned attention away from themselves by being an asshole to everyone else in the office. Mickey wondered if he needed to start watching his back.

He sat alongside Rashawn, turned on his laptop, and started pecking away. While hammering away at the keyboard, he maintained a running commentary toward his young colleague.

"Tell me how Avett South got two runs, old buddy."

"Big kid at first, Wehunt, hit a two-run homer after Brandon Cogswell walked the second baseman," Rashawn said.

Mickey pulled out a highlighter and marked the names on his lineup card.

"Locals ain't dead yet," Mickey said.

"Nope."

"See that kid on the mound, the lefty?"

"Hormel," Rashawn said.

"Yeah. He's about to start throwing meat. Hormel. Meat. Get it?"

"Sadly, yes."

"Plate umpire's pissed at him," Mickey said. "Count's three and oh. Two of them were borderline strikes. If he doesn't want to walk another batter, he's going to have throw it right down the middle, and that Keller kid ain't the one to have to do that to."

Mickey tapped away a while longer.

"You know," he said, "back when I got started, I used to think it was wrong for an umpire to behave like that. I felt there was no place for an ump who protected his turf. I felt like he let his turf get in the way of his ego."

"Exactly right," Rashawn said.

"Nope," Mickey said, "it's not. It took me twenty years to learn it. If someone shows you up, if he insults you, if he runs over you, sometimes you've got to let him know you mean business. I always say, 'Okay, hot shot, you better be perfect. Everything better go your way. Don't make any mistakes. I'm laying for your ass. One wrong move and I'm nailing you for all it's worth'."

"Damn, Mickey."

"I'm serious, Rashawn. They make more money. They got more power. All you got's the words, man. You've got to use them to keep the high and mighty chopped down to size."

Rashawn hadn't even thought Mickey was paying attention.

CHAPTER 4

Predictable ... in Retrospect

By nature, Mickey Statler was annoyingly early. It didn't fit the rest of his personality. He always allowed for disaster. A traffic jam on the way to the airport, for instance. On this day, the traffic jam was on the way to the office. He had time. It wasn't far. A wreck. A detour. For once, his silly punctuality was going to be beneficial. Mickey spent too much time sitting on a bench in a rental-car center, thumbing through his Twitter feed, or reading a book on his phone while waiting for one of his friends to be fashionably late.

Mickey was strangely relaxed. *Why worry about what cannot be changed?* He turned up the music and picked up his harmonica and jammed along. Occasionally, he glanced across at the people nearby, all red-faced and sweaty, not because their vehicles weren't equipped with air conditioners but because they were consumed in stress. It was self-inflicted.

Shit like that'll kill you, man. He hoped, when they peered back to exchange the glances, they thought him crazy. Crazy was okay. Mickey preferred to think of himself as irreverent. It served him well in his job.

When he pulled into the parking lot, his spot was taken. Son of a bitch. It was understandable, though. Mickey only rarely stopped by.

Maybe taking his spot gave some kid straight out of college a shorter walk when he got off at one in the morning.

He swiped his card at the side door. *What? Red?* Now he was going to have to walk around the building, but he was going to have to do that, anyway, to get the card recoded. He banged on the door a couple times and walked away. Three steps down and one foot on the sidewalk, he heard it swing open.

"Thanks," he said to some guy wearing coveralls who'd probably heard him while he was having a pack of Toastchees in the break room.

"Don't mention it."

The newsroom was getting ready to get busy. Half the people were sitting in front of desktops. The other half were leaning over wrap-around desks, chatting to the people sitting behind the desktops. As Mickey walked through the newsroom, the voices slowly quieted. He saw the people behind desks tilting their heads in his direction, signaling the visitors to cool it.

Uh, oh. No good can come of this.

The last time Mickey had seen a hush fall over the entire newsroom, it wasn't because one person walked in. Maybe it happened when a celebrity stopped by. Mickey didn't know. He'd never been there when that happened. No. It was like this the day management announced furloughs. Everyone went quiet and depressed, but then some started musing about the benefits of being relentlessly upbeat "associates," and others rationalized that it could be worse, but only Mickey had resisted counterintuitive optimism. The Human Resources Coordinator -- hers was a proper name, while his was strictly little "c" in columnist -- had told all the panting faces that they were fortunate to have to take two weeks of unpaid leave because it was better than a pay cut, and Mickey had raised his hand to point out that, across a period of a year, it was slightly worse. Inexplicably, this had seemed to make him unpopular among his peers, at least until they were out of the room.

So, Mickey reasoned, this was bad.

It couldn't be *that* bad, though. Just yesterday, he had been watching David Ortiz hit a home run, a single, and two doubles, and the latter double might have been a triple, and the cycle, had not the ball hit the top of a cushion and bounced into the stands for a ground-rule double. It had made him feel young again, or, at least, younger than David Ortiz.

Theoretically, following his customized pattern of life, Mickey should be on a hot streak for at least one more day. Probably two.

He pulled up a chair in sports editor J.D. McMahan's cubicle. They had a brief, uncomfortable "boy, those Braves sure do suck" conversation, and then it died after J.D. said "we sure could use some rain."

Mickey wasn't sure whether or not J.D. had been vaping in the I.T. den again. His eyes looked fine, or, as fine as they ever did.

Then the E.E. -- that's Executive Editor, not a row in the lower grandstands -- rang the sports department, and J.D. grabbed the receiver hurriedly so that "speaker" wasn't on, and talked real low, ended it with a hushed "okay," turned to Mickey and, "Well, Cynthia's ready, Shall we go?"

Mickey said something profound like "I reckon so," and off they strolled, the sports editor – J.D., who had replaced Jonathan, and Seth had been the one before that -- trying and failing to look relaxed. Perhaps this was a special occasion. Perhaps J.D. had vaped and hedged his bets with a few squirts of Visine. If he'd vaped, though, Mickey figured he would have been relaxed, if incoherent. He was seldom notably coherent. By the time they got to the E.E.'s office, Mickey had concluded that J.D. was likely straight and at least passable. His condition qualified it as a special occasion.

Still, Mickey was guardedly optimistic that it might be a cutback in his schedule, or maybe they wanted him to write a feature column on Tuesdays, or switch to another beat, or, horror of horrors, fill in with Legion baseball writing game stories, not columns. All had happened before in sixteen years, six months, and four days at the *News-Free Press*, the newspaper without irony.

The optimism crashed with the force of a Pinto, horse or car, into an oak tree, when Mickey noticed the presence of the Human Resources Coordinator, wearing the kind of smug impression one wears when secretly enjoying the dismissal of the smart guy who was always making smart-alecky questions in her *required* presentations.

Mickey thought the black cloak and glistening scythe made her look hot. Alluringly evil. He was already cascading into the waterfalls of absurdity that accompany the exhilarating freedom of impending disaster.

Not even Head Rollin' Cynthia Boland, of whom it was said a cash register should be played at her funeral, had much enthusiasm for the execution. She shuffled her shoulders -- "You know, we both knew this was coming," and Mickey said, "No, we didn't know. No one warned one of us" -- and tried to look empathic as, behind her steely-gray eyes, math was being quickly completed to indicate the progress toward a $5,000 bonus that would be achieved with just one more mercy killing.

J.D. was, by then, long gone, undoubtedly back at his desk, whispering to someone about how painful this was or commiserating with his fellow stoners amid the vaporous air of the I.T. hideaway.

Mickey had been toying with the idea of quitting and trying to make it as a freelancer. Part of his deal with the *News-Free Press* had been the freedom to write books, and on-line columns, and magazine pieces. As a result, he had never quibbled much about salary, even back in the days when money was still negotiable. They left him alone, and he left them alone. What had stopped him was revenue sharing, and the 401-K, and health insurance that got only mildly worse each year.

He'd thought about it, most often when frustrations with management mounted, but he had lacked the guts to take the leap of faith. Now his hands were being forced instantly. It was June the twenty-sixth, and the H.R.C. – Human Resources Coordinator -- was now telling him his final day was ... June the twenty-sixth.

"How convenient," Mickey said.

"I thought so," Jalene the 26-year-old H.R.C. (proper name!) said, failing to get the joke.

Cynthia excused herself. She almost offered Mickey her hand, but then she shivered a little because she realized he might leave it hanging, so she put it in her pocket. She was wearing pants, undoubtedly because she took pride in wearing the pants of the family ... newspaper.

"So I don't have to write a column tomorrow?" Mickey was overflowing with the type of one-liners that fit so well in a column.

"Uh, no."

"Cool."

Jalene, in spite of her relative youth, was already well-schooled in the subtle art of head-lopping. She explained an absurdly modest severance package as if it were some arcane, legal form of embezzlement. She provided detailed and easily understandable instructions on how one would go about filing for unemployment. She had him sign his career away in a variety of convenient ways.

I would not, could not, sue this rag. They might allege I was a fag, and claim I stole a box of pens or let a band of homeless in. As long as I can leave this place, I shall keep it in its proper place.

When it was over, Jalene sighed and asked if he had any questions.

Mickey stared at her directly.

"I really think you're hot," he said. "Are you married? I was, but no more. Want to have a few drinks?"

Jalene was shocked. Shocked, she told him!

Mickey left wondering if it was technically possible to be reprimanded for sexual harassment after one's employment had been terminated. Oh, well. He had no need to worry. He was fairly sure his permanent record had just been permanently sealed.

CHAPTER 5

Love in All the Wrong Places

Numbness was Mickey Statler's first reaction. He didn't think about it. He didn't think at all. He returned to the condo, kept the lights off, and closed the blinds. He closed his eyes and drifted off to sleep. He awakened thirty minutes later with that brief feeling of disorientation experienced by men who spend time on the road.

Where is this? Why am I here? Oh, yeah. World Series.

Mickey put on some coffee and looked at his phone to discover it was late afternoon. While he waited for the coffee, he turned on the TV and found an afternoon baseball game between the Tampa Bay Rays and the Los Angeles Dodgers. The Cincinnati Reds were playing the San Francisco Giants, too, but he stuck with the Dodgers because he needed Vin Scully. Leaning back in his easy chair amid the embarrassing disorder of makeshift home, a mug of Breakfast Blend at his side, Vin made him feel better, more patient, and hopeful. It wasn't the end of the world. Vin was, however, retiring at season's end. This was a time of great loss. Mickey's favorite people were falling by the wayside. David Letterman. Gone. Craig Ferguson. Gone. Now, late at night, Mickey watched Stephen Colbert, but then he switched to NBC, where the silly Jimmy Fallon gave way to Seth Meyers, and Mickey liked the way Meyers began every night with something of a *Saturday Night Live*-influenced take on the news. Almost every night he was home, Mickey made himself drowsy with Colbert and went to bed at the beginning of Meyers. Most times he was asleep by the time the news parody was over.

It was acceptable, Colbert replacing Letterman, and Lester Holt succeeding Brian Williams, the only man ever punished for lying about Iraq, on *The Nightly News*, and this would be David Ortiz's last year with the Red Sox, and nobody was going to replace David Ortiz. Mickey still missed Nomar Garciaparra, but three world championships had ameliorated the void. He discovered it was possible to keep his mind off the absence of a job by pondering baseball, what with Vin's soothing voice accompanying the visions in his mind like an orchestra.

It was nineteen forty-seven, and the baseball insiders of the day assured Branch Rickey repeatedly that the national pastime wasn't ready for Jack Roosevelt Robinson …

Mickey rummaged through the sights and sounds, recalling fine ballplayers who were barely now remembered. Tom Brunansky. Matt LeCroy. Jay Buhner. Bret Saberhagen. Mike Boddicker. He was going their way. He was reaching sportswriter's old age, the point at which one's value was less than the savings of hiring a kid just out of college, the point at which quality became irrelevant in the frightened fall of newspapers. Not only was he out of a job. No one was going to hire him. He would receive no package with benefits. He would have to fend for himself in matters of health insurance, retirement, and business expenses. He already needed more money than he had.

There he went getting numb again.

The phone he would shortly have to replace was buzzing constantly and slowly vibrating across his coffee table, which reminded Mickey of the players on the old electric football games of his youth and provided passive realization that word of his layoff was getting out. He knew there were texts, emails, tweets, posts, and messages imploring him to "pick up, goddamn it." He wasn't, though. Not today. Maybe not tomorrow. Right now, he wanted to do nothing. He wanted to think. He wanted to meditate. He wanted to ponder the great truths, not the ones involving paying bills and avoiding government aid. He figured he had at least a week before he needed to consider something so petty as self-preservation. Mickey was so listless that he didn't even have enough energy to drink. He didn't have the energy to read tweets, let alone write any. If anyone other than the police or fire department started banging on his door, Mickey wasn't going to answer it. He wasn't determined to overcome this setback. He wasn't depressed. He was uncaring. He was detached. He had become just another character in the tale of life. It didn't seem significant that he was the character, and the story was real, not imagined. The writer must be objective, even regarding himself.

Mickey counted the notches in his belt.

I never saw Eddie Mathews play, but I got drunk with him.

The best athlete I ever saw wrecked his knee in the tenth grade and became a doped-up dropout in the eleventh. What was his name again? I wonder if he's still in jail. I wonder if he's still alive.

I wonder what happened to the guy who used to do publicity for the Hornets. The first ones. He was a stand-up guy who never had a chance in that business. His main flaw was that he liked sportswriters.

My main flaw is that I became a sportswriter. I was good at it. I just didn't have any idea I was joining a dying profession. None of us did. The young ones, lost in their own delusional visions, think they are taking journalism where it has never been before. They're right. It has never been this cheap.

Eureka! Depression was setting in. The light dimmed outside, and he finally turned on the lamp so that he could read an obscure novel he'd plucked from a bargain table. He had the Democratic National Convention on TV with the sound muted, and occasionally looked up, thinking, *Huh, I bet Bill Clinton's giving a hell of a speech,* but he suspected, for the first time, that Martin Gaynes might actually win. He was at the vanguard of The Rise of the Bullshit Artists, and, because he gave the masses the red meat they so wanted to devour, they preferred to believe he was telling it like it was. Somehow, "straight talk" had come to mean "constant lies," and, *By God, let them have what they want! Let's just see how far we can sink!*

Mickey never ate. He just drank coffee and read the whole book, never knowing, even when he finished, whether he liked it or not.

The next morning, Wednesday, according to the phone, found him hungry, and after he kept nature at bay long enough to put on the coffee and take his blood-pressure pills, he looked at himself in the bathroom mirror from his nervous perch on the throne, and marveled at how badly a fifty-year-old man looked before a shave and a shower. Lines drooped below his eyes. His air looked greasy and unkempt. He needed a haircut. More than that, though, he needed the coffee, and a two-egg omelet with sharp cheddar cheese, and a slab of sausage, and two slices of toast.

Thus refreshed, Mickey mustered some enthusiasm for linking to the outside world. When he turned on the flat-screen, he granted it sound and listened to Joe Biden on *Morning Joe*. He started answering emails because they took longer, and he believed in doing first what he most dreaded.

I appreciate the concern, Fred, but I'll be fine. I'm just making a stop in the road.

You're right, Jay. Please delete this reply so that no one but you will know I think they're all cocksuckers.

No, ma'am, I haven't decided what I'll be doing next, but please don't worry yourself. Many, many people deserve your prayers more than I do. Much obliged, though.

I appreciate the offer, Mel. Please just give me a few days to make up my mind on just exactly what I want to do next. I'll get back with you soon.

Nope, Hollie, no warning. I found out yesterday that yesterday was my final day. I bear them no ill will, though. I think they compare favorably with ISIS.

Then he crafted a generic message, and started pasting replies and adding a personalized sentence. I took a while, and it took a toll. The messages piled up in his consciousness like toxic waste. The emails turned out to be the least of his dreads. Mickey mildly disliked text messages. What he really hated, though, were group messages on Facebook, the kind where some old friend wrote:

D'ya hear the news? The News-Free Press canned Mickey Statler! A new low. Hey, Mickey, I'm feeling for you, bud.

It was that modern, electronically empowered, "let's gossip about a colleague's misfortune, and draw him into the quagmire, as well" method of human interaction. The messages he divided in three groups: (1.) genuine concern; (2.) intelligence gathering; and (3.) hate it happened, and, by the way, what are the *News-Free Press's* plans on replacing you? The only upside was a bit more knowledge of who his real friends were.

The notes from readers were more touching, but the accumulative effect was a pall that descended over him as Mickey realized that the only people who didn't want him back on the beat, or some beat, were those capable of doing anything about it.

Gloom. Despair. Doom. Mickey thought he might start smoking again. He'd quit when Winston quit NASCAR. Ah, he shouldn't. He hadn't stopped drinking. He'd just stopped doing much of it. It only seemed proper that he should want to drink now. It was natural. He needed to look for love in all the wrong places because the right places were breaking his heart even faster.

CHAPTER 6

The Tangled Web She Weaves

It was a Thursday, but she didn't have a class until eleven, and then she had to meet her mother and her mother's new boyfriend, and then one more weekend at the beach before school started again, so Marcia didn't see any reason she couldn't have a couple beers, which, by five o'clock, had blossomed into quite the conservative estimate. She had two potential sorority sisters with her, and they were on their third pitcher of Michelob Ultra, because as of this very day, all three had reached the magical drinking age of twenty-one, which had been preceded by two years of drinking because they were in college, where rules were meant to be broken.

Marcia laughed along with Darcy and Felicia, but this particular brand of social life was growing tiresome. She wasn't any more the sorority type than she was the athlete. She was tired of frivolous talk. She'd been drawn to Darcy and Felicia because they liked to drink, but they seemed stupid all the time and silly to boot when they had more beers than a couple. They didn't really like her. They were advancing fall rush. They'd remain friends if they all agreed to pay for it.

She kept stealing glances at the boy standing at the bar. He had that fashionably shabby, frat-boy look, but she hadn't seen him in any classes. Navy blazer, khaki pants, striped tie loosened and unkempt … his cheeks were flushed, and he was sweaty. He had short, light-brown hair, almost the kind people described as sandy blond, and his blue eyes were pale and piercing, if also bloodshot. He looked accustomed to money but not presently supplied.

She liked all that and was feeling frisky. She had a nice buzz. She was interested in a *conquest*.

Tripp Fallaw noticed Marcia, too. Her baby blues caught his. He noticed the absence of any darkened roots and surmised correctly that this blonde was natural. He handed yellow cards to the men, older, thirty maybe, sitting on either side. Then he walked around the dining area, passing out two or three more. He walked out a door that led to a fenced-in, open area where a beach volleyball court was located. It was March, and the weather was just thinking about getting warm. The court needed a little work. Marcia figured he might be going out to have a cigarette. She wanted one, too. She excused herself, walked into the bathroom, washed her hands and, instead of returning to the bar, turned left, and walked outside.

He was, in fact, having a smoke. Marcia realized that, while she had a pack, they were in her purse, and it was at the table with Darcy and Felicia.

"Hi, I'm Marcia."

"Tripp." He put the cigarette between his lips so he could shake hands.

"Can I bum a smoke?"

"Sure." He reached into his shirt pocket. Camel Lights. Gave her a light. "I'm guessing you're at the college."

"Just transferred in," she said. "You?"

"I used to be at dear, old Triborough." He had a Tidewater accent. "I guess you could say I played out about a year ago. You want a beer?"

"Sure. Great."

Tripp dropped his cigarette and ground it into the sand with his docksider. He went inside. She finished her cigarette and sat at a table made from some sort of wooden, industrial roll. It had a canopy, though, green and white. Heineken. He came back with a couple St. Pauli Girls. Good choice.

Marcia took a sip. "It's good," she said. "I like these."

He inquired about her major, which pissed her off.

"Look, let's don't get into one of those 'what's your major?' conversations. What are those yellow cards?"

Tripp reached inside his blazer and pulled a small stack out. "These? A list of prices."

"Of what?"

"The drugs I sell."

Marcia shivered just a little. In her neck. Her pulse quickened.

"I'm kidding," he said. "You ever heard of parlay cards?"

"No."

"Really? You never heard of parlay cards," he said. "They're for betting. They set odds on ballgames. Right now it's mainly baseball, but there's, you know, World Cup, and golf, and shit. Look, last year, you know, I guess it wasn't one of my better ones."

"Tell me about it."

He offered another cigarette. She took it.

"Okay, I'll try to skip the unnecessary details," Tripp said. "I came to Triborough on a partial golf scholarship. I actually pulled a three-oh first term of my freshman year, then, in the spring, that was two years ago, we traveled all over, and I kind of got out of the habit of studying. Sophomore year, first term, I flunked Spanish and Western Civ. That made me ineligible in the spring, and, basically, I just stopped going to class. Uh, my dad got pissed, and then I fucked up in summer school, too, and he basically disowned me, said I'm on my own, so I just stayed up here and been making a living the best way I know how."

"I'm sorry, Tripp," she said and placed her hand on his. "You okay now? You making it?"

"Well, I got five hundred dollars in my pocket right now. Cash money."

"Cool."

"Uh, I don't suppose you … get high?" he asked.

"Not every day," Marcia said. "Most of 'em. You got some?"

"Let's go to my apartment."

Marcia walked back inside and got her purse. She told Darcy and Felicia she had a ride.

"Ooh," Darcy said. "We were hoping you'd be able to drive us back to the dorm."

"Sorry," Marcia said. "Fuck that."

As she walked out the door, Felicia said to Darcy, "What a bitch. What a hoe."

It was four in the morning. Marcia found herself fixated with the full moon casting an eerie glow through the open window in a rundown home near campus. The front faced the soccer stadium where, as best Marcia understood, the Triborough Patriots had once played football. She didn't feel bad, only restless. Gently, she extricated herself from Tripp Fallaw's arms and crept into the spare den. She found her purse, which held her cigarettes, and the lighter was on the coffee table, next to a glass ashtray that had probably been lifted from a restaurant. The ashtray contained several ground-out cigarettes but also a little less than half a joint. She lit it and considered the fact that she had smoked about as much cannabis in the past twenty-four hours as the month leading up to it.

It didn't seem like enough.

Marcia slipped into her tennis shoes, baby blue with pink laces, and hit the roach a couple times. She leaned back on the shabby couch, savoring the high, and looked around the darkened room. A Bob Marley poster. Obviously. A couple golf trophies sitting atop stereo speakers that were, in turn, sitting atop red, plastic milk boxes, undoubtedly stolen. Leaning against the corner was a street sign that read "Fallaw Street." Ah, and two orange traffic cones. Tripp probably sold weed, but he stole lots of things. He was just a little criminal, though, and Marcia kind of liked that. For her, this was a walk on the wild side.

And Tripp's last name was most likely Fallaw. Had to be. The street sign.

"I'm still a good person," said the sweet little girl on one shoulder. "Loser!" screamed the Goth on the other.

The moonlight drew her like dragonflies to a fishpond. The hours being wee, she knew she could probably smoke pot on the back porch, which was screened in, but one never knew, and she was afraid, though a bit irrationally. She already felt pleasant, so she put on her hoodie and walked, a little wobbly, in the dark, following a beacon of moonlight, with her lighter and cigarettes, through the sliding glass window to the porch. A rocking chair felt luxuriant as she let it drift to and fro, as it was wont to do. She lit a cigarette, inhaled deeply, and then watched it leave her lungs, not angrily, but as it wished, in its time, mingling with the bluish, lunar glow. She faced a little creek, a view of its course blocked by bushes growing along its banks, and, to each side, a line of nicer homes, the ones occupied mostly by professors, coaches, and moneychangers of the college. Marcia felt wonderful, relaxed by the weed, the cigarette, and the lingering sensation of physical love. This was going to put her back to sleep comfortably, but she didn't expect it to come so soon. She figured she'd just saunter back to bed, and while she considered it and thought of crawling back under the covers, and when the boy, and that's really no more or no less than what Tripp Fallaw was, awakened, she would kiss him, and their tongues would intertwine, and no telling what else might happen next, and … she never made it.

While she continued to rock gently, Marcia dreamed of her new man, striding purposely down a fairway, fans pressing against ropes on either side as Trip Fallaw worked his way inexorably toward victory. She was wearing a sun dress, tagging along tastefully nearby, and occasionally exchanging knowing glances with her man. No one knew the vital role she had played in nudging Tripp toward the fulfillment of his destiny. He had been a rascal, a hustler, bowing to the gospel of something for nothing, and then she had come along to smooth his rough edges and make him, solely by the force of her charm, the man he was meant to be. She awakened again with the sun coming up, rays jutting sideways through the trees, and she thought of Tripp in the lingering context of the dreams. She shivered. It was actually cold. She got up and went back inside but not to the boy's waiting arms. She found some coffee in the kitchen cabinet and put a pot on. She lit another cigarette and tried to remember what day it was.

Friday now. She had a class at eleven. She had to drive all the way to South Carolina in the afternoon. She had to get her shit together. Then

Tripp got up, and a switch, somewhere in Marcia, flipped on. She blew off class. And she served him. He returned the favor. They succumbed to each other's slavery. She bathed and made herself presentable. Once she got most of the way across North Carolina, she stopped for gas and bought a six-pack. She had a few and was half tight when she got there. *Three beers. Hah!* She had beer and tobacco on her breath when she kissed her mother. Had this occurred *ever before*, she would've at least been chewing gum furiously. She didn't care. Her older sister, Patti, and her boyfriend, Chance or Chase, or maybe even Chad, chatted amiably on the patio with Mom while Rodrigo grilled steaks. Rodrigo was an optometrist of Cuban descent.

Her mother smoked a cigarette, and Marcia decided she would, too. When she lit a Camel Light – she had adopted Tripp Fallaw's brand – the look on her mother's face would have dropped a grizzly bear, but she couldn't very well say anything, could she? She was smoking, too. Marcia enjoyed her predicament immensely. Mom didn't care. Mom was just wondering what Rodrigo would think.

Over dinner, Marcia informed her mother that she was seeing a golf pro. Rodrigo, who obviously wanted to play a fatherly role, invited himself into the conversation.

"An older man?" he asked, wondering just how in the world his co-ed daughter had gotten acquainted with a golf pro.

"Tripp's just a little bit older than I am, Dad," she said. "I guess he's not really a golf pro. He played on the T.C. golf team. Now he plays golf for money, so I guess that's why I said he was a golf pro."

And he sells pot, and he's a bookie, but that's not important. He is soooo good with his tongue. That's important.

Rodrigo frowned and cut all the pieces of his ribeye in advance, which few adults did. Mother devoted inordinate attention to her baked potato. The wind got chilly. Marcia left most of her steak and announced she was going for a walk. Instead, she just walked into the kitchen, grabbed the three remaining beers she had carried in from the car, and walked down to the boathouse. Rodrigo's house, now her mother's residence, bordered the Intracoastal Waterway. He was loaded. Marcia wondered why Vera didn't marry him. Her mother had been married twice. Patti was the daughter of a doctor. Vera had divorced well for herself, the first time, anyway.

She had a text message from Tripp.

When can u get loose, baby?

She was supposed to be there for a week.

Monday?

Cool. Wanna go to LA?

Hell yeeaahh!!!!

Meet u Roanoke airport. Let u know more when I do. Love u.

Marcia didn't tell her mother she was leaving until Sunday at dusk. It took her that long to conjure up enough of an argument to walk out in righteous indignation. She knew they'd all cry once she left. Her mother would put on a show. Then they'd all agree she was going through a phase.

Tripp told Marcia to be standing out front of the airport – it was allegedly "international" though most of its planes flew to places like Atlanta – and that didn't make sense to her. She'd had to park her Mazda. Why didn't he just meet her at the gate, or check-in, or a bar on the concourse?

Sure enough, though, he pulled up in his beat-up Olds – they didn't even make them anymore – punched the button that lowered the passenger window and told Marcia, who was mildly surprised it worked, to get in.

"We got more than an hour," Tripp said, pulling away.

"So, what? We're going to eat lunch?"

"No, silly, we're going to get high. Lunch is so much better if you blaze first."

What have I got myself into? It was fun, though. They just rode around the two-lane roads that circled the airport, outside the chain-link fences and the wind sleeves, passing a blunt back and forth and watching planes taxi. Tripp was even more buoyant than the weed made him. He provided just the right amount of scattershot details for Marcia to have an idea what he was talking about. The trip had something to do with golf, and a friend of Tripp's who was some kind of caddy to the stars, and them playing golf with celebrities, and somehow Tripp was going to make a bunch of money.

At the end of his diatribe, parking the faded Achieva, Tripp actually said, "Simple as that, baby."

Marcia was a little shaky in the airport. When the lady at the counter asked her if her luggage had been in the hands of someone "unknown" to her, she said, "Well, ma'am, like, if it was someone 'unknown to me,' well, then, how could I possibly know?" The woman requested assistance.

Tripp interceded and assured the humorless gentleman representing the airline that Marcia's bag was fine. In security, Marcia managed somehow to kick her shoes off under the x-ray machine, which caused some confusion, but all the interaction was somewhat convivial as the lines were short and the T.S.A. agents patient. All Marcia was guilty of was laughter.

When they got to the gate, passengers were already queueing up to board.

"God, I could use a cigarette," said Marcia, who was up to about half a pack a day.

"No place here," Tripp said. "They got smoking rooms in Atlanta. Flight's about an hour."

She looked at the other passengers. "Look at all these suitcases," she said. "We should've carried ours on."

"Not really. The suitcases can't be above a certain size. Neither of ours would make it." Tripp lowered his voice. "Besides, it's safer."

"How so?"

"I've got a certain something hidden in my bag."

"Couldn't you get busted?"

"They never check for anything but, you know, guns, anything metal, things terrorists might use. I've got it hidden. Trust me. It's cool."

"How do you know all this shit?" Marcia asked.

"Internet," he replied.

At Jackson-Hartsfield, the Atlanta airport, they landed at one concourse and took a shuttle train to another, where the Los Angeles connecting flight boarded. They had an hour to kill and began by visiting one of the glassed-in smoking areas. Marcia felt a bit paranoid, gazing outside as travelers hustled by, wondering if one of them would recognize her. She wasn't accustomed to smoking in front of random people, particularly not amidst the gaping maw of smoke that enveloped the room. Then they stopped for coffee and blueberry muffins, and sat a while in a dining area near the escalators to the trams. It was only then that Tripp explained the purpose of the trip in terms Marcia could fathom.

"I got this buddy, Wade," he said. "He's a caddy. Makes big money carrying the bags for big-time Hollywood celebrities. He's got games lined up for Wednesday and Thursday. We got tomorrow to sightsee, then I'll clean some cash, and we'll fly back Friday. I'm playing with some high rollers, and when I hustle their asses, we'll fly back home with a couple grand, easy."

"What happens if you don't?"

"You mean, if I don't win?"

"Yeah."

"Ain't happening," Tripp said. "Everybody knows it ain't happening. These guys got more money than they know what to do with. They throw it away on lessons, and play in pro-ams, and they just want to play a damn pro, Marcia."

"I take it you've done this before."

"Several times."

"Anybody I'd recognize?" she asked.

"You ever heard of Hector Iglesias?"

"I don't think so."

"Latino comic. He's got his own show on cable," Tripp said. "Funny as shit. Smokes weed like a fiend. Good shit, too. I played with him in October. Cleared about eight hundred dollars. This buddy of his, a rapper, played, too. He couldn't play for shit. He just tagged along. I didn't bet him. The main thing I remember is he had a gun in his bag."

"What'd you do?"

"I didn't do anything. What I said was 'shit.'"

They laughed, Marcia nervously.

"So, uh, what am I supposed to do?"

"Whatever you want to do, baby. Stay at the hotel, hang out at the pool, or you can come to the course. They'll probably have a pool there. You can tag along on the course, if you want."

"Will there be, like, carts?"

"Yeah, for sure. See, Wade's going to be my partner, so he won't be caddying. He's buddies with these guys. He's a hell of a player. Almost good as me."

On the flight to Los Angeles, Marcia noticed Tripp looking out the window. No, he was looking at the window: at himself, reflected. Marcia was in the middle seat, which was fine because she could sit in it easier, but it would have been nice for Tripp to offer the window. He tumbled off to sleep, leaning against the window. Marcia tried to read the airline magazine, but it just made her sleepy, too.

He thinks he's so cute, she thought, and he kinda is.

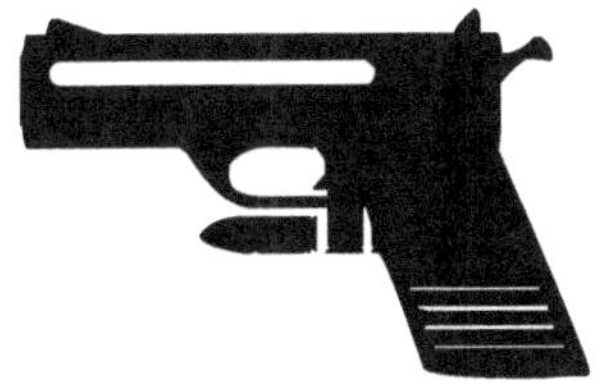

CHAPTER 7

The Inevitability of Drink

Did he hide from the world and wallow in self-pity? Or did he go out and show his ass? In the darkened living room of his condo, Mickey Statler felt there were only two choices. Oh, he could answer emails and write some more. He could seek employment, or, perhaps, guidance from his peers who, like him, were journalists, so they were sure to want to know all about it. He just didn't want to do anything constructive. He'd spent most of two decades being constructive. What he wanted was a day of quiet indecision. He didn't want to think about it.

Watch what you ask for. You might just get it. Mickey had talked about freeing himself of the bounds of journalism for years. He had wondered if he could make it work. He had fancied himself the author, not just the writer. He had written sports books on the side for years. Now he wanted to be more creative. Fiction he found appealing. Part of his deal with the *News-Free Press* had been the stipulation that he could do what he wanted on the side. The books had been modestly profitable. Could he make the profit ample if he devoted himself to it full-time?

It required thought. It required sitting in the living room like a zombie, failing to process for thirty minutes the fact that *Let's Make a Deal* was on TV. It required reading weighty pieces of elegant prose, only to set it aside because his eyes were running across the words without comprehending them.

The phone indicated it was Wednesday. He had little use for it. Time. Date. Occasionally, temperature. He was content getting the weather from the sight of rain splattering on the little stoop with the cheap plastic chairs, high above the courtyard and the swimming pool.

Gradually, Mickey's spirits rose as he found himself reminiscing about the good times, the highlights, almost none of which involved interactions with athletes. Mickey loved sports, but what he had mainly loved was being a sportswriter. It occurred to him that the writers were getting as young as their subjects in the Ice Age of journalism. Where revered, literate men had once filed their wisdom from their own private Mounts Olympi, now wisdom had been replaced by words that were, at best, clever, and, more often, self-absorbed. One of Mickey's longtime fascinations had been college newspapers. He'd roll into Chapel Hill, Charlottesville, or Athens, stop by a gathering place and pick up the student rag, oft times lying on the floor next to rows of mailboxes at the few institutions of higher learning that had not already turned their print digital and renamed their journalism departments "communications." Hell, that was a name suited more to an English major than a journalist. The school rags were hilariously pretentious, the goal being not to tell the discerning reader what happened but rather to provide an assurance that the writer was, indeed, very, very smart.

Mickey drank. He drank a lot. He just didn't drink often. Half a six of Ultra might sit in the refrigerator for two weeks. When he drank, it was usually in a sports bar, or a hospitality suite on the road, and he always aimed to be buzzed, not drunk. He got his buzz, it raised his spirits, and, from then on, he maintained and regulated. Beer was good for that. Vodka wasn't. He never drank vodka. It brought memories of his old man.

Unfortunately, these darkened ruminations had the natural effect of causing Mickey to start thinking about drinking. It was all he could do to fetch his electric shaver. It was still raining. That sucked. He felt dumb. He liked it. He didn't think he had suffered a stroke. He'd had no pain shoot through his cranium.

Mickey's job had just been eliminated. That's all.

He still had lots of time. He didn't want to wait too late. Might as well take advantage of Happy Hour. In the interest of alleviating lethargy, Mickey fetched himself a K-Cup and popped it into the coffee maker. Then, of course, he forgot about it. He had to pour it into another cup and microwave it, which, of course, boiled it, and having a simple mug of coffee killed most of an hour.

Maybe it was a painless stroke. I've got every excuse. My job was eliminated. I can't bring myself to say I was …. fired. I wasn't. Because they aren't going to replace me. I got … terminated. Exterminated, even. My kind is growing … extinct. Dinosaurs. I'm grazing on the leaves in the tops of trees. Huh? That flash in the sky! Wonder what that is?

Mickey showered and made himself presentable. He pondered the irony of going to a bar because he wanted to be alone. He had to do something, and he had already eliminated anything constructive. The last place he wanted to be was where other scribes, wags, and pundits were present. *Nah. Not at a bar! Surely not!*

Irreverence got in Mickey's way. He was a smart-ass. In fact, he had done it professionally. The term was "columnist." Inexplicably, he couldn't overcome the shame of not being one.

Mickey drove aimlessly, almost, mildly seeking areas where bars he had never entered might be located. Briefly, he considered the TallyHoe Tavern because such a place had existed in a Kris Kristofferson song, but then he determined from the array of vehicles in the lot that what might be tallied inside were hoes, and he wasn't feeling that decadent.

It was half past happy hour (five) when Mickcy arrived, more tired of indecision than acclimated, at the Lovable Loser Lounge. He was surprised he'd never heard of it. It had a feel that matched the name. It seemed like a merry place, and the bartender was fetching. He took what he judged to be the least conspicuous stool.

"Hi, I'm Laurie. Can I help you?"

Laurie had a mischievous smile and twinkles in her eyes. Mickey could tell she was fun and approximately half his age.

"What's good on draught?"

"Me? I like Shocktop," she said. "It's three dollars till seven."

He looked at the spigots. The Shocktop handle featured what looked like an Indian, American variety, fashioned out of an orange slice, with wheat sticking out the top. Shocktop. It looked a bit like an old mascot of the Atlanta Braves, Chief Nok-A-Homa.

"I'll have one," he said.

No more than a dozen patrons were there, but the regulars were drifting in. Laurie brought the beer. Mickey had been mildly expecting a slice of orange, but he appreciated the frosty mug. He took a good-sized slug.

"Umm. That's good. Kind of like …"

"Blue Moon," Laurie said. "That's what everybody says."

They took an immediate liking to each other. Laurie was worried that a man, Luther, had walked out on a tab, claiming he was going out for cigarettes. She asked the other barkeep, Louie, to ring him on his cell, but before Louie had the time, Luther wobbled back in, carrying a pack of discount full-flavor kings for himself and a pack of lights for Laurie.

"I just noticed," Mickey said. "People smoke in here."

"Outside the city limits," Laurie said. "They ain't never passed no law out here in the county."

"Fine by me," Mickey replied. "I've always thought it kind of absurd that people who come to a bar to drink can't smoke. It kind of defeats the purpose of going to a bar, in a way."

"I like you," she said. "You're a … sportswriter, ain't you?"

"Don't tell nobody. I used to be."

"When you give it up?"

Mickey looked at his watch, which, somehow, he'd remembered to wear.

"Uh, going on … thirty-two hours now."

"Ah," Laurie said. "That's why you're here. That's why I ain't seen you before."

Mickey just shrugged his shoulders and held up his mug. He was ready for another, and she was ready to pour it.

Luther was pouting. Mickey judged him to have a fancy for Laurie, which was even more pathetic than the same feeling growing in Mickey. Luther, with his bruised and damaged arms, his florid face, unshaven, and a lighter that wouldn't work, was either twenty years older than Mickey or ten harder lived. He was wobbly drunk and kept wanting Laurie to lean across the bar so he could better whisper sweet nothings to her.

Laurie brought Mickey's second draught and winked her left eye, the one Luther couldn't see. This time it was she who leaned across the bar.

"Don't mind him. I have to *indulge* him."

Mickey wanted to kiss her, and that's why he blushed.

"Understood."

"He's our best customer," she said.

Mickey reckoned Laurie was the reason for that.

By six-thirty, the Lovable Loser was overrun by Detroit Tigers fans – okay, ten or twelve – mysteriously gathered at the border between suburban and rural North Carolina for the purpose of watching them play on TV in Atlanta. The Loser must have made them some sort of deal, but several of them recognized Mickey Statler, the celebrated *News-Free Press* award-winning columnist, and, knowing Mickey's style, they thought it quite possible they'd wind up in some whimsical corner of a summertime column, and so they informed Mickey and Laurie, and quite possibly, Louie, that the sportswriter's money was no good here.

So it wasn't, and Mickey, the devotee of moderation where two kinds of spirits were concerned, got carried away and shoved the shame away for the longest time, telling grandiose stories of ACC finals and two Panthers Super Bowls, and being there the night Laettner's miracle jumper beat Kentucky. It wasn't until very late that Mickey became bitter, and the Tigers had already won, and most of their fans had drifted home before the few, the proud, the nearly as drunk as him, watched him blather about the sons of bitches at the *News-Free Press*.

Mickey held his beer, though he drank too much of it. Luther threw up on himself, and Laurie helped clean him up and get a cab.

"Second time this week," she told Mickey, and later, she got him home, too. She drove, he managed to give her somewhat decipherable directions, and Louie, whom Mickey had discovered sold weed on the side, followed in Laurie's Mitsubishi. He wanted her to stay with him, but Louie was behind them, and he seemed suddenly impatient – Mickey wondered why he didn't just bide his time rolling a joint – so Mickey promised Laurie that he could take the elevator just fine, and he hoped like hell their paths would cross again.

He gave her a business card – one that had been obsolete for, oh, thirty-seven hours by then – but he scrawled his cell number on it and said, "Laurie, darlin', look me up on Facebook. Or fucking Twitter. Just look me up, sweet Miss Laurie, 'cause, like, I'm everywhere. And nowhere at the same time."

Laurie liked him. He didn't think she was *indulging* him.

CHAPTER 8

Escaping Intact

Marcia learned shortly, and unsurprisingly, that Wade Sanderson was more than just Caddy to the Stars. He sold them weed. Sanderson drove a nice, burgundy SUV, a Ford Explorer for which he apologized and said he was aiming to trade up to a Lincoln Navigator. "You always have been a Ford man," Tripp said as they embraced.

"Well, my daddy sells 'em," Wade said. "Who's your friend here?"

"Marcia, Wade," Tripp said. "My best gal and my best friend."

"You done good, *bruh*." Wade sized her up and was pleased with what he saw. Marcia thought he looked "very California," whatever that was. He kissed her cheek.

They took "the Ten" east after driving a few miles on one of the other numbers to get to it. From the back seat, the pace was frightening. Hundreds, no, thousands, of cars were whizzing along at eighty miles an hour, just a few lengths apart. Disaster seemed inevitable, and it wasn't until, inevitably, all the traffic ground to a halt that Tripp and Wade managed to get a joint lit. Marcia was surprised at how they just took huge hits and exhaled clouds of sweet-smelling smoke out the windows. People who smoked pot in cars in the South, Marcia having been one for the first time just that morning, took precautions by partaking on rural roads, or, at least, on the interstates only when traffic was sparse.

"Yo," she said. "There's a cop two lanes over, three or four cars back."

Wade started laughing.

"It's cool, Marcia. He ain't gonna stop up this traffic no more just to bust a couple stoners."

"Make it three," she said, now bolder. "Little help."

When in L.A., do as the Angelenos.

"Oh, yeah, I'm sorry," Tripp said. "How fucked up of me."

Marcia understood the omission when she took a hit.

"Oh, my God," she said. "You buy this shit in stores out here?"

"Not that particular shit," Wade said. "I grew it."

He told her it was easy to get a medical-marijuana card. He said he had a card – "everybody does, mon" – but mostly as a precaution. Still backed up in traffic, he pulled out his wallet and showed his card to Tripp and Marcia.

Wade reached in his shirt pocket. "Know what this is?"

"A pen?"

He smiled. "A vaporizer."

Marcia took it from him. "No shit?" She wasn't completely sure what a vaporizer was and looked at it closely. She'd heard the name, though, and thought it was something like an e-cigarette.

"No shit," Wade said. "We'll hit it when we get to my place."

Tripp just sat there, silent, all knowing, stoned.

Marcia leaned back and tried to regain her bearings. She felt as if staring from inside a fishbowl. When traffic started moving again, she barely noticed. She just knew she'd come a long way from the Intracoastal Waterway. Flying.

Marcia spent Tuesday in a medicated fog, *medicated* being a popular cliché for using marijuana where it could be had for a prescription card and a song. Tripp and Wade said they had to "hone" their games, which meant they hit several buckets of balls at a driving range and took turns taking hits on essentially a ball-point bong that enabled them to ingest cannabis without exhaling smoke that was pungent. "See? It's vapor," Wade kept saying.

She loved it. Vapor. It made her feel like a thief. It made her want to live in California. It made her want to make love to life. She had never been to Southern California. This was supposed to be the day she and Tripp went sightseeing. They had talked about nightlife, and the beach, and going to some fancy restaurant where late-night talk shows sent audience members to dinners for two. Tripp and Wade played something called a par-three course, which apparently meant it was short. Tripp and Wade "hit balls" at the driving range. Tripp and Wade made a few deliveries. Marcia spent most of the day in the back seat of the SUV, thoroughly and blissfully stoned and talking about things she shortly couldn't remember.

"You know, I want one of those ..."

"Those what?"

"I don't know."

It was a benign haze. Marcia didn't want to fight. She didn't want to quarrel. She wasn't pleased that her man wanted to play golf, but she was vaguely aware that it was his ticket to stardom, or money, anyway. It was what he was good at. Marcia couldn't think of anything she was good at except she thought she was getting rapidly and enjoyably better at being high.

"Last week I wanted to get my degree," she said while they were stopped in traffic.

"So?"

"Now all I want is a cigarette."

Tripp and Wade laughed ... a lot. "Girl's a trip," said Tripp.

"Know what else I want?"

"What?"

"I wanna get laid," she said.

They smirked and tried to hold back more laughter. Failed.

"Now, tomorrow," Wade said, "we gotta stay straight. Serious business."

"Define straight," Tripp said.

"Don't get fucked up. Don't get baked. Don't get stoned. Don't get fried."

"What's the fucking use of playing golf?" asked Marcia, who had never played.

"Just get a buzz and keep it," Wade said. "Just get high."

"Yeah," said Tripp. "Just the way I play my best."

Marcia mustered what for her was laudable coherence.

"You gotta do one thing for me, Wade. I need a big, big, pretty please, favor."

"Name it, gorgeous."

"I've smoked weed from a blunt," she said. "I've sucked it from a bong. I've … v-vaporized the shit. Now I want to eat it."

"You want an edible?"

"Shit, yeah," Marcia said. "I'm a great cook. Could we, like, bake brownies?"

"I don't think so. It's harder than you think. You like candy bars, Marcia?"

"Who don't?"

"I'll stop by the dispensary and pick up a couple very special Reese's Cups."

"I'll do bong hits at your wedding," Marcia said.

"That's comforting," Wade replied.

"Marcia, I want you to look at these fuckin' … vehicles," Tripp Fallaw said as they arrived at the country club. "Shit."

Marcia was world-weary, cynical, burnt-out, and, of course, high.

So these were the Hills of Beverly.

That's about our fucking speed. Beverly Hillbillies.

Oh, why had she left the peace and tranquility of a South Carolina beach? Marcia finally saw what everyone at the Study Club undoubtedly knew. Tripp Fallaw was a bullshit artist, and now, three thousand miles away, she had an awful foreboding. Nothing was going to work. Tripp was a charmer, all right, and good in bed, but he'd reached the depths of sorriness the night before when she'd had to buy him condoms. "Uh, I'm a little low on cash," he'd said. *Jesus.* What had possessed her to run away with this two-bit hustler? She'd have been much better off with his weed-pushing friend, Wade Sanderson. At least he had a job, shady though it may be.

Wade had bought her candy. She had two packages of chocolaty and peanut-buttery goodness in her purse. Wade said be careful. He said don't eat more than half, or maybe just a bite, and then wait and see how it hits you. "Shit's pretty strong," he'd said.

Ahead of them, a white Porsche Boxster was unloading, clubs removed, the owner an elderly, tanned gentleman who must have been seventy. What was an old man doing with a car like that? Wade's Explorer might as well have been a covered wagon with a team of mules. That would have been acceptable. That would have been a novelty item. This occurred to Marcia because she was high. She wanted to write all this shit down.

Though she had no intention of accompanying them on their golf adventure, she wandered down to the first tee to see what stars of stage, screen and Hollywood were unwittingly going to get her and Tripp back to Virginia.

Marcia did, in fact, recognize Hector Iglesias, the comic Tripp had mentioned on the plane. She'd seen him on some sitcom, probably one that wasn't on the major networks. She vaguely remembered thinking he was okay. Marcia knew nothing about his partner, but he made quite an impression. He was undoubtedly a rapper, did not look particularly healthy, had at least two gold teeth, and all she could see of his skin was covered with semi-coherent scrawling. He perked up when he laid eyes on her, like she could be interested in his rich, decadent ass. He introduced himself as something silly she couldn't possibly remember. Little Something, though in print it was probably "Li'l." He started showing her his tats, referred to his "ink" as "art." She could barely keep a straight face. This bizarre apparition, who wasn't as tall as she was, sort of brought her out of her malaise. She really needed to take some notes on her iPhone.

The foursome was on the tee. Li'l Sumpin told Marcia he'd see her later, and *dey all was sho go pahtie when dis shit done.* Marcia told him to get on with his bad shit, then walked over and kissed Tripp smartly, just for show, and felt proud she was assimilating so well.

They were off, her pothead beau and his pothead friend, and the pothead comic and his pothead friend the rapper, and Marcia walked up to the clubhouse, and then the pool outside, and it occurred to her that she needed some pot.

They played for five hundred dollars a hole, this despite the fact that Tripp Fallaw might possibly have five hundred cents, and for nine holes, it went well. Iglesias could play, and he and Wade were fairly evenly matched. The rapper had been taking lessons, but he didn't have much skill. His drives were embarrassingly shy of Tripp's. They halved four holes, Tripp and Wade won four, and Hector won the eighth when he hit his tee shot three feet from the hole, and Wade missed a twenty-foot birdie putt after Tripp hit his tee shot in the trap. Li'l Sumpin had a double bogey. They were fifteen hundred dollars ahead at the turn.

Li'l Sumpin and Tripp were smoking up a storm, and it was really strong kush the rapper was stuffing into his little pipe, but that wasn't what did Tripp in. They had a cooler, and in addition to six beers, which they never got around to finishing, Li'l Sumpin had a waterproof container. In it was some aluminum foil folded around a few little mushrooms.

"Rehneck boh, ah eat me sevvul err day," he said, "You man up wit me? Thank you'n still hit im li'l balls straight 'n' shroomin'?"

"Ain't nothing stopped me before," Tripp said. He reached for a beer, popped two mushrooms, chewed a little, *eww*, and washed them down. The final four holes were fun. When Tripp hit a drive, and looked up, its path was etched in fluorescent orange tracks that gave him sunspots. On the seventeenth tee, when Tripp walked up to take his shot, he was walking through cumulus clouds, and the sky was the golf course. Then it flip-flopped back to normal, and Tripp nearly fell, and he shook his head and said, mysteriously, "Shit, man, that's hard to do."

Tripp was tripping.

Marcia ordered a glass of wine. When it arrived, she reached in her purse and got her faux Reese's Cup. She took a bite. Not bad. She sipped the wine. Had a cigarette. Asked for another glass of wine. So far, good. Took another bite. This one was better.

Then, after a slow while, everything slowed down more. She took out her iPhone and read her Twitter feed. She was on Facebook, but, then, so, too, was her mom. Fuck that. She wished she had a book. *Dr. Seuss might be nice.* She didn't have her iPod, but she could still listen to music on her phone. She didn't have her ear buds, though. *Where the fuck could they be?* She searched her purse. The candy was getting gooey. *Shit. It's hot. I hadn't noticed.* She ate the rest of the first pack. The other one seemed solid enough. *I know I'm not supposed to eat so much, but, shit, what's the worst that could happen?*

The rest of the afternoon might have been fact and might have been fiction. Most likely, it was a combination of the two. Some of it she dreamed. Some of it happened. She would be unsure later which was which.

A starlet came up. Sat down. Said her name was Jessica. Marcia recognized her from somewhere but couldn't name a movie, couldn't name a show, couldn't name a song. They shared the other candy bar. Jessica seemed like a really nice person.

She didn't awaken until nearly noon and was pleased to realize she was back at Wade Sanderson's place in Pomona. She tried to sleep longer. When she couldn't, she got up, reluctantly, and walked into the den where, surprisingly, Wade was sitting on the couch, waiting.

"I thought, like, you and Tripp had another golf match?" Marcia asked.

"Sit down, Marcia."

Jesus. Is Tripp, like, fucking dead?

"Tripp's gone," Wade said.

"Oh, my God." *As in, gone?*

"He ran off. Yesterday he got fucked up and lost a bunch of money. You know what he did? He paid off by giving Li'l Sleazy his golf clubs. Then the two of them went off to party. You wudn't in no better shape than he was. I let them go and brought you home."

"Thank you so much, Wade."

"That's not all. Sometime last night, Tripp came back. Stole a bunch of weed from me. Stole a '95 Mustang parked down the street. The cops are looking for him."

"Where you think he went?"

"Oh, I don't know. Vegas, maybe."

Marcia looked in her purse, which somehow she'd left on the coffee table. Her cash was gone. And her father's credit card. She found her plane ticket, though. It was zipped up in a side pocket.

The Cuban dentist reported the stolen credit card, wired her money, and switched her flight home to Columbia, South Carolina. Wade drove her to LAX. He told her, if she ever saw Tripp again, to tell him not to come see him because he was either going to kill him or have him killed. Marcia wished him good luck with that.

"You, on the other hand, are quite cool," Wade said. "I don't suppose you'd be interested in making a little money on the side."

"What you got in mind?" she asked. *Whoring?*

"You know, California produces the best weed in the world," he said, "and, most likely, the most. You don't think it all gets smoked by people with medical-marijuana cards, do you?"

Marcia couldn't imagine what he meant.

"You can do for me what Tripp was doing," Wade said.

"Which is?"

"Sell the shit out of some cannabis. There's not much risk. We don't send you a FedEx package or nothing. Too risky. Too much chance of being unlucky somewhere down the line. We'll deliver it to a secure place, probably one of those private storage complexes. You'll have a key. All you gotta do is go get it then make deliveries to, oh, five or six places in a fifty-sixty mile radius. One bundle is yours to sell on the side."

"Why do you think it's safe? Delivering it in a truck? What keeps you from being unlucky there?" she asked.

"You like cocaine?" he asked.

"Never tried it. Don't want to."

"Smart girl. Turns you into an asshole."

"You still didn't answer the question about the truck."

"Oh," Wade said, "it's a big one. Owned by the government."

"No shit?"

"I'll look out for you, Marcia," Wade sai. "When you get back home, there's a bag of coffee in your suitcase. Stuffed in the middle of the coffee, you're gonna find a bag of a sativa I really like. There is no chance of being caught by airport security. Trust me. Half the bags out of California got weed hidden in them. They're worried about terrorists. They don't give a fuck about a little weed. That's a gift. Because you're cool. Because it's not your fault Tripp is a loser."

They were at the airport. Marcia needed to take a deep breath. Being cool while traveling home with weed in the suitcase was easier said than done. She wished she was high. Wade gave her a card, scrawled his cell on the back, and told her to call him if she was interested.

All the way home, Marcia thought about how Tripp Fallaw was too cute and charming for his own good, and how he would come to a bad end because all he cared about was making the big hit, the big score. He wasn't interested in honest money. He was just interested in the con, and that was the way he was always going to be. She wasn't about to start selling weed. She liked the idea of having someone like Wade to get her some, though.

She had a peaceful day back at the at the waterfront house. She, her sister, and brother-in-law – his name was actually Chad, as it turned out -- went to the beach to body-surf for a couple hours. Afterwards, as the sun descended into the palmetto trees, Marcia sat alone on the patio and curled up with a good book, the Bible. She was drawn to the Old Testament and read about forlorn pilgrims who came to bad ends after deceiving the Righteous and Fearsome Lord. The next morning Marcia went with her mother to the Methodist church and decided that, the next night when she was back on campus, she was going to give in and go to the Fellowship of Christian Athletes because, even though she wasn't an athlete anymore, Christ didn't care. It was time, she knew, to grow up and make her way in life, the same way her parents had and her sister was.

It lasted for almost a week.

CHAPTER 9

Company Comes

Mickey Statler's hangover wasn't so bad. He got up when he got good and ready, which was ten, had his coffee, three Aleves, and found a three-quarters-empty bottle of Wild Turkey on the top shelf in the kitchen cabinet. He had to stand on a chair to get it, and that's when he noticed he was a tad wobbly, after all, but he braced himself a little with one hand while he grabbed the Wild Turkey with the other, sat it atop the microwave, and dismounted the chair. He took a big swig of coffee and replaced what he drank with a shot of liquor because that was as God intended for washed-up columnists.

So damned out of focus was he that good bourbon sharpened it a little. Mickey sat down and completed his only current assignments, which were opinions, or columns, or blogs – the terms grew fuzzy on the internet – for sites that had been paying him to do so for a decade.

It was off-the-top-of-the-head bullshit, but Mickey was good at it. Once, in a hospitality room during the wee hours, long after the final first-round game in the ACC basketball tournament, a similarly besotted scribe, Harrison Rawls of the old *Roanoke Register,* had proclaimed that Mickey Statler could write a column about taking a shit. Rawls, who was a snide drunk, had meant it as a denunciation, but everyone else, Mickey included, had thought it a wondrous compliment. It had followed him to the point that one of his more common requests was actually to write a column about taking a shit. He could get away with it, they all said. He could phrase it in a way that wouldn't be censored. Mickey had a website. He could do it. This wasn't the day. Nausea wasn't a sensation one would want to feel while writing about the process of ridding oneself of dung.

Besides, it might be best to concentrate on projects that offered the prospect of money.

What did he want? By two, he was done with the columns and had emailed them away to the far mainframes of Pittsburgh and Denver. He had a nice caffeine-alcohol buzz, a bit out of season in August but pleasant, nonetheless. He wasn't drinking because he was depressed. He was drinking because he wanted in the pants of Laurie, the bartender at the Lovable Loser Lounge and the patron saint of all who stumbled inside. He had his sights on her and not his overdue child support, hellishly vindictive ex-wife, and the impending need to make a living. He figured the two columns would pay for another few days of drinking and entertaining this fetching gal, and he didn't have to worry about much overhead because his prospective lover controlled the purse strings, located in the cash register of the Lovable Loser.

In the face of disaster, why not spit in the face of Fate by chasing pussy?

While Mickey tried his best to lay plans, a commotion ensued. Mickey's first thought was that the police were trying to knock in his door, but he actually remembered the details of the night before and could recall doing nothing illegal, right down to the sainted Laurie driving him home. She'd driven his car, so it should be outside, where she had left it and, unfortunately, left with Louie, her colleague and weed dealer on the side. Whatever gang had stormed his door was yelling and, yes, trying to knock the door in.

"I'm comin', I'm comin'," he said.

It was a random assortment of all the chums whose calls and emails Mickey hadn't been answering. They were united, apparently, in a willingness to be drinking at this hour of the day. Summer was slow for scribes, wags, and pundits.

"You fuckin' deadbeat," said Julius Parkinson, staggering in advance of the others. "Did you really think we were gonna leave you be? Really?"

Julius had a gambling problem, complicated, no doubt, by his enjoyment of scotch on the rocks. He'd had a reliable job until six months after his old man had sold the family newspaper to a conglomerate and two months after the old man died. He was living on his inheritance, but, in the long run, that was not going to be a good thing. Wife Meg was a bigger lush than he was, and Julius Junior had been in drug rehab the last Mickey heard.

Devin Sailer was an Englishman. He'd come to America to handle public relations for a pro soccer team and returned to journalism because he'd discovered he was too independent to be a flack, and then there had been the matter of being shot in the ass by the keeper whose wife he was screwing at the time. He'd remained in the States because he didn't have the money to get back to jolly old England, and he'd discovered that American women were often aroused by the sound of his accent. That had been twenty years ago. Now he was a nationally regarded expert on college football and basketball recruiting. Same gig. Different ball.

"Sorry to hear of your demise, Mickey, old boy. Cheers."

Julius and Devin, as different a pair as Mickey could imagine, were both held in high esteem by the bold young nerds of the younger generation. Have you ever seen two twenty-somethings who were both poised for adventure and scared shitless at the same time? They tramped in last, somewhat sober, each holding one side of a beer cooler. Mickey was a beer drinker. He'd always tried to be friendly and cooperative to these kids, but he hadn't a clue of their last names. He'd resisted the idolatry that Julius had encouraged and Devin had gotten by virtue of his funny way of speaking. Justin and Lanny weren't old enough to have learned that every single Julius Parkinson story had been stolen from someone who wasn't present when he told it. They actually believed it when Julius told them Hank Aaron had once told him he was "the only white man who has ever been truly fair to me." Devin's brand of bullshit was to regale them with tales of adventure beneath the sheets.

Mickey kept looking at his watch. He felt as if he was being inducted into the Committee of the Doomed. Julius still wrote about sports. No one could find out where. He brought his laptop. He pecked away at it afterwards. The broad suspicion was that he was paying his own way and doing what he'd always done because it was all he knew. Julius was ten years older than Mickey. At least he had money, for now. Devin was five years younger. His days were numbered, too. Justin and Lanny were safe for now. They still *liked* sports. They hadn't had their spirits broken yet, and they weren't making much money, and as long as that was still the case, they'd be fine. Then, one month, they'd get that fateful fifteen-percent pay raise, and, six months after that, after a change of management, it would be the justification for laying them off.

Maybe it was time to start pounding beer, after all.

Julius told the story about him and Jack Nicklaus, alone in the Augusta locker room, and Devin told the lads about the time he screwed Caroline Kennedy, and Julius asked Mickey to tell the story about him and Myra LeFlore, the Brown grad who had leapfrogged quickly from Memphis to Oklahoma City to the *Chicago Sun-Times* to the *New York Post*, leaving some figurative bodies in her wake.

"We were in the old Benny Kahn at Daytona, Speedweeks," Mickey said, popping a top. "Myra asks, to no one in particular, 'How do you spell intuition?' and I spelled it. She thanked me with this look of disbelief on her face, and I said, 'I won the state spelling bee when I was a kid,' and she looked back at me, right in the eyes, and said, 'What did you have to spell? Opossum?'"

"What'd you say back to her, Mick?" Julius asked, on cue.

"I said, 'Goddamn it, Myra, that may be the most snobbish thing I've heard.' She then accused me of being condescending toward *her*, but I couldn't help but start laughing because half the press room was already."

The laughter subsided. Devin said, "You know, all kidding aside, she really is quite insightful."

"You know who might come by?" Julius asked.

"No. No way," Mickey said.

"Tell him, Lanny."

Lanny gulped. "Justin and I ran into Myra last night in downtown Charlotte. We started talking, and she asked what we were doing, and

Justin told her we were coming over to see you, and, uh, she said she might stop by."

"Get this," Julius said, "she's doing a story on a transsexual, white-water rafter. From Linville Caverns. You can't make this stuff up."

"Though Myra might," Devin said.

Mickey lost his warm glow. Beer generally made him merry. Now he was turning mad. He didn't respect Myra LeFlore. He'd found her less than trustworthy in the honor among thieves that the media revered. Julius noticed the change. It might have been the smoke from Mickey's ears.

"Oh, don't worry, Mick," he said. "For God's sake. You know she won't come."

"She might want to see me on my knees," Mickey said, and, then, imitated her. "So, Mickey, how does it really feel to be … destitute?"

The bastards yelped in gallows humor, all but Justin and Lanny, who probably felt an obligation to get the old gods home.

"You ever fucked her?" Mickey asked Devin.

"Oh, God, yes," said he, predictably. "Several times."

"One more set of secrets the Russians got," Mickey growled. "Let's watch the fucking Olympics."

"Might as well," Devin said. "Gaynes is not speaking."

"Y'all know Myra's a Republican, right?" Mickey asked.

"No way," said Justin.

"I was at … it was outside … RFK Stadium," Mickey said. "I don't think I ever told this story. You head it, Julius?"

"Naw, I ain't. Do tell." Julius was starting to fade already.

"Well, W. was president and was throwing out the first pitch. Nationals Park hadn't been built yet. I was in D.C. for something else, probably the Heels playing Maryland or something, and the paper said go down to the ballpark, we got you credentials, and write a column on the president's visit, and, man, you know the hassle, intense security, all that, but W. sort of liked hanging out with sportswriters, not political, but, you know, he'd been with the Rangers and all that, so I'm hanging out …

Lanny, grab me another beer while you're up … and there's Myra, and, of course, she comes sidling up, and I told her I was just there to see if he committed some gaffe or said something stupid. Well, she draws up and tells me she had once been the president of the Brown University College Republicans, and I thought it was a joke, and I said, 'you're obviously shitting me because it would be the University Republicans because Brown is not a college,' and mine was a joke, but she didn't like it at all. About ten minutes later, the 43rd President of the United States arrives, and, swear to God, Myra LeFlore got his autograph."

Justin said "no way" again, and Lanny was suitably aroused to say "no shit."

Ten minutes later, Justin's cell rang. It was Myra. Mickey saw an opportunity to renew relations with Laurie.

Mickey got up, put on a Merlefest ballcap, and said, "Y'all boys just lock the door when you leave."

"What are we going to tell Myra? She works for the fucking *New York Post*," Lanny said.

"Tell her life's too short to deal with her snobbish ass," Mickey said. "Tell her I'd rather herd hogs for a living. Tell her the worst thing about having a job was bumping into her every now and again. Tell her now that I've been run out of the business, there's just nothing in the goddamned world that would make me want to be in the same room with her. Tell her anything you want. Tell her I despise her. She already knows it. I'm out of here."

"What are your plans?" asked Devin.

"My plans are to make passionate love to a young woman twice as good-looking as Myra LeFlore ever thought about being," Mickey said.

"No such woman exists," Devin said.

"Says you. I appreciate y'all coming to see me," Mickey said, "but friends are friends, and pussy is pussy, and y'all understand that."

"Aw, bullshit," Julius said. "You lie."

"Don't matter," Mickey said. "I'm gone."

He left them sitting there.

CHAPTER 10

A Bear of a Philosopher

Marcia had been back at Triborough College for three days. That morning she had jogged a mile on the track that surrounded the soccer stadium that was across the street from the shabby house where Tripp Fallaw had lived. Her own dorm room was a quarter mile away, so she jogged over, around the track four times, and back. By the time she had showered and dressed, it was still early. The fall semester didn't start for another week.

Whatever happened to sleeping in?

She decided to drive uptown with her Beat Generation sampler and have coffee and bagels at Auntie Em's Coffee and Creamery. For a few days after the California debacle, Marcia had read the Bible. Then she switched to Melville's *Billy Budd*, which she had read at least three times and still hated. Melville had been a bitter old man, desperate to find heavenly reward, when he'd written his obvious allegory on the life of Jesus. Melville already knew the story. All he'd done was foul it up. It provided a serviceable excuse to abandon the Lord and read some Kerouac and Kesey. Auntie Em's had a table outside, probably several when it wasn't so hot, but this particular Friday was overcast. A nice, cool breeze wafted through the street. Marcia was tired. She needed coffee to cure the mild queasiness of exertion's aftermath.

She also needed a cigarette, so she abandoned five whole days of self-restraint, reasoned that her growing physical fitness afforded her the occasional backslide, and bought a pack of Marlboro Lights and a Bic lighter at the tiny grocery store two doors down from Auntie Em's. She ordered a blend devised to accompany doughnuts, chose a blueberry bagel instead, and walked out to the table on the street, where she proceeded to slather her bagel and stir her coffee, and she ate the bagel hurriedly because the reason she had decided to sit on the street was because she wanted to break the seal on that pack and have a smoke. It felt good. The coffee felt good on top of it, cleansing the lingering tobacco from her tongue. Some might feel as if a jog and a smoke were antithetical. They didn't know how invigorated she now felt. She began reading a selection from *Sometimes a Great Notion*, a novel that was hard to follow in totality but gloriously irreverent in small doses.

Somehow, her eyes caught the approach of an enormous man, wearing cargo shorts and a Grateful Dead tee, walking up the sidewalk toward her with a faintly detectable limp. She returned to the details of Hank Stamper's stubbornness and was caught unawares when the large man spoke to her.

"Miss, I hate to intrude, but would you mind if I rested my legs across from you?"

Marcia was glad the sky was overcast because she could imagine squinting, the sun partly obscured by this hulk, on a sunny day. He had an appealing face, unusually bright blue eyes, long hair but freshly shaven.

"Sure," she said. "Help yourself."

"You're very kind," he said. "I'm Dylan Wannamacher. If you'll save this seat – I'm satisfied others will desire it – I'll go fetch me a cup of their finest."

He had a deep, rich Southern dialect, the kind that bubbled up from the delta of Mississippi, and yet it struck Marcia that his words were more like those of an Englishman. He might be a professor. He might be homeless. He was literate. She knew that, based on four sentences. She knew she liked him from the moment he opened his mouth. He was more interesting than Billy Budd, already. Then again, Marcia had found Tripp

Fallaw fascinating, and now she wasn't sure if she cared whether he was dead or alive.

"So what do you do, Dylan Wannamacher?" she asked when he returned.

"I teach English," he said. "I tell privileged white brats exploits of great adventure and tumult."

She introduced herself.

"Nice to meet you, Marcia. If you hadn't have introduced yourself, I'd have called you Mademoiselle or … Sweetie … or something," he said, surveying her looks. "Nah, you're not a Sweetie. Or a Honey Bunch. You might be a Honey. Marcia works best, though."

She inserted a mark and closed the book. Dylan wasn't an old man. He seemed too young to be eccentric.

"What brings you out this early?" she asked.

"I'm in the midst of the Breakfast of Champions, Marcia."

"And what, pray tell, is that?"

"Well, I have a pair of arthritic knees, and every morning, when I awaken, it's often quite difficult to get around, so I get up, enjoy a bit of cannabis, get myself presentable, and walk here to continue the medicinal practice with coffee and a cigarette," he said and fished out a Marlboro. "I asked if I could sit here with you because I can enjoy a cigarette in the cool morning air, and you are occupying the only available table. It's all just random fate."

"I take it that you have no teaching obligations today."

"Still more than a week from fall term," he said.

"So you medicate."

"Not legally," Dylan said. "After all, this is Virginia.'

"And why are you telling me all this?"

"Because you, too, get high."

"I do no such thing," Marcia said. "Not lately. And how would you tell? Are you psychic?"

"Just observant. I can tell you get high by the way you smoke."

"Oh, really."

"Really," he said. "Some people either don't smoke much or don't want people to think or know that they smoke. Like this."

Dylan lit his Marlboro and took a light puff, exhaling quickly. "Think they be bad."

He took a deeper draw and exhaled quickly. "People who smoke, who don't care who knows it, do so this way. But people who get high, particularly when they are high, they smoke a cigarette like it's a joint. They inhale deeply." He demonstrated, taking a deep inhale, holding it, and half-closing his eyes before expelling the smoke.

"That's me, huh?"

"That's you. Once upon a time, I fancied myself quite the observer. Then, one day, I realized I did exactly the same thing."

She laughed, fascinated.

"I live two blocks away. It's a building that once was a printing press, now divided into apartments. Not a bad deal," Dylan said. "By the way, I smoke Marlboro Lights most of the time myself. Two per bong hit. One Marlboro Red. In the mornings, I've gotten in the habit of getting high, getting dressed, and walking over here. If I still enjoyed the Breakfast of Champions at my place, I'd smoke a Marlboro Light as soon as I came down from the rush, then have another later. I am a creature of habit. Stoners always talk about getting the munchies. I get the smokies. Pizza doesn't bring back a man's buzz. Smoking cigarettes is bad, but, when you're high, it's good, and as long as weed is illegal, people are going to smoke cigarettes when they're high."

"It's going to kill us both," Marcia said.

"Life is fatal," Dylan replied.

Later Marcia googled Dylan Wannamacher. He had played football at Triborough. He had begun at the University of Virginia, undergone surgery on both knees, transferred to Triborough, which fielded a team but didn't offer scholarships, on a full academic scholarship, and been captain of a team that lost only once, in the second round of the Division III playoffs, his senior year. He was now thirty-eight years of age. He was a recipient of the Virginia Sports Confederation's Freckles Edmiston

Award, given to the Commonwealth's finest college defensive lineman and named for a Virginia Tech guard who had died a hero in World War II. One online account speculated that he'd won it because the Hokies and Wahoos both sucked that particular year.

Marcia had sworn off sports. She wondered why she continued to be attracted to athletes. Tripp had been a golfer. Now this roughhewn defensive tackle with a taste for literature and weed had materialized to intrigue her. On the other hand, Dylan Wannamacher, born and raised in Paulette, Mississippi, seemed to have cast sports aside, too. On the private school's website, no mention was made of "Coach" Wannamacher. Marcia thought it amusing that his biography referred to him as "beloved" English teacher. He had been Teacher of the Year in 2013.

No Wannamachers at all were listed in the phone listings. He probably didn't have a land line. Marcia decided she would be returning to Auntie Em's the next morning, and, quite likely, many more. Dylan was a man she wanted to get to know better.

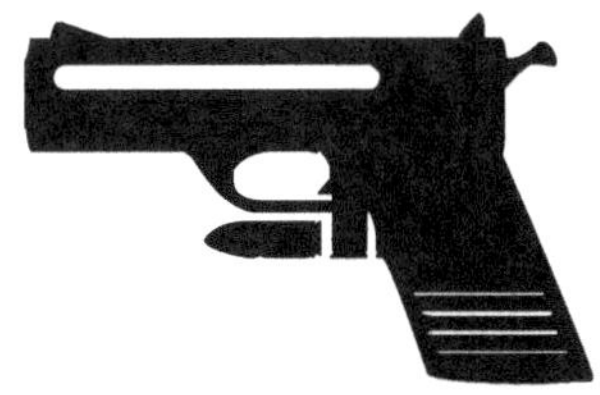

CHAPTER 11

Insider Trading

Mickey Statler left for the Lovable Loser. Julian Parkinson and Devin Sailer left for a watering hole of unknown origin. Justin and Lanny remained at Mickey's place. Myra LeForce had no interest in seeing her nemesis during his time of trouble. It would have been more masochistic than sadistic.

The reason Myra had leaped at a chance to write about a transsexual whitewater rafter because she wanted to see Justin and, especially, Lanny. Lanny Greenwell had grown up and attended college in the Bluegrass State, though, like Virginia, Kentucky considered itself a commonwealth, and not even Myra's Ivy League education had given her a clear idea of what was the difference. She wanted to see Lanny because he knew where to get weed. He almost always had it. He spent a couple thousand dollars on it every time he went home to dear old Corbin, and reliably had some for sale to a few of his colleagues on the Atlantic Coast and Southeastern conference beats. Myra had a web of intrigue in which she thought Lanny might have an interest.

It was sort of perfect, really. Myra took great pleasure in sitting with her younger, less accomplished peers, lounging comfortably in plastic chairs around a table on the fifth-floor patio of one of many fellow journalists she reviled, sampling Lanny's skunkweed.

"I can't ever get it straight," Myra said. "Is this sativa or indica?"

"Sativa," Lanny said. "It's leafy. Indica has little clumps. Usually fewer seeds."

Justin said, "Mickey would shit if he knew we were blazing at his place."

"I hope the hell he never knows," Lanny said.

"Fuck him," Myra said. "We gotta leave a hint. I mean, he's got no way of knowing we're even here, right?"

"He knew we were here when we left," Lanny said.

"Julius and Devin were here, too, then," Julius said.

"That means we've got plausible deniability," Myra noted. "Let's leave a couple roaches in the ash tray."

"You're nuts," Justin said.

"I'm high," she replied. "Let's go to Charlotte and find a good place to drink. We need to talk."

Mickey thought he detected a mild odor when he wobbled back into the condo, having carefully made his way, both hands on the wheel, back to home sweet home from the Lovable Loser, where he had sought Laurie in vain. A certain quantity of beer had the effect of numbing his senses, and he figured his smell might be impaired. It was ten o'clock, and when he turned on the TV, a political pundit was talking about Martin Gaynes's finances. The Igloo cooler that Justin and Lanny had brought over was on the kitchen floor next to the refrigerator. He opened it and found mostly empty bottles floating in the melting ice. Two of the Heinekens were intact, though, and Mickey pulled them both out, walked back to the living room, sat them on the table, and changed the channel to the Giants playing the Rockies.

CHAPTER 12

The Students' Choice

Dylan Wannamacher began the day as he began most, which was to enjoy the Breakfast of Champions. The season was changing. His life had two seasons, one taking up three fourths of the year. It was the first day of class at Enlightened Word College Preparatory Academy.

EWCPA. *Ewwwk-pah!* Not surprisingly, the school used EWA when initials were appropriate after first usage. Dylan taught three classes of American literature, one of "Appreciating the Classics," and one called "Directed Senior Seminar," which was more like managing a contest, or, in some ways, selling used cars. He tried to inspire his charges to pursue a career in writing, which was comparable to advising ancient Romans to build condos on Mount Vesuvius.

Dylan routinely referred to his employer as Enlightened Words. He felt better about teaching enlightened words than a single Enlightened Word. Dylan was somewhere between a Christian and an atheist but still not quite an agnostic. As with the old Gospel tune, Dylan and Jesus had their own thing going. If only Dylan and Jesus could get it all worked out.

He was wistful about his summer, as he was every year, because it was a time of personal growth and also because it was when he didn't have to take as many precautions to hide his enjoyment of cannabis. For instance, he could grow a beard. He had, in fact, grown a beard, but he'd shaved it a week earlier, allowing for some time to turn his pale face pink again. Beards were inconvenient for the teaching life because they often contained odors of stale cigarette and weed smoke. Dylan studied such matters diligently. He cut his hair, too.

Dylan looked dapper in his khaki suitcoat, so bought because any of six pairs of khaki pants went somewhat with it. For opening day, he wore the ones that came with the suit, along with a light-blue, buttoned-down dress shirt and a green-and-navy-striped tie. He walked inside Auntie Em's because it was, after all, still summer, and the inside was still air-conditioned, and when school started, he didn't smoke cigarettes in public, and when he smoked outside of the coffee shop, he generally wore something cool like a folk singer's tee shirt and cargo pants that conveniently held items like Swiss Army knives, lighters, rolling papers, and packs of Marlboros. He often rode over, moderately high, on his mountain bike.

Because he was straightening up and flying right, Dylan ordered a blueberry bagel and slathered it with cream cheese. Nothing was better with coffee except a cigarette. He diligently read the *Washington Post*, which was possible because it was six-thirty and the private school was only twenty miles away.

The drive was relaxing. He had no dread. Summer was pleasant, but getting back in the routine was a pleasant prospect. Dylan thought overly simplistic the notion that stoners were lazy. Writing a novel required discipline. It was hard. What weed did was make a man adore what he liked and revile what he didn't. After a bong hit —never a problem because his funky apartment building was a wonderful little colony of peace-loving hippies – Dylan loved to read, write, and post on Twitter under his fake account of honesty. He had a real account of hypocrisy, like most people, but under his *nom de tweet*, he dispensed nuggets of controversial wisdom, 140 characters at a time, on burning issues of the day such as single-payer health care, marijuana legalization, LGBT and whatever the new Q was, and, of course, stopping that authoritarian son of a bitch, Martin Gaynes. These were not popular sentiments at Enlightened Word. Dylan knew the Ten Commandments solely as a result of walking past the granite tablet on the lawn for ten years now.

In the summer, he'd written every day. He was pleased with his second novel. It, like his first novel, had not been published. Dylan was reluctant to have it published because he knew it wouldn't go over well at Enlightened Word, regardless of how enlightened they were. They felt more secure with just one enlightened Word. God. In three Persons. Blessed Trinity. God was complicated for just one word. Or Word.

As a consequence of Dylan's theory that weed turned likes into loves, his dislikes had turned his apartment into a bit of pig sty. Among the items he didn't like were tasks such as washing dishes, emptying trash, and washing, drying, and folding clothes. With steel determination, however, he had managed to perform all these tasks, even while making liberal use of his buddy the bong, and, as he drove into the teacher lot of Enlightened Words, he was entertaining the notion of entertaining his new acquaintance, dear, sweet Marcia. He'd pronounced the shabbiness of his humble abode as safely above minimum acceptable standards of cleanliness. He was thinking seriously of sweeping the floors.

All of his classes were the same. Dylan introduced himself to his pupils, eighty percent of whom already knew him well, sixty percent of whom either idolized or idealized him, and perhaps a quarter of whom were as high as he was. The marijuana was popular with the rich white kids, and Enlightened Word always had enough intelligent rapscallions – "Unless you straighten up, I'll send you off to a private school! That's what I'll do, Mister!" -- who knew where to get it. Dylan observed it all diligently, secure in the confidence that it took one to know one.

The kids knew he was cool.

The first day of class was one big press conference, so popular that the would-be scribes had to ask their questions in shifts. Dylan just threw the floor open, mainly to entertain discussion of what the kids had been reading, and, when invariably, he had no idea what they were talking about, he admitted it and let them tell him all about it. He didn't strictly confine the discussions to literature, but he had enough sense not to let some comment about drugs or politics escape back to the family dinner table at Thanksgiving.

Jordie, your mother found a packet of grass in your jacket.

Mr. Wannamacher said we should have an adventurous spirit, and that smoking pot is just a rite of passage into manhood.

Well, we'll just see what your headmaster has to say about that.

Dylan just played it all with winks and nudges. Winks and nudges were easy with a morning buzz and a righteous fervor for enlightened words.

It wasn't all fun. He passed out syllabuses (syllabi?). With the senior seminar, the faux press conference dealt with appropriate topics for the short story that was really the sole requirement for completing the course. He discussed the heinous nature of plagiarism, which, like masturbation, would eventually make a scholar go blind, and cautioned that, while all they had to write was one story of between 10,000 and 20,000 words, it had damned well better be good. His purpose was to make sure of it, and everything would be fine as long as they worked with him over several drafts.

At day's end, Dylan walked to the Accord and leaned on the hood, watching football practice from afar. The Fighting Smiths, he called them, for the natural relation of words and smiths. He didn't get along with the head football coach for the sole reason that he declined to take part in the coaching.

"Everybody pitches in," Waddy Pegler had told him, as if it were one of the Ten Commandments.

"I do, too," Dylan had replied. "I already advise the literary magazine and student paper. And the Beta Club. I'm the Beta Club adviser."

He'd almost forgotten. The Beta Club was only as active as it needed to be. The "magazine" and "paper" were strictly online. They counted, though. Pegler, the old water buffalo, had even brought Dylan's refusal to coach before the school board, and had it not been for Dylan's status as Teacher of the Year, he might have gotten his way. Dylan had tossed away the football on the last Saturday afternoon he walked off the Triborough field, and he didn't have much interest in taking part in a game whose final scores were typically forty-eight to forty-three, anyway.

"Hey, Mr. Wannamacher."

Dylan turned to find Milo Hirley, dressed in his practice uniform of dull white and ground-in dirt, trotting up.

"Running a little late?"

"No, sir," Milo said. "First day of school. A.W.S. meeting. Gotta set up elections for the frosh."

Frosh. An old-fashioned word. Must be making a comeback. Milo was everything at Word he wanted to be. A.W.S. was Association of Word Students. Milo ran it. Dylan didn't know for sure, but he figured Milo probably ran the football team. He hoped so. He had to be better than Waddy Pegler.

"It's fancy meeting you here," Milo said. "I was hoping I'd bump into you."

"Hadn't you better be getting to practice?

"Thirty seconds won't matter. I got an excuse."

Dylan sighed. "What's on your mind, Milo?"

"I was wondering if maybe me and the guys could meet and talk away from school," he said. "You know, totally off the record."

I shouldn't make any assumptions. I shouldn't be, uh, paranoid. Not now, anyway. Need to play this cool. Maybe they want to talk about girls, Libertarians, or where can this girl I know get an abortion without anybody knowing?

Nowhere, son. Nowhere.

"Sure," Dylan, who didn't get to be Teacher of the Year for nothing, said. "Next week sometime?"

"How about after practice? We'll be done at four-thirty."

"I don't know, Milo. That's awfully short notice."

"That's how it needs to be. How about five o'clock? Vissage Pizza."

"How you gonna get your friends together so soon?" Dylan asked.

"All my buds play football, Mr. Wannamacher. All the guys play football here. It's in the Bible."

Dylan smiled. The kid was charming. Not as smart as he thought he was, though. No one was that smart.

"All right," Dylan said. "Let's get this out of the way."

"Thanks a million, Mr. Wannamacher."

Milo was used to getting his way. It was hard not to like him, though. Dylan watched him trot down the hill. He figured him to be about five-foot-nine. He was sure he was the quarterback, just like he was sure to be the point guard on the basketball team and shortstop in baseball. Five-nine, and 165 pounds, was good size for an Enlightened Word signal caller. Five-nine, 165, was a good size for a Dragoon guard. The real name of the team was the Dragoons. That's why Dylan thought Smiths was better.

It wasn't unusual for complications to arise on opening day at Enlightened Word. Dylan made sure he had provisions. He watched practice for a while. He remembered those hot days in Mississippi, when they practiced three and a half hours, twice a day. By the time Dylan had reached high school, they'd actually allowed the players to drink water. These kids would be at the pizza parlor by five, and, after they feasted on pizza, they wouldn't have to run to the bathroom to puke because they'd eaten too soon after practice or guzzled too much iced tea. They'd probably be refreshed after their showers. Dylan was going to be refreshed, too. He drove to a nearby state park, set aside to commemorate a minor Confederate victory in the War Between the States. He sat behind a picnic table, overlooking what once had been a bloody pond, and vaped a moderate quantity of cannabis. He thought about the harsh conditions of a skirmish that had taken place a little over a century and a half before. He tweeted extensively of his thoughts and posted a photograph of the pond on Instagram.

Dylan seriously wanted a beer, just one, when he got to Vissage Pizza, whose name was not misspelled. It was just run by the only family of whom he had ever heard that was named Vissage. They did put a visage on the sign. The visage of an Enlightened Words Dragoon. Small world. Small pizza parlor. Small school.

"Hi, Mel." The owner was named Mel Vissage. Swear to God.

"What a surprise. Dylan. Where you been all summer?"

"Same as every summer. Back in Triborough, trying to write fiction."

"That's right. I forgot," Mel said. "You live in the big city."

They both laughed. E.W.A. wasn't even in a town. It was a cluster of businesses at a crossroads, with the academy campus separated by two hundred yards of pretty green lawn and a stately brick wall. Five hundred students, give or take, prepared for college there. Another three hundred lived there, and perhaps twenty had no formal connection with the school. The Vissage family made up four of that number. It cost about as much to attend private Enlightened Word as it did a public university. The students were housed in two large dormitories, one male and the other female, with all the other buildings, the gym, the football field, the baseball and softball diamonds, a four-hole, par-three golf course, and a natatorium.

"I'm meeting some of my students here," Dylan said.

"They're back in the corner booth," Mel said. "All hush-hush."

They hadn't noticed Dylan's arrival. Four were in a booth. Milo had assembled a quartet of scholars. He was the writer, the athlete, the politician, and the schemer, all rolled into one, which happened to be a recipe for being the big man on a snotty, prep-school campus. Next to him sat Walt Pegler, the coach's son, who seemed to think more of Dylan than he did his old man. On the other side were Jonny Heinsohn, something of a pre-med sort, and that rare combination of thespian and athlete, Marty Drummond, whose father happened to be the headmaster.

One reason the meeting time had appealed to Dylan was that he had time to get high beforehand. Another was that the football players didn't.

Milo greeted him, rising from the booth.

"Man, Mr. Wannamacher, we been talking about getting together with you all summer," he said. "We even drove over to Triborough one Sunday afternoon, trying to find you."

"My whereabouts are a closely guarded secret," Dylan said. "I should pull up a chair."

"No," Marty said. "We can move. Let's take the booth with the curve-around couch."

Trixie – Dylan fancied her a Trixie – took the order. Naturally, it was a lowest common denominator based on an absence of ingredients anyone didn't like. They got mushrooms, sausage, pepperoni, and bacon, along with pitchers of all eligible beverages, those being Coke and Diet Coke.

"What size?" she asked.

"The size of a monster truck tire," Milo said.

"Don't make 'em that big. I think what you want is Jumbo."

"Jumbo it is."

"Well, what's on your mind, you inquisitive Smiths?" Dylan asked his gifted charges.

"Well, like, we kind of wanted to have a bull session," Milo said. "Only no holds barred. Everything we say stays here."

"I've always tried to be honest," Dylan said, "but I reserve the right to be tactful. Ask me what you want, and I'll tell you what I think. Tell you what, though. In the spirit of confidentiality, let's all cut off our cell phones. It's not that I don't trust you, Walt, but your father does despise me."

Pegler's son looked disappointed.

"Look, I know you wouldn't do that, try to catch me on tape saying something that might get me fired, but your dad has tried to do that in the past, and, Milo, you just got done saying everything stays in this booth, so it seems reasonable to me."

They all powered down. No live podcast or video feed.

"Why don't you coach football?" Jonny asked.

"Uh, probably, because when I became a man, I gave up childish things," Dylan said, "and because it would give Coach Pegler too much satisfaction. I mean, I don't think so, but it's … possible I might have volunteered to show the linemen a few things, but Pegler tried to force me into it, and that I could not abide."

"Have you ever seen us play?" Marty asked.

"Uh, I watched the second half of a game the year before last. I parked outside the fence," Dylan said. "You beat the snot out of whoever it was you were playing."

He paused. "I read all about you in the papers, though."

"Ain't much there," Milo said.

"Ah, there's a pretty lengthy account in the Grenadier most weeks," Dylan said. "Online."

"Sucks," Marty said, smiling. "Milo writes for it."

The president of A.W.S. gave Marty the finger.

Having completed the "pleasantries," everything got quiet. Dylan figured the topic would turn either to the abortion-responsibility question or weed. Surely, he thought, they had enough sense to use protection.

"What do you think about medical marijuana?" Milo asked, signaling that it was time to get down to business.

Dylan sighed. "I think it's absurd that it isn't allowed everywhere. I mean, at the very least, it probably has the medicinal value of things like vitamins and minerals. I read where, like, seventy-five percent of doctors were in favor of it."

"In Virginia, it's only allowed for oils," Jonny said.

"And they don't get you high," Walt blurted none too subtly.

Another sigh. Dylan was sighing a lot. He could use a cigarette. Instead, he poured himself another Diet Coke. The pizza arrived.

"Dig in, Dragoons. It's on me. Maybe you can swap me some weed." Dylan watched their eyes widen. "I'm kidding."

They did, in fact, dig in. The boys had the hunger of a recently completed period of exertion. They were obviously cutting supper in the dining hall. Dylan had the munchies. Not as much as he had the smokies, but the pizza was appealing. When he got his first bite headed to his innards, he said, "Give me a break. Half the old people in this county are popping pills to keep 'em stoned and alive. Now you're telling me that some 37-year old coal miner, dying of cancer, can't even get a buzz with his last gasps. It's hypocritical is what it is."

Dylan was playing their song.

"What'd you do this summer, Mr. Wannamacher?" Marty conveniently changed the subject.

Against his better judgment, Dylan said, "I just sat around and smoked weed. … I'm kidding again."

Actually, no. He got the feeling they sensed this. *Huh. Why so paranoid?*

"I finished my second novel. And y'all can call me Dylan. Here. And I'll start calling you Messrs. Hirley, Drummond, Heinsohn, and Pegler."

"It's all right," Milo said. "Where can I buy it?"

"You can't," Denny said. "It isn't published. Neither is the first."

"Have you ever thought about, you know, self-publishing? Or, what? Kindle? I read books on my phone," Milo said.

"I've got to have something up front," Dylan said. "My novels are pretty frank. When they're published, that's when I'm going to have to move on. This novel – the latest one's name is Life Is Fatal – would not go over well at Enlightened Word. It would be a bigger problem than your father, Walt. It'll happen. I just can't give up my real job now. That's all."

"What do you think about recreational marijuana?" Walt asked

Dylan knew he was smirking as he thought about the coach's son, sneaking around behind his father's back. Most of the kids at E.W.A. were boarders. It occurred to Dylan that Walt and Marty were not.

"Okay, here's my view," he said, "and here's my background. My daddy and my granddaddy were both alcoholics. Both of them died too young as a result. I think weed is bad, but it's not anywhere close to as bad as alcohol. One reason I think it ought to be legal as that it would make it harder for kids like y'all to get high. Kids are gonna do shit, particularly when they're off on their own, and, believe it or not, living in a dorm room when you're seventeen years old is a lot more on your own than being at home, as, I'd wager, Walt and Marty can attest. My view may be jaded, but I think there's kind of a common denominator between people who develop a problem and those who start doing it, whatever it is, booze, weed, hard drugs, when they're too damned young to handle it. One of the reason you delinquents are sucking on reefer is that ain't nobody selling it to you who's asking for an I.D."

After the flicker of a guilty glance, Milo opined, "By the time it's legal, we'll all be old enough."

"Maybe for social security in the Commonwealth," Dylan said.

They hadn't gotten around to phase three, which was if their inspirational icon, Mr. Wannamacher, actually medicated, partook, and/ or blazed at this particular point in his rapidly approaching middle age of life. People started talking about middle age at forty-five. Dylan didn't figure he'd make ninety. He figured his life expectancy was seventy-five or six. He was midway there.

"Okay, enough about me," Dylan said. "Let me ask some questions. Let's put y'all's honesty to the test. Why do you smoke pot?"

"Pussy," Marty said. "It helps."

"I've heard that's true," Dylan said.

"It's just living life," Jonny, who wasn't into intangible concepts, being scientifically and mathematically inclined, said.

"Walt?"

"It's a good way to give my dad the big 'fuck you'," he said. "Without him even knowing, of course."

"I've been looking forward to this. Milo?"

He'd been looking forward to it, too. Why he waited till last was obvious. He'd thought about it. Milo Hirley thought a lot.

"It makes me creative," he said. "It gives me enlightenment. I can write better. I can play guitar better and enjoy it more. I even read better when I've got a buzz. When I was late for practice today, Mr. Wannamacher …"

"Dylan."

"When I was late for practice today, Dylan, I was smoking a roach."

"You dog," Walt said.

"Well, watch it, boys," Dylan said. "I know this sounds like something your dad would say, but don't get carried away."

"My dad said something like 'I'm going to send your conniving ass to a private school'," Milo said.

"Out of curiosity, are you guys blazing in the dorm?" Dylan asked.

"Hell, no," Walt said. "Behind the natatorium."

"We like to swim," Marty said.

"It's like, you know, four-twenty, where kids in California blazed at that time. They got together at some statue. Luther Burbank, I think, whoever he was. We meet at the Arnholdt Eliot statue. I think he was a swimmer," Milo said.

"And how is that a safe place?"

"The security guard is cool. He looks out for us," Marty said.

"He sells us our weed," Milo added.

"Well, I got to get back to Triborough," Dylan said. "Believe it or not, it's been almost real. What I really don't understand is why in hell you feel compelled to tell me all this. I mean, what makes you think I won't tell? Never mind that I said I wouldn't. I'm way over thirty. What makes you think you can trust me?"

"Aw, hell, Dylan, I've always known you were cool," Milo said.

On the way back to Triborough, Dylan thought about what he'd lost and what he'd gained. He probably shouldn't have done it. He wanted the students to like him too much, but the trouble was that, when most kids asked an adult what to do, the answer was "don't do it." What if they *were* going to do it? They needed advice from someone other than one another. Back in Mississippi, he'd overheard his high school coach talking to an assistant.

"You know what the secret is to coaching these kids?" he'd said.

"I don't know. What?"

"Don't ever, ever, ever let the little shitasses make up they own mind about nothing. They sure to fuck it up."

It was a long way from Paulette, Mississippi, to Enlightened Words, in more ways than one.

Marcia was sitting on a bench outside the Beauregard Press Apartments. Miraculously, Dylan found a parking space right across the street. She was reading her phone. He watched her, lost in her novel, expecting her to look up and notice him sitting there. Finally, he got out. Even while he was fetching his briefcase from the trunk of the Accord, not because he needed it but because his weed was stashed inside, she didn't notice him. He walked across the street and stopped in front of her.

"Waiting for someone?" he asked.

She jumped. "Oh, it's you. I guess I was distracted with this novel. Have you ever read Chekhov?"

"Grew up across the street from Chekhov," Dylan said. "Graduated high school with Chekhov's sister, uh, Jimmie Sue. Want to come in?"

CHAPTER 13

Back to the Grind

With Laurie nowhere to be found, three days of drinking had grown wearisome for Mickey Statler, and he decided he needed to do something unmotivated by the bottom of a glass or a crumpled can. He awakened smartly and, after relieving himself, put a bagel in the toaster and a K-cup in the coffeemaker. The day's first problem, lack of creamed cheese, was resolved by slathering peanut butter across it, which was particularly unconventional because peanut butter was not a condiment often associated with a blueberry bagel. They were cheap, though, and not particularly flavorful, and the peanut butter melted on the surface of the toasted bagel gave it something of a glaze. Washed down by hot Donut Shop, it did the trick. He mused about life and watched the latest tropical developments on The Weather Channel. After firing up the laptop and rolling its table in front of his easy chair, Mickey sought work, not the kind that makes a living but the kind that keeps one occupied and away from bars.

He announced his availability to nearby newspapers for free-lance work. The timing was right. High school football teams were now playing. He was exceptionally well qualified for a quick 400 words on the battle for the Beltway Bell, or the Tri-County Trophy, or the Midstate Medallion.

An offer arrived within moments. The area "paper of record," the one that had showed little interest in hiring him, was now excited to have him as a correspondent, also known as a "stringer." "Stringing" the Hedges Hogs against the Benson Barons would bring him the princely sum of seventy-five bucks. Mickey waited thirty minutes to reply.

Sold!

After an almost worshipful opening paragraph, the Sports Deployment Editor of the Statesman-Advertiser got around to the gory details:

We'll need 375-400 words by midnight. Sneak down to the field and take some photos. See if you can transmit them at halftime. Tweet after each score and at the end of each quarter. See the stats form attached. Try to shoot some video of the winning coach. You can post that on the paper's YouTube site sometime Saturday morning.

Can't wait! – Gus Trevelyon IV, Sports Deployment Editor.

Mickey Statler was glad he didn't have to write four hundred words about why a newspaper needed its writer to be "deployed," as if Benson and Hedges were battling for the Midstate Medallion with air strikes and artillery barrages. *But, first, the prayer by Becky Boombah, head cheerleader and president of the Fellowship of Christian Athletes!*

The fanciful name Becky Boombah made Mickey think of Laurie, and he knew that, in his mind, her last name was going to become Boombah. Where'd that come from? Oh, yeah. Rodney Dangerfield's doctor., Vinnie Boombatz.

Nothing to it. Fire off an email. Work comes within minutes. Let's see. A ballgame for seventy-five bucks. Small college on Saturday. Seventy-five more. Wonder what they paid for the volleyball, or girls' tennis, or cross country, on a Tuesday? If he played his cards right, and the *Statesman-Advertiser* had no problem with him peddling his wares to other rags, he might even wind up going to a game every night, with the stray cross country meet every day, and then, why, he'd be making upwards of … 450 dollars a week. Don't take Sunday off, and he could clear, oh, two thousand dollars a month as a free-lance workaholic.

That would take care of the monthly mortgage payment. He had that going for him.

Mickey spent the rest of the morning and most of the afternoon sipping coffee, fiddling around with a camera that lacked many of the features associated with professional photography, and pondering the logistics of interviewing a football coach while, at the same time, shooting video of him through either the aforementioned substandard camera or, quite possibly, his cell.

Oh, yeah. His cell. He had to get the bill switched to his name. The *News-Free Press* would invariably discontinue its service at any time, preferably not while Mickey was trying to tweet that Skippy Johnson had just kicked a thirty-seven-yard field goal for the Kirkland Kickstarters.

High schools would be so much better off if they allowed him to select their nicknames. They were so obvious. They should've been the Lawrence Arabians, the Union Labels, the Mayo Nays, and, of course, the Augusta Wind. *The Fighting Wind? Nah. The Swirling Wind.*

Mickey managed to get his cell billing changed, while maintaining his address book and number, and endured many of his own free minutes on hold waiting for someone to ask a few questions and transfer him again. The good news was that he watched half of *Marriage on the Rocks* with Frank Sinatra and Deborah Kerr, and that was the bad news, too. Dean Martin was in it, though, and he liked Dino.

As he was driving past the Lovable Loser, en route to Benson, it occurred to Mickey that he was about to cover Benson & Hedges, a cigarette name. This almost led him to stop by the Loser and regale Louie with a joke about Benson & Hedges, since he definitely wasn't going to be able to squeeze that pun into his lead. He knew Louie would get a kick out of it, because Louie would be stoned, but what if Laurie was there? Well, there wouldn't have been any four hundred words about the death struggle between Benson & Hedges for all the cancer sticks. Mickey remembered the time, when he was twenty-four, and decided to cover a game from the television set in the dorm room of a cheerleader with whom he had slept. Neither got away with it. She got kicked off the squad, and he got relegated to the desk for a month.

Those were the good, old days, and reliving them made him want to drink, but duty called. Sometimes a man had to sacrifice in the name of money.

Even without a pitcher of lager in front of him, Mickey was in a decent mood. The irreverence that had fueled many a column now descended over him as a consequence of sheer desperation. He had nothing to lose! He was free! It was time to recreate the adventures of his youth. He might as well pick up somebody's wife, because, regardless of whether or not he did it with her, he was fucked.

Somehow this made him feel giddy. He had nothing! What an adventure! Perhaps he could knock off a liquor store later. He was too nice a guy for a three-state killing spree, and a man had to recognize his limitations.

Benson was forty miles away. Mickey hadn't been there in twenty years. He hadn't even driven toward it in ten, that is, unless he counted recent visits to the Lovable Loser, which, now that he thought about it, might be a stop on the way home. He could file from the bar. He was reasonably sure they had wi-fi.

Bring me a beer, and keep 'em coming! I've got journalism to weave!

The phone, now uniquely his in the sense that he had a truly authentic sense of ownership, directed him to Benson High School. The Barons were perennial powers. Mickey thought it odd that his trusty Samsung was directing him to where the stadium used to be. It was a middle school. Behind the middle school, though, was the same Home of the Barons that had been there twenty years before. In spite of several state championships in the interim, the miserly people of the town had apparently not raised any money to retire the old dump in which they played. Mickey was appalled. The Atlanta Braves were about to move into a new park twenty years after they built the old one. Charlotte had wrecked a lovely coliseum so that it could build another one in the middle of the city. Mickey rode around town a while, noticed the dilapidated mill neighborhood and the ruination all around. It wasn't hard to tell that when the mill shut down, the funds for public works dried up, too. What a column this would make. What a lack of a place to put it he had. He entertained the notion of a website. There was a way to bring in a few more righteous bucks.

For now, though, just the facts.

CHAPTER 14

Not Much, but It's Home

"Ten years," Dylan Wannamacher said. "I've been living here ten years."

Marcia squinted. It was dark. Dylan turned on a lamp. Cobwebs hung in the upper reaches of the windows. He noticed she was staring at the webs.

"I'm sorry about the mess," he said. "The light on the ceiling fan stopped working a while back. I should get it fixed. I guess I just don't to have an electrician poking around when I'm gone, and I damned sure don't want to have to deal with one when I'm here."

"Might get into your stash?"

"Something like that. Would you like a cup of coffee?"

"Sure," she said. "How'd you wind up here?"

"Here? As in, the apartment? Or, as in, Triborough?" He walked into the kitchen. "I have mine black, with Sweet 'n' Low. I got some sugar, though. Low-fat milk. I might even have some of that powdered creamer. I don't reckon age matters much with that stuff. You could probably use that after it sat on a shelf ten years."

"Has it?" she asked.

"Not quite," Dylan said. "I probably didn't buy it till at least a couple years after I moved in."

"I'll have low-fat milk and sugar, then."

Marcia couldn't see him. His words just drifted in from the kitchen, where, apparently, from the sound, he was refilling ice trays. He place a metal tray on the aptly named coffee table. He took his mug away and left her to make appropriate use of the jar of sugar and a pint of milk he'd poured through a funnel into an empty Gatorade bottle.

"Not exactly elegant, I know," he said. "I just don't believe in bottled water. I use old plastic bottles and fill them with tap water."

"You know, we've got something in common," Marcia said. "We both have sports backgrounds. I went to Low Country Carolina on a soccer scholarship and transferred here. You went to UVA on a football scholarship and transferred to Triborough. But you kept on playing. I gave it up."

"Been studying up on me, huh? I'm pretty sure we've got something else in common," Dylan said. He reached over behind the couch, and from a precisely comfortable reach, he pulled out his bong. It was white and made of crockery, medium-sized, nothing ostentatious.

"Well, there's that," Marcia said.

"I've had an interesting day," Dylan said, pulling out a tinted pill bottle about two-thirds full of ground cannabis. As he packed the bowl, he said, "I had some of my smarter students ask to meet me in private after school. First day of school, like they had been planning it all summer. We met in a pizza parlor nearby after they got through practicing football. I spent an hour reading a novel on my cell."

Dylan flipped the switch on a window fan, pointed outward. He hit the bong, and, when he exhaled, the smoke dispersed quickly out the window.

"Come over here," Dylan said, motioning to the loveseat. "Kinda good news and bad news. The bad news is this building has no central air. I've got a window unit in my bedroom. This place ain't so big. Keep the lights off, and it never gets too hot."

"And the good news?" she asked.

"Well," Dylan said. "Most everybody who lives in this place blazes. Either that or they don't mind those who do. We got a pretty, uh, laidback vibe in the building. We got artists, musicians, poets, professors. We even got the county chairpersons for the National Association for the Reform of Marijuana Laws and Greenpeace. Actually, they're the same person."

"You?"

"Oh, Lord, no. He's a good friend, though. It's all I can do to teach my students and write my novels. I've attended a few meetings. I'm sympathetic to Greenpeace, but I don't have much interest in it. I'm a generally good liberal, but I'm more of a pragmatist than the Greenpeace folks. Probably because I'm a little older."

Shortly after her own hungry bong hit, Marcia sized up Dylan Wannamacher. He was a lot to see. He wasn't fat as much as he was massive. As weed seeped into her bloodstream, she wondered if he was well endowed. To curb her impulses, and enhance the high, she pulled out her pack of cigarettes.

"You mind?"

"Lord, no," he said. "The fan'll get rid of the smoke. I kind of like the smell of weed. You know how they say the smoke from a vaporizer has no odor?"

"Yeah."

"It does. A little. I can smell it in the hall."

"So, you've got this hippie writers' colony living here."

"Not just writers, but, yeah."

"So how do you keep, oh, drug dealers away?"

"What makes you think we want to?" he asked. "Seriously, I know what you're saying. Maybe it's peer pressure."

"What?"

"Peer pressure. I hate to be snobbish, but it's probably intimidating for your garden-variety drug dealer to be around such a distinguished group of stoners. I'm not saying nobody ever stops by to make a delivery. I haven't seen it, but maybe I'm just naïve. I'm satisfied a few people grow it."

"You?"

"Nah. I'm no horticulturist."

"So … are there students here?"

"Nah. Not undergrads. Grad students, teaching freshman classes while they're working on a master's."

"How would I go about moving in?"

"You can apply for the waiting list," Dylan said. "We're pretty much full up right now. If you occasionally need a place to crash, I got a spare bedroom. Give me two weeks, and I could probably clear it out enough for habitation."

Marcia could see the possibilities.

"Tell me," Dylan asked. "Why come you stopped playing soccer?"

"It's sort of a long story."

"It's not quite dark yet. I got nothing to do, nowhere to go, till school tomorrow."

"Well, it's like this," Marcia said. "I was on the team, not playing much, and this senior kind of took an interest in me."

"As in?"

"She was in love with me. She introduced me to weed. The problem, obviously, is I'm not so inclined. Sexually. I liked the weed."

"Not that there's anything wrong with it," Dylan said.

"Nah. Course not. It was just a sticky problem. I bolted. Quit the team. I almost went into hiding. I sort of buried myself in studies and discovered that I liked to write. I kind of fell in with the coffee-shop, literary crowd."

"Worked right well in terms of weed," Dylan said. "That's my guess."

"That's another thing we got in common. Only you didn't stop playing football when you transferred here."

"Well, I haven't ever been propositioned by another football player," he said.

"Fair point. But how come you left, you know, Mr. Jefferson's University for here?"

He sighed. "Long story, too."

"Like you said. We got plenty of time."

"Another bong hit?"

"Oh, hell, yeah," she said.

Dylan let her go first.

"Okay, you've already looked up everything you could find about me," he said. "It's okay. I'm flattered. You know, I'm from Mississippi. Paulette, Mississippi. I don't know, I like to think those of us from Miss'sippi kind of got literature in our bones. We also got hatred and gentility, bigotry and sentimentality. We're just a mass of contradictions. It's not without its good points, but, when I started getting recruited, the last thing I wanted to do was stay in Miss'sippi. I visited UVA, and, you know, it all seemed so … enlightened."

Marcia chased the bong with a Camel Light. Dylan took his turn.

"Freshman year at UVA. I only spent a year there," Dylan said, "and somehow I managed to tear up not one, but both knees, one blocking on a punt return against Wake Forest and the other in spring practice. I'm like you. I kind of got into my studies and realized I was good at other things besides football, but it was a torturous time, man. The second surgery, on my left knee, was in March. Ides of March. Mostly, I limped to class every day on crutches, and I spent a lot of time in rehab, and even when I wasn't doing anything but reading a book or writing a paper, I pretty much had ice on my knee all the time, and I switched roommates so that I could pair up with this other guy who was laid up just like me, and he smoked weed like it was going out of style, and I got to where it suited me fine. I still sorta loved football, but I didn't want to stay in that meat grinder. The coaches and I didn't get along. We weren't any good. I still wanted to play, but I wanted to have fun doing it, so I transferred here to Triborough, and it turned out that I got pretty much a full ride just based on my modest writing skills, so I came here and had a big time. I don't regret it one bit."

High, Marcia saw possibilities in this overgrown wordsmith and his respectable colony of stoners, right in the middle of Triborough and two blocks from the county law enforcement center. She might turn this into a place where she could peddle a bit of California weed from her friend the Caddy of the Stars. She had to struggle to remember his name.

Wade something-or-other. Sanderson. Wade Sanderson.

"So … you play guitar, huh?" Marcia noticed the Martin leaning against the end of the loveseat in which she was sitting.

"A little," he said. "I can play it by ear, but I'm never going to be a picker. My fingers are too big and clumsy. You know, I'm a writer. Lyrics are what matter to me. I know enough about guitar to write songs. I always tell people I just chase my voice with the strings. They all nod, but half of them don't really understand what I mean by it. Particularly the good musicians. They all had lessons. We got a couple classically trained musicians living here. I taught myself when I was laid up getting my knee rehabbed. Sit around, get up in the morning, fix some coffee, hit the bong, smoke a cigarette while the coffee cools, play a little guitar. Those were the days."

"What's different now?" Marcia asked.

Dylan smiled. "Not a damn thing. Not really. I'm just biding my time till I get world-famous."

They stayed up to two in the morning, telling stories, singing songs, and maintaining a buzz. After eleven, Dylan fetched a miniature guitar, a Little Martin, he called it, and he strummed it because it wasn't as loud, and he didn't want to keep the neighbors awake.

"The walls are thick," he said. "There's really not much chance of bothering anybody. Most of the sound escapes out the window. If it's ever bothered anybody, they didn't say anything."

She was attracted to Dylan. She might have been attracted to anyone when she was stoned, and that had played a role in her infatuation with the dirtbag Tripp Fallaw, too, but Dylan Wannamacher was respectable, and he had a good heart, but she could tell he wanted to screw her brains out. He was a gentleman, and she was probably going to have to get a bit ornery in order for him to succumb. He had a certain courtliness. She got him to tell her about his meeting with his roguish students, and it occurred to her that a group of filthy-rich prep-school kids might make for better commerce than a three-story apartment building of struggling-artist stoners. She thought about it, and the notion of dealing pot appealed to her. She put Dylan on his back and rode him like a mechanical bull. The next morning Dylan went off to Enlightened Word, and Marcia slept in.

On day two of the EWA calendar, Dylan Wannamacher drank coffee. Lots of coffee. Back at his apartment, Marcia smoked lots of his weed.

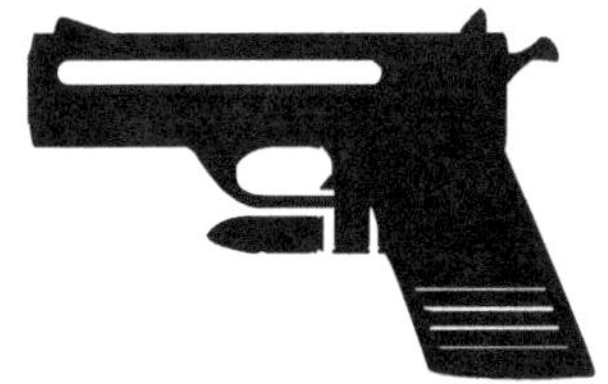

CHAPTER 15

The Master Plan

Marcia burned with ambition. She was dedicated to writing a novel, and not just any novel, but one that would bring her fame and adulation. She was not quite ready to go all the way with fiction, though. It was not uncommon for a first novel to be at least loosely based on the author's life. Some never strayed far away. Pat Conroy, who had recently died, made a career writing about his wildly dysfunctional family. Marcia's life wasn't as colorful as Conroy's. She needed experience. She needed to live the story she wanted to write, and everything was falling into place.

Fate was with her. It had led her through an attempted lesbian seduction, a wild, drug-impaired road trip to California, an offer to make a lucrative, illicit living as a weed dealer, and now a sexual relationship with a teacher and ex-football player who was her match in terms of literary aspiration and dogged independence. She wanted to do Dylan Wannamacher justice as much as she had done him in bed. He excited and fascinated her.

She liked to screw. She resented the sexist notion that, as a woman, she was supposed to play the games that men never had to. They could be unabashed hunters. She had to seduce. They could just hunt freely. Women were notches on their belts.

Marcia wanted to learn what it was like to deal drugs. She wanted to live dangerously. She wanted to make the money that could form the foundation of her success. She called Wade Sanderson several times and made arrangements. Easy as pie, he told her. Everything was cool. She had influence behind her. As long as she exercised proper care, no one would catch her. Wade assured her that the fix was in. It wouldn't be long, he said, until recreational cannabis was legal. With the foundation he was setting, he and his associates from entertainment, sports, government, and, yes, law enforcement, would be prepared to hit the ground running when the War on Drugs ended in defeat. She suspected that he overstated his own importance. Wade was a caddy, not a criminal mastermind. That was something Marcia thought she might become. She figured she could found her empire by setting up a local network, something like a paper route, with a band of free-thinking artists and another of privileged rich kids. Dylan Wannamacher was the man who could put her and her weed in circulation. She wondered whether or not she should let him in on her plot. She tended to think no, partly because he might not be bold enough to embrace it, but partly because she thought it more adventurous to deceive him. She craved his love, but she craved excitement more. It's not like she was peddling crack in the projects. She would deal with people smart enough to be cool about it. A pretty girl could get away with murder if she knew how to act like she knew what she was doing.

She walked to Auntie Em's stoned on her ass, sipped coffee, had a bagel with creamed cheese, and a banana-nut muffin that seemed more delicious than any she'd eaten before, and killed two hours reading about the weed business on her iPhone. Then she stopped on the way back at Walgreen's to buy two legal pads, two packs of Camel Lights, and some genuine cream for her coffee. When she got back, she turned on the window fan, hit Dylan's bong, and started mapping out her plans for regional weed domination. At about one in the afternoon, Marcia realized that she'd forgotten her creative-writing class. Because of the weed, she didn't get alarmed. What got her alarmed was the realization that she had locked herself out of Dylan's apartment. She figured, though, that she was going to have to go back to the dorm anyway because that's where her laptop was stashed. Once she cranked out the short story that was almost half-finished and presented it to her professor, he wasn't going to get bent out of shape about some group discussion she'd blown off.

What the hell. Maybe she'd screw him, too.

Dylan Wannamacher was happy, too, though his back was hurting like hell. It wasn't debilitating. He wished he had some marijuana to be medicinal, but he kept a small bottle of Meloxicam in his backpack for just such an emergency. He was supposed to take one each day but skipped it if he wasn't in pain, and then he took two when he was. He was opening the semester by having two of his classes read John Knowles' *A Separate Peace*. Paperback copies were atop their desks. A few looked as if they might have been opened.

It was a good introduction for prep-school kids, and a prep school was what Enlightened Word purported to be. A teacher at such an institution was what Dylan purported to be. The purpose of opening the term with such a book was to provide his students with a morality tale in which they could relate. Next up was Faulkner's *The Reivers*, and then another Mississippian, Larry Brown, who wrote harsh prose about dirt-poor Southerners. The goal was have the kids dismount slowly from their high horses so that they could relate to the simple problems of poverty and innocence. After those three, Dylan planned to move out of the south and west to Steinbeck's *East of Eden*.

Dylan wanted to move out of the South himself. He was hopeful one of the two manuscripts he had in circulation would be published, and that he'd get a decent advance, and he'd move out west to a place where cannabis was legal. The coast of Oregon was the current object of his fancy. He'd been there once and found a humanity in the gentle people there that seemed lacking in the South, particularly the deep part of it where he'd been raised.

The good news of this Friday was word that one of his short stories had been published. He had in his possession a crisp check in the amount of a hundred bucks, which, given the time Dylan had put into it, amounted to significantly less than minimum wage.

A hundred bucks wouldn't get him to Oregon, but he was going to make that move as soon as he could swing it. He remained hopeful in spite of his having been trying to swing it for roughly as long as the current president had been in office.

At five, Dylan returned to Triborough to find Marcia, once again, sitting on the bench out front, smoking a cigarette, her eyes so red that they reminded him of a Japanese battle flag from World War II.

"Sit tight," he said. "I reckon I need to go to the hardware store and get you a key made," he said.

"Cool beans," she said. "You sure you don't want to go upstairs and get laid first?"

"Tempting," he said, "but you are an energetic young woman whose ardor requires a certain period of recovery, and if we screw again right now, I'll never make it to the True Value, and, goddamn it, Marcia, I need to go to the hardware store."

Love at first sight was not uncommon for Dylan Wannamacher, but it seldom had required this kind of staying power.

"Let's engage in some strenuous writing when you get back, Dylan. First we'll fuckin' write."

"Then we'll fuckin' fuck?" He grinned.

"Exactly," she said.

"Why don't you go with me? Then we can fuckin' eat."

CHAPTER 16

The New Deal

Mickey Statler wasn't clinically depressed. He was depressed for a damned good reason. His job had been eliminated. He wasn't making enough money. His prestige was gradually declining. Calls and text messages from friends were getting less frequent. He understood. They didn't want to talk anymore about how sorry they were about what had happened. Most of them were scared shitless that it was going to happen to them. They were dinosaurs watching a comet streak across a barren sky. For those still safe, Mickey was a symbol of what they didn't want to confront.

He didn't want to talk about it, either.

Days he spent applying in vain for jobs for which he was over- or under-qualified. Nothing fit. Either it was a job clearly meant for a kid just out of college or some kind of teaching job which listed a master's degree, which Mickey didn't have, as preferred. What he thought was an interview, at a nearby newspaper, turned into a session in which the executive editor asked him for advice on whom to hire. He kept on applying, knowing nothing would come of it, until he finally just quit. He'd reached a point in his career where applying for a job was futile. If there was something out there, it would come to him.

He'd fucked up. He'd dedicated his entire life to a profession that was dying.

A wide range of depressing situations bombarded him at home. Martin Gaynes made him madder and madder. He no longer wanted Gaynes just to lose. He wanted him to die penniless. He'd settle for him going to prison. He was ashamed of himself for wishing such harm on his fellow man, but he couldn't help it. He asked Jesus to forgive him, but it was mainly just superstition, his religion. He recited the names of people he liked, asking for blessings upon them. He asked forgiveness of his own sins, of which there were many. He started looking for a cheaper place to live and even thought about moving back to his South Carolina home. He was afraid to call his ex-wife and was vaguely surprised that she wasn't hounding him for money. Maybe she was getting married again. That would be super.

The world was closing in, and it was never so apparent as when he was mulling the wreckage of his life. Getting out helped him get his mind off it. He had been a guest speaker at the Lovejoy Kiwanis Club, regaling a room full of businessmen and women who were like everyone else. They hated what had happened. They wished there was something they could do. There wasn't.

Writing about high school sports was fun. It took him back to when he had youth, and his ambition hadn't been batted down. He thought about how his best times had been back when he was young and poor, drinking beer with his colleagues with the money left over from keeping the electricity on. He was too old for fun now. He couldn't escape the ignominy.

Mickey ate Chinese food and played Powerball with the lucky numbers in the fortune cookie because they included the high school football numbers of himself, his brother and his late father. The other two were his favorite baseball players, Nomar Garciaparra (5) and David Ortiz (34). He played 5, 10, 33, 34, 50. He wouldn't win but judged the purchase a success because Laurie called. She was seductive on the phone. She was probably seductive in the grocery-store line. She said she'd missed him and wanted to catch up. He told her he felt like he'd just won the lottery and that he'd be at the Lovable Loser in an hour.

He was in a convenience-store line with his Powerball ticket when she called. He also bought a pack of cigarettes and a lighter because it seemed like the thing to do. He drove the two blocks back to the apartment, took a shower, made himself presentable, poured himself a gin and tonic and watched a few minutes of Martin Gaynes at a rally while he smoked his first cigarette since the last time he had been at the Lovable Loser, searching in vain for Laurie.

Mickey Statler was on a bad run. He needed some relief.

When Mickey checked his email, he found more evidence that his book on the heroes of the Atlantic Coast Conference wasn't going to be a blockbuster. He had hoped it would provide more aid paying his bills without having to dip into his retirement account. When a man gets in a bind, the solutions get more and more drastic, not to mention less and less likely to succeed. Mickey was betting. Hell, he was taking bets. He was quite a bit better at taking them than making them.

Mickey could have done something productive. He could have rolled up his sleeves and gone to work, making proposals for free-lance stories he could have written, or he could have delved into his growing financial problems and tried to make a plan to stanch the bleeding of his accounts. Any comprehensive plan for long-term relief required short-term relief, so Mickey headed for where he knew he could get good advice, the Lovable Loser Sports Bar.

The best mistakes were always comedies.

Laurie was there with an open stool next to her. Their eyes met significantly when Mickey walked in the door. He ordered a beer, but she said "fuck that" and told Louie that Mickey needed "a drink of liquor," and, by God, so he did. He ordered a gin and tonic to match up with the one he'd mixed himself at home. His had been stronger.

"I'm off," she said.

I'm on, Mickey thought.

"Actually, I got fired."

Laurie said she'd been peeling off a small piece of the action from the cash register for years, and it had been just fine, kind of understood, as long as she and the boss were "seeing each other," but then he broke up with her, and she kept on taking her "commission," and tucking away her usual share turned out to be against the law.

"Aw, well, fuck it," Laurie said. "How the hell has your day been?"

"Peachy," Mickey said.

They finished their drinks and had another, and Mickey cut the bullshit after a while and admitted to her, through the depressive effects of drink, that he was having trouble paying his bills and was starting to wonder if there was any way out. In time they each grew tired of discussing the other's problems, and Mickey asked her if she'd like to step outside for a cigarette after he drained the latter gin and tonic.

"I got a better idea," Laurie said. "Follow me."

She led him through the kitchen to the storage room.

"I thought you were no longer an employee," Mickey said.

"Sonny spends all his time at the place in Olive Heights." Presumably, Sonny was the owner who had jilted and fired her. "Trust me. I still got the run of the place."

Laurie reached in her purse and pulled out a lighter and a joint.

"It's, uh, been a long time since I've done that," Mickey said.

"Relax, honey. You're not philosophically opposed to it or nothing, are you?"

"No. I kind of like it, but …"

"See that big fan, built into the wall? It blows outward. Me and Louie get high back here all the time."

Laurie lit the joint, hit it, and handed it to Mickey, who took a small hit and coughed when he exhaled.

"Shit."

"You ever took a gun?" she said.

"Yeah," Mickey said. "Been a while."

"Lean your back against the wall." Laurie turned the joint backwards, place it lightly between her teeth, cupped her hands on each side, and mumbled: "Okay, now, on three, just slowly inhale. One … two … three."

She blew the smoke into his mouth. He drew it in for as long as he could stand, then, finally, waved his hands to signal that he could hold no more. She took her own hit while a plume of smoke exited Mickey's lungs forcefully. She looked at him, eyes dancing, and flicked on the wall switch that activated the fan. It howled to life.

"Louie knows what we be doing," Laurie said, laughing.

Mickey continued to lean against the wall, not sure if he could maintain his balance otherwise. He felt euphoric and numb. Laurie kissed him passionately, her tongue sweeping across his and occasionally sweeping out and slathering his lips, nose, and chin with pungent saliva. She unzipped his fly and began fondling him, but then she let him go, pulled away, and stepped back to get her breath.

"Better back off," she said. "Don't want to get you spent too quick, nowumsayin?"

Mickey wanted to keep going, but most of the boxes contained bottled beer, and they would bust if he and this gorgeous woman tumbled across them, and the floor was hard and concrete, and, by the time he got his breath back, the heaving somehow enabled him to get a better grip on his balance.

"I need to sit down," he said at last.

"Here," Laurie said. "Have a stick of gum. And wipe your face off."

Mickey had nothing to clean off his chin but his forearm, but he grabbed a couple cocktail napkins as Laurie led him past the bar. She ordered more drinks, and they went out to the courtyard where people sat around and smoked at the picnic tables.

They smoked. It was one of the better ones Mickey ever had. The drinks arrived. They didn't talk much. They regrouped. Being stoned helped Mickey curb his passion, but only for a time. He was about to get laid, and it hadn't happened in a while.

If they had decided to hang around the bar a while longer, and if Ronnie Shingler hadn't spotted Mickey and Laurie leaving the Loser, and if Mickey hadn't covered the game where Ronnie's son John Lee dropped the game-winning pass in overtime, and if Mickey hadn't been too ashamed to bring Laurie back to his disheveled apartment, and if he and Laurie hadn't been smoking marijuana when the police came knocking, then Mickey wouldn't have wound up spending the night in jail and wondering, at some point, why Laurie wasn't there, too.

Maybe it was all just fate.

Mickey decided not to make his one phone call. He would just rot there, for two whole weeks if he had to, because they had to feed him, so maybe they'd just let him go after a while. Stranger things had happened. Mickey wasn't going to hang himself or try to find something to slit his wrists. No, he was going to do what God intended and just rot. He could be stubborn.

It never seemed as if he slept. The jail cell wasn't exactly the Hilton, though neither had been the motel room where he and Laurie had been cavorting. His mind had been alive, considering the depth of the hole and paucity of ways to get out of it, but no solutions had presented themselves. It was going to hit the papers, most notably the one which had relieved him of a job. It would look nice and polite in the *News-Free Press*, but other nearby rags wouldn't be so discreet, and TV would get hold of it the way it usually did, by reading about it in the papers and then blowing it up out of all proportion.

Mickey had to admit, though, the proportion was pretty large.

He must have slept some. It was inexplicable that all the thought had taken up six hours of brooding and despair. If they were dreams, they were full of images of his sobbing daughter, reproachful ex, and the managing editor of the *News-Free Press*, who would surely be delighted at the opportunity to erase the sports columnist's remaining severance pay. Mickey was in the clink, a term he knew because he liked old movies. He'd been busted for pot, which was only, by the way, because Laurie had some. He hadn't smoked weed in pursuit of anything but sex since he was, oh, thirty or so. He saw his predicament for what it was. He'd beaten the odds too many times, skated his way through a license check with his offhand affability, claimed he'd been desperately trying to get home to see a sick child or a dying mother, whatever it had taken to charm his way out of trouble. Mickey, for all his faults, was a charming guy, and, at long last, he had staggered, quite literally, into a fix where charm was irrelevant.

That hanging-in-the-jail-cell option wasn't looking bad, but it was just Mickey being dispirited. Gallows humor had spiced up his columns on occasion. He wasn't going to end it all. He just couldn't figure out a way to make earth much better than hell.

Mickey figured the noise had something to do with breakfast, but the trusty, or jailer, or whoever he was, walked down the hall to where Mickey was thankfully confined alone. He opened the door.

"Statler?"

"Yes, sir, that's me."

"You're free to go."

There wasn't much to the "processing." They just gave him back what had been "on his person": wallet, change, car keys, a plastic room key, a lighter, half a pack of smokes, and a condom, the one he hadn't used, safely packaged and sanitized for his security and convenience.

Seeing Laurie Bigelow, whose last name he had only learned when they were being arrested, at the counter would have seemed a miracle. She wasn't there. A deputy was waiting.

"Mickey, how are you? Been reading your columns for years."

"Why, thank you, sir." Mickey was wary and disbelieving. The tag above the badge said the deputy's name was Shingler. "What's … the … deal?"

He ought to have been able to do better than that.

Shingler led him through the first of two double doors. The fifteen feet or so between them was vacant and thus private.

"Nothing ever happened," Shingler said. "All charges dropped. As a matter of paperwork, they never existed."

"So …"

"You won't lose your job. If you do, you won't lose your severance or unemployment eligibility."

"I hope it doesn't come to that."

"Me, too, Mickey, but you *have* got a commitment."

"Oh?"

"Yep," Shingler said. "I want you to meet me, oh, at, uh, five or thereabouts. I get off at four, you see. You remember the motel room where you got arrested?"

"Vaguely." Mickey smiled.

"That's where I'll be waiting," Shingler said. "That key in your pocket? It still works."

"See you at five," Mickey said, bewildered.

Still clueless, Mickey Lowndes knocked on the door of Room 227 of the Nocono Lodge, where last he had been arrested. A voice from inside said, "Use your key."

Amazingly, it did, in fact, still work.

"Sit down," said the deputy who had delivered Mickey from incarceration that morning. "I'm Ronnie Shingler. We've got a lot to talk about."

Lowndes certainly suspected as much. He'd wracked his brain all day. Was he getting some kind of informal sentence of community service? Of course not. What was the need for setting him up, which was obviously what had happened? He was grateful for not being ruined, but what was the need of holding that ruination over his head? He'd called Laurie, but it had not been a lengthy exchange.

Mickey: "You set me up."

Laurie: "You had it coming. But I'm sorry. I am. I had to."

Click.

Now it was time to find out what the hell was going on. He sat down.

"This is going to take a while," Shingler said, "but I want you to know what you're getting into."

Shingler made no mention of there being any option.

"The county administrator is a fellow named Bob Siderowf," Shingler said. "A few years ago, Bob got together with me and the sheriff, and he talked about the need to raise some money. Every government entity has run into the same thing over the past decade. We've had this rise of hard-ass conservatives who have taken this solemn oath not to raise any tax for any reason, so we've started running our law-enforcement operations for profit. We send our cars out on the interstate to horn in on the Highway Patrol's business. We run speed traps just over the top of every hill. When some kid gets arrested for anything, we tack on mandatory collect calls and service charges and court costs, and we say folks got to pay for the cost of services like fire and ambulances, which might be fair if it weren't for the fact that all those salaries get paid whether the personnel is hauling ass out to some house or not. So the people who got money don't have to spend more of it, and we stick it to the people who ain't got none. Me and some of the boys got together and figured out a new way to bring some money in. It works real well, but it's got to be a secret 'cause it just happens to be illegal."

"It sounds like I'm poster boy for who you trying to help," Mickey said.

"Well, Mickey, you are ideal, I'll give you that," Shingler said. "What we still do is try to keep the county free of drugs. Where the money comes in is when we take the pot we confiscate and spread it around to other places. We use some of it for the purposes of law enforcement. For instance, some of that marijuana was used to nab you."

"Deputy Shingler …"

"Please call me Ronnie."

"Ronnie, I don't even smoke pot as a general rule. If Laurie hadn't pulled some out …"

"And if you hadn't been interested in getting in her pants …"

"That's right."

"Obviously, we had factored all that in, Mickey."

"Obviously."

"Be that as it may, let me finish what I got to say. You travel a lot, and you don't just cover one sport. You go to the races at Charlotte and Martinsville and Richmond. You're at the ballgames in Chapel Hill, Raleigh, Durham, Winston-Salem, sometimes even Boone and Greenville. We just need somebody to make deliveries, and it can't be just anybody 'cause it's got to be safe. Having you transport it is as safe as we can get."

"Jesus, Ronnie."

"Look, there's nothing to it. Everything is set up. We can cover you here in the county, but we need somebody who is smart, reliable, relaxed, and professional. It's easy. Maybe you walk into a hotel lobby to check in. You carry a briefcase. You set it on the floor, talk to the clerk, get your room key. Then you turn around, leave the briefcase and pick up the one sitting on the floor that the fellow behind you brought with him. He takes yours. Same way at a restaurant. Maybe it's a little backpack. Dude meets you for dinner. He doesn't look suspicious, either. You leave. He takes yours. You take his. There's a variety of methods, all of them safe and all of them foolproof as long as we ain't got fools doing them. We ain't never had one yet, and you're not going to be the first."

"How do you do it? You know, don't you have to account for everything you confiscate?"

"Yes, but it's all a matter of getting the right people in the right places. One of the things that makes it tough to be a cop is it don't pay much. If a cop ain't on the take a little, he can't support a family. It ain't getting no better and ain't gon' get no better 'cause the money's not there."

"So, you're saying that the county's selling drugs so that school kids can get their books," Lowndes said.

"That's not the case directly," Shingler said, "but that's the basic idea. Not only do you not need the expense of being busted for marijuana, but you're like a cop, Mickey. You need the money, too."

"Damned if that ain't true."

"Five hundred bucks a week, minimum. More if, you know, it's more than once in, say, a week. I'm generous."

"Again, at some point, doesn't there have to be some … certification of what happens to the pot?"

"Let's just say something gets incinerated," Shingler said. "It may be shredded paper. It may be grass clippings or pine needles. Like I said, it's just a matter of having the right people in charge. We've got a good bit of control over how people are slotted, and believe it or not, there really aren't all that many people who know what's going on."

"And I don't have any choice."

"You don't have any choice." Shingler pulled out a newspaper clipping. "This is a column of yours, Mickey. Let me read to you what you wrote."

One of the great myths of journalism is that a reporter can't keep a secret. Oh, he can keep a secret. You tell him it's a secret, that it's off the record, and he won't even tell his mama. The trouble is, if you don't tell him it's a secret, it's his job to tell the whole world.

"I'm really hoping, Mickey, you weren't just whistling 'Dixie.'"

"I was writing about the NASCAR Hall of Fame, Ronnie."

"You were writing about this job, Mickey. You just didn't know it."

CHAPTER 17

Teen Spirit

Having another writer at his apartment was a difficult adjustment for Dylan Wannamacher, who was accustomed to a routine of coming home, putting on some coffee, hitting the bong, turning on the TV – a ballgame, or an old movie, or MSNBC – and writing. Only the presence of Marcia, sitting across from him, typing away at her laptop behind a folding table while he pecked away at his on a small, rolling desk, was different.

Oddly, Marcia, who had played soccer, preferred football on TV, and he, who had played football, preferred soccer. His main love was baseball, the Boston Red Sox, somehow, even though he had grown up in Mississippi, a state divided between Cardinals and Braves fans. Dylan loved the Red Sox because his father had loved first Ted Williams and then Carl Yastrzemski, and he had loved first Nomar Garciaparra and now David Ortiz, who was retiring, and Dylan was already grooming Mookie Betts as his replacement.

Dylan hadn't even written while the Red Sox had been occupied being swept by the Cleveland Indians in the first round of the playoffs. He was still interested in how the rest of the season went, but baseball obviously bored Marcia, so he watched politics, which had become the biggest sport of all. That was the trouble. People were treating politics as sports and sports as politics. It was a fascinating line of thought but not one that would bear inserting in his manuscript. He wasn't interested in tinkering with it. The first novel, the one that was ready, had just been rejected again. He wasn't ready to begin another. What profundity was seeping out of his brain came in random fits and starts, suitable to be stored away in the unformed-projects folder. He seemed unable to create anything other than a few pungent paragraphs, here and there.

Meanwhile, the living room was dark enough that he thought he could see sparks flying off Marcia's keyboard.

He just stopped and stared. After a minute or so, she noticed.

"What?"

"I was just marveling at how productive you are," he said. "I'm stuck."

"I'm writing about this girl who works her way through college selling weed," Marcia said.

"Just weed? No coke? No meth? No smack?"

"Nah, she's not that bad a girl. Just trying to get by."

"I'll be damned," Dylan said. "Wonder if there's a living in that."

He loaded the bong and took a hit.

"I'm guessing she partakes herself from time to time," he said, exhaling.

"Yeah, a little," Marcia replied. She got up and took the bong from him. "You know. Quality control."

She had her own weed. After she finished hitting it, she packed the bowl again and returned the bong to Dylan.

"I'm buzzed enough," he said.

"Next time," she replied.

"Cool."

They both sat silent, both pushing their laptops away, and watched the latest adventures of Martin J. Gaynes on TV.

"Let me guess," Marcia said. "You voted for Artie Thomas, the socialist."

"Yeah. It was a good run."

"Now you're voting for Katharine?"

"Uh-huh. It's the fall. The leaves change. The weather gets colder. Gotta take what you can get."

"I think my main character would vote for Gaynes," Marcia said. "Not because she agrees with him. Because he'd be fun. No telling what he would do."

"He wouldn't legalize weed," Dylan said.

"That man might do anything. Shit. You don't know. He don't know."

"This is true," Dylan said. "Besides, it's funny. Gaynes makes me laugh my ass off, right up until I start to weep."

"Katharine won't legalize weed," Marcia said.

"No, but with her, there's hope," Dylan said. "Weed and elsewhere. Hey, you know what a Libertarian is?"

"What?"

"A conservative who smokes weed. I mean, did you know that some Bernie fans now say they'll vote for John Garretson? He's the opposite extreme."

"But he'd legalize cannabis."

"Sometimes I wish I were a one-issue voter," Dylan said, "but I'm not. I want peace, love, *and* understanding."

"Me, neither. If I was, I'd vote for Garretson."

"You mean … your character."

"Yeah," she said. "My character."

"I gotta grade some essays in a little while," Dylan said. "I think I'll do it after I sample your bud."

"It's good."

"I wouldn't even think about grading papers straight. They'd all get F's."

"I want to meet your adviser brats." Marcia had a way with coining terms. She was already calling the apartments Hippie Arms because of its former status and present tenants. What's more, he was already calling it that, too, and it had never occurred to him in more than a decade of living there. Dylan thought "adviser brats" was a bit imprecise – and grammatically misleading – but he knew it would stick between the two of them.

"Okay," Dylan said. "Next time they request an emergency session at the pizzeria, I'll alert you."

"I'd kind of like to get to know the place you work, Dylan. I'm getting used to a private college, but I don't know anything about a private, you know, secondary school."

"Is this you or your character?"

"Oh, both."

"I've got no room to talk," Dylan said. "That's what I've been doing. I was just writing about the hypocrisy of Enlightened Word. The school's kind of behind the politically-correct curve. There's still a smoking lounge for the faculty. Officially, it's a lounge, but in the time I've been there, the only thing that's changed is the amount of air freshener and ventilation. The teachers still smoke. They just feel bad about it. I don't go in there much. I just have a cigarette on the way over and a cigarette on the way home. I'm really the hypocrite I'm writing about."

They went back to writing. Dylan thought he might have a short story. Unlike his novels, his short stories often found publishers. They didn't make him much money – a hundred dollars here, fifty there – and he wrote them under a *nom de plume*, but every time he read his own words in print, it gave him a small bit of sustaining confidence that he could pull everything together in novel that would pull him away from adviser brats and to a literary world beyond. Marcia watched closely when he finally got around to trying her weed.

"God Almighty," he said after a long stare at the ceiling tiles, where his mind spelled words like "poesy" and "onomatopoeia" in the blocks. "Where'd you get this?"

"Kah-lee-for-nya," she said in a Latino lilt. "Vacuum-packed for my convenience and delivered safely and conveniently."

Dylan stared at her through reddening eyes. "You? Or your character?"

"Like I said, Dylan. Both."

Marcia had gone to bed by the time Dylan finished grading the essays. He gave thirteen A's and four B's. The only C went to Milo Hirley, and Dylan wrote in the margins:

Your protagonist is a substance. Make a person the protagonist. Rewrite and I'll raise the grade.

The more Dylan Wannamacher pondered the woman who was sharing his bed, the more he doubted that he was in love with her. He had a habit of talking himself out of true love. He was aroused by her, and not just sexually. He was intrigued. He wanted to know her. He wanted to come to grips with her essence. He envisioned her as a character in his fiction.

Marcia envisioned him the same way.

Was sex so good because they were suited, or was it because it was the ultimate examination of another's soul?

Marcia was either blowing off a lot of classes, or she didn't have any that started very early. Dylan was always up at least an hour ahead of her – fixing his coffee, reading the paper, hitting the bong before he headed out the door for Auntie Em's, more coffee, more reading, a bagel – and he didn't know when she awakened each day. It might not be before he began lecturing at Enlightened Word. Dylan admired her ambition. He could use more of it. He sensed her calculating nature, imagining the little engine in her brain, whirring away with plans and aspirations. She was unusually resourceful for a woman her age, barely old enough to drink, seventeen years his junior. On most days, when Dylan got home, Marcia either had dinner on the stove or freshly ordered. She paid for it. He had made no such request or suggestion. She figured it was the least she could do, given that she was mostly living there. A dorm room at Triborough was listed in her name, but Marcia didn't care for her roommate and said she just dropped by every few days to get some writing done in private. She didn't shy away from living with an older man, and the fact that she didn't ever seem ashamed of him meant more to him than she knew. She mentioned from time to time that she'd like to attend some function at Enlightened Word with him. Dylan laughed it off at first, saying he would never subject her to such indignity and boredom, but she kept bringing it up, and the more he thought about it, the more he wanted to show her off.

"The homecoming picnic is Friday after school," he said one night, making a point not to look up as he typed something nonsensical in the name of fiction.

She stopped whatever she was writing. "Are you asking if I want to go?"

"Well, I can't imagine you or anyone else enjoying it. It's an outdoor picnic, and they have a homecoming parade with our pitiful little band playing," he said. "But, yeah, if you want to go … I'll have to meet you there. I don't think there's enough time for me to make a round trip to come and get you."

"Cool. You'll have to show me how to get there."

Dylan caved. He sent her a text saying that he could skip sixth period and drive back to Hippie Arms to pick her up. It was office time, and Friday, and he only had one appointment, and he took care of it by talking with a senior cheerleader while they ate lunch in a private corner of the cafeteria.

Now he felt stressed about showing off Marcia in front of the faculty. Fifteen minutes home. Fifteen minutes back. Quick bong hit in between.

They bickered a bit on the way back to Enlightened Words. She instigated it. She wanted to play.

"You know, I've been thinking about it," she said, "and I really think I might be a Republican."

"Are you registered as a Republican?"

"In North Carolina. But it's too late to file absentee, and I'm damn sure not driving to North Carolina. I don't even live there anymore."

"I guess, as a pragmatist, I should be happy you're not voting if you'd vote for Gaynes."

"I wouldn't vote for Gaynes."

"You'd vote for Katharine?"

"Noooooo. I'd vote for John Garretson. Maybe."

"Weed," he said.

"Yeah. Fuck yeah. Why not?"

"He doesn't know anything," he said.

"The difference between the two main parties," Marcia said, "is that Democrats think good comes from good, and Republicans think good comes from money."

"The higher angels," Dylan replied, "and the lesser angels."

"No. You know when weed is going to be legal? It's not going to be because it's not as bad as alcohol. It's not because it's a waste of money to try to stop it. It's because there's a bunch of money to be made. Big money. And big taxes. Politicians love a new way to waste money."

Dylan decided it was good she wasn't voting. She'd vote for Gaynes. He just knew it. He changed the subject.

"I've got to give this bullshit speech. Well, not really a speech. A short talk."

"About what?" she asked.

"Nothing. I'm not saying. I don't want to talk about it. The speech is nothing."

"And life is fatal," she said. He laughed.

Much to Dylan's surprise, the picnic had been moved inside to the cafeteria. The weather was clear. Someone said scattered thunderstorms were forecast later. As best he could figure, the logic was that, since the tables would have to be hauled back inside in the rain, if it did so, then they decided not to set them up at all, even though it wasn't raining, because it might.

"This is the first time I've ever been to a cookout that was in," Dylan said to Marcia, who laughed at it too much because she was stoned.

Being high made Dylan level off into a benign world of satirical thought, just trying to revel in the absurdity of it all. Everyone went outside to watch five flimsy floats, convertibles carrying the various members of the homecoming court, and the marching band pass by. Waddy Pegler gave his pep talk outside. Everyone else had to wait until after the hamburgers, hot dogs, potato chips and coconut cake were served, prayed for, and consumed.

Dylan steered Marcia to a tastefully mid-range table, over to one side, conveniently near the exit, second row back from the podium. He was proud that his young lover wasn't ashamed of him, but he was acting mildly as if he were ashamed of her. This didn't bother her at all. It seemed to please her.

Milo Hirley and Jonny Heinsohn arrived late, frantically peering around the cafeteria before finding Dylan and Marcia. No one else was sitting at the table, so they did. Walt Pegler and Marty Drummond joined them, and they all exchanged knowing glances that Dylan immediately deciphered. Milo and Hirley had been smoking pot behind the natatorium because their security-guard friend, who probably sold the weed, watched out for them. Walt and Marty had been unable to make it because Walt's father was the football coach and Marty's was the headmaster. Jonny, such a serious young man, surprised Dylan. Milo, though, was charismatic. The force of his personality made friends follow him into and out of trouble. It occurred to Dylan that Milo and Marcia were a lot alike.

Six people now sat at the table. All ate with a bit more enthusiasm than would be expected for charred burgers, adorned with cheese, lettuce, tomato slices and a squirt of mustard. Milo went back to the chow line, which was deserted because the headmaster was calling for order and getting ready to start the program. The band was lining up, probably to play some hymn like "Onward, Christian Soldiers" or something. Wearing a suspicious grin, Milo took a plastic plate and stacked hamburger patties haphazardly. Coach Pegler gave him a dour look.

"Gotta be strong and healthy," Milo said, too loud. "Beat O'Halloran!"

A ripple of laughter drifted through the crowd as Milo returned with the hamburger patties. He had a bottle of ketchup in one of his back pockets and a wad of napkins in his front. He passed the plate around. Dylan passed, as did Marcia. Milo and Jonny were hungrier than the other two. As soon as they were done eating, everyone except Dylan took out phones, Marcia included. Dylan wondered if they were texting one another while sitting within earshot. He tried to pay attention to what Dr. Nathan Drummond had to say, in part because what he had to say was going to suffice as his introduction. Dylan had no idea what he was going to say but was confident he would come up with something. He thought it prudent at least to ponder the matter.

Marcia was looking up the four adviser brats on Facebook. It wasn't difficult. She sent each friend requests that were almost immediately accepted. Then she sent them direct messages with her phone number, suggesting that they save it in their phones and text her back. Dr. Drummond beckoned Dylan to the podium. He strode gracefully to the front, began by introducing his "friend" Marcia, which, after a short delay, led her to sit her phone on the table and stand up for recognition. It wasn't like anyone there had failed to notice her. Applause was forbidden. The sound that rose was that of several hundred people whispering something akin to "shiiiiiiitttt" under their breaths. Some of the wives probably whispered "welllll." She was young, beautiful, and his, for now.

"I want to talk to you a few minutes about winning," Dylan said. "It's been a long time since I was an athlete, but the feeling of it is with me every day. When I was a kid, in Paulette, Mississippi, I played on a state championship team, and it left me with this wonderful feeling of accomplishment and confidence that I carry with me to this day. When we were riding home on the bus, after winning another game, I was acutely aware of what that meant. It made me feel, irrationally perhaps, but it made me feel like I could do anything."

Marcia sent Milo a text: *Can you keep a secret, Milo?*

Sure.

I mean, from Dylan?

OK.

How would you like some high-grade, Northern California weed?

Cool.

Three hundred an oz. Four of you split it, 75 bucks each. How's that sound?

Great. Deal.

"But I remember, sitting on the bus and wondering what the effect was on the teams that we had just beaten," Dylan said. "I mean, I came out of that experience thinking I could do anything. Did those poor kids leave that game with an inferiority complex? Did they leave that field, go out into life, expecting to fail?"

How'd you like to sell enough so that you get yours for free?

I'd like that.

I'll sell you an oz. Meet you in the morning, oh, 10 o'clock, at Auntie Em's Coffee Shop in Triborough? Can you raise the money?

I think so.

See how that goes. We'll talk.

"Here's my point. When I hear people say that all this emphasis on winning takes the fun out of sports, I laugh," Dylan concluded. "Nothing is as much fun as winning. Nothing. It doesn't matter if it's the Super Bowl, or homecoming tonight against O'Halloran, or an English essay, or a history exam, or running a business. Nothing beats winning."

Dylan couldn't hide his smirk as he returned to the table. Some of the faculty was probably taken aback by his fervor. Waddy Pegler might say something nice to him. They might get along for as much as a week. It was such bullshit. A certain amount of it came with the job. He couldn't possible have done his minute on the stage sober.

He hadn't fooled Milo Hirley.

"Way to go, General Patton," Milo said. The others laughed, especially Jonny, because he was high, too.

Dylan smiled. Those boys were so going to get their asses beaten by O'Halloran. He was glad he didn't have anything to do with it.

CHAPTER 18

Somebody's Gotta Do It

Mickey Statler hated himself. It was going to be nice having money again, though.

After his meeting with the figurative devil, Deputy Ronnie Shingler, Mickey hadn't done anything. He'd had the TV on. It might have been a football game. He felt as numb as a man could feel while still alive. He wasn't excited. He wasn't drowsy. He wasn't proud of himself. He wasn't ashamed. He thought for a while about what a wonderful occasion it would be to commit suicide, but he had neither a firearm nor the motivation to use it.

Shingler had given him a backpack taken from the trunk of his own car. So numb had he been after being shanghaied into the Illegal Legal Drug Ring of Cops (ILDROC), Mickey didn't even think it odd that Shingler had returned property that had never been taken from him. Shingler said there was some "paperwork" in it.

Just about the time that Jerry noticed the Cubs were leading the Dodgers, 1-0, with one out in the top of the fourth inning, he noticed the backpack, which had his laptop, binoculars, and other items conducive to the coverage of ballgames, sitting at his feet. In it, he found the weed that wasn't his but had been assigned to him as a means of throwing him in jail. A little parting gift. Twenty-four hours earlier, Mickey had been smoking it with Laurie Bigelow, the strumpet who had screwed his brains out and consummated the wreckage of his life. Twenty hours earlier, he had been caught in the act. Eighteen hours earlier, he had been in a jail cell. It seemed to him that his experience was a perfect argument for the existence of Fate, with a capital letter in front.

Hah. A pack of rolling papers was in the baggy. It took him three tries to roll a joint. He got high. It was Fate. Inexorable. Irresistible. He didn't care that someone could smell it in the hall. They'd never evict him before he paid his overdue rent if they thought there was any chance he'd have it. It didn't seem as if many other tenants were at home. It wasn't until he got high that he started hearing little sounds that were a result of paranoia, he reckoned. He wondered if his cigarettes were in the car. It took him a while to cultivate the motivation to get up and go see. Once cultivated, he also had the energy to put a K-cup into the machine and brew some coffee. He found the cigarettes, but when he returned to the apartment, he realized he had no lighter, so he used the elevator again. Gladys Whitford was waiting for the elevator. He kept his distance because he knew he smelled of cannabis. Gladys smiled, and he didn't know if it was because she loved him or because she could smell his breath. Gladys was married. Her husband had always seemed mean to Mickey.

He forgot about the coffee for a while. When he remembered, it was lukewarm. He poured it into another cup and microwaved it. It was scalding now. He sat it on the lamp table next to the recliner. Maybe he'd remember it. The Dodgers had a man in scoring position in the middle of the fifth.

Howie Kendrick stole third on a play that was overturned. Jon Lester was facing Adrian Gonzalez. Both were ex-Red Sox. That's the last Mickey remembered. He nodded off to sleep, and the coffee didn't get drunk again.

The next morning Mickey awakened feeling great, even though he had never made it to bed. For perhaps five minutes, either what had happened to him didn't appear in his mind, or he subconsciously thought it a dream. He microwaved the coffee again. It was still good. He fetched the laptop from the backpack. It occurred to him that the backpack might not be the best place to keep the weed. For the time being, he placed it in a drawer on the lamp table. He turned on the laptop, pulling the coffee table closer to the recliner.

When his email came up, Mickey found a job offer. In fact, he found a contract attached. A contract stipulated that he was to receive a salary fifteen thousand dollars higher than his old job at the *News-Free Press*. He sent the paperwork via wi-fi to his printer in the office where he never worked because no TV was situated there, and when he fetched the printouts, he discovered that, upon filling out the paperwork, he was to receive a "signing bonus" of three thousand dollars. Mickey had only heard of athletes getting signing bonuses.

He filed the paperwork quickly. Scanned it. Faxed it back. Worked on his joint rolling. Why did he ever start drinking in the first place? Learn to love the bomb. It was Fate. It was The Ultimate Sporting Life. The name of the website. The Ultimate Sporting Life. He sifted through it. Not bad. He'd never heard of it. It must have lots of money to launder.

Stoned, he wrote the first song of his life: *Marijuana loves me this I know / For the police told me so / Pay the way to write my shit / First I'll take another hit.*

Really, it was a jingle, but a jingle based on Jesus. "Jesus loves Me." Perhaps he could come up with more verses in time.

Time flies like an arrow. Fruit flies like a banana. There was a way to say it that was funny without being Groucho Marx.

Whoa. It was Saturday. Mickey thought he might have a small-college football game to cover. That wasn't going to happen. He called the sports department of his part-time client, the *Statesman-Record*.

"Sports, Gus Trevelyon."

"Gus, Mickey Statler."

"Hey, Mickey, how you?"

"I'm fine, Gus, but I'm not going to be able to cover the Catawba game tonight. Something's come up."

"Sorry to hear that. What's wrong?"

"No, I'm fine. I just got a new job, that's all. I'm off the market."

"Well, that's great. I don't mind it if you write one more game for us."

"I appreciate that, Gus, but I'm just not going to be able to go. I think what I'm going to be able to do is get drunk celebrating."

"Oh, okay. Well, we'll make do. Thanks for calling."

Mickey figured correctly that Gus Trevelyan was probably thanking his lucky stars right now that he had not hired Mickey Statler full-time. He might tell others that, neglecting to mention that he'd never had the slightest inclination to pay a salary befitting someone of Mickey's experience. Maybe word would spread that Mickey was a drunk. Maybe that would make everyone at the *News-Free Press* delighted because it would provide them a justification for their pitiless act. No one was ever going to know that Mickey had spent six hours in the Lovejoy County jail, though.

Mickey was safe. He was selling weed for the sons of bitches.

CHAPTER 19

The New Ball Coach

Dylan Wannamacher awakened because the phone was ringing.

It was the headmaster. Something terrible had happened at Enlightened Word. Dylan's presence was needed as soon as he could get there. Dr. Nathan Drummond said he'd fill him in when he got there. He had too many people to call to elaborate.

Click.

Dylan found it difficult to get a move on, but he took the hottest shower he could stand, roused Marcia enough to tell her he had to go somewhere and would explain later. He was fatigued and stiff as a board. The Breakfast of Champions – weed, coffee, cigarette – would only offset the invigorating effect of the shower, but it didn't last long. He had to stop for a huge mug of coffee, and the drive to Enlightened Word was only fifteen miles.

Marcia sent Dylan a text once she arose and regained some measure of coherence. He replied quickly, divulging that there had been a tragedy, that he was busy, and he'd tell her all about it once he got home, which wouldn't be any time soon. She seized the opportunity to run some errands and complete a few business transactions. She hadn't long been back to Hippie Arms herself when he trudged in well after dark.

Dylan still didn't want to talk about it. Dylan wanted to get stoned. Not buzzed. Not high. Baked. He parked himself in his shabby chair and took consecutive bong hits of Marcia's delightful California bud. She took one, which provided her the patience to wait.

"I don't know whether to … tell the tale … logist- … no … chronologically … and save the best … and worst … for last," he said. "I think it might be simpler for me … at this point … just to tell it … in order."

Marcia watched him, mentally trying to swipe at the cobwebs of his mind, with some amusement. Something tragic had happened at Enlightened Word, and a single bong hit was enough to make her see absurd humor in tragedy. She had a cigarette and watched him.

"The Coach is dead. Long live the Coach," Dylan said. Then he laughed, too. Marcia thought he'd flipped his lid.

"Dylan, honey, would you like a cigarette? A drink? You have a quart, or maybe it's a fifth, of Tanqueray Number Ten, and three bottles of tonic, and some relatively fresh limes," she said.

"Getting drunk is not a good idea. It's a thoroughly inferior buzz. And tomorrow is gonna be worse than today, and the day after that, worse still. And so on."

"Well, Tuesday is Election Day."

"Gaynes's not gonna win," he said. "Surely not."

Marcia waited through another silence, then said, "Uh, and what was it that happened?"

"Oh, yeah," Dylan said. "Okay, first things first. Waddy Pegler died last night in his sleep."

"Who's Waddy Pegler?"

"The football coach. The Enlightened Word football coach. My arch enemy on the faculty. You met his son, Walt, at the Homecoming deal. I spent the whole day counseling kids, trying to help them handle grief. I talked to Walt. He said he felt guilty because a part of him was glad his dad was dead, and he said he thought it was his fault."

"Aw, that's terrible."

"The funeral is tomorrow. They called off football practice."

"That seems appropriate."

"They're gonna have football practice Tuesday."

"Why are you, all of a sudden, obsessed with this football team?"

"Because," Dylan said, "now I'm the coach."

"What did you say?"

"I'm the fucking football coach. It's only got four assistant coaches. Two are part-time. Two are volunteers. None of them's qualified. I'm qualified, Dr. Nathan Drummond, says. Tragedy puts one in a uniquely inferior bargaining position."

"How many games are left?"

"Three."

"It won't be so bad," Marcia said. The notion of Dylan being occupied from morning till night had some appeal for her.

PART TWO
THE REALLY BIG PICTURE

CHAPTER 20

The Consortium

Security was tight. The Consortium was dutifully concerned. It gathered only infrequently, where its members could discuss vexing issues frankly – not honestly, for there was nothing honest about them – and face to face. The air strip was suitable for corporate jets but had no room for them all to park. Each had to land and leave the representatives, then take off again and fly to a small public airport that could accommodate them. Then they would return, one at a time, to pick up the important men who owned the planes. Only one plane remained at the strip. It belonged to the tobacco tycoon who owned the strip and the sprawling home that adjoined it.

The tobacco executive wanted to diversify. He was weary of legal battles and machinations. The senior official of the Federal Bureau of Investigation had first resigned himself to the changing attitude of the nation and then decided to profit from it. The lieutenant governor of a populous state in the Northeast was about to leave office, having been successfully targeted by the Tea Party in a Republican primary. Abandoning Martin Gaynes had been a mistake, and the experience had made him bitter and greedy. The past president of the National Confederation of Law Enforcement Officers was there. So was a general in the Army Reserve. The owner of a powerful right-wing website lived in his own mansion elsewhere in the mountains. He flew in, too, because the retreat was ten winding miles from the nearest public highway, and the tobacco executive frowned on receiving visitors by land. A Hollywood producer, famous for action movies and special effects, needed money for expensive projects because his last two flicks had been losers at the box office.

They were all pragmatic, dedicated, white male capitalists who had prospered by being amoral. Their goal was to corner the market on legal cannabis, and the plan had been set in motion by participating in the more risky domination of the market in illegal weed. They needed one another for protection and propaganda. They also needed one another to multiply the millions they intended to make.

Bentsen Lilley knew as much about cannabis as a man who had never smoked it could. He knew that consumption of weed by the young was going up and consumption of tobacco was going down. He knew the rates had almost intersected, and he knew there was a strong correlation. Kids who smoked weed were likely to smoke cigarettes afterward. One could protect the other. As one rose, so would the other. He already had his marketing experts and advertising visionaries on the case. They were veterans of the old campaigns, men who had expanded the legend of the Marlboro Man, rallied feminists to Virginia Slims, concocted Joe Camel, and marketed Newports to the African-American community at the expense of Kools and Salems. Most had fallen out of favor until Lilley rounded them all up, paid them all generously, and gotten their creative juices flowing again. Soon it would all be worth it.

Alyssa, whom Lilley had met while she was dating Martin Gaynes, greeted all the guests, then gathered the kids, herded them into the Lear Jet, and flew to Denver for a connection to their home in Puerto Vallarta, where her husband would join them in a few days, once the elections were over.

The lieutenant governor delivered a prayer, and the general led the Pledge of Allegiance. Coffee pots and freshly baked muffins were passed around while Lilley began the discussion with an update on the ballot initiatives in nine states, five of which were voting on the legalization of recreational marijuana and the others for medicinal use. Lilley said he expected the votes to pass in every state except Arizona, and it was going to be close there. He said they'd be safe if Katharine Franklin won because she had expressed respect for the wishes of states on the matter. Both candidates had avoided the matter. What little Gaynes had said had been discouraging, but Lilley thought it unlikely Gaynes would win.

"What if he does?" the police chief, who was from Texas, asked.

"First of all, I don't think Mr. Gaynes has the slightest bit of conviction about anything," Lilley said. "Secondly, it's such an easy pivot. We Republicans have always believed in states' rights. Gaynes can ill afford to ignore the will of citizens in each state, let alone California."

"He's going to get beaten badly there," the lieutenant governor said. "Why would he care? What if he decides to punish California? He's a vindictive son of a bitch."

"It's not at all likely to happen," Lilley said. "If it does, and he makes an issue of it, we'll get rid of him."

No one said anything.

"To clarify, he'll be impeached, or threatened with it." Lilley turned his gaze to the FBI deputy director. "You'll see to that, won't you, Eddie."

"I don't think it'd be a problem," Edmund Kingsley said quietly. "Russians. Putin. Trust me. It won't be hard to turn that issue against him. His hands are dirty."

Lilley punched a button on a remote control, and oak paneling parted to reveal a large video screen. They reviewed shipping patterns and the flow of product from Northern California, the legal states in the Northwest and Colorado, the mountains of Kentucky, Tennessee, and North Carolina to carefully protected distribution capitals, at least one of which was in each state. Authority and security came from official sources – law enforcement, military, private trucking, cargo planes, and rail – and high-quality weed was being delivered in airtight shipping containers to airports, railroads, and private storage facilities that had been quietly purchased by the consortium. It all worked because, at every level, fixes had been inserted. Inspectors ignored the containers. Bureaucrats skillfully manipulated the numbers. Marijuana grown legally for recreational use was being exported through official channels that had been sanitized through money and intimidation. Cops made deals and backed them up by instilling fear in the hearts of their victims, some of whom were innocent. It required lots of money. It required discipline. The men in the room had discipline. They carefully demanded it in those beneath them.

"We have to be resourceful," Lilley said. "We have to be smart. I want to tell you one of our success stories. At one time, we considered trying to hire political reporters, and even operatives, to act as delivery agents while traveling around the country. The problem of that was that it wasn't organized and reliable. All the candidates and campaigns traveled to primary states, and, then, once the Democrats and Republicans had made their candidates, the whole election was really only contested in swing states because everyone knows how the outcomes in most states is going to turn out. We couldn't make the needs of our business match up with the … migration of the presidential campaigns.

"One of our associates, a deputy sheriff in North Carolina, stumbled into something that has really worked well. He got together with Garlin (Samuelson, head of the NCLEO), and Garlin came to me with the idea, and Patrick (Trintignant, the web developer) and I funded a website that has been reasonably successful in its own right while existing as a cover for distribution. As you are aware, lots of journalists have lost their jobs. This deputy, a fellow named Ronnie Shingler, has been with us from the start. In fact, he's had his hands in an undercover weed operation since before I even thought of it. His department started fabricating the destruction of confiscated weed and redistributing it in other parts of the state. When we got into a … similar business, our operations sort of bumped together, and we got together with Deputy Shingler and turned him to our side. He has, uh, gotten us a really valuable operative, a sportswriter, a fairly well-known one at that, and having him on the website has been a popular addition, and, you see, what's really convenient about a sportswriter is you can send him almost anywhere. This guy – his name is Mickey Statler – can write about anything. He's really good. You want to tell us more about him, Patrick?"

Trintignant said, "We've got a number of writers on the payroll, but Mickey Statler is something. I wish I'd known about him sooner. I don't think he's interested in writing about politics, but he could write humor columns five days a week. The thing that makes Statler so valuable is you can send him anywhere. He's no snob. He'll write a fucking great column whether it's an NFL game or the Little League World Series. I mean, honestly, I read him no matter what he writes. He's just an old-fashioned, ruggedly independent, voice. Most people absolutely love him, but those who don't love to hate him."

"They love him wherever weed is sold," Lilley said. "Which is everywhere."

"He's, you know, comparatively honest, too," Trintignant said. "He's no pothead. We were lucky to get him. His longtime paper eliminated his position. Shingler kind of set him up because he knew Statler was desperate. Got him hooked up with an attractive woman who set a trap for Statler because Shingler had already trapped her. We made the guy a deal he couldn't refuse. Now he's happy with what he's writing, he's making good money, and all he has to do is swap a briefcase full of product for one full of money. He didn't much like dealing weed, but now he doesn't mind because he needed the money and he's getting used to having it. He's the best thing The Ultimate Sporting Life site has going for it, and he's the best middle man in this whole operation."

It was an upbeat ending to a meeting that had begun with a group of men nervous about the election, and they celebrated appropriately. The FBI man and the metropolitan police chief retired to one room to enjoy good bourbon, scotch, and cigars. The politicians and Trintignant sampled the consortium's fine weed, and a bus arrived on the premises containing cooks to prepare steaks and co-eds from the state university forty miles away to provide genial hospitality and comfort. They owed Lilley a few favors there. His name was on the coliseum.

In reality, the girls weren't students. They were classy strippers, the same ones who posed as students when football and basketball prospects visited the school.

The police chief sampled a little weed because one of the young women allowed as how she had a taste for it herself.

Near nightfall, the private jets started returning, as did the athletic department's sleek bus to campus, and all the masters of the universe returned to their respective constellations happy, impaired, and sexually satisfied. Trintignant was the last to leave. That way he and Lilley could do some lines without having to share that particular addiction with the others. It had been coke that had forged their friendship back in the nineties. Neither had any interest in legalizing it. They thought, particularly after snorting it, that it required a certain level of wisdom and breeding that the general population lacked. Cannabis kept them contented. Cocaine could only stir them up, and Gaynes had done enough of that already.

CHAPTER 21

The Rank and File

Being named Jalloquille Means means, in turn, never having to say you're sorry. And never being called by your full name, relegated forever to "Quill" or "Jolly." Something about it gives you a desire never to look back.

Everything about the Fairborn State flanker cries out for the future. His emotion looks forward. His brain concentrates on the task at hand.

Recruiters thought the NCAA's Football Bowl Subdivision had Means overmatched. When he arrived at Fairborn State, he brought an attitude with him. Means sashayed out in front of a half-full Vaught-Hemingway Stadium and made the Ole Miss Rebels pay.

"That was for little guys all over," he said simply while a battalion of Fairborn State enthusiasts pounded his shoulders and prepared to hoist him upon their backs. The little band played the fight song over and over. The pep squad kept dancing. Ole Miss fans wadded up their programs and left them littered in the aisles and portals of the great Southeastern Conference monstrosity. They craved no reminders of this unfortunate Saturday afternoon.

Means caught 15 passes, four for scores, in the Skylarks' 38-36 stunner in Oxford. Heroes were common. A spindly freshman from a private school in Elba, Arkansas, stepped up and won it with a 42-yard field goal that was three yards longer than any other he'd ever kicked with a real clock running. Back in Elba, they play their football eight to a side.

But get this. The Fairborn quarterback, Terry Totteleau, hoisted up 61 prayers. Only 27 were answered. More than half of them were processed by Means, who just happens to be unusually righteous for a big man on a small campus.

"Jesus brung me through some hard times when I was growing up," he said, once escaped from his fanatical followers. "I had to find my humility. When the big schools didn't come calling, it made me question myself, man."

Means caught 93 passes during his senior year at Mozell County High School in Blarney Stone, Alabama, where he was not among the local Irish. Twenty-seven wound up in end zones. Thirty-four took him 40 yards or more down the field. No one in Blarney Stone, Irish or otherwise, had ever seen anything like it. Means was fast. He was sure-handed. He was 5-foot-9. In the SEC – where Alabama, Auburn, Arkansas and, yes, Ole Miss stretched him out and sized him up – he didn't meet the minimum. The SEC was a ride at Six Flags, and a high-school hotshot, no matter how hot, couldn't get aboard if he couldn't make 5-11.

Just up the road from Blarney Stone, Hardy Heights had a five-star a recruit who was five inches taller than six feet. Ole Miss signed Stephen Lavalle to much fanfare. Lavalle didn't make any of his 28 receptions Saturday. The Rebels dismissed him two weeks ago for "violating team rules." Lavalle's high school Harriers fell to Means' Tigers in the Alabama AA semifinals of 2012. On Saturday, while Ole Miss was losing on the field, Lavalle was exercising his non-competing clause.

"I'm sorry for Stephen," Means said. "I know him a little. He's a great athlete. I hope he gets himself straightened out. I'm gonna pray for him."

What were the Fairborn State Flatlanders doing in Oxford? Making money. The Rebels paid them $400,000 and hoped they'd be duly appreciative. Money didn't have much corruptive influence on Means and his teammates. They weren't getting any.

"We might get them nicer jackets for the awards banquet," head coach Archie Siemer said, "if we can lock up the conference next week in Grinder Shoals."

The Flatlanders lost early in the season to Tulane. At the time, undoubtedly, they had no idea how good they were. Provided they can slip past Ozark Mountain Home – yes, it's a thing, or a school, in southern Missouri

— they will probably earn a home slot in the first round of the FCS (Football Championship Subdivision, i.e., once Division I-AA, i.e., the culled part of the herd, playoffs), where the Flatlanders fell in the first round to Villanova a year ago.

"We gonna win it all this time," Means opined, allowing himself momentarily to look past the impending challenge of Grinder Shoals. "I know it's in us. I know it is."

Means never met his father until he was 19 and didn't even let it bother him that it was his dad, Herman, who had given him the name Jalloquille.

"My mama says he was drunk when he did," he said, smiling. "It wasn't no bad thing. It give me something to hang my hat on, you know what I'm saying? I've forgave him. He wasn't no bad man. He just had to go away. We prayed when I seen him. I'm so glad I had a mama who loved me and cared for me. I'm glad I come up in Blarney Stone. There wasn't, you know, that much trouble nowhere to get into."

Means said he found Jesus after his aunt died in a car wreck when he was 15. No one in Vaught-Hemingway Stadium found any evidence of back-sliding.

Mickey Statler edited his work, emailed it in, and bided his time organizing the game notes and explaining to an editor in Colorado that he had written "Means means" intentionally, but it was a lousy pun and he wouldn't mind it if the editor wanted to change it. He said it worked for him, but the reason editors existed was to make those judgments for themselves. Mickey fetched himself a Coke and two leftover slices of cold pizza, then just killed time until the ill-tempered Ole Miss traffic cleared out. Time in traffic was time wasted. Then he bade farewell to a few old chums he'd run across in the press box and drove back to the Hampton Inn in his rental car. He'd have left for home but was staying over in Oxford because he had to make another transaction. That morning, he'd swapped briefcases with a kid in khakis and a rugby shirt who looked like rush chairman of the SAEs. He had another switch to make in the room. He was driving all the way back to North Carolina and wouldn't be home until Tuesday. He had a side trip to Johnson City, Tennessee. He figured it would be a pickup there.

Back in Room 424, Mickey sat in his chair, reading a John Grisham novel because it seemed like the natural thing to do in Oxford, when a knock on the door occurred right on time. He opened the door. A small, nice-looking black kid wearing purple coaching shorts and a Fairborn State golf shirt walked in. Mickey had been impressed with the quality of people who brought him briefcases full of money in exchange of others full of vacuum-packed, odorless weed. The group, or company, or cartel, whatever it was, knew how to deal drugs with class. If any of them was armed, Mickey had never noticed. The cartel featured impeccable law and order.

"Hey, there," the kid said. "I'm Gerald."

Mickey didn't want to know any names. "I'm not," he replied.

"Oh, yeah, I forgot." The kid had a big smile.

"No worries," Mickey said. The young had replaced "no problem" with it.

"Well, I reckon you can't help but know I'm from Fairborn State," Gerald said.

"Yeah. I was at the game today. That was quite a win."

Gerald couldn't help but open the briefcase. Mickey told him not to mess with the bags. He didn't want to let any smell out. He nodded.

"I'm the head student equipment manager. The equipment van is parked outside. Everybody else went home on the bus, even the three other managers."

"Well, congratulations … Gerald."

"Oh, yeah," he said, "This is obviously some real good shit."

"I was, uh, talking about the game," Mickey said.

Gerald laughed. "Oh, yeah, right. Well, I'll be going."

Mickey looked in the other briefcase.

"Looks all right," he said. "I'm not gonna count it. I'm just delivering it. If it's short, I reckon somebody'll be in touch."

"You ain't got nothing to worry about there," Gerald said.

As the kid started out the door, Mickey said, "I wrote a story today about Jalloquille Means today."

"Cool," Gerald said. "Me and him do some business."

Everybody, Mickey thought. *Fucking everybody.*

"Tell me something before you leave," Mickey said. "How they get away with it. I mean. Fairborn State is the NCAA. Isn't there drug testing?"

"Oh, yeah. Everybody gotta pee in a cup when they report for practice. They gotta be clean, oh, I'd say, three to four weeks beforehand, then, ain't no more unless'n you make the playoffs, which we gonna do. So the players what smoke, they done cut it off already. Most of this going to the basketball teams. And spring sports, baseball and track, mainly. They way ahead of time enough to set down the pipe."

"Do equipment managers get tested, Gerald?"

"Nuh, uh," he said. "Not never."

Gerald seemed like a nice kid. He was making a good living, screwing on facemasks and selling weed. Working his way through college. It was heartwarming.

Tuesday was a grueling day. He counted out half the money and then divided that again. He used it to pay for one briefcase – the damned company must have bought them in bulk because they were all alike – in Johnson City and another in Boone, North Carolina. The bearded fellow in the overalls looked like he grew it. The one in Boone he met on a golf course. He looked like he sold cars. Mickey got back to the apartment at one in the morning, and it wasn't until the next morning that he even thought about it being Election Day.

The story on Jalloquille Means gnawed at Mickey all the way home but especially through the Blue Ridge Mountains. He felt a bit disillusioned. Maybe Jalloquille's religion wasn't a sham. Maybe he was a Rastafarian. Marijuana was some kind of religious sacrament. It made him feel spiritual. What right did Mickey have to question another's religion? He was the one selling the shit.

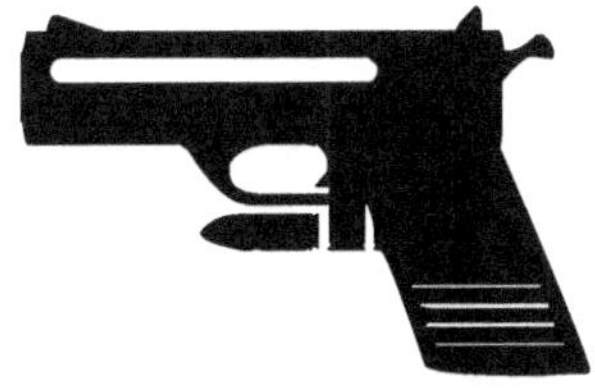

CHAPTER 22

The Role Model

Dylan Wannamacher felt ridiculous. He was wearing cargo shorts, the kind he normally wore when he needed lots of pockets, particularly the ones behind his thighs where no one ever thought to look. He had never been frisked, but if, by the wildest of misfortune, he ever was, surely the cops with whom his relations were nothing but the best would overlook those back pockets, where a bag of weed he had recently purchased might be located. It was in the range of his minor precautions. Minor precautions were a harmless form of nuclear weapon. He took them so that he would never have to use them. They were deterrents. He was high. As he began most every day with a bong hit before he drove to Enlightened Word, it didn't occur to him to stop just because he had to coach a football team.

He hadn't been much of an English teacher that day. Between pondering just how it was he intended to coach the team, and being mindful of a presidential election taking place, and coping with the difficulty of mourning the death of a man he had despised, the works of Thomas Wolfe bored him silly, so he held back on assigning *You Can't Go Home Again* and moved three decades ahead to the Beat Generation. Milo Hirley and his own Merry Pranksters would take to Kerouac, Burroughs, Kesey, and Ginsburg with aplomb, Dylan figured. The lads were similarly undisciplined. This he also discovered to be true on the playing field.

Dylan had no gear. The late Waddy Pegler had passed out all the caps, golf shirts, and shoes to the other coaches. Now his office was the lair of a dead coach, and not just any dead coach but a dead coach who had been his sworn enemy. It was good Dylan didn't believe in ghosts. Waddy would have been all over his ass. He lingered, though, in the dusty office, the wood in his desk redolent of the cheap cigars he had smoked there. Dylan imagined the smoke curling around in the flickering light of a projector, but then he did the math and realized Waddy wasn't even old enough to have graded football players through anything but video. Dylan finally found some old coaching shirts in a cardboard box under a shuttered counter. Every single one was XXXL, which was perfect. Dylan was twice the size of Waddy, who had been stocky but short. Undoubtedly, that's why the shirts were leftover. There hadn't been anyone who could wear them. He imagined some burly teacher signing on as an assistant coach and then getting tired of Waddy's shit. Waddy would have said "good riddance" but mourned the money he spent for the shirts.

He walked in the bathroom, pulled one of the white shirts over his teaching button-down, and stared at himself with amusement. The shirt smelled musty. How else could it smell? He turned around and looked at the back. No speckles of mildew dotted the white mesh. Why were there no pockets? He needed a place for writing utensils. The cargo shorts wound up being more functional than he thought. He was going to be taking a lot of notes. Some of them would be about how in hell he was going to do this. He knew football. Coaching football? Not so much. He would coach it on the fly, and maybe, just maybe, it would give him material for writing. That was the only possible good from this unwieldy predicament.

How ignorant was he? Dylan didn't know his own assistant coaches. Allegedly, there were four. Two were part-time. Two were volunteers. He didn't have any way of knowing which were which and thought it might be ticklish to ask. As time for practice approached, none showed up. Dylan didn't feel like waiting. He walked quietly through the locker room, mumbling a few greetings, and then walked down the hill to the practice field, which was the baseball field in the spring.

The seven-man sled appeared to be in working order. A two-man sled looked like it hadn't been used in ages. It was lodged against an outfield fence. The presence of a form-tackling sled – two slides resembling pontoons, or cigars, with an upright, padded dummy meant to simulate a ball carrier – cheered him. He had a feeling his team needed work on tackling. Every team he watched nowadays did.

The assistant coaches appeared and identified themselves by the whistles around their necks. Dylan realized he needed one. It could wait until Wednesday. Two appeared to be no older than twenty-five. One was probably about Dylan's age, another, thirty-two, or thereabouts. Dylan surmised that the part-timers were the young ones. The volunteers were the old guys, probably former players themselves, now selling insurance or used cars. The oldest assistant carried the bearing of a preacher. Dylan hoped he wasn't one. He introduced himself. The would-be preacher, Bonds Wiltson, was the assistant director of the Triborough Family YMCA. The other volunteer, George Grabarkewitz, ran a sporting goods store in Triborough. Shawn Celestine was a former soccer player at Triborough. Dylan bet he coached soccer in the spring. He also figured he was in charge of special teams. Stiller McGwire couldn't wait to tell Dylan that his junior varsity team was undefeated, leading him to suspect that Stiller coached the JVs. So inquisitive was his crack staff of assistants that they had waited to show up on the practice field at the same time as the players. Dylan guessed he should have called a meeting. When it appeared as if all the players had arrived, he told them to sit down in the wood-slatted baseball stands. He didn't tell the assistants anything, but they lined up, side by side, behind him, legs spread to shoulder length and arms folded behind them. The army called it "parade rest," or so Dylan recalled from an ROTC crib class that one year at UVA.

The new coach made it up as he went along.

"Men, as you are undoubtedly aware, I did not choose to be your coach," Dylan said. "I chose only to be your English teacher. Many years ago, in an earlier life, I did, in fact, play football. I remember this every morning when I get out of bed. I know a little something about how the game is played. My goal is to concentrate on fundamentals. My goal is to teach you football the same way I teach you literature."

A bigger bunch of bloodshot eyes he'd last seen at the only Grateful Dead concert he'd seen before Jerry Garcia died. At least half the Enlightened Word Dragoons were lit. He could see the weed in their satirical glances and a chorus of thoughts firing at him, all summed up in two words: *yeah, right.* School had only been out an hour. Where did they find the time? Where did they find the weed?

"Look, nothing is going to change in terms of the basic way we do things," *we* sounding strange coming out of his mouth. "I don't know what offense you run. I don't know what defense you run. I'll catch on, but we're going to rely on your assistant coaches for X's and O's. Three nights from now, they're going to call the plays. What I'm going to try to concentrate on is fundamentals – blocking and tackling – and I'm going to try my best to motivate you. Right now, my thinking is that's going to be a difficult task."

Dylan saw no hint of initiative in their eyes. He quickly and approximately counted twenty-seven players. Surely this was the varsity only. Where was the junior varsity? When did it practice? Two kids who looked like JVs were in shorts and tee shirts. Trainers? Equipment managers? One of each. He sent one up to his new office to fetch his leather briefcase, which had paper and ink in it. He told the boy, whose name was Trent, to see if he could find a whistle while he was at it.

"Today, we're going to go sort of backwards. We'll start out with some warm-up exercises. Who are the captains?" he asked.

Milo Hirley and Walt Pegler raised their hands. A day after his father's funeral, Walt was at practice. He looked high, but he was at practice. Good.

"Milo and I are the permanent captains," Walt said. "Dad always named a game captain before we went out on Friday nights."

Dylan looked for tears in the boy's eyes. He was stoic. His eyes were watery, but it was probably from weed.

"All right, Milo, Walt, you lead the team in calisthenics," Dylan said. "Then we're going to scrimmage. I'm just going to watch and evaluate. When I've seen enough, we're going to work on individual improvement. Backs and receivers, working on pitch and catch. I'll take the linemen. We'll work on blocking and tackling fundamentals. At the end of practice, you're going to run the forty-yard dash. Not wind sprints. I just want to get a time on everybody. Don't worry about that. Speed is overrated. Economy of movement is underrated. Playing football isn't about pure speed. It's about getting from where you are to where you need to be in the least amount of time. It's about intelligence. And instinct. Now get out there and start going through a series of calisthenics: jumping jacks, push-ups, sit-ups … the drills don't change. Everybody who ever played football knows them. While y'all are doing exercises, I'm going to meet with the coaches for a couple minutes."

They walked away. A couple may have broken a trot. Dylan was going to set some rules. Run, not walk, everywhere. Helmets on. No sitting down. Taking a knee would be all right. Now, though, he wanted to see his players in their natural states. He'd watch how they did things, then put his foot down. Today was an exploratory mission. Before he could coach them, he needed to observe them.

"All right," Dylan said to the assistants, who sat around him on the bleachers once the players had vacated them. "I just need to make sure we're straight on a couple things. First of all, where are the JVs?"

"I gave them today off," Stiller McGwire said. "I just figured it would be best for me to stick with the varsity only today, what with so much to do and all."

"Okay, fine," Dylan said. "Who's a back coach? Who's a line coach? Who's better at offense? Who at defense? Shawn? I bet you're in charge of special teams."

"That's right."

Bonds Wiltson took the offense. George Grabarkewitz took the defense. Dylan told Stiller he'd need his help with the linemen's drills.

"How many kids we got playing both ways?" Dylan asked.

"Five full-time," George said. "One or two more on occasion."

"All right, start out with first offense, against the one-way starters and some fill-ins on defense. Then, when I let you know, switch to the opposite: first defense versus fill-in offense. I'm going to back off and take notes. Y'all run things. I'll get more into it tomorrow and learn as much as I can. Everybody good with that?"

They all nodded.

As Dylan watched, he grew more pissed off. This was not what he wanted to be doing. He was no disciplinarian. But, as much as he tried to resist, as much as he tried to remain obstinate, as much as he wanted to go through the motions, it was coming back. He shuffled from place to place, keeping a distance as he scribbled notes. Milo Hurley had some ability at quarterback. They passed three fourths of the time. That would have to change. The passing game was fine, but a team had to establish the run in order to make passing more efficient. A defense that had to respect the run was less able to stop the pass. Passing for a team that couldn't run was, all else being even, a one-in-three proposition. For a team that could run, it was two out of three. Given Milo's obvious skills, it was probably forty one way and seventy the other. The linemen didn't know how to run-block. Dylan decided that was job one.

Once they sweated away the lethargy, things perked up. The defense was okay, other than the expected inability to tackle. Even in what little he saw of modern football, Dylan could see that the art of tackling was in sharp decline, even as the art of forcing fumbles was progressing. He had noticed while drunkenly watching Triborough lose that players on both teams ripped away at the ball, so much so that they didn't pay enough attention to stopping the ball carrier. Dylan didn't think it took much of a statistician to conclude that they were losing more than they gained. Contact caused fumbles. Pressure on the quarterback caused interceptions. Concentration prevented turnovers. Dylan wanted a team that would cause turnovers rather than commit them.

Who didn't?

Dylan was going to have to get a haircut, not because it was any kind of requirement but because he felt as if the Everglades were flowing through his locks. Undoubtedly, he was going to start wearing a cap to shield his face ever so slightly from the sun, and his dark-brown, slightly graying mop was too thick to abide a cap for long. He couldn't remember the last time he'd worn one. It didn't seem like he was doing much, and it wasn't hot, but more than his hair was sweating. It must have been nervous tension. He mildly craved a cigarette.

No seeds of revolt took hold until Dylan started drilling them in fundamentals. He had Stiller work in shifts with linemen on pulls, double-teams, and reach blocks. He took the rest to the sleds, only to discover they didn't know how to use them. They had only pushed the seven-man sled in unison. Dylan showed them how to hit and roll, hit and roll, down the line, all seven dummies, and then they fired out, kept their feet under them as they bounced back and hit alternate dummies, four to a run instead of seven. It appeared as if the lads had never done anything so strenuous.

They didn't know how to form-tackle. It involved approaching the sled low, lifting it up, and turning it sideways. It was humorous to watch them pushing the sled for twenty, thirty yards, never lifting enough to upend it. Dylan had to demonstrate himself, and that was going to ache in the morning.

Then he brought them all together and worked on angles of pursuit. Milo would pitch to a running back who swept around end, and, without contact in the line, each defender would have to tag the runner. Those in the area where the runner was headed tagged him at the line of scrimmage. Others would run down the line and tag him as he turned upfield. The poor slobs on the far side would have to haul ass down the field at a forty-five-degree angle, intersecting the runner at the sideline thirty or forty yards downfield.

"You gotta quit with this trailing the runner," Dylan yelled. "You're wasting your effort. Doing this properly, and getting the hang of it, is the difference between allowing a first down and a touchdown. The last thing I ever want any of you to do is make up your damned mind about anything. This game, at this level, is about always, always, knowing what to do. I'm going to teach you simple things that, if you were as smart as you think you are, you'd know from your own experience."

Dylan didn't just have to teach the players. Even out of the side of his eyes, or watching from his perch behind the seven-man sled, he could see that Stiller McGwire was no teacher. He didn't know anything about footwork, or having his blockers make their moves economically. Now, though, Dylan had taught them how to hit sleds, Stiller couldn't mess that up much, he reckoned. Dylan would take over the contact drills on Wednesday. It would take some tact. These coaches had been here. They either didn't make much money or none at all. Dylan didn't know how much extra he was making, come to think of it. He knew if he didn't take up the matter with Dr. Nathan Drummond, the school wouldn't give him a coaching stipend at all. He figured he'd better do that before Friday when his bargaining position might decline by virtue of the Smitties getting their pot-smoking asses clobbered again.

Practice ended when it became too dark to continue. Dylan felt like he must have been more exhausted than the players, but when he asked if anyone had anything, he got an earful.

One budding clubhouse lawyer said, "Man, we got homework. This school is a demanding place, Coach. You know that. The biggest problem I got is completing the assignment you yourself gave out."

Yeah.

The boy's name was Peter Baxter. He was a sober, sensitive fellow, one that Dylan suspected wasn't a stoner.

"Look," Dylan said, "I want you to have fun. I'm sorry some of you didn't have it today. But I want to tell you something about fun. You hear people say this emphasis on winning at all costs takes the fun out of sports. Oh, bullshit. Do you know how much fun winning is? How much of it have you done? When I was in high school, I played on a team that kicked ass every week, and when I was riding home on a school bus from a road trip, I used to think about those poor slobs we'd just torched forty-two to nothing. I knew then how much victory meant to me. It made me believe I could do anything, and I thought, well, what's the effect of losing on those guys from the other team? Do they go into other areas of life thinking they're gonna lose? Athletics has to be a positive experience. If it ain't worth winning, it ain't worth doing. Maybe you don't know that now, but you're going to learn it, and you're going to thank me. Probably not in my lifetime, but one day, you'll visit my grave, and you'll thank me then. Do you get this? Do you understand what I'm trying to say to you?"

Yes-SIR! It was good to see a little spunk in them. They trudged up the hill, looking like Napoleon's army leaving Russia, and Dylan started organizing his notes and trying to place everything back in his briefcase in some modest semblance of order.

"Hey, Coach." It was Milo.

"Yeah."

"I'm kind of hungry? You? How about splitting a pizza? On me."

"You're not bringing the Algonquin Round Table with you?" Dylan replied, doubting seriously that Milo knew what that was.

"Nah. They all got your paper to write."

"I'm starving. I need a shower bad as you. We both get dressed, I'll meet you there. Vissage, I presume."

"Ain't no other place," Milo said.

Dylan knew his back was going to ache in the morning. He dawdled. It was all he could do to get dressed. He sat a while, and it tightened while he was still. When he got to Vissage Pizza, Milo was picking up the pie – pepperoni, beef, mushrooms – and directing him to a booth in the far corner. He'd purchased a pitcher of root beer, which Dylan couldn't stand, but it was wet, and he was thirsty.

"Can I still call you Dylan here?"

"I reckon. I doubt we'll have dinner together every night."

"You know football, man. It's pretty impressive," Milo said.

"Well, thanks. I know enough to be dangerous." He half drug and half lifted two slices onto a paper plate. "I also know my quarterback came to practice high today."

"I was fine. It don't last long. I'm not telling you nothing you don't know."

He's letting me know he's got me by the balls.

"Let's just set all this shit aside," Dylan said. "What I said was legit, Milo. For football to be worth it, it's got to be worth doing right. Losing ain't worth it. If that means betraying my liberal sensibilities, so be it."

"D'you get high when you played ball? Dylan?"

"Not before practice. Not before games. Never before. Occasionally after. You want me to be honest? That's honest."

"Cool," Milo said. "Did you get high before practice today?"

"No. Was this not apparent by my demeanor?"

"I'm just fuckin' with you. I didn't mean to make no issue. I was out of line, all right. No more getting high before practice."

"What I don't see is how you did it? When y'all got to practice, I'd say at least twenty of you looked like zombies, at least until you got some sweat up. What? You have, like, a team hot box. Did you all come bursting out of some conversion van, all smoked up, in uniform?"

"If we had, it would've been a lot cooler." Apparently, Milo was familiar with the movie *Dazed and Confused.*

"Seriously," Milo added, "I don't know about everybody else. Me and Walt, he's having a hard time with Coach Pegler's death. Me and him blazed down behind the natatorium."

"Go easy on that shit," Dylan said.

"Yeah, Coach. Honest. I want to win some ballgames, too. It's complicated, though. You don't know the whole story about Coach Pegler."

"I don't need to know."

"Yeah, you do. Walt's daddy had a drinking problem. He was drinking Saturday night. Walt thought he was tore down. He lifted his daddy's keys, and met Shoneka Salley at the gym."

"Black girl."

"That didn't help when Coach Pegler walked in on them in the training room, them going at it on one of them padded tables."

"Christ."

"That's what Walt said, I'm guessing. Anyway, his old man beat him up pretty good. He was drunk, but he had enough sense not to punch him in the face. He pounded him in the gut, and Walt wouldn't hit his daddy back. Don't nobody know but me and him and her. And now you."

"And Waddy went home, passed out, and died."

"That's about it."

"I don't think nobody else needs to know," Dylan said.

"Nope. You needed to, though."

They ate in silence for a while.

"Look, Milo, I think life works better, the less you have to be a hypocrite. I don't expect you to believe what I'm about to tell you, and it's only based on what's happened to me in my life, but just take this under advisement, would you? When I was growing up, in Mississippi, kids smoked weed, too, but it was kind of … optional. Back then, you could buy beer when you were eighteen. Liquor was twenty-one. When eighteen was legal, it made it a lot easier buying if you were sixteen or seventeen. I never drank beer till I was a senior in high school. I never smoked weed till I was in college. I've often thought it was less a problem for me than some of the kids I grew up with because I didn't start doing it till I was old enough that my body could handle it."

"It's not fucking addictive, Dylan. Not physically, anyway. I've researched it. It's psychologically addictive. That means people smoke pot because they love the shit out of it. They don't go into withdrawal when they hadn't got it."

"Yes," Dylan said, "I believe you to be correct. Can I tell you something you might not have experienced?"

He nodded.

"This has been my observation, Milo. The people who get fucked up on drugs are the ones who are compulsive. The ones who drink or smoke or snort their way to oblivion are the ones who can't stop. They're the ones who start smoking crack or shooting heroin. The ones who, every time you see them, they're, like, 'hey, man, let's get fucked up.' They're not satisfied with just having a buzz. They've gotta get fucked up, and it keeps taking more and more to do it, and, pretty soon, just splitting a joint with your buddy don't get it, and you're trying something else, and that's when something I heard somebody say about alcoholism kicks in. It's a difference between drinking from the bottle and the bottle drinking from you. I don't drink much. It's, like, I go a month without drinking a beer, but then, you know, I have fun when I do it. The night Waddy Pegler died, I was getting drunk at the Triborough Homecoming game. I had a good time, but I just don't drink that much. It scares me. My daddy was an alcoholic. Supposedly he died of cancer, but that wasn't it. It was a lot simpler. He drank himself to death, and I was off at college. I didn't even know it was happening. Now call that bullshit, but would you just tuck that away in the back of your mind? Because, if you don't, one day you're gonna know damn well it's true. … I'm done."

"Yes, sir, Coach." Milo dropped the Dylan.

On the way home, Dylan felt a little ashamed because he'd almost started crying. It wasn't so much Milo who worried him. Maybe he was exaggerating, but it seemed to him that he was coaching a team that had celebrated the arrival of a new head coach by getting stoned the first day before practice. Was it the trauma? Was that an excuse? Was it standard operating procedure? Was it he? Why, of all people, had fate saddled him with this predicament?

The answer, of course, was that Jesus had a wicked sense of humor.

When he got home, Marcia had prepared lasagna, and he had little appetite, but he knew better than to admit it, so he ate as much as he could but not enough for her to believe that he liked it, and then it pissed her off more when he said wasn't in the mood for weed, which was a first, and she knew that if he'd just hit the bong once, they would have patched things up, but he wouldn't, so Marcia had no sympathy for the difficulty of trying to take over a football team after the previous coach had died, even though the man's son was still on the team.

She let it drop, but she hoped like hell he wasn't actually thinking about quitting. Weed was most of what Marcia liked about him.

Dylan drank lots of coffee. He was up late. He was tortured at the awful state of affairs confronting him. He thought he was in a crazy world, or maybe an alternative universe, where the anarchy of his own life was a result, not a cause, of general collapse.

Martin J. Gaynes was elected President of the United States. Marcia did a poor job of concealing her glee. He might not have hated her had he gotten high with her, and it might not have been such a bad move to help himself to the gin he had brought home from the Homecoming blur. It just didn't seem right, though. He wasn't of a mind. He made no resolution. He'd get high in the morning if the mood struck him as it had every morning since the last time he ran out of bud. Against his better judgment, he left Marcia to hit the bong alone. He didn't know what had gotten into him.

CHAPTER 23

Regaining Status

Mickey Statler put his journalist's inquisitiveness on the back burner where his extralegal activities were concerned. He was making good money and didn't ask any questions. As promised, it was safe. He might as well have been delivering office supplies, and he didn't really have to deliver. His clients made house, or, rather, motel-room, calls. He felt as if his life had a bit of a pall drooped over it. It wasn't why he had made the unfortunate decision, many years ago, to write about sports for a living. He watched what he saw and wrote it. It was honest. It was fun. The world never hung in the balance. Sometimes he had to deal with tragedy – he had been in Daytona Beach, Florida, on the day a crash took the life of Dale Earnhardt, and he had written about the deaths of several other athletes in the prime of life – but it was still a matter, however distasteful, of seeing and writing. Mickey saw many events that were conflicted, but he was never conflicted when writing about them.

Though he had no practical choice, being a marijuana mule made Mickey feel conflicted. He didn't have the guts to quit. He didn't like it, but he didn't want to put himself in harm's way, and cops who moonlighted as criminals were capable of conjuring up copious amounts of harm, if crossed. Twenty-five years of watching gifted athletes who were human in every other way had cured his naivete. He had even written that the central experience of journalism was disillusionment. Mickey had learned to appreciate athletes for what they did within the boundaries of their games and not expect any particular nobility in the rest of their characters. It was healthy and anathema to any fan.

The country, spooked at the threat of terrorism, was turning angrier. A rash of police shootings, caught on video and widely watched, had created civil unrest in many cities. They all seemed to involve what appeared to be the unjustified shootings of African Americans by policemen who were often, but not always, white. It had even happened in Lovejoy. A city policeman had yelled for a man trying to escape to stop. When he failed to do so, for almost two seconds, the cop shot him dead. It turned out that the cop had mistaken the dead man for another. But, by the logic of the initial explanation, the man had it coming. He'd been in possession of marijuana.

An innocent man who just happened to have a bag of weed on him might well run for that reason. Mickey had every reason to believe that local authorities were in possession of lots of cannabis that might be planted on a dead man who could offer no defense. Mickey wondered if cops were eliminating competition. Were they self-defense or cop hits? He couldn't see a constructive conversation on the matter coming out of lunch with Ronnie Shingler, his personal laison and partner in crime.

Shingler trusted him. He had been obedient and punctual. All his transactions had gone off without a hitch. He couldn't help but wonder but asked no questions. Most of their communication had been via text, and, occasionally, when he had a few days at home, Shingler had sent Mickey to a privately owned business where an old man worked on phones out of an office in his home. The man wiped his phone. He *really* deleted the messages. Mickey had a notebook where he scribbled items he needed to remember.

His schedule was generally mapped out two weeks in advance. The alleged job couldn't have been much better in terms of journalistic independence. Mickey went out and found something to write. It was his specialty. He just traveled from place to place in search of something interesting. It was easy. Inexplicably, it seemed that many others found it hard. He noticed that his trips were never to places where marijuana was legal for recreational use. That made sense. This would eventually cost him trips to California, which had just passed a proposition making it legal for the thousands, perhaps millions, who were not already buying with medicinal permits. He hadn't been to the West but once: Phoenix for a stock car race. He'd been as far north as Foxborough, Massachusetts, and as far south as Coral Gables, Florida. He flew on private planes for reasons that were fittingly private.

Mickey had money. Money was important for the man who hadn't had it. He was even caught up on child support. When the *News-Free Press* job had been eliminated, he had been both afraid and angry at himself for lying low and avoiding his estranged wife, but, most damnably, his daughter. The problem had never been her, and he had to go see her. Next up, though, was a mid-week basketball game near Myrtle Beach, South Carolina, and the Atlantic Coast Conference Football Championship in Orlando, Florida. Thanksgiving had come and gone without so much as a turkey sandwich, but he'd catch up at Christmas.

The critically acclaimed columnist of The Ultimate Sporting Life wasn't on a regular beat, so he didn't see all his old running mates regularly. He knew people everywhere, but he was seldom familiar enough to socialize, so varied were the events he attended. This worked conveniently for cannabis delivery. He didn't have to make last-minute changes in dinner plans. No one came knocking on his hotel-room door that he would have to shoo off before the kid in the equipment van showed up.

His prestige was returning. He was becoming quite the sensation. Colleagues who had commiserated his fate two months ago were now reinventing him as a lucky dog. He wondered if any of them smelled something fishy in his sweet gig. A few of them still remembered what it was like to be a reporter.

CHAPTER 24

Tangled Weed

Dylan Wannamacher rose early with time on his hands. Marcia had apparently spent the night in the dorm. He missed her company but was accustomed to failed relationships, not that this was one, or wasn't. Three times he'd fallen in love with women who were not similarly enchanted. Old news. Each failure had left him more cautious and reticent to stick his neck out. It was entirely possible that he no longer believed in love.

He had affection for Marcia. He didn't love her. He thought her a good writer, but he hadn't really read enough of what she'd written. He expected her fiction was a true account of her life with the names changed. That's the way many first-time novelists rolled. Some couldn't roll any other way. She hadn't asked for his help, and he hadn't offered. What could he say she'd take the right way? He made a conscious effort, in short stories and the two unpublished novels, to write about people different from him. He inserted himself into them. *What if I were this guy, in this place, at this time? What would I do?* He didn't want to drift into old age, writing the same story over and over, growing more embittered with each telling, descending through radicalism and drugs to a hackneyed fate and an early grave.

For now, he'd concentrate on actually achieving success and deal with the problems if they arose. Without success, problems were a bitch.

All considered, it was a good time for solitude. Dylan was conflicted by an issue with which he did not wish to deal. He had always been aware of students smoking the occasional joint. Avoidance of hypocrisy had been a factor in keeping the issue of teen drug use safely confined to the recesses of his mind. He was a stoner, but he was *of age*. On the other hand, cannabis was equally illegal to those not of age. He understood why kids got high. Weed was easier to acquire than beer. The high didn't last as long. It was easier to hide.

Less than four months earlier, Dylan had met with four students at Vissage Pizza and they had asked him what he thought about marijuana. They distinctly suspected him of using it himself, and he had done little to dissuade them. Fate was both cruel and hilarious. Little did he know that he would become not only their English teacher but their football coach. Marijuana might not be an obstacle to their lives, but Dylan had reluctantly concluded that it was an obstacle to their success on the playing field. He didn't know how it had happened. In the spring, he had smirked at times over the occasional suspicion that some goofy kid had gotten extra-goofy at lunchtime. Then he'd seen it in the brightest kids in class. Now he stood in front of a team on the practice field that was one-third stoned and two-thirds high. Dylan could only sweat out of them so much.

Dylan had a weed problem. He'd never thought it possible.

The morning was the time, and the Enlightened Word natatorium was the place. The pool didn't open until ten. The janitor was always there at seven. The janitor would always let them in. The janitor liked his job. He liked the kids. He liked to sell them weed. The natatorium had a small, enclosed room with a built-in hot tub. The air was heavy and pungent with the smell of chlorine. It served the purpose of air freshener. The stench of weed didn't linger long. The Merry Pranksters were relaxing in the tub and passing a joint.

Marcia, "Coach" Wannamacher's woman, had given them the name. She said they should all read a book called *The Electric Kool-Aid Acid Test*. Milo Hirley might actually do it, once football season was over, and he was back home in Fairfax, peddling good shit like Santa Claus to all his buds at *chrimmus muhfuh time*.

"Hey, Walt, how's the mourning coming along?"

"Good, man."

"No, not the morning, like, sun be up. Mourning, like, mourning your old man."

"About the same."

"Dulls the pain, eh?"

"What pain?"

Milo and Walt. Senior co-captains. They exercised their leadership by being able to converse in the hot tub. Sparingly. Marty Drummond and Jonny Heinsohn were there, too, silent and floating via both hot, roiling water and mind. It didn't last long. The morning brought what seemed like a general cleansing of body and mind. The only danger was letting time get away from them. It seemed so slow but was so fast. Bryne looked out for them. He ducked in and told them it was time to go.

Bryne wasn't Brian because his full name was Brynildson. Brynildson Hiers. He was a janitor who had been selling Milo and other Pranksters weed since the spring of their sophomore years. He was a major factor in the Pranksters' success. He kept them merry. Milo, Walt, Marty, and Jonny showered and gargled at the sink outside the showers. They took their own sweet time getting dressed, slowly drifting ashore on the beach of relative sobriety. As they filed out, Bryne said to Milo that they needed to talk. Milo told the others to wait for him outside.

"How's it going, Bryne?"

"I been better," he said. "Y'all boys been getting high too much."

"That's hilarious. Man sells me weed thinks I'm smoking too much of it."

"That ain't exactly it."

"No?"

"Y'all be smoking too much weed you ain't getting from me."

"Ah," Milo said. "Be not alarmed, my good man. I just got hold of some really robust indica, mon. It won't last long. It's from way off. Northern California. Probably Humboldt County, I'm guessing. You want in on it?"

"What? Now you selling to me?" Bryan asked, a mite menacingly. "Man, I done a lot for y'all boys. You ain't oughtta be fuckin' with me."

Milo stared at him and tried to look sincere.

"You're right," he said. "Just give me a day or two. I'll make it up to you. You know me and you tight."

"I know it," Bryne said. "I just wanted to be straight with you."

They embraced and bumped fists. Milo walked out the back door and squinted at the sun breaking above the pine trees that lined the horizon. Walt and Marty were smoking cigarettes. Milo asked if he could bum one. That way they could bravely face the day's academic challenges. The natatorium was a perfect place in so many ways. Their eyes were bloodshot. They had been swimming. Nothing beat a refreshing swim at dawn. That and a healthy breakfast, featuring all the major food groups: weed, tobacco, then proteins and carbohydrates. Fuck a glass of orange juice. They drank black coffee like a boss.

"Who got a hundred dollars on him?" Milo asked.

"I got it," Jonny said.

"When you got P.E.?

"Third period."

"Buy some weed from Bryne with it. I'll pay you back after practice tonight."

"Why we need that homegrown shit, Milo?"

"We don't. Just gotta keep our boy Bryne halfway satisfied till I think of something. He's pissed we ain't been buying his product."

"What you gonna do with it?" Marty Drummond asked.

"Aw, sell it some sophomore or something," Milo said. "I'm picking up some more from Marcia on Saturday. I'll discuss the matter with her some. We gotta figure out a way to get Bryne in on the plan without him thinking we hanging him out to dry. Which we are, but that don't mean we ain't gotta look out for him."

"Don't forget, kids," Marty imitated his father's tone. "The Enlightened Word is …?"

"Titties."

"That's right. Hey, man, you like titties? Oh, yeah. I love 'em. You ain't no leg man? Aw, naw. Strictly titties. I love me some titties."

The Enlightened Word was code for weed. It changed from time to time, usually as a result of stoned enlightenment.

Coach Dylan Wannamacher had found his running game in the defensive line. Seriously. His stopwatch discovered that the two fastest runners on his team were twins Lenaius and Denaius Paterson. Lenny and Denny. They were two of the Dragoons' three African Americans. The other, 300-pound Ja'Tarik Guest, would remain in the offensive line. Dylan knew he needed to pair the Paterson twins in a split backfield or an I, but he didn't have time to change the offense, so they'd have to both play defense and swap time on offense. The jet sweeps, with the forward bloop tosses, were already in the playbook, and Dylan found it easier for Lenny and Denny to catch the little tosses than to teach them how to receive handoffs. They were rushing yards that counted officially as passing, and Milo Hirley was happy because they would pad his statistics absurdly. Dylan, in the name of simplicity, made every handoff a pitch, and the running game showed up statistically in forward laterals. Milo also darted into the middle of the line himself, after receiving the snaps. He was shifty. He read the holes better than the twins, who hadn't learned enough to do anything other than go where Dylan told them. Dylan didn't know if it would work, but he was confident it would be better. The changes gave their own defense fits.

Other members of the faculty complained that his practices were too long, so he must be doing something right. Doctor Drummond let him be. Having shanghaied him into the job, Drummond couldn't very well tell Dylan how to do it. It was the same way Dylan couldn't turn down a job that opened due to tragedy.

Touche, Nathan.

Morale was improving. Milo held up his end of the bargain. It was Dylan's knowledgeable opinion that neither he, Walt Pegler, Marty Drummond nor Jonny Heinsohn was high when practice began. Dylan wondered where the Merry Pranksters nickname originated. He had assigned them Beat Generation writers, but neither Ken Kesey nor Tom Wolfe. Surely they hadn't read Wolfe's *The Electric Kool-Aid Acid Test* of their own volition. The biggest problem was the reserves, all but one of whom was an underclassman. They apparently saw no reason to come to practice straight. It took a while to get them going. Some days they never got going. The various cliques were hard to identify. The Pranksters knew Dylan was onto them. The others were afraid of it. Paranoia was not an attractive trait in a football team.

CHAPTER 25

Potential Complications

The Consortium did not often meet. Its prime investors and participants had obligations, and they were growing as the country prepared for a new administration. The election of Martin J. Gaynes had been a shock to the Consortium. The eventual legalization of cannabis had seemed inevitable until the Republican insurgency swept an impulsive billionaire into office. In its previous get-together, Bentsen Lilley and his associates had paid lip service to a Gaynes takeover. Lilley, who had delayed his Thanksgiving with the family in Puerto Vallarta, had returned early, as well. Now he and his closest partner, Patrick Trintignant, were cloistered in his home while the first big Rocky Mountain snow fell outside.

"Gaynes hasn't said a word," Trintignant, who had deep ties with the Right, said. "There's been a lot of speculation, but that's all it is. We'll be all right."

"Oh, yeah, we'll be all right," Lilley said. "The son of a bitch just named the biggest opponent of weed in the country as his attorney general. We'll be fine, Pat, Just fucking fine."

"Relax, Ben. The man who's *gonna* build a wall isn't. The man who's *gonna* take on Wall Street is taking half its richest money manipulators with him to Washington. He's cutting deals. He's *gonna* cut one with us, too. We're *gonna* provide product for his resorts. He's *gonna* be a preferred partner. He's *gonna* get the best weed. All these little hipster shitheads who flock to the weed cafes of Amsterdam are going to have a cheaper domestic option. Gaynes is obviously not going to set his personal business affairs aside, at least not to the extent of every other president in history. One of the sons is pro-weed."

"Martin Jr.," Lilley said. "Knowing Gaynes, it's another bait and switch. He needed one of the kids to come out for weed, just for a little boost in pro-weed voters. I'm not sure there's much stake to be put in what Little Marty says. They probably have an agreement that Andrew remains silent."

"Maybe," Trintignant said. "As you know, this has been my point all along. It's so easy to get the GOP to use states' rights as a crutch. It's a fallback. Make it worth their time, and they'll rationalize weed away. 'I'm against it, but who am I to override the choices of citizens of a state to do what they deem appropriate.' In his campaign, Gaynes gravitated toward the propagandists. My site's power is with the Libertarians. The trick is to build a grass-roots movement from the right with the Libertarians, and make it worth Gaynes's time with his own business, make it worth his sons' and daughters' time, and, well, there's another angle to pursue."

"I'm listening."

"Anger from the left. First of all, the polling shows that there is a considerable gap between marijuana opinions among the Democratic Party's voter base and the policies of the party. If Katharine Franklin had gone stronger on the issue, and got off the fence, that same polling suggests she would have won."

"The same could be said for other issues, too," Lilley said. "She lost to Gaynes, and she lost to Pathan for the same goddamn reason. Too careful. Too slick. Too calculating. But, getting back to the Left, just what do you mean for us to do?"

"Get 'em out in the streets, just like the goddamned hippies of the sixties," Trintignant said.

"I can't believe you're saying that, Pat. It's hard for me not to laugh."

"Just stir things up, Ben. We already know how to do it."

"White cops killing black suspects."

"Bingo. We just, uh, turn up the heat a little more on our campaign to eliminate opposition. It's not like we aren't already doing it," Trintignant said. "We can't go on being extralegal forever. At some point, just by random actions, something's going to happen that's major enough to expose us. That's why we've had to liquidate some of the people we can't trust. Most were just thugs. Criminals. But a few were whistle-blowers, extortionists, trying to be paid off. Do-gooders, they're the worst."

"And we don't play that shit," Lilley said.

"No, we do not."

"So, you're saying, we try to play ball with Gaynes, but if it doesn't work, we make it wild in the streets."

"He hates to be made to look bad," Trintignant said.

"If he doesn't get the message, we'll really make him look bad," Lilley replied. "That's why we've got the best working for us. Best lawyers. Best politicians. We've got the FBI. We got all the police we need. Fuck Gaynes. He's not gonna stop us. If he does, we'll stop him. I'm gonna call Samuelson. Hell, I might even drop in on him, if the weather improves. Garlin will know how to set it up. You think we need to talk to Kingsley? Maybe wait a while?"

"I'll talk it over with him," Trintignant said. "The FBI can cause lots of trouble for Gaynes."

"They damn sure helped bring Katharine down."

"Yeah, and I can't understand it. Tell you what we could use, Ben. We need Ed as the head of the FBI. I bet that could be arranged. I'll get in touch with some of our allies on the Hill."

The last person Marcia thought would contact her was Tripp Fallaw. She wouldn't have answered the phone, but she thought it was a contact in California. At first, she didn't recognize the voice as anything but strung out.

"Baby, I'm fuckin' desperate. You gotta help me."

"Who's this?"

"You know who it is."

"I said, who the fuck is this? … Tripp? Goddamn you."

"My fucking life is in danger, Marcia. I gotta get out of here. I gotta get out of the whole fucking West Coast. I probably gotta get out of the country, but first I got to get back east."

"Tripp, why in hell would I help you? You left me in the middle of L.A., no money, no way home. Fuck you."

"Don't hang up, Marcia. I got money. I'll give you ten thousand dollars to come get me."

"Just suppose I would do something to help your sorry ass. How the fuck am I supposed to get you on a plane? Are the cops chasing you?"

"Not officially," Tripp Fallaw said, "but I can't trust 'em."

"Shit," she said. "I'll call you back."

"This phone is stolen."

"What?"

"I gotta get it back to the guy I stole it from. I'm just outside a casino. He's probably looking for it. I can't use my phone. In fact, I don't have one. I threw it off the pier. I think somebody was following me."

"You're fucked up on something, Tripp."

"I'd hate to go through this shit sober."

"Well, how am I supposed to get back in touch with you?"

"Fly to LAX. I'll be back in touch."

"Tripp …"

"Gotta go, Marcia. Thanks. I won't do you that way again."

Hung up. Damn him.

Marcia called Wade Sanderson, who had put her in the weed business. He didn't answer. She texted him that she'd heard from Tripp Fallaw. He called straight back.

"Where is he?" he asked when she answered.

"I don't know. Somewhere in Southern California, I gathered. He said his life's in danger. Begged me to come get him. Said he was on a phone he'd stolen from some guy in a casino. Said the guy was probably looking for the phone right now, and he needed to get it back to him."

"Gimme the number."

"I told you it's not his," she said.

"Just give me the number. I'll call the guy and find out where *he* is."

"Is it you who's aiming to kill him, Wade?"

"Hell, no. I'd like to whip his ass. I might shoot him in the knees. I wouldn't kill him, though. I'd like to see him in jail, getting butt-fucked by some motorcycle gang member, but I don't quite hate him enough to kill him. Like they used to say back home, Tripp Fallaw ain't worth killing."

"He says he's got money," Marcia said.

"I wouldn't know. He's got some enemies, Marcia. What money he's got, he owes five times as much. For God's sake, stay away from that fucker."

"All right. Don't kill him, Wade."

"I told you it ain't my business. I'm not in the murder department. Don't fucking try to help Fallaw out. You'll regret it. But, Marcia …"

"Yeah."

"I'd love it if you'd fly out to see me. We can spend some time together over the holidays, know what I'm saying?"

"I hear you," she said. "I'll see what I can do."

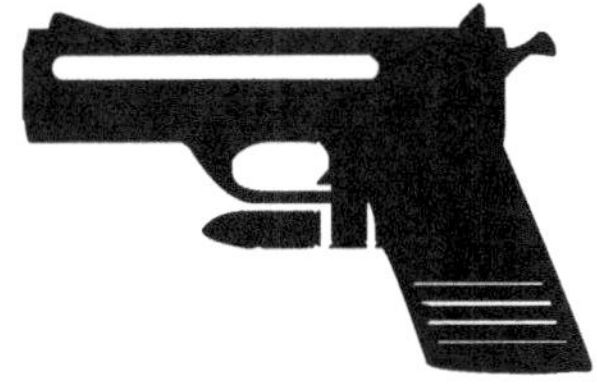

CHAPTER 26

Mickey's Beat

Mickey Statler couldn't write *anything* he wanted. He didn't know the bounds. What he knew was that there was a clear conflict of interest.

An inordinate amount of his cannabis deliveries were on college campuses. In fairness, an inordinate amount of his traveling was to college towns. No surprise there. Mickey had never thought of himself as naïve. Three decades of chasing sports stories had made him world-weary and hard-bitten. He knew that athletes were no more paragons of virtue than the general population. They were adept at sports. Many were fine human beings, but nothing about sports made them that way. Football, for instance, was cruel, ruthless, and dehumanizing. The game cultivated toughness, not compassion.

Athletes at the big schools were tightly protected. When a one-on-one interview was allowed at all, it wasn't altogether one-on-one. A representative of the athletic department sat in, taking notes as carefully as the reporter. He still found anecdotal evidence from auxiliary student figures – equipment managers, trainers, tutors, grad assistants – who showed up at his hotel rooms to exchange money for product. When Mickey had been in college, thirty years earlier, athletes were no saints. As a young student journalist, working for the campus daily, he had partied with the ballplayers. Marijuana had been in widespread use even then, but now it had less stigma attached. Drug testing policies varied school to school. He suspected some schools used lax testing policies for a recruiting advantage. He suspected some schools had much to hide, hence the tight control over their athletes.

Small schools were less protective and more naïve. At a small, church-related college in Missouri, he'd gone to write an inspirational story on a star running back who had skipped the previous year to be a missionary in Costa Rica. He was a great kid. The sports information director had freely given Mickey the kid's room number, and when he arrived on the third floor of the dormitory where mostly athletes were housed, the smell of burning marijuana leaves hung heavily in the hall. When Ellis Anderton, twenty-one, of Sargasso, Iowa, opened the door, he told Mickey he'd been expecting him, so please come in and have a seat. Mickey apparently wore a suspicious look.

"Don't mind the aroma," Anderton said. "You get used to it."

"I would imagine."

Anderton sighed. "I get my, I don't know, high, buzz, whatever, from the Lord Jesus Christ. The righteous man cannot spread the Word of God in a sinful world without himself being a part of it. That's the most important lesson I learned in Costa Rica. My roommate smokes pot. He goes down the hall. He's still a good dude. He comes to Scripture reading, too."

Mickey hadn't pulled out his recorder yet. *A pity,* he thought. Anderton was direct and forthright. Weed wasn't his scene, but he clearly didn't consider it a big deal. The Fellowship of Christian Athletes had changed. When Mickey had been in school, the stoners hid from the FCA, the Campus Crusade for Christ, and the Baptist Student Union. The Wesleyans he hadn't been sure about.

The interview continued, and Mickey knew his popularity at The Ultimate Sporting Life would come into question if he wrote a story about how marijuana was more popular than bottled water among the nation's sporting elite. It would be a hell of a story, though, if he didn't have privileged information. He'd left the campus feeling slightly dirty, driven to Paducah and filed his story while he drained a six-pack, then retired to the hotel bar, where it occurred to him that it was wasteful to drink liquor when he had enough weed in his room to keep Coachella going for a day. For Mickey, weed was bad luck, even though circumstance had forced him to sell it.

Then there was the story of Jalloquille Means, which he'd written, and the hearsay evidence from Gerald the equipment manager, which he had merely filed away with all the other tales of mild, weed-induced corruption.

At the same time, it was easy to rationalize. The stuff must not be too bad because it damned sure seemed as if everyone was smoking it. California, Nevada, Maine, and Massachusetts had just legalized it, and close to half the country had now approved it for either recreational or medicinal use. Mickey wondered if it was a coincidence that so many college football teams in weed-legal states seemed to be rapidly improving – Washington, Washington State, Colorado, although Oregon was down – even though they didn't condone its use among their athletes.

Yeah. Right.

At a bar in Atlanta, Mickey had been having dinner with friends, and they'd stayed late, watching Southern California knock Washington from the unbeaten ranks. Mickey had consumed enough bourbon to crack, "Move over, Huskies. Now Southern California's got legal weed, too."

That brought a silence to the table until someone nervously chuckled, and then everyone started laughing. *Mickey, old man, you're funny as hell, you know that? You'll say anything.*

The journalist in him wanted to write the story somewhere. Under an assumed name, perhaps, though it would be dangerous. Maybe this was a book. Maybe he could write it. Maybe he could find the time if hell froze over, which was entirely possible with Martin Gaynes in charge.

The more he thought about it, Mickey concluded that cannabis ought to be legal. It didn't produce a hangover. It didn't wreck a whole day. It didn't last very long. It may have been catastrophic for a team to go out drinking the night before a game – when he was in college, the weekly beer bash had been on Thursday nights – but have no effect at all if they'd sat around taking bong hits. Weed had been an option back in his day. There was booze, and there was grass. Booze had seemed manlier. Grass had seemed more seductive. What separated the kids of today, he reckoned, was its accessibility. Nowadays, it was socially more acceptable and easier to get. People selling weed never checked IDs. Mickey never checked IDs.

Of course, he was just a wholesaler. He hated his involvement every minute, but he didn't hate the money he was making, and, wonder of wonders, he had the cops surreptitiously on *his* side. It was a double-edged sword, police protection. Like having a wife. Can't live with her. Can't live without her. *C'mon, baby, let the good times roll.*

Damn Laurie Bigelow. He sure would like to screw her again. He was weakening. Now he could get *her* high. No one would get busted. He could get the shit at cost. He didn't want to marry her, or make an honest woman out of her, God forbid, or marry anybody, for that matter. Weed didn't seem like a big deal, but marriage, that was frightening. Devastating. Destructive. Mickey was just interested in recreational sex. Sport fucking, as it were.

In Nashville, Mickey had a police escort for an exchange in the alley behind Tootsie's Orchid Lounge on Lower Broadway. A narc who knew where it was safe and could watch out for honest cops showed him the spot of the exchange and monitored it from a safe distance. It was the first time he'd made an exchange out in the open. Any streetwise panhandler would've known exactly what he was doing. The briefcases contained exactly what they looked like they did. The narc didn't care. The customer was a bassist between sets. Once he picked up the product, he was on his own. The narc stayed with Mickey because Mickey had the money, and one green was superior to the other.

Damned if crime wasn't easier than obeying the law when the police were the criminals. Life was good when the fix was in. Mickey was beginning to enjoy the exhilaration of the criminal life. Journalists turned bad the same way the cops did.

The Atlantic Coast Conference championship game had been an entertaining one. Clemson, en route to the Bowl Championship Series, had had to earn it, squeezing by Virginia Tech, 42-35. Mickey had failed to find a particularly unique column angle and had settled for an analysis of the rising Heisman Trophy prospects of the Tigers' quarterback.

He'd spent Sunday whistle-stopping through several college towns – Deland, Saint Augustine, and Statesboro, Georgia – and even spent a couple hours in a Saint Augustine mall signing copies of his ACC basketball book from the spring before. He made his last product exchange at ten that night at a Hampton Inn bordering the Georgia Southern campus. The next day he drove back to Lovejoy, where he left the cash in a roll-top desk under lock and key, inside a storage warehouse that was also under lock and key. He had gathered that the entire warehouse was the property of Ronnie Shingler and his associates. No one else had ever been there at the same time he was. He wondered if the warehouse had been confiscated from undesirable drug dealers so that Shingler's desirable ones could use it as something of a distribution center. Mickey had also gathered that it was unlikely the Lovejoy authorities acquired enough weed locally to keep the enterprise going. The operation was quite a bit larger than Shingler had ever intimated or Mickey imagined.

Mickey couldn't help but see the evil. He had to look no farther than his eyes could see. Colleges would soon close for the holidays, but there would be no break for Mickey. He expected to be assigned minor bowl games and holiday basketball tournaments. He had few loved ones with whom to spend Christmas, anyway. He'd grown up in a family that was always struggling to make ends meet. He'd been the first in his family to graduate from college. What he was doing now wasn't the most honorable way to make a living, but it sure beat working in a cotton mill, not that such sweatshops even existed anymore.

Newspapers would soon go the way of the cotton mills. It had been a good gig back before the goddamned *USA Today* came along. Now a man had to moonlight. Mickey had the modern equivalent of a paper route, except that the subscribers changed week to week.

CHAPTER 27

To the Victors Go the Spoils

After three days, Dylan Wannamacher could see improvement.

Not in the Enlightened Word Dragoons. In him.

He was getting around better. His back didn't ache as much. The bad knees kept him from doing more than occasionally breaking into a trot. That was the reason he had bought a bicycle in the first place. The smooth pedaling motion didn't cause the arthritis to flare up as much. He couldn't take the wear and tear of running anymore. The wear and tear of running had worn the knees out more than college football ever did.

As for the football team, it was too soon to tell. The notion that he could teach them how to block and tackle in three days was absurd. They looked better in practice. Throw in the tension of a game, and who knew? He hoped the next opponent, and one of two remaining, would look right past the slumping Dragoons. They must be unprepared for the unexpected. Those teams knew the head coach had died, and Dylan hoped it was spreading far and wide that the team was now coached by some English teacher who had never coached before.

They would not be prepared for Lenny and Denny Paterson. Powders Pointe, a public school, was next, on the road. Because they were the Pointers, no one ever called them anything but the Powders Pointers.

Dylan wondered if the girls' teams were called the Powders Pointers Sisters. They wore blue and white. Yes. Powder blue.

This was most of what Dylan knew. He watched the Pointers on video. In contrast to the Dragoons, they had started slowly but gradually improved. They were Double-A in class to Enlightened Word's A. They were at home. They were widely expected to win.

Dylan had concluded that the best assistant coach was Stiller McGwire, though he was a bit of an ass kisser. It was understandable, Dylan reasoned. From the Triborough practice field to the Enlightened Word faculty, he had always marveled at the susceptibility of otherwise intelligent people to be blind to ass kissing. In part, this was because it was functional, but that didn't come close to accounting for the fawning and the results it seemed to foster. Dylan tended to distrust those who heaped lavish praise upon him. What did they want? What was their angle? He recognized that every positive term had a negative counterpart. One man's team player was another's ass-kissing weasel. Dylan's suspicions just leaned to the side of the ass-kissing weasel on most occasions. He respected McGwire's competence but didn't know if he could trust him.

Stiller kept saying that they ought to get together for beers one night after practice. Dylan finally told him he'd take him up on it once they'd played a game and they had more to talk about. Bonds Wiltson was an obedient, civic-minded jock sniffer who probably doubled as a spy for his close friend, Dr. Nathan Drummond. George Grabarkewitz was a businessman protecting the money his sporting goods store made from supplying the Enlightened Word athletics teams. Waddy Pegler had doubled as the athletics director, and as a result, Enlightened Word didn't currently have one. Dylan could rely on Grabarkewitz if for no other reason than he figured Dylan would become athletics director, too. He had no idea that Dylan would rather be co-chair of the county Tea Party than athletics director of Enlightened Word. Dylan thought it functional not to tell George that. Then there was Shawn Celestine, who Dylan found about as quirky as every other placekicker, soccer player, distance runner, and pole vaulter he'd ever known. Shawn had one sticking point. He insisted on having a specialist to kick field goals and extra points. He said the punter could play other positions, but a sidewinding kicker – and what other kind was there nowadays? – had to have the leg flexibility that the grinding nature of football did not allow. The trouble was that the kicker, Eli Shouse, was an above-average athlete that Dylan wanted to use in the defensive backfield or at wide receiver. Shawn was passionate. Dylan had to give him that. He dared Dylan to name one proficient, soccer-style kicker who had played another position. He couldn't think of one, so he let Shawn have his way. The soccer player was the only assistant who had stood up to him, and Dylan liked that. He even drew a laugh from Shawn when he said, "All right. That little fucker better not miss from forty in."

They all seemed to like it when he talked dirty, as long as he didn't do it too often.

Everyone took the team bus to Powders Pointe except Bonds Wiltson, who drove separately because he had some YMCA meetings to attend. Youth basketball, as everyone knew, was right around the corner. Bonds made arrangements with a Burger King to have Whoppers and fries ready for the trip home. Dylan had him order a few extra for hungry linemen, especially Ja'Tarik Guest.

During a rambling pregame pep talk, Dylan drew heavily on Pat O'Brien in *Knute Rockne, All-American*; George C. Scott in *Patton*; and Sylvester Stallone in *Victory*. He considered Alec Guinness in *The Bridge on the River Kwai* but didn't think it would work without an English accent. The team didn't seem to be stoned, whether because the Merry Pranksters had exerted their newfound leadership or because the bus trip had dissolved the collective buzz. In part, Dylan had used the pep talk as an experiment. Not only were their eyes not bloodshot. They didn't exchange glances and roll their eyes at his wholesome words. That was scary in itself. Dylan hoped they weren't stoned, but he didn't want to coach an army of dull automatons, either.

Every team occasionally has a game where the field seems forever slanted against it. This was such a night for Powders Pointe. The Dragoons, conversely, got some delightful breaks in the first quarter, in which the Pointers could have scored three touchdowns, should have scored two and a field goal, and did score one and miss the extra point. No one blocked Ja'Tarik on a fourth down, and he sent a Powders Pointe wingback to the hospital right after the poor kid took the ball on a jet sweep. The fullback fumbled shy of the end zone on "first down and goal to go."

The Enlightened Word offense shoved the ball out far enough to punt comfortably, and Milo got a fortuitous roll on a punt that wasn't nearly as good as the forty-eight yards for which he was credited.

Then the Pointers overreacted. They got antsy, concerned more about running up the score than winning the game. They abandoned the running game that had worked well in the first quarter. The only player the Dragoons couldn't cover was the wingback who was entering a concussion protocol at the nearest emergency room. In the second quarter, Enlightened Word's running game came alive because what the defense didn't know, Lenny and Denny Paterson, caught them unawares. Lenny's series in the backfield took the Dragoons sixty-seven yards in sixteen plays, but Dylan failed to overrule Stiller McGwire's decision to go for it on fourth and three, and it failed. Denny scored on a thirty-yard run with thirty seconds remaining in the first half. Eli Shouse kicked Enlightened word into a 7-6 halftime lead, and Powders Pointe ran six offensive plays in the whole second quarter.

The second half was more of the same, though it took an inordinately long time to play because the Pointers' quarterback kept trying long passes he couldn't complete. Jonny Heinsohn and Milo each had interceptions in the fourth quarter, and Eli's 38-yard field goal made the final score 10-6.

About fifty Enlightened Word partisans saw it. At midfield, Dylan shook hands with an opposing coach who wore a look that said he was worried about his job. He met Milo's wild-eyed father and Waddy Pegler's widow, to whom he'd never spoken, only seen. The Whoppers were fine, but the fries were stale on the way home. Milo Hirley managed to ride home in a van with the cheerleaders without their adviser noticing. One of the cheerleaders, the femme fatale Shoneka Salley, was alleged to have jacked off Walt Pegler in the back row of the bus, though some claimed they were only french kissing. When Dylan caught wind of what happened, he was glad George Grabarkewitz had opted to ride back to Triborough with Bonds Wiltson. Stiller drove the bus. Dylan read a book on his cell. He neither heard nor saw the evil but found out about it. Peter Baxter, the team malcontent and undoubtedly a future attorney, texted him. Dylan laughed to himself when he thought, *Well, son, I'm going to let you get away with it this time, but if I ever hear of you getting a blow job after a loss, well, that's where I draw the line.*

Walt had an unorthodox, but obviously functional, method of receiving grief counseling.

Enlightened Word had its own golf course, a devilishly difficult but short test that had been designed by a famous course architect whose son had graduated from Enlightened Word in the 1930s, when work on golf courses was hard to find. The course, even though it had been designed during an age when shafts were made of wood, turned a tidy profit because of its history and because old people who couldn't hit it very far loved it. Out of longstanding tradition, the course was closed on Sundays but open to students willing to walk through a narrow gate on the seventh hole and carry their own clubs. The Merry Pranksters got together there every Sunday, and owing to the fact that this particular Sunday was cold and brisk, they had it all to themselves. They played through the turn and halfway up the second fairway, at which point they retired to the woods and smoked weed in what was probably the safest place in the Commonwealth of Virginia. They sat on the trunk of a tree that had been felled by a summertime lightning strike and was far enough into the woods that no one had cared to remove it.

They didn't just get high. They got stoned.

"Okay, like, I get it how you got in the van," Jonny Heinsohn said, "but what I want to know is how you got out of it."

Milo Hirley, whose interception had sealed Powders Pointe's fate, asked, "Hey, that 'got' one more hit in it?"

Jonny took one more puff and passed. Milo took a hit and gave what was left to Marty Drummond and told him to go ahead and eat it. Marty didn't much care to swallow the roach without anything to wash it down, but he wasn't going to defy Milo's orders.

"Kimmie got sick," Milo said.

"What?" Walt asked.

"Kimmie got sick. I put her up to it. As soon as the van stopped, she went crashing out the side door, and she staggered away, about twenty yards, and started retching like she was puking. The others started squealing, said, 'Miss Hopkinson, Kimmie's really sick!' and when Miss Hopkinson chased after her, out I slipped. I just sat over behind the hedges, smoked a cigarette, froze my ass off, and waited for the bus to get there. I even managed to sneak over and get my shit out of the belly of the bus."

"That's slick, bruh," Walt said.

"What about you, lover boy?" Milo queried in reply.

"Wasn't nothing to it," Walt said. "Everybody on the fuckin' bus had their plugs in, listening to tunes. We could've fucked and nobody would've noticed."

"Next week is my turn," Jonny said.

"Next week is a fucking home game," Marty reminded him.

"Then the last game."

"You're fucking taking dibs," Milo said. "Ain't the way it works. Every man for himself. Be bold. Like Coach Wannamacher. Who gotta pack of smokes?"

Walt had a pack of Newports. He smoked Newports because his girlfriend was African American, and, for some reason, African Americans seemed to prefer menthols. Milo took one. Since he was a beggar, he could not be a chooser.

"Why y'all smoke, man?" Marty asked.

"Because it's very, very good when you're high," Milo said.

"Shit."

"Man, it's hard not to smoke a cigarette when you're high," Walt said.

"I ain't never thought about it," Milo said. "Out of all the times we done got high, you mean to tell me you never smoked a cigarette."

"I learned how, but that was way before I started blazing," Marty said.

Milo took a deep draw. "Well, my nigga, it's like this. A cigarette is good after things. It's good after football practice. It's good after a cup of coffee. It's very good after a joint. You know when it's very, very good?"

"When?" Jonny asked.

"After sex," Milo said, "but you wouldn't know about that, would you, Jonny boy?"

"I get laid," Jonny said.

"Shit," Milo said, "my brutha ain't had pussy since pussy had him."

Jonny's face was already red because it was cold. He had to grin because the other three were laughing.

"Shit, boys, it's back to the salt mines tomorrow," Milo said. "What does that, like, even mean?"

"We won a game," Walt said.

"That's three," Marty added.

"Yeah, we're gonna be straight while we're still playing football, but know what? We don't play that shit on weekends. Get high once a week," Milo said.

"All day long," Jonny said.

"Damn straight," Milo said.

Dylan Wannamacher's Sunday was quite different. He actually watched pro football. The Steelers beat somebody. Marcia dropped by at about the time the four o'clock game started. Dylan didn't say anything. He just removed the bong from the cabinet without leaving the recliner and passed it to her.

"What? You quit?"

"No," he said. "I just haven't felt like it."

"Being a role model?"

"Nah. I might get back in the mood in five minutes. It might be five days. Five weeks. I haven't quit. I've just stopped. I'm sure it won't last too long," Dylan said. "I haven't quit writing, either. I just stopped. This coaching is time-consuming."

"It sapped your creativity," she opined. "Without weed, you got no shot."

"Might be," Dylan said. "Might be."

Marcia hoped the aroma of smoke might tempt him and she exhaled it across the room in his direction as far as she could, but he didn't budge and she lost interest after a while.

"I got some work to do," she said. "I guess I'll head on back to the dorm."

"Suit yourself," Dylan said, "but please do keep in touch."

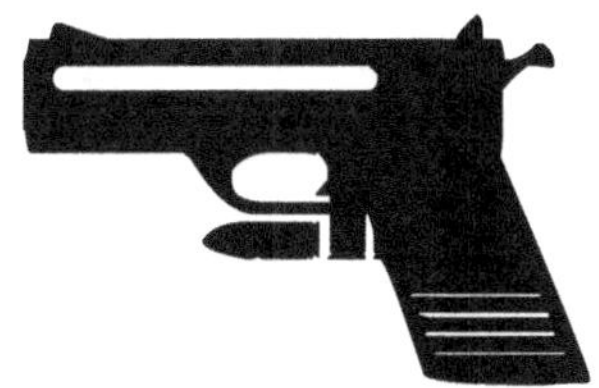

CHAPTER 28

The Tangled Webs

Marcia's mobility was not altogether a matter of choice. Her roommate, Alexis, was regularly banging a basketball player, which meant she spent most of her time in his off-campus apartment, but now the season had started, and Alexis generally gravitated back to the room when her lover was on the road, and it seemed that, early in a season, that was a lot. Alexis was a Super Trooper, which meant she performed dance routines at halftime. It was obviously a vital part of her life because she talked incessantly about it. Marcia took mild enjoyment in noticing that Alexis had gotten a little heavy to be cavorting about with her midriffs bare. She was pleasant and guileless enough that Marcia didn't hate her, but they had little in common. Marcia rotated her supply of product between the room and Dylan's apartment at Hippie Arms, depending on the presence of her roommate and the convenience of supplying her clients. She didn't worry about Dylan knowing of her activities, but she felt compelled to hide the range. She certainly didn't want him to know that Enlightened Word was a source of great commerce. She liked to spend her nights in the place where she could speak freely on the phone.

Wade Sanderson was her confidant. He kept her in business and valued her skill in navigating the complications of the cannabis trade. He handled her cell phone with a generous bonus that more than paid the bill. He gave her advice she trusted and was the only person with whom she could freely confide. She thought him good for her. She wanted to go to California over Thanksgiving. Rescuing Tripp Fallaw was really a small part of it. She wanted to see Wade. Tripp was a lowlife, but she had a lingering attraction because she had enjoyed him in bed. She had even enjoyed his selfish irresponsibility to a point. The point had been when he left her stranded in Los Angeles. She couldn't keep him completely off her mind, but she grew ever more attracted to Wade, a more reliable pirate. Tripp could never go straight. Wade, she thought, was as straight as a dealer could be. Wade was going to be a major player when weed went legal. It was his whole plan. He knew how to be cool. She wanted to cruise around in L.A. again. She was moving there when Triborough made her wealthy enough.

"I don't know what happened to Tripp," Wade told her via phone. "Maybe he figured out a way to get into Mexico. He might be laying in a gutter in Tijuana, for all I know."

"If you ever find out, tell me, would you?"

"He hasn't called you anymore?"

"Not a word," she said.

"Well, maybe no news is good news. How's your supply?"

"It's good. I could use a pound or two by Thanksgiving."

"Damn, woman, you must have that whole college majoring in philosophy or some shit," he said.

"The pharmacy school's near the top of the rankings, too," she said. "I got a couple stoners in the seminary."

"Praise Jesus," Wade said. "All is well."

"I got a little problem to deal with at the private school."

"Triborough's private, right?"

"Yeah, but I mean the little boarding school down the road. Enlightened Word. A lot of kids there got kicked out of somewhere else. They got money. Several of them drive sports cars."

"Selling under-age can be dangerous," Wade said.

"Everybody's under-age for weed," she said. "It ain't no more illegal than it is for college kids. There's nothing to it. These kids been hiding weed since they were fourteen, fifteen years old. They're smart, and they been learning how to hide weed a lot longer than I have. I kind of stumbled across it. I had an in, you might say."

"And the problem is?"

"They been buying their weed from a janitor that works at the school, and now they got used to my good shit, and it's cost him some business, and my main man at the school, kid named Milo Hirley, says he's making some trouble about it. I can take care of it."

"Don't worry about it, Marcia. This happens all the time. We'll shake him up with a little visit from the police. Just enough to scare him. What's his name?"

"Get this. His name is Brynildson Hiers. Funny spelling. B-R-Y-N-I-L-D-S-O-N. And Hiers is H-I-E-R-S."

"I take it Mr. Hiers is of the African-American persuasion," Wade said.

"That is my suspicion, Wade. I can't say that I've met the man yet."

"You don't need to. Give me a week, and we'll have him either buying from you or out of the business. Anything else?"

"All is cool, otherwise, Wade."

"Okay. Marcia?"

"Yeah?"

"Don't you fly out here."

She didn't reply.

"I'm coming back east for a few days at Christmas," he said. "If you'll have me, I'll come see you for a few days more."

"I'd like that," she said. "Bye."

"I love you, Marcia. Merry Christmas."

It was the first time Wade Sanderson had said that to her. Merry Christmas, too.

Peter Baxter had too many irons in his fire. He was in the Drama Club at the same time he was on the football team. He was the editor of the Enlightened Word yearbook. The Merry Pranksters despised him. He wasn't popular, but his old man was a financier who wrote an annual check to the school that was three times as much as the cost of boarding him there. Coincidentally, Peter won lots of honors. He fancied himself a Method actor and claimed to be playing sports as a means of preparing for the starring role in *Damn Yankees*, which was scheduled to be the spring play. He was too intense to be any good on the football field, or the baseball field, or the basketball court, but he played all three and complained constantly that he ought to be playing more. So far in the season, Milo Hirley had attempted to throw him seven passes, and he had dropped five of them. He was a passable defensive back who had a knack of failing at the worst times.

Peter was scoring Adderall from Bryne Hiers. It was the reason he was so intense. It was the reason he had time for all his activities. It was the reason his eyeballs practically popped out of their sockets when Dylan Wannamacher tried to teach him something. Had he suffered from attention deficit disorder, the pills might have done him some good, but since he had no such malady anywhere but in his imagination, they made him self-absorbed, bombastic, and insufferable. He seldom slept. No one considered that Peter might be on the verge of a breakdown. He had a rich daddy. Bryne knew it. Bryne tried to get him to slow down, but Peter always paid up with cash, and money was no object. Bryne loved the kids at Enlightened Word, but he hadn't even sold anything but weed until Peter came along. The habit had been growing since his sophomore year, when the Adderall just helped him ace his exams. Now he wanted to ace everything, unable to perceive that he was starting to fall apart. The Merry Pranksters loved to chill. They didn't care enough about Peter Baxter to whip his ass, although Milo Hirley might have been willing to part with a dime bag of weed to anyone who'd break his leg.

The Merry Pranksters were subtly divided. Milo Hirley and Walt Pegler were one pair. Marty Drummond and Jonny Heinsohn were the other. Milo and Walt had each suffered at the hands of their fathers. Milo only had to deal with his from a distance. Walt's was now dead.

Chick Hirley owned five used-car lots. He'd once raced stock cars. He had seldom had much time for his son, who resented him. When Milo had turned sixteen, he managed to get along with his father long enough to get a car, which Chick could easily provide since that's what he did for a living. He almost got busted with some friends in the spring because they stupidly thought it was safe to sit in a 1995 Camaro in the parking lot of a shut-down factory and pass a joint around. The police monitored such sites, and they would have all gotten charged had it not been for the fact that three of them were white kids from respectable families. Chick got it all covered up. Word of the scandal only leaked out by word of mouth, but Milo's mother put some effort into getting her son, a fine athlete, a scholarship to Enlightened Word. Then, having performed her motherly duties, she divorced Chick and moved to Dallas with a massage therapist she had been screwing on the sly since Milo was in middle school.

If Walt Pegler had told anyone but Milo what an abusive drunk his father was, they wouldn't have believed it, but they had become immediate friends when Milo had shown up at Enlightened Word. Walt had been enrolled in the school since kindergarten and showed his new friend the ropes. He had been open to doing anything of which the Coach would not approve, and Milo had showed Walt how to smoke weed and be cool about it.

The Merry Pranksters were living the life of Riley, as Chick Hirley was fond of saying. They were playing ball. Things were looking up. Their favorite teacher was coaching the football team, and Waddy Pegler was dead. Walt didn't say he was glad his father was gone. He didn't have to.

Marty Drummond, son of the headmaster, had no dysfunctional family to cite for his transgressions. He had the cultivated grace of a pastor's son, and the timing had been perfect when the Reverend Nathan Drummond started calling himself Doctor and took responsibility for the best and only United Methodist-supported academy in the Commonwealth of Virginia. Marty's dad was a good man. His mother was a fine woman. His older brother was following in his father's footsteps. Marty asked forgiveness each night, on his knees, for his sins, but forgiveness, as he'd been taught, was a cleansing in the eyes of God. His father never taught Marty that he could sin endlessly as long as he asked forgiveness, but

Marty concluded this from what he'd been taught and didn't care to delve into the theology of it further.

Sin was fun. Sex was the best kind. Smoking pot was right up there. Jesus loved him. This he knew.

Being the fourth and least colorful member of the Merry Pranksters had unquestionably brought Jonny Heinsohn, the son of science, out of his shell. Jonny's father and mother both taught at Triborough. They were mathematics professors of regional renown with a son less and less interested in polynomial functions.

Only Milo lived in the dorms. They all owned cars. The natatorium and golf course weren't the only places they got high. They blazed in Triborough when Jonny had the house to himself. They blazed on the manicured grounds of the headmaster's home, which was also Marty's. Milo had little to do with his roommate, a musician he suspected was gay. As long as Sandy Hostetler didn't advance on him, Milo didn't care. To each his own. Milo typically left practice and either blazed outside the natatorium as darkness descended on campus, or, when he was really desperate, riding around the backroads in his five-year-old Chevy Cavalier. Then he'd go back to the dorm, cut out the light on the balcony at the end of the hall, and smoke a cigarette in the darkness.

Enlightened Word was not a smoke-free campus, but it was supposed to be so for its impressionable, tuition-paying adolescents. As church-supported academies went, it was a decent preparation for the world beyond. Everyone played the system, and as long as all used discretion, no one got in trouble. The football coach had been an alcoholic, and when he died, he had been replaced by an English instructor who was the school's most beloved faculty member. The English instructor was a pothead.

Things were looking up. Milo pondered all these weighty issues at length when he was high, and he was high a lot.

CHAPTER 29

Too Big to Succeed

The fear in Mickey Statler's soul entered a second phase. The first had been assuaged by resignation and made palatable by money. He figured he was paddling the same boat as innumerable cops, politicians, and attorneys, most of whom tended to be generally law-abiding people who had been corrupted gradually by the lure of easy money. It was easily rationalized. Marijuana wasn't that bad. It was bound to be legal everywhere eventually. The flow of history was on its side. *This* was doomed to fail, though. Someone was going to slip up. It didn't matter how smart the ringleaders were. It didn't matter that the fix was in. Somewhere, somehow, the fix was going to fail.

Mickey had a slogan from years of sportswriting: *If you do something that stupid, God will turn on you.* Most cops were good people. Many were honest. He wished he knew someone he could trust. He didn't. He knew he had been drawn into an operation bigger than it had been described. He knew it was big enough that fighting it was dangerous. He suspected it was bigger than he could imagine. He had never considered himself particularly conspiratorial, in spite of the profession he was in. Now, though, he was suspicious every time a hapless black or Latino was gunned down in the streets by a cop. Surely, some were just a consequence of paranoid, embattled cops, worried of being casualties of the dangerous line of work they had chosen. But there were too many cases. Mickey started reading the details. A suspect misidentified and wrongly detained. Panicked, he ran. Shot in the back by cops with itchy trigger fingers. Sometimes the cops were charged, but seldom were they convicted. He suspected the ones who got off were the corrupt ones, the ones sent out to eliminate competition. Were they just shootings? Or executions? He didn't want to be shot, whether it was an execution or not. Mickey was fortunately white. He had that going for him, and he hated racism, but not so much that he was willing to forfeit the advantage of the pigment with which he had been born.

Add in the rising indignation in the streets of every major city at the outcome of the election. Things were getting too hot. Winds were fueling the brush fires. The president-elect was doing what he had done to get himself elected. He was bullshitting his way to the White House, and he obviously planned on bullshitting his way through the presidency. Mickey saw no hope in the republic. He saw only the devils of nature infecting the human soul. The last thing Mickey wanted was to be caught in the crossfire, but he was trapped in the middle of a dodgeball game, being pummeled from one side and unable to rely on any empathy from the other.

Mickey didn't want to see his ex-wife, but he missed his lovely daughter. He knew she was in college. He didn't know which one. She didn't have his cell number; he didn't have hers. At the moment, he didn't owe Vera a dime. He still dreaded calling her. She'd drum up some reason to raise hell. He googled his daughter. All he could find were pictures of her playing sports. She hadn't touched her Facebook page in two years. He couldn't find her on Twitter. She hadn't been interested enough to contact him. Mickey was still on Twitter and Facebook, though all he ever did was post links to his stories as per persistent urgings from The Ultimate Sporting Life. He was busy. He wrote his stories and buried himself in them. He enjoyed it. In exchange, all he had to do was swap briefcases with someone every few days. He didn't grow weed. He didn't smoke it. Thanks to the vacuum-packed plastic baggies, he didn't even smell it. There wasn't much to the selling. Being a briefcase swapper was easy. Mickey had always heard yarns of assistant coaches who cheated while recruiting. *He's [insert head coach's name] bagman.* Mickey had become a bagman. Or maybe a drug mule. Unofficially, he was a government mule, a criminal operating with the approval of those charged with stopping crime. It was a sweet job for a man who could look at himself in a mirror without remorse. Mickey wasn't such a man.

A couple human-interest stories were coming up. Mickey liked those best. He didn't have to fight the big-time fog. He didn't have to face the traffic hassles or the imperial coaches with their imperial guards. All he had to do was crank out a profile of a star point guard from the inner city who was inexplicably majoring in agriculture and a football coach who was winning in spite of never having coached anything before.

Every day Mickey marveled at the places a market for cannabis could take him. He'd be going to the National Shit-Shoveling Finals in the middle of Montana if the nation's great shit shovelers had a need for three pounds of marijuana.

And he knew they did. Why should shit shovelers be any different from fraternity brothers, sorority sisters, golf pros, sporting goods salesmen, administrators of port authorities, recruiters of soldiers and athletes alike, directors of retirement homes, and equipment managers? Those were just the ones he could remember.

On Thanksgiving, Mickey ordered from the drive-through of the first junk-food joint he could find that was open. He drew attention away from his problems by watching the Detroit Lions beat the Atlanta Falcons and the Dallas Cowboys similarly edge the Washington Redskins. A third-of-a-pound bacon cheeseburger and greasy fries gave his stomach a nice cushion as he took on the task of drinking himself to oblivion by the time the night games, one pro and one college, came on. He wanted to carouse but didn't have the energy. The booze had the effect of knocking him out instead of stirring up his carnal impulses. His last thought before he passed out was a sad, general realization that he was getting old.

The unofficially socialized marijuana trade was making him money and restoring Mickey's professional prestige, but it left him with the same feeling he had always had with family. Mickey drank but never with his family. If Uncle Fred got drunk and wrecked his car on the way home, Mickey didn't want to have anything to do with it. He didn't want to be the bad influence. He was a hypocrite, but that was just the unavoidable consequence of being tactful. He carried scars from his old man that he'd never wanted to pass along to his daughter.

On Friday morning, Mickey awakened with a brutal hangover that was richly deserved. If he'd awakened feeling merry and bright, there'd be no reason not to get snookered every night. Hell, all those kids smoking all that pot never got a hangover at all. No wonder their heads were fucked up. No wonder they felt no guilt.

By the evening, Mickey had recovered enough to swing by the mini-warehouse to pick up his latest instructions and enough product to fulfill them. He needed to get back out on the road, so that he could walk sidelines, tell old tales in the press box, and write new ones. For better *and* worse, a man had to do what he had to do.

CHAPTER 30

The Media Darling

The Enlightened Word Dragoons were going to the Class A playoffs with a record of four wins and six losses.

More importantly, the 23-14 victory over Plaintiff – yes, it was the name of a town – gave the team a Region Four record of three and two. Three and two gave them a third seed of the four schools that qualified for playoff slots in the six-team region. On the night of December 4, the Dragoons were to play another private school, B. Henry Lashley Academy, the second seed from Region 1, on the road. Lashley had been ranked first in the state until being upset by Slayton County. In the entire Commonwealth, the only matchup of private schools in the first round was Enlightened Word at Lashley.

Dylan Wannamacher had allowed something terrible to happen. He thought the team had a chance to win. He cared. The English teacher and would-be writer had vowed that he was just going to try to get through the year in a respectable fashion. He hadn't dreamed they'd win both games he coached. He hadn't entertained the possibility of making the playoffs until he'd read about it in the *Triborough Standard* before the Plaintiff game. Back when Dylan had played football, the idea of four teams from a six-team region making playoffs would have been deemed absurd.

Since the *Standard* had a web site, a story had been within the Google capability of one Carson Carmine, whose job it was to find assignments for writers representing The Ultimate Sporting Life. One of the most common questions asked of Mickey Statler in press boxes and over drinks was, "Where do you *find* these stories?"

Mickey answered honestly. "They just assign them to me. Someone back at the office looks for human-interest stories. They call or send an email. The only thing I've got to do with it, other than writing the damned story, is saying, 'Got it.'"

No one really bought that. They preferred to think Mickey was some sports version of Charles Kuralt, on the road. Mickey made his modest answer and let them think what they would. The basic story was true. The more complicated truth was that Carson looked up a place where a weed delivery was needed and found something to keep the writer occupied legitimately and the records plausible.

Doctor Nathan Drummond got the news via email from Mickey. When he told Dylan that Mickey Statler was coming to practice on Thursday and then going down to Lashley, seventy-three miles away, Dylan didn't know who Mickey Statler was but could tell from Drummond's expression that Statler was someone important.

"*The* Mickey Statler?" Dylan asked, his whimsy going right over the headmaster's head.

"Absolutely," Drummond said.

"Cool."

Dylan looked up Statler on his cell phone. Award-winning sportswriter now working for The Ultimate Sporting Life. Dylan had never heard of that, either, but he clicked on it and discovered it was a reasonably interesting site. He read a couple of Statler's stories. The guy could write. Dylan found the pop-up ads annoying. He was trying to have lunch at the faculty table, playing with his phone as he picked at his mystery meat, when a video popped up with loud rap music in place of narration, and Dylan couldn't figure out how to get rid of it. Several outbursts of vulgarity violated the sanctity of the faculty table before Dylan somehow found a little "x" to click on that made the video go away. Then another popped up, so, at wit's end, Dylan cut off the phone and hoped the pop-up wouldn't still be there when he "powered up" again. Six other teachers sat at the table. Three were now staring at him over the top of their eyeglasses.

"Dylan," Bob Wasdin said, "for God's sake …"

"Sorry. I was trying to read this article, and a video popped up from nowhere," Dylan said. "That's probably why a man shouldn't fiddle with his phone when he's supposed to be having lunch."

Wasdin was the basketball coach. Dylan's football team making the playoffs was aggravating Wasdin's preparations. The Merry Pranksters all played basketball, too, and three would play baseball in the spring except for Jonny Heinsohn, who ran track. Making the playoffs meant that Wasdin's version of the Dragoons was going to suck early in the season. If football somehow managed to win a game or two, Wasdin figured they might suck all year. How an English teacher, seldom if ever seen at an athletic contest, could take over, win two games, and earn a playoff berth with a team that had lost four consecutive games before, of all things, the coach died, was unbelievable. Wasdin had not planned for it at all. He had to be sportsmanlike, rah-rah for the old school, and all that, but his pissy mood had been growing. This 4-6 football team was getting more attention than his 2007 team that advanced to the state finals. The faculty's resident eccentric – Wasdin tended to think of Dylan as a hippie but knew no modern equivalent of the term – had been transformed by a couple mild upsets into some kind of poet-philosopher of football. Every day, when Wasdin walked across the campus green to the gymnasium, there to direct his depleted basketball team, at least one brightly covered TV van was parked next to the practice field.

Mickey Statler arrived punctually to practice in his Buick rental, stuck a notepad in his back pocket, unplugged his phone from the charger so that he could use it as a recorder, and walked down to the field. He couldn't introduce himself because Dylan Wannamacher was being interviewed by a local TV guy. Mickey just stood behind the camera, pulled out the pad and a pen from his shirt pocket, and eavesdropped. He didn't steal any quotes – the questions were, as usual, stupid, and few were questions at all – but observed the prime subject of his story.

The sports guy seemed oafish. Mickey wondered how these guys got their jobs.

"You seem to be an unusual guy to be a football coach, Coach Wannamacher."

"Oh, really," Dylan replied, grinning. "Why do you say that?"

Mickey scribbled. *DW eating that shit up. Friendly, but mocking.*

"Well, you never coached till, what, two weeks ago?"

"Three."

No homework. TV guy knows nothing. Doesn't know he was star player at local college. DW playing with him.

Since Corky, or Biff, or whatever nickname he must go by, had no reply to a single word, Dylan helped.

"I know something of football fundamentals. I played the game myself when I was younger."

Now he's playing dumb.

"Oh."

TV guy dumb, natural born.

"You know, Josh, when I played football, at Triborough, my head coach was a man named Halleran Gibbs. Long before I played for him, he had been brought in at a time when Triborough was close to dropping football. The story was that he had gotten up in front of the faculty, and told them, I'm paraphrasing, 'If football isn't a vital part of the educational experience at the college, if the discipline it takes, and the dedication, and the diversity of the student body isn't useful because it gives kids a chance at an education who wouldn't get one, or at least as good of one, if not for football, if all of what I just said isn't true, then you ought to get rid of it.' Then, you know, they voted to keep football. I've never forgotten that. I had no interest in being a coach, but circumstances dictated that I would become one by accident, really, and once that was established, I felt like it was my duty to do my best."

Josh got his story. Now he'll be a rally killer and ask something stupid about the opponent.

"Now B.H. Lashley, Coach, that's quite a team."

Too easy.

The coach was patient. He walked away to begin practice. This didn't concern Mickey. He knew, if he hung out for a while, taking notes, Wannamacher would stroll over. He needed to know what Josh's last name was so that he could properly satirize him, so he watched as the cub reporter took four takes to get his stand-up right.

"From Enlightened Word Academy, this is Josh Slezak, Action Nine Sports."

When he finally got done, Mickey offered a handshake. "Great job. I'm Mickey Statler. The Ultimate Sporting Life. I'm doing a little piece, too."

Josh Slezak actually gulped. He knew the name. He blubbered something about "really, really" enjoying Mickey's work. *Josh Slezak. It's possible that might be his real name. Gotta get the spelling right.*

Forty-five minutes into practice, Wannamacher walked over. It was chilly but bright, as December days tended to be. He wore khakis and a navy jacket. Orange cap with an interlocked "EW" in navy. Mickey introduced himself and asked if he minded if he called him Dylan. Mickey didn't like the subservient connotation of "Coach Wannamacher." Dylan said "no problem" and Mickey encouraged Dylan to call him Mickey.

"Why don't we go over to the baseball bleachers? We can sit on the back row so I can see what's going on better," Dylan said.

"I can wait until after practice."

"That's okay. I don't call the plays," Dylan said. "When I first took a look at the team, what I concluded was that what it really needed was work on the fundamentals. They couldn't block, and they couldn't tackle. They threw on most every down; the linemen didn't know how to run-block. The defense was a sieve, but it wasn't because they were getting beat physically. They were in position to make tackles. They just didn't know how. Right in the middle of the season, I figured I had to work on the weaknesses. I let the assistant coaches call the plays. I'm getting it. Most teams have the same basic terminology. Even numbers to the right, odd to the left. Higher numbers outside on both sides. All I do is make suggestions. 'Let's run a screen in the left flat,' I'll say, and that's a Thirty-Nine Screen, because the setback who flares out there is the three back. That sort of thing."

"Since it's been, oh, more than fifteen years since you played, have you had any difficulties adapting to changes in the game?"

"Oh, sure," Dylan replied. "We never used the shotgun when I played. The basic problem is that it's hard to run any kind of quick opener. It's hard to get a runner into the line with a head of steam. Most running plays look more like draw plays to me, but that's why teams have come up with these inside laterals, shovel passes, and jet sweeps. It puts speed into the equation, and the first day I was out there, I noticed that we had two kids, Lenny and Denny Paterson, who could run the ball, and they hadn't even been playing in the backfield. I think the biggest difference in the team has been that we've managed to develop a running game, and that makes the passing game – Milo Hirley is a good little quarterback – more efficient."

Dylan started fidgeting, eyes darting around. Something had displeased him.

"Excuse me," he said. "Uh, I guess we aren't as much on auto-pilot as I thought. I gotta go shake these kids up."

"We can talk after practice," Mickey said. "I'd like to chat briefly with a couple of the players. Maybe … Lenny and Denny, uh, Paterson, and the quarterback. The Patersons are twins, I presume?"

"Yeah, twins. Tell you what, Mickey. What if you talk to Lenny, Denny, and Milo as soon as practice is over, and then I buy your supper. We can go split a pizza, have a beer. That work?"

"Sure, that works." Mickey hadn't had an athlete or coach buy him a meal since Danny Ford left Clemson.

As Dylan made his way back out to reinvigorate his charges, Mickey fiddled with his phone. Four pages back in the notepad was a number for him to text.

A little backed up. How bout we get together at 9?

He watched practice from the bleachers until he felt the phone buzz after about five minutes.

Cool. Be there 9. Rm 322, Marriott, right?

CHAPTER 31

Small World

Mickey Statler got done with the interview a bit early and was back at the Marriott a little after seven-thirty. He opened his laptop and began transcribing the interviews with Dylan Wannamacher and players Lenaius Paterson, Denaius Paterson, and Milo Hirley. That killed an hour. He began writing the story, working on the body because he didn't know how Friday night's game between Enlightened Word and B. Henry Lashley would come out. Lashley was heavily favored, so Mickey wrote with a mild slant, anticipating the probable outcome. He became a bit lost in the thought required to consider such matters, and it caught him unawares when the expected knock on the door occurred at about ten minutes after nine.

He had also forgotten about the coffee he had brewed in the room-provided machine. He yelled, "Hang on. Coming." Quickly, he emptied a packet of Sweet 'n' Low and poured the coffee. He stirred it and took a sip. It was rather lukewarm, having been sitting in the carafe for about a half hour since the brewing ended. He opened the door to find a comely young woman looking at the floor as if studying the texture of the wood.

Mickey choked on the coffee and very nearly executed a spit take that would have made Danny Thomas envious. He coughed, and the girl looked up.

"Daddy?" Marcia Statler asked, rather in disbelief at what her eyes saw.

"Marcia. Come in."

It wasn't a surprise party. She had a briefcase identical to the one sitting on the couch. Mickey had not a clue of what to say.

"Jesus," she said. "I need a cigarette. I … bet this room is non-smoking."

"We can go out on the stoop," he said and opened the sliding glass panel. She walked out and sat down. He put on the jacket he had draped across the chair while he had been writing and joined her. It was cold but windless. Freezing rain was forecast for Friday.

She lit a cigarette and placed a pack of Marlboro Lights and the lighter on the circular iron table. He took the liberty of lighting one for himself. It would kill some time while they both considered the situation.

"Mom said you had come into some money," she said.

"How is Vera?"

"I haven't seen her since the summer. We talk on the phone occasionally."

"I didn't have your number," Mickey said.

"It's okay."

"Your mother pretty much shut me out. It wasn't until recently that I got caught up. I've been traveling all over. In another week, I was planning on taking some time off. I gotta be in Shreveport day after Christmas for a crummy little bowl game. N.C. State and Vanderbilt. Then I'm done till past New Year's Day."

Mickey knew she wasn't interested.

"You got some time?" he asked.

"Yeah," she said. "There's no need to keep beating around the bush."

"How'd you get into this? Did they bribe you? Set you up?"

"I just needed the money, Dad. It's a good way to make it. I just stumbled into it. Met a guy in California, said he'd set me up. He did. I'm making good money. You?"

"Yeah, Marcia. I'm making good money. I got set up, though. I didn't have any choice. It's complicated."

"I reckon it doesn't matter, Daddy. So it's complicated."

Another silence ensued.

"So …. how's school," he said. "You're in school, right?"

"I dropped two classes. I'm still taking two. Mainly, I have to write poems and short stories. By dropping the classes, I lost my scholarship money, but just for this semester. It costs about the same it would have, anyway. I paid for it."

Mickey digested it without a word.

"I know this is going to sound like bullshit, like I'm justifying my actions, but I'm writing a novel, and the main character is a writer who pays her bills by selling weed, and she has an affair with one of her professors …"

"It'd be a good defense if you get busted," Mickey said. "Research for a novel. I need to come up with something like that. I got an idea. It'd probably be best to get a contract signed, huh?"

"I hadn't thought about that."

"I was kidding. Who's the professor?"

"Well, everything's not literally true," she said. "Actually, he's an English teacher at a private school."

"Shit."

"It's not that bad, Daddy. He's a really talented writer."

"I don't suppose he's at a place called Enlightened Word Academy?"

"Why, yes, but …"

"And he didn't recently start coaching football because the previous coach died?"

"How did …"

"I spent three hours today watching the team practice, and another hour sitting at a pizza parlor interviewing Dylan Wannamacher."

"Vissage Pizza."

"Yeah."

"That's fucking incredible," Marcia said.

"Not really. Coincidences come in clusters. Like a guy making a drug deal with his daughter, then finding out she's in love with the guy he just interviewed. Happens all the time. It's like luck. Mine is seldom mediocre. Either everything goes right, or everything goes wrong."

"What's this?"

"I'm leaning toward the latter at the moment," he said.

She laughed. "You've got to admit, it's really funny."

"Hilarious."

"Daddy, would you like to split a joint?"

"That's what got me into this mess," he said. "Why not? Why the fuck not?"

Mickey told his daughter about how he'd been laid off, and how he'd tried to make a little money writing free-lance stories, and how he was about to be evicted from his apartment, and he'd been drinking quite a bit, and he fallen for this barmaid, Laurie, and how she'd taken him to a cheap motel room, and they'd smoked weed, and screwed, and the cops had started banging on the door, and busted him, and how he'd been let go on the condition that he would deliver weed while he was traveling around the country writing sports columns for a website that paid him as a way to launder the money, most likely, though he didn't know for sure, and it all got more and more irreverent as he and his precious daughter, the younger, the only one that had ever loved him, got high.

"It was all a setup," he said. "Old man falls for this young gal who, ridiculously, takes an interest in him, and it's all a setup. She trapped me to get herself out of trouble. Good-looking gal, though. They'll do it every time."

Marcia didn't go back to the beginning. She skipped the sordid tale of how a soccer teammate had tried to seduce her and started with the day she encountered Tripp Fallaw in the sports bar during the summer, and how she'd slept with him, and let him persuade her to go with him to California, and they'd had a wild time until he blew a pile of money in a failed golf hustle, and left her stranded, but that a friend of his, who lived out in L.A., had told her he could set her up selling weed if she was interested.

"Rodrigo, that's Mom's boyfriend, paid to get me home from California, and I straightened up for a while, but, when I came here for school, I kind of started partying again, and that's when I met Dylan, not at some bar, but at a coffee shop, and we kind of hit it off, and the more I thought about it, I got the idea about writing a novel, so I called Wade – he's my friend in California – and I've been making money like it's going out of style ever since," she said.

Mickey looked at her, saw the curvature of her breasts in the dim light, and realized just how beautiful his daughter had become. She had been a bit gawky, stretched out, when she was playing high school soccer, and he was still living with Vera. He'd always known she got her athletic ability from her mother, who had been a struggling pro golfer when Mickey had met her. He also knew she got her writing ability from him. It was not the best time for pride.

"So, the weed in that briefcase came from California?"

"Humboldt County. Best in the world. Shit sells itself. It probably arrived on a freight train, or in a tractor-trailer. They stash it on a government vehicle – postal service, maybe, or military vehicle, maybe even a transport plane – and it gets distributed across the country."

"I thought it was all weed that had been confiscated by the cops," Mickey said.

"Nope."

"How you know all this?"

"My contact, Wade. He's a big shot, I guess."

"Damn," Mickey said. "I knew it was big, but I didn't know it was anything like this. Is Dylan in on this?"

"No. He knows I sell a little, but he just thinks it's a few artists in his building. It's kind of a full-time job, really, but it's not dangerous. If I got into any trouble, somebody else would take care of it. My one phone call would be to a cop. He'd come in and tell the honest ones I was an undercover agent, and, even though they'd tampered with the operation unwittingly, it might actually be to their advantage."

"I had a cop accompany me to a drop-off in Nashville about a week or so ago," Mickey said.

"What I think is, they're gearing up to pot being legalized, and they'll have all the distribution plans in place when they're ready to go public."

Mickey fetched another of his daughter's cigarettes, pondering all this information through the mental haze.

"They'll gain a lot of overhead once they lose the free delivery system," he said.

"Yeah, but they're probably making a shitload now," she said.

Mickey cringed a little at his daughter's language. It was a lot of information to process. He was writing a story on a man who was probably fucking his daughter, and she was apparently on the way to becoming either a criminal mastermind or a best-selling author, or both. She was using the unconventional profession of pusher as a springboard. She was doing it by choice. He was doing it because he had no choice. Once the dominoes began falling, his explanation had less chance of being believed than hers.

He looked at his watch. Ten-thirty.

"You hungry," he said.

"Ravenously."

"I am, too. I ate pizza with your English teacher turned coach. I should't be hungry, but, of course, I am. We can order room service."

"I'd be good for some pizza," Marcia said, "but I'd also like some ice cream. Maybe even first."

They went back inside. He took a good look at her in the light. Beautiful. Her hair was a bit darker now, more brown than the dirty blond of her high school years. He thought it had just naturally changed. He saw none of the coldness in her blue eyes that he suspected. She got those from her mother, too. They were eyes that could change a man's opinions. They were eyes that could get what they wanted, but not because they emitted lasers. They had the appeal of a puppy but the hue of a cat that was content and curled up beside you. Mickey shivered. He wondered what those eyes could do. He wondered if those eyes could kill. He thought those eyes could convince someone else to.

Marcia had been his ally when the family fell apart. Patti was four years older, close to married, he expected. She had swallowed Vera's propaganda and stopped speaking to him even before he moved out. He hadn't spoken to Patti since. She might as well have disappeared from his psyche. He held bitterness and tried not to think of her. Marcia had been on his side, but he was a sportswriter, always on the road, and he couldn't have taken care of her properly, so he'd reluctantly let Vera have her, knowing that she'd try to poison Marcia against him. They had so much to talk about besides how the government was secretly selling illegal weed from coast to coast.

"I'll get the pizza with my cell," he said. "You call room service and have them send up whatever you want."

The sundae, vanilla covered with oozing chocolate and sprinkles, arrived first, and she devoured it. She offered a bite, but he declined. Then she walked back out onto the cold balcony, undoubtedly to have a cigarette but perhaps a joint, as well. He didn't need to get any more stoned, and someone had to pay for the pizza when it arrived. He'd ordered a large pepperoni because he remembered that's what she'd liked when she was younger. He knew guilt would descend upon him in the morning, but now that he and his daughter had been revealed to each other as partners in crime, neither had any motive of secrecy. They chatted in ways they never could before.

"You know I never wanted to give you up," he said between pieces.

"I know, Daddy."

"Your mother insisted I couldn't possibly raise you right, what with the travel."

"I guess the joke's on her," Marcia said. "I went and became a stinking drug dealer, anyway."

"Just like your old man." Mickey said it haltingly.

Mickey insisted that she stay over and sleep in the bedroom. He took the roll-away in the couch. They reheated the pizza in the microwave for breakfast, and then she left. He had to drive to Lashley, or wherever B. Henry Lashley Academy was. After Marcia left, Mickey finally wept for the first time, and he couldn't stop for an hour. He finally gave up trying and took a shower, and that somehow served the purpose of stopping his tears. In no way was he in any condition to write about a football game, but he'd developed an ability to put private matters aside over the years. It was the job, and he had to do it. He'd fought hangovers, a messy divorce, grief at deaths of colleagues with whom he had been close, whether instantly, via heart attacks, or agonizing, via cancer, and he could damn well handle a simple bout of overwhelming sadness. As it turned out, B. Henry Lashley Academy was located in a town called Pettigru, and he instructed the nice lady in his phone to route him through the hills and small towns rather than swiftly down the interstate, and that way he could listen to appropriate music, and absently study the barns, windmills, and country stores. He even stopped to buy a basket of Granny Smith apples, knowing that he could finish them off on Saturday, when he was to drive back to North Carolina. Marcia had taken all the product he had left to deliver.

Marcia Statler went back to Dylan Wannamacher's apartment, knowing that he was at school, and from there Dylan would go to Pettigru to provide Marcia's father with an award-winning story, while, meanwhile, she'd take thirty-two vacuum-sealed bags of potent marijuana and divide ounces into eighths and quarters, and head off to dorm rooms, apartments, a Gold's Gym, and a pool hall, there to peddle what she already had committed. Her beauty made it a little easier. No one suspected a good-looking girl with a wholesome face. She was less affected than her father, but a small sentimentality gave her pause. She would write on Saturday in the dorm room, leaving Dylan a note expressing either congratulations or condolences at the outcome of the big game. In a week, the briefcase delivered by her father would gross fifteen thousand dollars, net nine thousand, and three thousand would be hers. She'd deposit a thousand apiece in three checking accounts, and she planned on buying herself a lavish Christmas present that might be a new car if she could find one that suited her fancy.

She looked forward to surgery on Sunday. She was going to have to tinker with her outline and make room for some unexpected plot twists.

CHAPTER 32

The Storm Before the Calm

Mickey Statler drove the winding roads to Pettigru, trying to get his mind off being a drug dealer, discovering that his daughter was a drug dealer, and writing a story about a football coach who was fucking his daughter.

Other than that, Mickey felt splendid. Jam-up. In the pink.

His phone took him to E. Henry Lashley Academy, but that's not where the football stadium was. The Lashes – he didn't really know the nickname – shared a stadium with the local public school, and when he got there, he learned that Pettigru High was the Hillcats because they apparently controlled the scoreboard. The Lashes and the Dragoons were playing at the Home of the Hillcats. Mickey was hours early, his punctuality cultivated through decades of similar complications. He drove back to the quaint downtown, saw a café whose looks struck his fancy, parked his rental Buick, and strolled inside for a good, greasy cheeseburger with fries. The sweet tea was as good as the food. He was glad to see the sugar line was north of here. Up around D.C., ordering iced tea was a bit of a risk.

Mickey felt calm, tranquilized, even. He was charming to the waitress. He let it go when the burger came with onions he'd hoped to do without. He didn't even remove them. The burger was so good that the onions' flavor blended seamlessly into the beef, lettuce, tomatoes, and mayonnaise, the way that God intended. Onions were okay if they didn't overwhelm everything else. He munched away pondering this and other weighty issues of life.

Grundy's Café had apparently once been a small shop. Mickey imagined a men's store. On each side of the front door were squared-off stages where mannequins had once posed for passersby. Now each cubicle had a round table. He could imagine the mayor sitting there so that he could wave at everyone strolling by. Now, however, the two women who sat at the table were smoking electronic cigarettes. They had those black cylinders that glowed blue at the tip when the women took draws. Mickey thought about the old putdown: "He thinks his shit don't stink." With those cigarettes, the smoke didn't stink. He just couldn't get past the weirdness of it. The two young women looked out of place. E-cigarettes in a café on the square in rural Virginia made Mickey wonder if the smokers had been invaded by body snatchers.

"Got room for dessert, hon?" the waitress asked.

"What you got, sugar?" Mickey knew the small-town sweetness. He'd grown up in this world, back when a man could still work and still would. After all, he hadn't always been a weed mule. Once upon a time, he'd sat on his ass in press boxes for hours.

"Bread pudding with raisins and sauce. Apple pie a la mode. Lemon pound cake."

"Which you like?" he asked.

"That pound cake ain't been out of the oven an hour," she said. "I told Ursula it didn't make sense to bake that thing this late in the day, but she said if it weren't gone in a jiffy, it'd still be scrumptious tomorrow. Sometimes folks want cake for breakfast on a Saturday, know what I mean?"

"I'll have a slice." It would have been cold to ignore such a sales pitch. Mickey was satisfied the waitress's name must be Millie. She had a husband named Rock. He was a welder. They lived in a duplex and went to the Church of Christ.

Dylan Wannamacher got his team to Pettigru too soon, too. The assistant coaches tried to get him to wait, but he was excited and fretted about flat tires and insisted on heading down the road. When they got there, with ninety minutes to kill, he told the players just to relax and think about the ballgame. This wasn't unfamiliar. When Waddy Pegler had been the coach, they'd always had such rituals of contemplation before home games, where they took down the cushions that hung behind the baskets in the gym and lounged around, thinking not about the game but about practical jokes and detailed conversations about which cheerleaders they wanted to screw. As a general rule, they lied about those they had.

The Merry Pranksters gathered at a safe distance from everyone else. It would have been unthinkable for them to socialize with teammates with whom they had a business relationship. Most everyone else was listening to rap music on their iPods, anyway.

"So, whatcha think?" Milo Hirley asked Walt Pegler.

"We gotta play like hell if we're gonna win."

"What if we don't?"

"We get turnt as hell tomorrow," Milo said.

"And if we do?" Marty Drummond asked.

"Same fucking thing," Milo said.

Dylan appeared from around the corner of the grandstand, making the rounds.

"What's on your mind, fellas?" he asked.

"Titties," Milo said.

"Good topic," the coach replied.

Mickey Statler had little problem parking the Buick. He just leaned out the window and told the fellow with the Lashley Boosters golf shirt on he was with the press. He didn't have to flash a card, which was good since he didn't have one.

The front gate was another story. Mickey told the man standing there that he was with the press.

"I ain't never seen you," the fellow, who also wearing Lashley Boosters gear, said.

"I'm writing about the visitors. I work for a national website. I'm doing a story on the Enlightened Word coach. He'd never coached before until Waddy Pegler died, and the team has won three straight since he took over. I spent half yesterday interviewing him and his players. Now I've got to wrap up the story based on how they do tonight."

"What's the name of that there website?" the man asked, probably not unduly concerned about how the enemy had an inspirational story to tell.

"It's called The Ultimate Sporting Life. Here. Hang on a minute. I'll call it up on my phone and show you a story I've written," Dylan said. He ran his fingers up and down the screen and clicked on his story about Jalloquille Means. He handed his phone to the gatekeeper, who read a paragraph or two.

"So … I reckon you're what they call the mainstream media?"

"You know what the mainstream is, Mister? The mainstream media is the media you don't like. For me, the mainstream media is Fox News, so, no, I'm not in the mainstream media."

"Well, Mr. Libtard, you ain't running things here at B. Henry Lashley, and 'less'n you got a High School League card, you ain't a-gettin' in for free."

"Could I have your name, sir?" Mickey swung his backpack around and pulled a notepad out of a side pocket.

"Lamar Ellington. Want me to spell it?"

"Nah, that's all right, Lamar. I'm not sure I can trust you to spell your own name."

"Why, you sonuvabitch." Lamar motioned for a police officer. When he strolled over, he said, "Fred, I want you to do me a favor and throw this ignorant bastard in jail. He threatened me with personal harm."

"That's twice he's cussed me, Officer," Mickey said. "I haven't cussed him once. I'm a legitimate member of the media, as this man knows."

"You better come with me, boy." Fred wasn't saying it to Lamar.

The only likely reason Mickey got in the game before kickoff was that he'd had the presence of mind to activate the recording device on his cell. Once he'd settled down listening to the sleep-inducing lecture of Fred the Cop, Mickey played the recording for him. He got in the game, but they told him there wasn't room for the press in the press box, this being a playoff game, bad weather rolling in, and all. Mickey thought to himself that he could have gotten a seat in the grandstands, where good seats were still available, for eight bucks and not had to deal with Lamar of the Tea Party. It started sleeting while he was walking down the steps onto the playing field. The B. Henry Lashley Marching Christian Lions were playing their routine double time so that they could flee the premises with their instruments undamaged. The national anthem took forty-seven seconds.

Mickey pulled the hood over his head and yanked the drawstrings to keep it there. His notepad was going to be useless. His cell was supposed to be watertight, and that was about to be tested. He'd have to talk into it and record his observations, but his memory was going to need to be sharp. Bad things sure did come in bunches. He'd been so angry that he'd forgotten about his problems, but then he saw the huge, seemingly friendly giant who was screwing a sweet little, weed-selling dish, who happened to be Mickey's daughter, and the sleet was nothing next to what flooded back into Mickey's brain.

"Well, this sucks," Dylan Wannamacher said, extending his hand.

"You have some idea," Mickey said, and Dylan wondered if he might be drunk.

Dylan walked away thinking that was odd.

Mickey thought to himself, *Virginia and North Carolina. Just two states. I'll need one more for a killing spree.* He watched the Lashley Lions run out on the field and thought them the most athletic bunch of white boys he'd spied in a while. Lashley was one of *those* kinds of schools, the ones founded in the name of Jesus, a fundamentalist reading of His teachings, and creating a Promised Land where boys and girls could avoid mingling with black folks. Lashley was quite obviously the Rome of a failing empire. Mickey was quite convinced B. Henry Lashley, whether alive or dead, must be some kind of evangelist who either was or had been adept at separating Christians from a hefty share of their money.

He badly wanted Enlightened Word, cradle-robbing coach and all, to kick B. Henry Lashley's ass. And his football players, too.

It was not to be. The Christian Lions rolled down the field and scored touchdowns on their first two possessions. Meanwhile, the weather worsened, and it seemed unlikely that the Alabama Crimson Tide, let alone the Enlightened Word Dragoons, could score two touchdowns during the entire forty-two minutes that remained. Mickey thought seriously of leaving right then, but something happened that piqued his interest.

On the Dragoons' third possession, Milo Hirley pitched the ball forward to Lenny Paterson, who was hit as he darted toward the trenches. The ball came loose and floated into the air. Milo grabbed it and started retreating. Past the hash mark, he saw Peter Baxter wide open, and, as much as he hated it, had little choice but to heave the ball in his direction. Miraculously, Baxter caught it and hightailed it with a touch of cowardice toward the sideline, where Mickey found himself backpedaling to keep from being run over. He managed to keep from being toppled but a Lashley linebacker hit Baxter three yards out of bounds. Baxter got up and fired the ball at the linebacker, Number 53, hitting him in the small of the back. The linebacker charged and screamed, "You fucking stoner!"

As he rolled over backwards, Baxter yelled, "I ain't no fucking stoner. It's the rest of them, you stupid sonuvabitch!"

The brawl that ensued was in the middle of the Dragoons' bench, though a large contingent of Christian Lions joined the fray, growling. Mickey backed into the fence, grabbed his phone and started talking into it. Milo had no interest in defending Peter Baxter, but the rhubarb had quickly escalated into a general assault between the fundamentalists and the Enlightened. Milo rather cleverly dove at a Lashley safety just as Number 53 punched Baxter for the umpteenth time. All but the dumbasses kept their helmets on, and they were sliding through ice and mud, so no one was hurt. Baxter and Number 53 were ejected, but the officials were reluctant to banish anyone else because they couldn't begin to keep up with the widespread anarchy.

Both teams got personal fouls. Still third down and eight yards to go at the twenty-three. Lashley needed Number 53 more than Enlightened Word needed Peter Baxter. The Dragoons rallied. Four plays later, Eli Shouse kicked the ugliest field goal that ever went between uprights. The game came alive at the same rate as the prospects for Mickey Statler's story. Mickey had shoved his phone in his pocket and helped separate the players from one another. He got muddy. It couldn't possibly make him any colder.

Enlightened Word controlled the rest of the game. Lashley had worsening weather on its side. The second and third quarters were scoreless. Enlightened Word scored five minutes into the fourth because somehow Denny Paterson slipped through the muck and outran his white pursuers for a fifty-seven-yard touchdown, and Dylan Wannamacher had enough sense not to let Shouse kick again. Lenny replaced his winded twin and rammed in for a two-point conversion that brought Enlightened Word within three points. That was the closest they got. At the end, Shouse could have tied it with a thirty-five-yard field goal, but it never had a chance. Sebastian Janikowski would have been no more than fifty-fifty in conditions that a pro player never had to face. The grass was gone, and the mud was frozen.

When Mickey placed his recorder in front of Milo Hirley, he had only three words: "What a pisser." Both Paterson twins were weeping uncontrollably. Walt Pegler was on his back in the mud, his body convulsing as if in the throes of religious cataclysm, and Mickey didn't try to talk to him because he knew of no English-to-Charismatic-Tongues dictionary. The Dragoons got beat fourteen to eleven by the Reverend Doctor B. Henry Lashley, Lamar the Ticket Taker, Mother Nature and President-Elect Martin J. Gaynes, or that was the way Mickey was tempted to portray it. He needed the perilous drive back to Triborough to moderate the tone. He took the interstate back, and when he walked into the lobby of the Marriott at half past twelve, he looked as scruffy as any homeless wino. Mickey shrugged his shoulders and flashed his room card, and the lords of the lobby let him pass. He hung up his clothes on the shower rod, changed into dry clothes, and polished up the story that he filed at damned near four. He wrote it in first person and called Enlightened Word "the best by God four and seven team ever I seen," adopting the grammar of his late father. He read it and thought it worked. If the editors thought it didn't, that was their responsibility.

It was unfortunate that Mickey had to check out of the Marriott at noon on Saturday, but his idiotic punctuality kicked in, as usual, and he was up at nine. His left hip was sore, undoubtedly a result of favoring his left side because of the arthritic knee on the right. He grunted a lot but still enjoyed the shower, and when he got dressed and packed, called the daughter whose number he now possessed.

"I've got to hit the road, Marcia," he told her. "I just wanted to tell you I love you, even though I know too much about you and you about me. I'll keep in touch and come back to see you as soon as I can."

"I love you, too, Daddy. How'd the game come out?"

"Oh, Enlightened Word lost, but they played a hell of a game," he said. "The weather was awful. I got a story out of it. Look here, I was hoping we could get together and have a cup of coffee before I hit the road."

"Oh, Daddy, I can't," she said. "I'm out of town right now, running some errands."

He had a suspicion about what kind of errands she had. A familiar one.

"Damn it all," he said. "Well, I'm not gonna make it very far without a good cup of joe. Where's that place you mentioned going to."

"Where I met Dylan?"¬

"Yeah."

"It's called Auntie Em's. From where you are, it's right on Main Street, on the left once you get past Montague. I hate you got to leave."

"Me, too, sugar, but I do."

When Mickey limped into the little college-catering emporium, Dylan Wannamacher was sitting along the left side, alone in a booth.

"Well, I'll be," Dylan said. "Have a seat. I just read your story. It's fantastic. Let me buy you something you'll like."

He came back with a mug of the coffee Mickey presumed to be the best they had and a brown-sugar-caked muffin that was steaming and moist.

"I reckon we gave you something to write about," Dylan said.

"It was the best game I've seen in a while," Mickey replied. "You still got no plans to coach anymore?"

"I enjoyed it. I hate to admit it, but I did. I'm no coach, though. I'm a writer, not too different from you. I don't have to document everything with fiction."

"Mark Twain, I think, was who said truth is stranger than fiction because fiction has to make sense," Mickey said.

"Truth sure is stranger than fiction these days. In about every way I can figure."

"I've got something I need to tell you," Mickey said. "I'm glad I bumped into you. It's better than calling."

"Oh?"

"Yeah." Mickey took a long, thoughtful sip. "Marcia is my daughter."

"I'll be."

"Don't worry. She told me everything. We learned a lot of secrets about each other. Her mother and I had an ugly divorce. I really didn't even know she was here. I hadn't seen her in, I don't know, maybe a year."

"How'd you get together?"

"Oh," Mickey said, "let's just say we bumped into each other. I have no bone to pick with you. She's got her flaws, but she's a good girl. She says you're a good man. I haven't seen anything the past three days to doubt it. Just be good to her, all right?"

Dylan simply nodded.

"You're a damned good coach, Dylan. You're so good, I just wrote the best story about a four-and-seven team that was ever written. Lest I seem immodest, it might be the only good story about a four-and-seven team."

Dylan laughed. "A toast. Here's to four and seven."

"I can't help but wish you'd keep on coaching. I might be getting back up here from time to time."

"It won't hold together," Dylan said. "They'll run wild next year, and not in a good way."

"Isn't that why you need to stick with 'em?"

"Shit. They're out somewhere smoking weed somewhere right now. It's hard for a man to hold that line when he ain't altogether agin' it. I'm assuming, having discussed such matters at length with your daughter, you know something of my own personal habits. Those kids, though, they're too young, and I wish they wouldn't grow up so fast, but I'm not enough of a hypocrite to handle it in the long run."

"Well, Dylan, I know a little something about hypocrisy myself. You can't live with it. You can't live without it." Mickey paused, then decided to go ahead and say it. "Like my daughter."

Mickey stood up and put on his gray hoodie, which, unlike his parka, was clean, and said, "Let's keep in touch. I got the tip."

He opened his wallet, left a five on the counter, and handed Dylan his business card.

PART THREE
FLAWS OF
PERFECT CRIME

CHAPTER 33

Tightening Up

Bentsen Lilley was nothing if not mobile. He could jet in and out of wherever he wanted. The Consortium's greatest advantage was its relationship with the law. Garlin Samuelson, president of the National Confederation of Law Enforcement Officers (NCLEO), had been instrumental in building the network. A call or an email from Samuelson could influence the hiring of certain people in certain positions, whether county, state, or local. Edmund Kingsley was the other associate occupying a lofty perch in law enforcement. Lilley hoped that Kingsley would soon become director of the Federal Bureau of Investigation, but that was out of Lilley's hands. No impending change in administrations had ever been so unpredictable. Lilley did what he could with a trip to Washington. With what little he had learned, Lilley flew to Texas and met Samuelson at a Mexican joint outside Galveston.

Samuelson was waiting at a booth in the back, his gray Stetson lying on the table in front of him with a mug of draft beer and a basket of tortilla chips.

"I been tied up in three days of goddamned meetings in Austin," Samuelson said. "Legislature's knocked off for the year. Sons of bitches expect us to do all the work while they're away. Want a beer, Bentsen?"

"Why not? I don't have to fly the plane," Lilley said.

Samuelson motioned to the bartender.

"Javy's making a good living off of us, Bentsen. He sells a good bit of product out of here. He's a good man, and he's got police protection."

"Strictly weed, I reckon."

"Oh, yeah. He knows if I find out he's involved in cocaine, or meth, it's his ass," Samuelson said. "There's nothing to worry about. We put him in business. He was clean till we approached him with a deal he couldn't refuse. He's sending his boy through the University of Houston. Truth is, little Javy is working his own way through, if you know what I mean."

"It's a family business, Garlin."

They had a laugh. Lilley's beer arrived. The waitress said Senor Barcenas was sending complimentary fajitas. Samuelson thanked her in Spanish. Gracias and all that.

"How things look in D.C.?" Samuelson asked after she walked away. Lilley took a healthy swallow of his Shiner Bock.

"Ah, like we knew," he said. "You can't predict what they're going to do. Best I can gather, the country's up for sale. The president-elect doesn't waste much time on principle. He's nice to people who are nice to him."

"You being nice to him?"

"I've never met him," Lilley said. "I got in to see a couple big-time players, ones Kingsley said would speak with me frankly. They expressed some sympathy for our position. They listened to me extol the good Republican virtues of states' rights and home rule. The main thing I learned, though, is that we've got to cool it."

"What's that mean in English, Bentsen?"

"All right, I'll cut through the bullshit. The blacks are all riled. They're unhappy at the outcome of the election. They're, especially the young ones, all into this Black Lives Matter bullshit, and the new president-elect wants it to stop. Two things. Number one, things have got to quiet down. No more of this 'shoot a colored down, then plant weed on him.' There's been too many videos. The dirty work has got to be cleaner. The police have got to back off. We're going to have to take care of these missions underground. It won't be that different. We've still got great capability to cover it up. We've got to neutralize this riffraff outside the public view. We do that for the president? He'll get out of the way of weed legalization."

"So what you're saying, if I get the drift, is that … security … isn't a police operation anymore?" Samuelson asked.

"That's right, Garlin. Security, as you put it, is an FBI operation. Not so much formal FBI, but Kingsley said he can provide the personnel for such operations."

"What? Mafia? Retired agents? Ex-military?"

Lilley waved off the question. "I ask no questions. Don't want to know too many answers. I'll leave you and Kingsley to work out the details."

Wade Sanderson knew that Tripp Fallaw was on Santa Catalina Island, which wasn't a large place. It had one decent-sized town, Avalon. It had an airport, miles away. The island had few roads and two other harbors that came together near the north end, almost cutting off a tiny island but not quite. Tripp was also strung out on whatever drugs he had left and clueless. He'd probably fled to Catalina because, in his twisted logic, he'd figured it was a relatively safe place to make the money he desperately needed. The trouble was that the Avalon Casino wasn't a casino at all. It had a grand movie theater on its lower level and a banquet hall above. It amused Wade to consider Tripp's latest grand misadventure.

Even December was pleasant on Santa Catalina. The flight from the mainland had been delayed, waiting for fog to dissipate. A golf cart had taken Tripp to Avalon. The driver said he had to refill the gas tank after every round trip.

Wade knew that Tripp had lied to Marcia Statler. He hadn't stolen the phone from an unsuspecting gambler because there were no gamblers. He'd made the call from Santa Catalina, all right, and he'd told Marcia he was at the casino. The man whose cell had been used was a shopkeeper in Avalon. Why had he lied? Maybe it was because Tripp was so complete a bullshitter that he'd just done it as a part of his character. Perhaps he'd done it to present himself as slicker than he was. Perhaps he was distrustful, as he should have been, because even though he'd sworn Marcia to secrecy, she'd told Wade about it, anyway.

Because Wade was Tripp's friend.

Simon Tibbetts was a tall, balding, rather effeminate merchant of souvenirs and artifacts. He told Wade that a young man, somewhat disheveled and ill, had paid cash for a tie-dyed "Lovely Catalina" tee shirt, and he remembered him distinctly because he had returned some time later to inform the shopkeeper that he'd apparently placed a cell phone in the bag with his tee shirt. Tibbetts said he couldn't imagine that being true, but that he had been prone to absentmindedness for all his life, and, as much as he hated to admit it, silly mistakes had become more common since he'd reached his sixties. He said he hadn't even noticed it missing. Tibbetts described the man. It was Tripp, all right. Wade gave Tibbetts a card that purported him to be a private investigator and told him to call if he happened to see "the young man" again.

Wade, who had never visited Santa Catalina, rented himself a bicycle. He thought that there was no such thing as an automobile, but while he had lunch at a street-front sandwich shop, a SmartCar idled past. It was cute, two-tone, blue and white, for the man who had everything, including a car on a tiny island that didn't have many. Wade had never even considered there being a place where cars were unnecessary.

Tripp had to be holed up somewhere, stoned. He couldn't gamble. He couldn't play golf. The island had no place to play it. No wonder Tripp had called Marcia. He needed a way out. Wade was there to give him one. Wade bicycled up in the hills, just so he could find a nice, safe place to smoke a joint. He needed to relax. Tripp would come to him. It was just a matter of time.

CHAPTER 34

Dealing Is the Deal

"How do I get out, Ronnie?"

The Panorama Lodge was the kind of place where daddies took their families because their daddies had taken them. It had private rooms, each equipped with little jukeboxes mounted in the cheap, paneled walls. Deputy Sheriff Ronnie Shingler had discreetly made sure an unoccupied room was on each side of the one where he and Mickey Statler were seated.

"Merry Christmas to you, too, Mickey." Shingler put on his reading glasses and picked up the menu. "Last time I was here, the trout was delicious. I think that's what I'll have. You?"

"What's it been? Almost six, okay, five months," Mickey said. "I've done everything you've asked."

Shingler looked at him over the top of the glasses.

"Have there been problems? Did I deceive you? Aren't you making enough money?"

"No, no problems. No, you didn't deceive me. Yes, I'm making enough money," Mickey said, "but, this thing, it's a whole lot bigger than you ever let on. The weed I'm delivering isn't confiscated here in Lovejoy. It's coming from California. Humboldt County, wherever that is."

Shingler motioned for Mickey to hold it down. A teen-aged waitress opened the door. Shingler ordered the trout dinner for both of them and sweet tea for himself.

"Would you like a beer, Mickey?"

"No. Tea will be fine."

"I'm on duty. You know how it is," Shingler said. He looked sideways at the waitress. "Darling, how about bringing us an order of jalapeno poppers to start."

"Ooh, them's good," she said as she finished writing up the order. "I'll get 'em put in right away."

Once she left, Shingler said, "You know, Mickey, you've done a jam-up job. I read every damned story you write, and I don't read all that much. You ought to make a book out of them columns. They told me you could write about anything, and that's the truth."

"That's kind of you, Ronnie. Imagine how well I could write if I could really *concentrate* on it."

"It boggles the mind," Shingler said, "but, you know, that writing of yours is all gravy. The important part of your job is delivering those briefcases and bringing back another one full of money. As it turns out, you do that as well as you write, and I mean that as a compliment. Why you got cold feet?"

"Because it's too big, Ronnie. You've got to know that. Running with the law what's against the law? You can't get away with that forever. Somebody's gonna slip up. Somebody's gonna get jealous. Somebody's gonna demand a bigger share of the pie."

"You're right. It can't last forever, but it can last until such time as cannabis becomes legal everywhere medicinally and, eventually, recreationally. We'll have everything in place. It's a good plan. The more you knew about it, the more you'd see how painstakingly it's all devised. But I don't believe you need to know no more about it than you do right now."

"I didn't sign up for it," Mickey said. "You did."

"Your dick signed you up for it, Mickey. You made a mistake, and you've got no choice. You're part of the club. You can get out once we go straight, but, shit, you'd be a damned fool to do it then. You'd be a damned fool to try and do it now. We've had several people wanted to get out. They didn't do so good."

"Is that a threat, Ronnie?"

"Don't be silly, Mickey. Of course, it is."

The waitress returned with the poppers.

"You know, on second thought, honey, I think I will have a drink," Mickey said.

"What'll it be?" she asked.

"You know what a boilermaker is, honey?"

"Huh-uh."

Shingler intervened. "It's a draught beer and a shot of whisky," he said. "Don't matter what kind. Bourbon probably be best. Bring my friend one."

When she left, Shingler's look turned hard.

"Now what the fuck has got you scared, Mickey?"

Mickey didn't want to tell Ronnie Shingler that his latest contact had been his daughter. He was surprised the son of a bitch didn't already know.

"Nothing," he said. "I just sort of fancied getting back to being a law-abiding citizen again, Ronnie."

"You might as well get that shit out of your mind," Shingler said. "Here. Have a popper."

Enlightened Word Academy's student body consisted of 727 inquisitive souls. Twenty-seven played on the football team. Six more were equipment managers and student trainers. Twelve more were cheerleaders. Thirty-eight played in the band. Six hundred forty-four were home for the Christmas holidays. Twenty lived in the area. Twenty were playing in holiday basketball tournaments. That left eighty-three holed up in the two dorms, the majority in A Dorm because it was for boys.

They all got back from the Lashley game safely, but, when they awakened on Saturday morning, four inches of snow were on the ground, and four more fell that day, and it was still too cold for it to melt. Mobility was limited, but behavior was not. Preston Breen, the science instructor and bachelor who lived in A Dorm's ground-floor apartment, had been devastated by the onset of snow. It didn't take much to devastate Mr. Breen. He was here because he couldn't handle pressure. It was a low-pressure environment. Pressure that wasn't low made him susceptible to drink, and, by Monday morning, he was to the point where all he could do to control the liquor was drink more of it. The lights were off, the lamps lit, the shades drawn, and Mr. Breen thought about killing himself. Suicide, of course, was too much pressure for him to handle, so he was doing it gradually with cheap vodka. The juice, grapefruit and orange, was gone, but he had a six-pack of lime Gatorade and two more quarts of Heaven Hill.

No one knew where Miss Glynis Dockery was. Apparently she'd strayed from her apartment in B Dorm and couldn't get back. One girl said she thought Miss Dockery was from West Virginia. Miss Dockery might be the last person at Enlightened Word or, for that matter, the Commonwealth, who didn't believe in cell phones.

For the fourscore and three holed up at the closed school, freedom sure was nice, what with snow on the ground.

It was conceivable that Mr. Breen might stagger out of his cave, growl at the miscreants, and maybe even do something rash like call the authorities, so the boys, most of them, made an exodus to B Dorm, where word had spread that no supervision was in place at all. As luck would have it, Milo Hirley and Walt Pegler provided weed for all who desired it. Milo had braved the elements on Saturday for a tortuous trek into Triborough, there to strike a mother lode. Some of the more righteous, boys and girls alike, retired to their rooms to read books and talk to their parents about when they might be able to get home, but they also holed up there because they didn't really want to know what mischief was going on, the better to avoid being tempted by it.

Poor Jonny Heinsohn missed out. His parents had gotten him home before the snow shut down lines of transportation. Marty Drummond took part in the sinning that ensued, but he had to get himself straightened up enough to slog back to his parents' stately campus dwelling. Walt Pegler was supposed to be home at dark on Saturday himself, but he wasn't scared of his mother now that his father was gone. All that Walt and Milo suffered was a shortage of condoms.

It was this shortage – and a modest sense of social responsibility – that led Milo and Walt at last out into the blinding glare of a pristine, albeit frigid, snow-covered afternoon, for the kind of exposure to the elements that invigorates young men who have been blissfully stoned and sexually promiscuous for two days and one night. It seemed unbelievable to be sitting calmly on a bench, right in the middle of the common, completely unconcerned that anyone would see them. They split a joint neither felt because it was so cold that even their brains were frozen. Milo lit a cigarette because it was what he usually did when a weed buzz faded. Walt didn't see the use.

"When did you start smoking menthols?" Walt asked.

"When I found these Marb menthols in Kimmie's desk drawer. Shoneka smoke?"

"She vapes. It seems like all the girls vape."

"Yeah. Kimmie, too. That's probably why these smokes were tucked away," Milo said. "I was looking to see if she had any condoms. You know, I don't see why people vape. If it won't kill you, what's the fucking use?"

"You expect the girl to provide them?" Walt asked, sounding as if he'd never imagined such a thing. "Condoms, I mean. Not cigarettes."

"Nah. It didn't hurt to look. I don't want to get nobody knocked up."

It was quiet. Eerily quiet. Even quieter because they were high.

"Guess we'll have to report to basketball practice tomorrow," Walt said.

"Yeah," Milo said. "You know, Dylan was right."

"About what?"

"It's not worth playing football unless you play it to win. Damned if we didn't almost pull it off."

"We'd've won if it wasn't so stinking cold."

"Football's not basketball," Milo said. "I hate it's over. Basketball is for fun. I'm gonna get high before every practice. Besides, I got a shitload of weed to get rid of. You want in?"

"Shit, yeah," Walt said.

"By the way, everything's cool with Bryne."

"He ain't pissed no more?"

"Nah," Milo said. "I got him to smoke some of mine. He realized he couldn't compete with that shit. Next chance I get, I'm gonna put him in business for me."

"Goddamighty," Walt said. "Fuckin' Bryne's working for you."

"For us, my man. How much product can you handle?"

"Um, maybe, three ounces."

"I hear you, bruh."

"Two to sell. One to save for personal consumption."

"That'll just about break even."

"Maybe a half-ounce for personal consumption."

"It's the American way, mon," Milo said.

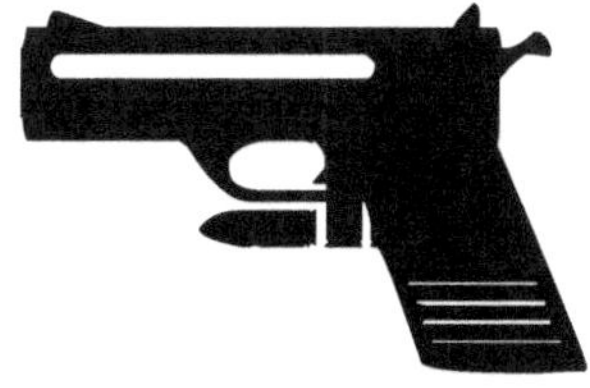

CHAPTER 35

Nothing to It

Wade Sanderson wasn't much disguised. He had grown a neat beard since the last time he'd seen Tripp Fallaw. He was wearing sunglasses. He looked a bit more like a tourist – backpack, bicycle, camera, cargo shorts, flowery shirt – than usual, but lots of people dressed that way in Southern California every day. Sanderson, who had grown up in Conover, North Carolina, thought his home now was the American Dream gone bad, and he was a typical inhabitant. When he spied Tripp, looking like hell and accompanied by a hippie chick who looked zonked and must have been because she was with Tripp, he knew they would be headed to a room, either hers or hopefully his, there to take drugs and perform sexual acts upon the other. Wade envied the little bullshit artist his way with women. He'd gotten Marcia Statler to come all the way to L.A. with him, left her stranded, and, yet, she still felt sorry for him and wanted to help him out. Wade wanted Marcia to fly to California, too. He just didn't want Tripp to be there.

Now Wade had to wait him out. He circled blocks on the bike, picking them up again, even riding past, until they arrived at a shabby little inn, one with a gift shop and all sorts of claims of famous people who had spent the night there. Most were dead and couldn't deny it. He noted the room number and figured he'd wait until the one-night stand had run its course. That girl with the faraway eyes might be willing to whisk him away to Mexico, but she wouldn't know how. She'd wake up, and in the cool, gray light of dawn, slip away because things were starting to get too weird. Besides, Santa Catalina Island was a wonderful place for a carefree ride up in the hills, there to smoke a joint in peaceful serenity. Wade wasn't the only visitor to whom it had occurred. Cannabis made him merry. It took away his edge. He enjoyed the opportunity to relax. Every storm needed an accompanying calm. That night Wade went to peaceful sleep and dreamed of old times back in the Carolinas. He was out by nine and awakened long before dawn. He got up, shaved and showered, packed his bags but paid for another night anyway, just in case, and rode back to the Casa Aventuras, room 203, inside terrace, overlooking a pool that was still open even though it was December. Wade never got used to that.

Sure enough, the girl emerged at first light. She stopped by the office, likely to pay for the room. Tripp had plied her with drugs and sex. He'd earned it. Wade thought about approaching her. Nah. He knew all of her he needed, and she need know nothing of him. He was confident that Tripp wasn't going anywhere, not for several hours. Tripp pedaled off and found himself a café for a nice breakfast of a western omelet, coffee, and orange juice. He read the paper. He checked his text messages and Twitter feed. It was going to be a long day. A long night. Wade was going to show Tripp Fallaw, his old friend, the time of his life.

Eleven-thirty was about right. Wade turned in the bicycle. He didn't want it stolen and didn't want to take the precautions necessary to prevent it. He had the cell of his new friend the cart driver, and the man, whose name was Enrique, had assured him that he'd be glad to take him back to the airport, or to Two Harbors, at any time, for what Wade had tipped him for the ride into Avalon.

Wade knocked on the door of Room 203. Hard. Several times.

"Tripp! It's me! I come to get you out of here! You hear me? I got you a ride! Clean break!"

Tripp Fallaw squinted at the light when he opened the door.

"Shit. 'At you, Wade? Wade? Come in." He'd had a pistol behind his back. Wade caught a glint of it before the door closed. Tripp sat on the bed and turned on the lamp. He looked at Wade.

"What? Oh, this thing? I didn't know who it might be. At the door, I mean. It sounded like you, but, shit, a man don't know who he can trust anymore."

"Ain't that the truth," Wade said.

"So … what's up?"

"I heard you were here. Being as how I heard it, I figured that itself means I had to get you out of the country. I just happen to have somebody owes me a favor. I been looking for you two days."

"Damn, Wade."

"Nah, listen. Tomorrow morning, I'm gonna put you on a plane, at the other side of this very island, and it's gonna fly you to a place called Loreto. I doubt you've ever heard of it. I know I hadn't until the day before yesterday."

"Where's it, like, in New Mexico?" Tripp asked.

"No, Tripp, it's, like, in Old Mexico. Baja California Sur. Middle of nowhere. On the inner coast. Closest place I could find to the end of the earth that has an airport."

"Shit, Wade, I doubt I got my passport."

"Ain't nobody gonna check where they gonna set you down."

"Well, damn, I know, you know, I gotta get out, but, like, this is hitting me fresh and all, and …"

"Take a shower. I'll make some coffee," Wade said.

"Ain't no coffee machine."

"I'll go get some. You just take a shower."

Wade waited until he heard the shower come on. He stood at the door, listened for the sound of the curtain rings, sliding across the rod, and heard the flow of the water change as Tripp stepped under it. He found the plastic card in Tripp's pants, pocketed it so that he could get back in, and strode off in search of coffee. It wasn't hard to find, though the pot was empty in the office. A little shop was about thirty yards away.

When he got back, Tripp was in his underwear, putting on his pants. A pair of khakis. Wade handed him the coffee. He reached in his own pockets, pulled out packets of sugar and powdered creamer, and tossed them on the lamp table next to the bed.

"Oh, thanks," Tripp said, though he apparently took it black.

"You finish that coffee, you wanna do a line?"

Tripp grinned. "I fucked an old gal for some coke last night."

Damn him and that grin. He is one likeable douchebag.

"I bet you been here long enough to know where a couple buddies can go out drinking," Wade said.

"I thought …"

"The plane ain't till in the morning, Tripp. You don't think I went to all this trouble just so I could go to Sunday school. Me and you probably ain't gonna see each other for a while. I just wanted you to know it's all water under the bridge. Let's get fucked up, find us a couple sluts, like the old days. It'd be a shame for you to get on that plane, leave the good old U.S. of A. behind you, and not be hung over."

"I'm out of money, Tripp, and I ain't got this room no more."

"I paid you up for one more night when I got the coffee. Don't worry about it. On me," Wade said. "While I was looking for you yesterday, son, I sold a shitload of weed. Before I come over here, I made a few arrangements so I could turn it into a business expense, so to speak. Hey, we got a lot of partying to do tonight. I'm up for snorting away some of the profit."

Tripp found an empty paper cup with a plastic top and a straw sticking out of it. Then he yanked the straw out of the cup and took a dirty napkin from the trash can and dried the straw, squeezing it so that the moisture seeped out.

"You don't happen to have a straight razor, do you?" Tripp asked.

"No, but I got a business card from the man who's gonna take us to the airport in the morning. I reckon it'll do. Here, Tripp. This ought to perk you right up."

"I met Maddie at this place where she says, if ain't hardly nobody there, people snort shit right off the counter."

"I reckon that's where we need to go."

"Maddie, she's the gal I screwed last night."

"I gathered as much," Wade said.

Tripp Fallaw was charming, but he was also alarmingly guileless, and his concept of reality was affected by drug addiction. Wade thought, *Well, if he'd just been able to stick to the weed, but he's one those compulsive types who'll do anything for a buzz until he gets bored enough with one that he tries the next one.* Wade didn't understand people like that because he wasn't one of them, but they sure were a dime a dozen. Potheads might be slow and lazy, but they generally kept up with their bills. Besides, Wade made a prosperous living, and he was a pothead. Weed made people love what they already liked, and Wade sure enjoyed selling it.

Wade took a token line, but then he found the ash tray, made himself comfortable across half the crummy couch, and thoughtfully sucked down a joint. He was a bit of a contrast to Tripp, whose eyes were wide and face sweaty. Wade announced that it was time to get religious about drinking, rummaged through his backpack for a can of Lysol, and sprayed the room thoroughly as Tripp made his way to the door. Wade made sure the "Do Not Disturb" was hanging on the knob when they left for Tripp's preferred watering hole. He slipped has baggy of coke back in the backpack and left it in the room. He also made sure to put the business card back in his wallet. Tripp didn't need anything else to perk him up. From here on out, he needed things that would lie him down.

They drank a lot, and caroused a little, and Wade surreptitiously slipped a good-looking brunette forty dollars and told her to beat it because he didn't want Tripp occupied while he was still up to the task.

It shouldn't have been a surprise that Tripp overdid it. His whole life had been overdone. At nine o'clock, he'd already puked into some kind of a bush near the bar's side door, lost the capacity to walk, and damned near lost consciousness. Wade couldn't have carried him five blocks on his back, but that, not scraping cocaine, was the reason for the business card, because it had been given him by his new friend, Enrique, driver of the gasoline-powered cart. Enrique loved Wade. Enrique loved weed. Wade had been lying about selling weed. He had just given some away.

Enrique helped drag Tripp back into the room. He needed the help getting him up the steps. He gave Enrique a C note and told him to come back to pick him up at midnight. They were going back to the airport. Enrique said he had to fill up the cart with gas again.

In the room, Wade smoked a joint to relax. Weed made him love what he already liked. He removed a zip-up bag, the kind doctors presumably used. He removed a syringe, filled it up, and even squirted a little out the needle, just like in the movies. He pulled a chair over, next to the bed, and watched Tripp, dead to the world in a way. Wade injected the needle. Tripp didn't even flinch, and Wade made him dead to the world in another way. He pulled out his .38, made sure it was loaded, and tucked it in the front of his pants. Then he walked out into the night air, breathed deeply, and sat on a bench, under a street lamp. He called his buddy in the Los Angeles County Sheriff's Department, explained the situation, gave him the address and the phone number, and waited for Enrique. It was almost cold. Wade put on his windbreaker. Enrique looked like he was bundled up for the Iditarod. They split a joint on the way to the airport. When they arrived at the airport, Wade handed Enrique another hundred bucks, and half an ounce of weed, and told him not one damned thing had happened.

It hadn't been clean, but it hadn't had to be. Wade sent Enrique back on his way before the six-seater with Los Angeles County lettered on the side landed in the darkness. Four deputies got off. Wade Sanderson got on. It didn't matter that his fingerprints were everywhere, including Tripp Fallaw's body. The deputies knew how to clean everything up. Tripp had a rap sheet. Tripp had been busted. Tripp was on the lam. Murder was much easier because the law was on Wade's side.

CHAPTER 36

For Old Times' Sake

Dylan Wannamacher spent most of three days snowed in, getting back to his writing. It would stand to reason that, since he now considered his career as a football coach over, and he could go back to being no more a role model than the normal demands of an English teacher required, he would spend this solitary confinement smoking marijuana again.

He didn't. He didn't know why he didn't. He had stopped. He hadn't quit. Nothing prevented him from resuming a habit of which he had been fond for close to two decades. He was just contemplative, not high and contemplative.

Dylan had become unpredictable to himself. As such, on Tuesday night, he decided to attend the scheduled Enlightened Word basketball game. This was unusual as he had never, in fourteen years as a teacher there, done so.

Owing to his size, Dylan wasn't adept at slipping in and out of places. He tried. He tried to pay his way in, but Stiller McGwire, sitting at the table in the lobby selling tickets, refused to let him do so. He walked through the portal at the end of the court and sat down on the front row. What had drawn him to the game was Milo Hirley. He wanted to check on him. Milo was an unrepentant rogue, but Dylan had hope for him. It came as something of a surprise to find that Milo wasn't playing in the game, which was against a team wearing green that had "Hornets" in script on its jerseys. Milo was sitting at the end of the bench, wearing khakis and a sport shirt with black sneakers. Along with most in attendance, Milo spotted Dylan sitting on the front row at the far end off the court, opposite the benches and scoring table. At the end of the first quarter, as the team huddled around Coach Bob Wasdin, Milo used the opportunity to walk behind the benches and scoring table, around the court, and sit next to the man who had briefly been his football coach and had been his English teacher since the time he transferred into Enlightened Word.

"'Sup, Dylan."

"Ah, nothing to do. Decided to drive over and see how y'all doing. Wasdin tell you to come over and pick my brain on matchup zones?"

"No," Milo said, "he just kicked me off the team for tonight."

"Very little you tell me ever surprises me, Milo."

"He should have. I mouthed off at him at practice, and then we pretty much had an argument, and he pretty much told me to get the hell out. He said I was 'on something'."

"Were you?" Dylan asked.

"Not by then."

The Dragoons were leading by eight points. The Hornets, from wherever, weren't particularly good. Enlightened Word looked like a team without a leader. Dylan suspected he was sitting next to him.

Both of them were aware that more eyes were on them than the game. Not even the other Merry Pranksters would have guessed the topic of conversation. Most everyone figured the football coach of the modest miracle was concerned regarding his team's, and this team's, best athlete and, as a result, felt the need to counsel him about his attitude. Instead, they were chatting amiably about whether either was, at this moment, high on drugs.

"How 'bout you?" Milo asked.

"What?"

"Are you 'on something'?"

"Nope. Just a metal mug of coffee I drained on the way over."

"Well, haven't you been stoned for the last three days, getting that terrible loss behind you, and regaining a sense of resolve in the face of adversity?"

"No, Milo. I'm just Dylan Wannamacher, not Vince Lombardi. I just fooled around with a football team for a month."

"Which is all the more reason," Milo said, "for you to be stoned on your ass right now. I am so disappointed."

Dylan smiled. He could see people across the court, staring at him and Milo, smiling when he and Milo did.

"I don't know why. I just stopped smoking when I started coaching y'all. I haven't felt the inclination to start again. I might tomorrow. I might on the way home after talking this shit with you. I'm being a totally spontaneous person, letting one moment decide what the next one holds," Dylan said.

"You're stoned on your ass, Dylan."

Dylan stared at him.

"Whatever you say," Dylan said. "My eyes are clear, or they ought to be. The same cannot be said of yours, but I didn't come here to lecture you. That's the whole problem. I have no right to talk."

"So, obviously, you're gonna keep coaching here," Milo said. "You'll be the fucking athletic director. You'll go to clinics. Start leading the fucking Pledge of Allegiance. You'll be just like Waddy Pegler, except you don't have a son to beat up. And you won't be able to take the pressure, either, and some time in about ten years, you'll keel over dead, too."

Dylan bit his lip. As much as he wanted to take Milo Hirley outside and strangle him – and as much as some of their observers would have loved to see it – he held his thoughts.

"I'm out of line," Milo said finally. "I'm just frustrated. I didn't mean it."

"I'm not coaching anymore," Dylan said. "School's out. I've been snowed in. I haven't had any discussions. I haven't seen Drummond since he shook my hand after the game. I'd probably best get my ass out of here now. No telling who's gonna come running over here once the half ends."

"Well, it's got two minutes and eighteen seconds," Milo said. "I like that way of phrasing: 'best get my ass out of here.' I'd best mosey my ass back over to my new home at the end of the fucking bench."

"Hang in there, kid," Dylan said. He got up and drove back to Triborough.

He decided that he was going to Mississippi to spend some time with his mother. He hadn't even called her in a month. Being busy was no excuse for not calling Mama. He reckoned he'd start working his way back home as soon as he felt good and ready.

Marcia Statler was already headed south. She dreaded seeing her mother, who had moved near the Atlantic coast just to have her other daughter nearby. That hadn't worked out, and it had been a bone of contention between them, and then there was Marcia having abruptly left the condo to fly off to California with some golf pro who had left her stranded there. Vera had gone so far as to compare her to her father, and she had no idea just how true that comparison had become. Marcia had distributed her product in record time. She hadn't seen Dylan partly because he had been busy coaching football, but the truth was that she had been just as busy.

She planned to spend whatever time it took to placate her mother. That would definitely encompass Christmas. She hoped to slip away on the day after and go to Lovejoy, where she hoped to see her traveling man of a father, and she had in her bag an ounce of weed she might be able to sell to whichever stoner classmates she could find from high school who might still have the money to buy some. It was optional. She had some small urge to let them know she had learned to party and that she had become a *playa*. School didn't resume until January fourth, a Wednesday. She might even have time to fly to California, but she'd heard no more from Tripp Fallaw, and Wade Sanderson hadn't answered her text messages. When she tried to call him, the message said he was out of his office until after Christmas, and his mailbox was full. A drug dealer should never allow his mailbox to be full. She wondered what was going on. Maybe Tripp was in Mexico. Maybe Wade was helping him get there.

Marcia spent a night in Raleigh. After she found a room at a Hampton Inn, she got stoned and went to a nearby mall where she bought her mother an insanely expensive brand of perfume; her sister, Patti, a more moderately priced fragrance; and then there was Rodrigo, the Cuban dentist, undoubtedly in a festive mood since the evil Castro had died. Marcia owed dear Rodrigo something nice because he had rescued her by buying an airline ticket that got her back from Los Angeles. He was a thin, somewhat desiccated, man, probably a medium if she chose a jacket, but she had a difficult time being practical. She considered a leather, fur-lined jacket that would make him look like a fighter pilot. Then she wondered where she could find a semi-automatic rifle. Maybe some kind of beret, something that Che Guevara might wear. The image delighted her. She passed on at least a dozen gun dealers nestled at various locations on U.S. 220, finally found one seedy enough to strike her fancy, and settled on a nickel-plated revolver, based on the principle that Rodrigo could bravely protect her mama if roving bands of maniacal ne'er do-wells invaded their subdivision.

Daddy. What could she get Daddy? He was the one who needed the nickel-plated revolver, but he'd never accept it. She knew he had been wounded by their unanticipated meeting at the Triborough Marriott. She thought about some kind of signed painting or photograph of one of his favorite athletes: Willie Mays, or Johnny Unitas, or Richard Petty. She had plenty of money to spend. Maybe she could find one from a hero who was dead. Unitas. He had kicked the bucket. What a shame the road to the Grand Strand didn't run through Baltimore. She thought about Amazon, but she needed to ditch some cash. Something would come along. She felt a sense of destiny in her quest.

Had indeed Marcia bought him a nickel-plated revolver, Mickey Statler would have been sorely tempted to use it. He was bummed but far from ready to kill himself. He just didn't know what to do. The notion that he had been trapped was hard enough to accept on its own merits, but the addition of his own daughter into the equation lent his predicament a certain desperation.

He, too, felt the call to Mama.

Mickey's father had lived to see his son become a sportswriter but not a successful one. He often thought of how much his father would have enjoyed his tales of behind-the-scenes conniving. Lex Statler had been a rogue and a hustler, but it was the alcoholism that killed him at just about the age slot Mickey was occupying now.

The farm that had been out in the country when Mickey was a boy was now almost in town. Now Mildred Fischer Statler rented it out to a nearby cattleman, but the renter mainly used it for hay and deer hunting. When Mickey pulled in, his mother's Oldsmobile wasn't in the carport, so Mickey drove down the dirt road that ran past the house and made his way carefully across terrain more suitable for trucks and tractors than a Japanese midsize. The barn was falling in. The woods were overgrown. It's what happened when there were no cows and horses to make their paths through the woods, munching away at leaves and branches as they wandered.

Mama's Achieva had been the last car he'd bought her, back before the expense of divorce and the decline of his career eliminated what had been disposable income. He was going to buy her something nice, but he wanted to talk to her in order to gain some idea what he could give her that she wouldn't, in turn, give someone else. Fred and his sister Jan lived across town. Mickey sure hoped that Olds made it one more year. By next Christmas, he'd be able to buy her a brand-new car, not an Olds, because they weren't making them anymore.

Three people -- two men and a woman -- all took a break from their deadlines and commitments to go see their mothers. It was natural this time of year, the irresistible attraction to the person who had brought them into the world. None of their movements had been coordinated. Dylan Wannamacher was taking his own sweet time making his way from Triborough to Paulette, Mississippi. Marcia Statler was headed to Vera's home at the beach. Mickey Statler was at the farm, in the South Carolina upstate, where he had grown up, and then he would drive through Georgia, then Alabama, then within twenty miles of where Dylan was headed. If everything happened to fall just right, the paths of Mickey and Marcia, his daughter, would intersect when Mickey came back from the Independence Bowl.

What did they all have in common? In three different places, just before they faced their mothers, they'd deem it necessary to get high.

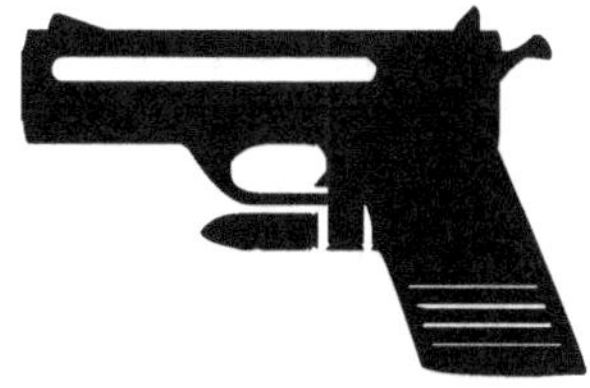

CHAPTER 37

Hearts to Hearts

Mickey Statler was unaccustomed to withholding information from his mother. Over the years, one of his favorite press-box sayings had been: "People always think a journalist can't keep a secret. I can keep a secret. You tell me not to tell anyone, and I won't even tell my mother, but you've got to understand that, if you don't tell me, it's my job to tell the whole world."

He was proving his point.

Cynthia Lee Statler had come from the country. She had dropped out of high school to marry Mickey's father, who had been dead for eighteen years. Of her two sons and a daughter, Mickey was the only one who lived within three hundred miles of home. He traveled, though. She mainly saw him when he was passing through. That's what he was doing this time, too. She never let on, though. The pressure had gotten to him. He hated himself for times like these. The guilt of not having visited in a while – not even having called in a month – had contributed to his absence. Guilt for staying away made him stay away more. It was inexcusable. Mama, though, she'd excuse anything. She'd endured his daddy. Mickey remembered how his grandmother, rest her soul, had commiserated. "Oh, I just hate it for your mother."

Mickey had told her, "Well, Granny, you're right, but if it's any consolation, my mama manages to be happy. It doesn't matter how bad things get. She finds something good to dwell on."

Mickey couldn't face her without smoking half a joint in the car. This was new. He needed the buzz to tell her of his recent journalistic triumphs, how he was making good money again, and the sky was the limit, and how, for the first time, this website, this Ultimate Sporting Life, had been a godsend. He could write what he wanted, and he'd proven true what he had claimed for decades. He wrote what interested him, relying on the assumption that, if he thought it worthwhile, there would undoubtedly be thousands, maybe even millions, who would like it, too. His modesty pleased her, but she didn't know his prosperity came from dirty money. Mickey was a cool, unflappable marijuana mule. The fact that he could write was a bonus for his employers. Luck was often conditional.

Mama didn't have a cell phone. Mama didn't want one. She just wanted to smoke her cigarettes, drink her coffee, and read her novels. They shared a love of John Steinbeck, and, occasionally, with some time to kill, Mickey would go to a bookstore and look for some old buried gem of Steinbeck's – a book of World War II stories from the front, or a volume of correspondence between Steinbeck and his agent during the writing of *East of Eden* – to bring home to Mama. Together they had discovered the underrated Wallace Stegner, known to most as a teacher of other writers but to Mickey and Mama as better than any he had molded and inspired. Stegner had died in a car wreck, in 1993, and, sitting there, high and contemplative, it occurred that an underrated country singer, Billy Walker, had also died late in life in a traffic accident. It wasn't enough just to live life unappreciated. The poor wretches had to suffer a gruesome death, too.

They talked about "your daddy," long dead now but more lovable than when he had been alive. They'd had the conversation many times.

"Mama, you remember that time when we had those two stud horses break out of the barn and jump the fence?"

"Oh, Lord, yes," she said. "Them two wild things lit out toward town. I can see you and your daddy jumping in the pickup truck and taking off after 'em."

They both started laughing. "Remember? They were having a big drawing in the parking lot of the Piggly Wiggly store, and them two horses come through there, running wide-ass open, and all the people scattered, and me and Daddy tried to catch them, but then they took off through the mill hill, running through clotheslines."

"They'd shit several times right in the middle of Main Street," she said.

"Maybe it was best Daddy died when he did," Mickey said. "They'd th'ow you in jail if that kind of foolishness happened now."

"They th'owed you in jail back then," she said, looking at her son over the top of her reading glasses. "Not your daddy, though."

Cynthia noticed Mickey was getting drowsy. "I expect you need another cup of coffee," she said. "You must be tired from that long drive."

"Aw, I drive twice as far all the time."

It wasn't the drive, Mama. It was the weed.

He drove her to the Fins 'n' Tails, the local fish camp, and they both had the Tuesday-through-Thursday baby shrimp/baby flounder special. Mickey ate voraciously. His mother asked for a box and took half hers home. That night Mickey slept in his old bed. It wasn't as comfortable as he remembered. The next morning, he got up and headed off in the general direction of Shreveport, Louisiana, there to uncover something interesting about one of the players from either Vanderbilt or North Carolina State, likely to be determined by which team won.

She waved goodbye, knowing her son was troubled. Mickey spent Christmas Eve on the road and Christmas Day in a hotel room writing and a Shreveport casino gambling. He cleared a hundred bucks on blackjack and fifty playing the slots. A hundred fifty was nothing next to gambling with an ounce of weed.

Marcia Statler's visit to Mother's was rife with tension. She felt sorry for Rodrigo the Cuban Orthodontist, whom she learned had finally decided to stop living with Vera in sin. Marcia wasn't particularly adept at hiding her feelings, anyway, and being obviously non-plussed at the lovebirds' exciting plans was an obvious buzz kill for overly dramatic Mother. Vera wasn't a Mommy or a Mom. She was a Mother. Icy formality was her most noteworthy virtue. Marcia played the rebellious bohemian to the hilt. She got there stoned and quickly advanced to drunk, pointing out to anyone who would listen that she damned sure couldn't get along with her mother sober. Poor Rodrigo had the thankless task of trying to get along with both. Vicki had the same blasé boyfriend – Case or Chase or Chance, whichever one Marcia used was invariably the wrong one – and when Marcia introduced the possibility of her mother's and sister's getting married at the same time, she was surprised when neither recognized it for the joke it was. They embraced the prospect. It was the only time in the three days she was there that anything she said or did pleased anyone, and it pissed her off that it happened once.

Dylan Wannamacher was thankful that his brother, Fred, and Fred's wife, Jan, were still in Paulette to keep a watch on Violet, his mother, still living in the house on Bosley Circle where he and Fred grew up. His visit was a surprise, which he intended. When he'd left Triborough, Dylan hadn't been sure if he'd make it or not. Word of his modest coaching triumphs had not reached Mississippi. Literary prominence had been common in the Magnolia State, so success in the manly art of football was appreciated more. Mississippians were always looking for a coach who could beat Alabama. Dylan aspired to be Faulkner, but his lifelong friends wished he was Johnny Vaught, or Jackie Sherrill, or anybody who had ever enjoyed some smattering of success against the Crimson Tide. Knowing this, Dylan, who preferred not to discuss the matter of his football coaching where it actually took place, told the family all about it.

It was a welcome break. Dylan, Mama, and Fred sat at the kitchen table, while Jan tended to the newborn, Little Fred, in the den.

"I remember another time I drove home from Virginia," Dylan said. "Fred was playing in the state championship game, he scored the winning points on a two-point conversion, and me and Jordan Crosley got drunk before the game, and when we got there, we filed past you and Daddy, and Daddy was drunk, too, and Grandma Wannamacher was there, and that was the only time in my life that, instead of kissing my grandma, I shook hands with her because I reeked of beer. I came all the way home, and when I saw my grandma, I shook her hand."

"You couldn't stand it that you had a brother who played tailback," Fred said.

"When I played, Fred, my position was what I wanted it to be."

"Oh, okay, I got it."

"I done all right," Dylan said. "Caught thirty-seven passes my senior year, scored twelve touchdowns receiving, which I expect is still the school record."

"Nah," Fred said. "That was before the shotgun and the, what they call it? The air-raid offense. They score twelve touchdowns in two games, and the other teams get nine. I think they had a kid caught nineteen touchdown passes just last year. It's a track meet nowadays."

"Well, when we played, Fred, men were men," Dylan said. "And sheep were nervous."

Dylan was starting to like football again. No good could come from that. Fred asked him if he wanted to go see Southern Miss play in the New Orleans Bowl. Dylan said he'd rather watch Little Fred play in the toilet bowl, which made Fred laugh, Mama turn red, and all of them thankful Jan was out of earshot.

They spent Christmas Eve snacking on boiled peanuts, ham biscuits, and pigs in blankets, and sipping Ancient Times with "spring water." Jan took the baby home at nine, and Fred and Dylan snuck out in the parking lot and smoked a joint. They had been doing this since Fred was seventeen, and the first time was late that night after the state championship game.

"People don't change," Fred said. "They just get too old to keep up with the young'uns."

"Old, hell," Dylan replied. "You and me might as well be, oh, twenty-five again. We got no more sense than when we's eighteen. Ain't nothing changed except our relative health."

When in Paulette, talk as the Pauletteans talked. If Dylan stayed there three more days, he'd sound like Uncle Remus. It was good to see Fred. He didn't have the slightest idea what his brother did for a living. He didn't care. They had better things to talk about stoned. It was the first time they'd seen each other in three years, and what they did then was almost exactly the same.

"I had just about give up football until I got shanghaied into coaching it," Dylan said.

"It's in your blood," Fred said. "You'n bury it, but it ain't never going away."

"Some things never change."

"No," Fred said, "not really."

Amid the tedium of North Carolina State's easy Independence Bowl victory over Vanderbilt, Mickey Statler wrote a feature that paid tribute to it. He lampooned it. The Wolfpack fans probably wouldn't like it, but they'd all read it. Mickey had learned that the best form of criticism was satire. Write in a way that makes the critics look silly responding. The truth of what he'd written was irrefutable. That limited the responses to the profane, the stupid, and the silly. The best the crazies could muster was a variation on the old "everybody does it, but we got caught" or the "how is this any different from what [insert team] did in [insert year]?"

The crazies invariably changed the subject. The sane just held their tongues and quietly plotted the author's assassination.

When he finally got back to North Carolina, Mickey pored over the rules and regulations he had never bothered to read because, in all his other stories, there hadn't been a need. This time, before he polished the story, he transmitted a detailed list of confidential footnotes, divulging to the editor all the identities of the unnamed sources that could not be revealed publicly in the story he was about to send. Mickey hadn't learned his policy on unnamed sources from a textbook. He'd gone to college, but he hadn't majored in journalism. He had four requirements that had been cultivated through trial and error for two decades. To be cited anonymously, a source had to be: (1.) in a position to know, with (2.) nothing to gain, and (3.) revealing his name had to have a catastrophic effect on his job, or his life, or, to boil it down in the manner Mickey was prone to use in a bar, "his ass," and, (4.) what he said had to be true. Mickey was responsible for that.

What he wrote was a story about the rise in marijuana usage among college athletes. He detailed the many athletes who had been suspended "reportedly for a positive marijuana test," the ways many more used knowledge of the process to avoid it, and the way many schools crafted the process in order to assist them. Mickey quoted the players who felt the substance helped them overcome pain, and how it was an informal part of the rehab process because, once they had suffered serious injuries, they weren't subject to drug tests anymore. An assistant coach at a prominent school fretted about how the schools in weed-legal states were getting an edge in recruiting, as detailed in the performances of such teams in football and men's basketball. The conditions of Mickey's employment had made him uniquely qualified to see "the extent of the problem," if, indeed, it was a problem at all. Head coaches, directors of athletics, and officials of the National Collegiate Athletic Association and conferences were sometimes willing to discuss the conditions on the record. Many of the athletes had developed a certain righteous indignation. Some of them were even serious when they referred to cannabis as "medication." All said it wasn't so bad. All said it wasn't as bad as drinking. Some said it was good.

Before he emailed it to The Ultimate Sporting Life, Mickey applied humorous touches like a coat of wax. A basketball player from the Midwest had responded to talk of a medicinal cannabis that had its active components removed so as not to cause impairment by saying that his own head coach popped prescription meds like candy.

"When he got his ass on his shoulders, we all know that prescription be done run out," the player said. "Then they say, if I'm gonna take weed for pain, it's gotta be in a form that don't make you high. Shit. They don't make it that way with Vicodin, Oxycontin, I done had teammates got hooked on that."

Most of them were under 21. Even where cannabis was recreationally legal, it was illegal on campuses. So was alcohol. Weed was easier to get. Dealers never asked for I.D.

Mickey didn't think the website would publish it. He was wrong. It went viral, made the *CBS Morning News*, and they wanted him to be on the show, as did quickly *The Today Show; Good Morning, America;* and *Late Night with Seth Meyers*. Mickey didn't have an agent. He needed one.

All the way home, as Mickey had made his obligatory, slightly out-of-the-way stopovers, he'd imagined himself as Willy Loman in Death of a Salesman. He'd decided to write the piece because he needed to buck up to the infernal system in which had been snared. He'd hoped it would be rejected. He'd hoped it would get him fired. Instead, it seemed to be having the opposite effect. It was good for business, as it turned out.

It put Mickey under scrutiny. He stopped answering the phone. Fortunately, he did see a text from his daughter. Marcia was coming to visit.

The story, on balance, was somewhat neutral, but neutral was uncommon in the journalism of illegal drugs. Most stories were propaganda, one way or another. The Ultimate Sporting Life had previously steered clear of the business its owners intended to master. Mickey's story could only help, but a number of people up and down the chain of command, from Bentsen Lilley to Ronnie Shingler, from Patrick Trintignant to Wade Sanderson, took notice. The problem wasn't what Mickey Statler had written. It was that it hadn't been part of any plan. He was approved to swap briefcases of weed for briefcases of cash. They couldn't quibble with the results of what he had done.

They could only quietly plot his assassination.

Mickey was glad to hear from his daughter that his ex-wife was still maddening. His relationship with Marcia had undergone shock treatment. Mickey was still tingling, but somehow it had made them close again. She breezed in on him with perfect timing. He was exhausted both from the work and the stress of writing the story ("Hypocrisy Abounds with Athletes, Colleges and Weed"), and he shut off his laptop and phone and watched Marcia fire up a joint. She seemed to have no angst lingering from the great Triborough surprise.

She offered it to him. He declined.

"No offense," Mickey said. "I'm trying to cut back."

"Not quit?"

"Not quit. It's too easy. When you drink, there's a price to pay. You wake up the next morning, feeling like hell. If it wasn't for that hangover, you'd do it all the time," Mickey said. "With weed, there ain't no hangover."

"It doesn't last too long. It doesn't make you act like an asshole. It makes you creative. It makes you love the things you like. It's perfect," she responded.

"I'm just getting drug along by the culture shock, Marcia."

"Do you write high? Have you written high?"

"Recently."

"Did you write well?"

"Yeah."

Marcia laughed heartily. "So what's not to like?"

"Too much to like," Mickey said. "In spite of my being your father, I'm the last person who has any business telling you what to do. I'm trying not to, but aren't you worried that something bad is bound to happen? That you and I have gotten ourselves into this huge mess that's out of control and, most importantly, out of our control?"

She lit a cigarette and stared at him.

"No," she said. "Not at all."

Mickey wished he had something to say. He couldn't remember ever being in a worse bargaining position.

Marcia's cell rang.

"Oh, hey," she said. "What's up? … Okay, settle down." Marcia stood up, placed the cigarette between her lips, raised the free hand, and motioned to Mickey that she'd be right back. She stepped out on the balcony – it was cold out there, and she was wearing only a hoodie – and closed the sliding door behind her. Mickey noticed that the hoodie had a silk-screen depiction of someone who was alleged to be "The Poet Laureate of San Francisco." It was obvious that Marcia was having an animated conversation. Mickey got up and made coffee. When he came back, Marcia was hanging up and calling someone else. Finally, she returned, shivering. Mickey had a tray waiting with coffee, sugar, and powdered creamer.

He didn't say anything. She'd tell him if he needed to know.

"It's nothing," she said. "Ooh, coffee's hot. It's good, though. Someone who works for me got busted. It's taken care of. Just had to make a call."

"Who's the woman on the hoodie, Marcia?" he asked, out of the blue.

"A poet. Diane di Prima. One of the few Beat Generation poets who was a woman. She's still alive, believe it or not. In her eighties. I'd love to meet her."

Mickey wished he'd split the joint. He tried to look calm. He wished he had a story to write. Unfortunately, it was more a story to tell.

"Kid went home," Marcia said. "He's a student. He got together with friends. They wanted to know if he knew where they could get some weed. He said 'sure do.' Word must have gotten around. It has a tendency of doing that. Next thing, you know, he got busted at some youth center. You can't get out of your element, off your territory. He knew that. I can't say anything. I sold some to some friends when I was at Mama's. You know what this kid's mistake was?"

"What?"

"They were black people he was with."

"What's wrong with that? I mean, apart from what naturally comes to mind. Uh, racistically, which is likely not a word."

"You didn't raise a bigot, Dad. For white kids from decent families, weed's practically legal now. You know that. The kids Milo was with, they'll get off, too, because, at least, by God, *they were with a white kid. They must be decent kids, too."*

"Milo," Mickey said. "That's the name of the kid who plays quarterback for Enlightened Word Academy. Surely not him."

"Yeah," Marcia said. "There's not a buttload of Milos running around."

"And his coach? Dylan Wannamacher?"

"Oh, no, Dylan's got nothing to do with it. Honest. That's just a coincidence. Besides, I haven't seen him in, oh, couple weeks, maybe. I mean, I met Milo through Dylan, but, no, he's just a cool guy. I love him, kind of, you know, literarily."

"Oh, yeah," Mickey said. "Literary love. The best kind."

If all of what Marcia said about the mystical and soul-enriching qualities was true, Mickey needed a joint.

"How'd you like a drink, Marcia?"

"I'll tell you what, Daddy. You split a J with me. I'll have a drink with you."

"It's a weekend," he said.

"Thursday," she said

"Close enough."

CHAPTER 38

Milo Come Lately

Dylan Wannamacher came back from Mississippi depressed at having left it. He couldn't remember the last time he'd enjoyed home. Now it seemed the fleeing had been in vain. It had been good to see Mama, good to see Fred, good to experience football again. The past didn't seem so painful.

Also, he had no weed. He'd left what he had with Fred. Surely, Jan wouldn't find out. Dylan didn't want to be responsible for a divorce. Fred was a grown man, though. That meant he knew how to hide his vices. He knew the principle of "don't ask, don't tell." Jan wouldn't know because Jan wouldn't want to know.

Dylan couldn't sleep. It was vexing. He had to confront the notion that cannabis might be his crutch. He sat in his darkened apartment, brooding about causes and effects. It was an issue he must confront. Did that morning bong hit, that routine of going to Enlightened Word high and then returning to the comfort of its charm each night, assuage his depression or aggravate it? The thrill of victory had worn off. He felt trapped in futile existence.

He wished he could teach, but school didn't resume till Tuesday. He read in the paper that Enlightened Word was playing in some holiday tournament in Richmond. He thought about self-publishing his first novel, the one that had been rewritten the most, because at least then it would be out there. Enough people would read it to have him boiled in oil or placed in stocks on the public square. As long as he could piss a few people off, it might make him happy.

At the moment, though, Dylan couldn't do anything productive. All he could do was think. He tried to play his guitar, but his mind was so dulled that he couldn't remember half his own lyrics. Supposedly, that was what weed did. Also, apparently, vice-versa.

Around noon, Milo Hirley sent a text message, asking if he could come over. Milo had never come over before, but Dylan didn't mind the company and was interested in what Milo had been doing. He gave him directions to Hippie Arms and gave him the apartment number.

When Milo arrived, Dylan realized almost immediately there was something he didn't know. He thought Milo might be high. That wasn't what surprised him. Milo didn't say he'd done anything wrong.

"It's like everything else, I reckon," Milo said. "It was because of a girl I knew. We just bumped into each other outside the mall in Virginia Beach. She was sitting on a slab of concrete near the entrance, smoking a cigarette. I didn't even know she smoked. I walked up and asked her if I could bum one, and we got to talking, and one thing led to another. … Anyway, I was hoping Miss, uh, Statler, would be here."

Something had happened, something Milo thought Dylan knew. Dylan had no desire to know whatever it was. He changed the subject.

"I just got back from a few days at home myself," Dylan said. "I'm not sure, but I think she went home, too. Visiting her folks. Did you know the writer who was here last week, who wrote about our team and that game for that website – Ultimate Sports something or other – was Marcia's father?"

"No. Not at all."

"He didn't know it, either. I mean, he didn't know we were friends. He stopped by before he left, and we had a nice chat. Seemed like a nice fellow. Hell of a writer, too."

"That might've been the best story I ever read about a losing team," Milo said. "I might be a tad prejudiced."

"Yeah. We'd have won, though, if the weather hadn't been so damned rotten. Lashley could've put it off a day, but they played in that weather because they thought it would hurt us more than them. It didn't. We just made a couple mistakes early, and that cost us. We dominated the game in every other way."

"And, yet, you still not gonna coach no more."

"Probably not," Dylan said. "Hell, they probably won't even ask me. I been home. I wish I hadn't told my mama and my brother about it. They were tickled to death. I did enjoy it, but I like my life the way it was before, too. Right now I want to get back to normal."

"Well, I ain't gonna be around," Milo said. "I do wish you'd keep on coaching the team. You taught us a lot in an awful little time. If you coach, I'll violate my rule and come back and see you. I been swearing for two years I'd never set foot on the EW campus again if I could get myself graduated."

"What's next?"

"I was thinking about Old Dominion, but it wouldn't do me no good to go to school at home. There'd be no peace from my old man, and I probably need to be away from there as much now as when I came here."

"I checked my email this morning," Dylan said. "I got an inquiry about you from the University of Richmond."

"What? D'you tell him I'd be a great quarterback and, besides, they wouldn't have no problems keeping the team supplied with deadly marijuana?" Milo laughed. He was definitely high.

"Well, I haven't replied just yet, but don't worry. I think your virtues greatly outweigh your vices."

"I appreciate that. I mean, now that we're not involved in a player-coach relationship, and since you want to get back to normal, I don't reckon you'd like to split a 'J'?"

"No, sir, Milo. That wouldn't do. I think teaching you English is just as important as teaching you football. Be careful, will you?"

"You mind if I smoke a cigarette? I'm dying for one."

"Go ahead. The rules in the classroom aren't quite as restrictive as the football field."

Marlboro Reds. Good God.

"I gotta go in a minute," Milo said. "I'm back on the team. Take the bus down to Richmond. We got a game at seven. Or seven-thirty. Somewhere's around there."

"Don't be surprised if you run into somebody who looks like a coach wearing a Spiders jacket."

"I'm gon' need somebody to pay my way through school. My dad says he'll put me through Old Dominion but only if I live at home. I ain't got no home, Dylan."

Dylan smiled. "I'll pray for you."

"You sure you won't split a joint? I find it's real good for my spiritual life."

They laughed at the mutual sacrilege.

"I don't even have any," Dylan said.

"Oh, I can fix that." Milo reached in his letter jacket pocket. "You take this. I got plenty."

"No, damn you!"

Milo got up, pulled out his little zip-lock bag, and stashed it behind the stereo on the rack next to the television set, where the sound was muted on an infomercial about some oven that apparently made chicken delicious, succulent, and juicy.

"Throw it away, if you must," he said. "Give it to Miss Statler. Tell her I 'preciate what she's done for me."

Never mind the absurdity of leaving a gift of weed to the woman who was providing it. Milo just wanted to make sure Dylan had it.

"What'd she do for you, Milo?"

He stopped. Obviously, it was something he thought Dylan knew.

"Oh, nothing," he said. "She's gone out of her way being nice to me and Walt and Marty and Jonny. She's a good lady. I gotta go get my ass straightened out and play some ball in Richmond. I'm sorry I'm late on Merry Christmas."

He walked out the door before Dylan could inquire further on what he was talking about.

Dylan got up and locked the door. He sat back down, picked up the remote control, and tried in vain to find quality television programming. After about five minutes of rumination, he popped a K-cup into the coffee maker, fetched Milo's weed and his own bong and smoked himself a moderate bowl. He played a little guitar while his coffee cooled. He sipped it and thought a bit.

Stiller McGwire wasn't selling weed to the Enlightened Word football team on the side. Marcia Statler was.

CHAPTER 39

Intentionally Vague

Bentsen Lilley had some important news to share with Patrick Trintignant. He summoned the Consortium's propaganda expert to the chalet in the Rockies because, he said, what he had to tell him was so important that it had to be communicated face-to-face.

When Trintignant arrived, Lilley greeted him at the door, and when they walked into his study, sent the housekeeping personnel home for the rest of the day. Just to be safe, he locked the doors and got right to the point.

"Patrick, I've talked to the president-elect."

"In person?"

"In the flesh," Lilley said. "I spoke with Mr. Gaynes frankly. He lived up to his reputation as a deal maker. Gaynes promised me that Edmund Kingsley will be the next director of the FBI."

"That's wonderful news."

"Would you care for a cigar, Patrick? Soon to be president Gaynes presented to me a box of Cubans. He said he was going to reinstitute the Cuban restriction on trade, but this wouldn't affect him, he said, because he had been conducting business with the Castro regime for a decade or more. Now that the dictator is dead, and Gaynes is soon to be president, reinstituting the trade embargo will only eliminate competition from other American companies.”

“Gaynes doesn’t plan to give up his business activities as president?” Trintignant asked.

“No. He’s dividing it between his three adult sons. He thinks his business is going to boom, and it would be foolish to give up the advantage of being president of the United States,” Lilley said. “He’s not ever going to release his taxes, either. I have made a deal with Mr. Gaynes that will be mutually beneficial.”

“And this involves the Consortium? This involves legal weed?”

“Precisely.”

“And how does this jibe with the intense, public opposition of the attorney general?”

“Yes,” Lilley said. “Martin Jerald Gaynes informed me that, if we were worried about the legal opposition of the Justice Department as run by Nathan Beale, we should get rid of him.”

“Get rid of him?”

“Get rid of him.”

“What does that mean, Bentsen?”

“The president-elect didn’t specify. What I take it to mean is that we should use the information Kingsley has acquired to derail his Senate confirmation. If that fails, it might require another means.”

“That ... being?”

“Senator Beale has visited me here before. Pending confirmation, of course, he remains a sitting senator from a state that has one of the higher smoking rates in the Union,” Lilley said. “While negotiating with him regarding the tobacco industry, I paid for a family skiing vacation, and, while his wife and kids were enjoying themselves on the slopes near Aspen, I flew him up here. As I recall, after quite a few bourbons and a night of pleasure, he referred to himself as ‘a cash-and-carry Christian.’ The next day, when he left, he informed me that he would have to be sensitive to his evangelical base in Mississippi. In all the years since, we haven’t talked, but I haven’t forgotten that Senator Beale, in effect, subsequently reneged on our agreement. I don’t think he has forgotten that he double-crossed me and the rest of the tobacco industry in the interest of a reelection campaign in which he won seventy-one percent of the vote. I believe, with the president's urging, he might feel obligated to get back in my good graces."

"So, a man known nationally for his deep opposition to marijuana legalization is going to change his view?"

"Either that," Lilley said, "or he will face rejection by the august body in which he presently sits."

"That seems like a long shot," Trintignant said.

"It is. Failing that, well, let's just say that the Federal Bureau of Investigation, and it's soon-to-be director, our friend Edmund Kingsley, in particular, is rather adept at liquidation. The Central Intelligence Agency is more noted for its knack in that area, but … they've been known to work together and hide each other's … indiscretions."

"As in, assassination."

"Oh, let's not use that untidy term," Lilley said. "Let's just say the FBI is in a position to arrive at a conclusion that no such thing occurred. Do you want me to be more specific?"

"No. I'll leave that to you and Edmund."

"I hope it doesn't come to that, Patrick, but such an important problem requires a solution with several contingencies."

"These cigars are exquisite, Bentsen."

"Yes. I'm rather fond of them."

The sheriff of Triborough County always did his homework. He entrusted reactive police work to his staff but participated personally in planned operations. In his recent reelection campaign, he had coordinated the normal publicity stunts. Round up the hopeless drug addicts that he could arrest any day of the week. Cite their arrests as a great advance against the pernicious effect of the organized criminals who were corrupting the minds of the young. When his deputies erred, when they acted overzealously, when they shot down innocent men and women, and when no other explanation was credible, B.F. "Popcorn" Quinne had always called them "the result of a drug deal gone bad."

His most trustworthy deputy, Lorne Antony, did the homework and proposed a plan. Popcorn was generous to Lorne, who was like a son. Lorne had learned what most policemen do. A man couldn't make a living on his salary. He ate for free. He drank for free. He got his share of the take Popcorn derived from protecting the Consortium. Hundreds, maybe even thousands, of law enforcement officials benefited from turning a blind eye to certain criminals and harassing others. The Consortium was big business and above indulging the annoyance of independent drug dealers. Popcorn particularly wanted to come along on this particular mission because it was not his intention for the suspect to survive the raid.

"What say I buy you supper tonight?" Mickey Statler asked when he caught Rashawn Ling at the *News-Free Press* offices.

"I think I can make it. I got the Tar Heels and the Wolfies in Chapel Hill tomorrow. Anything up?"

"Oh, I just wanted to catch up." Mickey didn't trust that his phone was secure. "Let's see. I'll pick you up outside the office at seven. I haven't been inside since they laid me off, and I'm not particularly interested in giving them the opportunity to tell me how glad they are that I landed on my feet, and how they knew I wouldn't have any trouble finding a new job, and how, you know, it was probably a good thing in hindsight. They've got no fucking idea. They tried to ruin me and damn near succeeded."

The two sportswriters, one white as the Mayflower Compact and the other African-Chinese American, met at Lovejoy/Killjoy, a sports bar that specialized in wings, nachos, and craft beer. By the standards of the community, it was as exotic as Rashawn was.

Mickey wanted to drink. He trusted Rashawn. He wasn't afraid of a loose tongue. He was proud of it.

The beers were Carolinas-themed. Carolina Wren. Carolina Moon. Sassafras Mountain. Grand Strand. Outer Bank. Pilot Mountain. Caesar's Head. Kitty Hawk. Durham Bull. Cold Mountain. Queen City. Pee Dee. Mickey started working his way through the list with a Kitty Hawk. Rashawn had a Caesar's Head. They ordered two dozen wings, half hot and half garlic parmesan.

"Rashawn, there ain't five people in this whole town I trust," Mickey said. "One of them's the mailman. I used to trust a barber, but Jimmie Lee

Williamson passed away. There certainly ain't nobody else at the *News-Free Press*. Does Jon David McMahan still go straight to the I.T. when he walks in the door."

"Five o'clock budget meeting every day, eyes red as a wolf," Rashawn replied. "If they didn't lock that place up at seven, we'd be putting out some funky sports pages."

Mickey took a healthy slug of his Kitty Hawk and remembered one of J.D.'s headlines. "Fatal accident didn't stop Dunn."

It had been the story of a snow skier who had recovered from an avalanche.

"How about that time he ran mug shots of the five Lovejoy High basketball starters right above an A.P. story about a gambling scandal? 'Five indicted in point-shaving probe.' I had to cover the Llamas that night," Rashawn recalled.

"Ah, the good old days," Mickey said. "As it turns out, I'm one to talk."

"Toking up on the road, are you?"

"Rashawn, what would you give to get out of this town? To break a story so big that it would have other papers begging for you to come to work for them?"

Rashawn motioned to the waitress that he needed a refill. "I've already offered the *Herald-Examiner* my left nut. I'd hate to give up both of them."

"This isn't a sports story, Rashawn. This is a news story. A big one," Mickey said.

PART FOUR
WORLDWIDE IMPLICATIONS

CHAPTER 40

Coincidences

"If I could play every club like a fairway wood, I'd be a pro," Patrick Trintignant said to his frequent caddy, Wade Sanderson, as he stood over the ball on the seventh fairway of Torrey Pines' North Course. Trintignant made solid contact but opened his club face on impact. The ball curled majestically into the ravine that separated North course from South.

"You may never hit one farther," Wade said. "It's still bouncing. The canyon may funnel it clear into the Pacific."

Trintignant dropped another, rolled his wrists as he swung through, and watched the ball land on the green.

"Who's counting?" he asked aloud.

"Not I, Pat," Wade said.

Today they were partners. Wade could, in fact, play more than fairway woods proficiently. They were not there for golf, though it was a lovely place to play. They were there to plan and conspire. Wade had become a troubleshooter for the Consortium. Trintignant admired the unemotional dispatch with which he had liquidated his onetime friend, Tripp Fallaw. Tripp's remains were likely in the bellies of several different sharks that had fought over him in the warm waters off Baja California.

Wade played a five-iron just left of the green.

"Tripp, how would you like to take a trip back east?" Trintignant asked.

"Where 'bouts?"

"Virginia. Triborough, Virginia."

"I have a friend there," Wade said.

"Yes," Trintignant said. "Marcia Statler. Are you familiar with Mickey Statler?"

"The sportswriter?"

"Yes. Marcia is his daughter."

Trintignant two-putted for a tainted par. Wade chipped on, missed a four-foot putt, and scored five.

When they returned to the cart, Trintignant said to Wade, "Here. You might want to hit this vape again."

The eighth hole, a par-three, was backed up a bit. Trintignant stopped shy of the other carts. One foursome was still waiting to tee off, and the next would wait still longer until those in front completed the hole. Trintignant was a V.I.P. at the prestigious municipal course near San Diego. A twosome headed by Trintignant was allowed, even though the rules said it had to be four.

"That little coincidence – the girl being the writer's daughter – had eluded us," Trintignant said. "We might have a problem there. Maybe not. You're close to Marcia Statler. I want you to find out."

"Yeah, I'll do it. When you want me there?"

"Oh, as soon as you arrange it. Week, maybe?"

"That'll work. You just want me to find out what the deal is?" Tripp asked.

"For now. Here's the rub. Okay, on one side, we may have gone a bit too far involving the troublesome competitor Miss Statler complained to you about. We have an arrangement with the sheriff of Triborough County. He set up the dealer – I believe his name was Brynildson Hiers – and, uh, shot him. It's a rural county, and no one made a big deal of it, but he had been a janitor at a nearby school where Marcia Statler had established a network, and the kids there – and, apparently, Marcia, as well – had worked out their problems with Mr. Hiers and became a bit traumatized upon his demise."

"That's kind of a ridiculous overreaction."

"Agreed," Trintignant said, "but instructions get garbled, and people try to impress their bosses, and sometimes, it's just overkill, forgive the pun, but let me you about the other side of the story. A journalist from North Carolina, Rashawn Ling, has been, uh, snooping around and seems to have some knowledge of how the Consortium operates."

"I guess you're going to tell me that Rashawn Ling is half-Chinese, half-black?"

"Yes. Yet another coincidence, of sorts," Trintignant replied. "Mr. Ling was interested in collaborating on the story with a journalist in New York named Myra LeFlore. Fortunately for us, and unfortunately for Mr. Ling, Miss LeFlore is affiliated with us. She writes on a semi-regular basis at Tignant.com."

"I see," Wade said. "Just out of curiosity, Pat, why is it Tignant.com and not Trintignant.com?"

"Oh, Trintignant is too unwieldy, and Tignant was originally a slang term for 'totally ignorant,' the idea being that it's what the ideas of the Left are. Mickey Statler is the best-known columnist at our affiliated sports site, The Ultimate Sporting Life. Mr. Statler recently wrote a piece, a very well-received piece, on the increasing use of marijuana among college and professional athletes, and the fact that many consider cannabis a useful alternative to pharmaceuticals in managing the pain inherent in their sports."

"That's good, right?"

"Yes," Trintignant said, "but it was unauthorized. That, in itself, is just an interesting sidelight. Mickey Statler and Myra LeFlore have little connection and, apparently, little regard for each other. The final coincidence, rather, is that Mickey Statler and Rashawn Ling worked as recently as six months ago on the same newspaper staff, the *Lovejoy News-Free Press*. We can deal with Mr. Ling through the auspices of an associate who is a county deputy sheriff. What I need you to do is investigate the situation involving Mickey Statler, his daughter, and whatever is going on in Virginia."

"I met Marcia through Tripp Fallaw," Wade said. "He brought her out here with him, and then he proceeded to get wasted, lose money he didn't have, steal a car from my neighbor down the street, steal Marcia's money, go on the lam, and leave her stranded. She's sharp, way above Tripp's class, but she just came with him for the adventure, I guess. Her mother's boyfriend – I think he's, like, a Cuban dentist – sent her a plane ticket and money to get home. I offered Marcia a chance to make some money selling weed at Triborough College, where she had enrolled, and, about two weeks, maybe a month, later, she took me up on it. Her mom and dad must be divorced. That's why I never thought about her last name."

"Clearly, Wade, you're the man for the job," Trintignant said. "It's not a big thing, but we need to take care of it before it develops into a problem. We've got some major operations underway in Washington with the Gaynes Administration, and we don't need any inconvenient scandals to undermine what we're trying to accomplish."

The North Course had recently been renovated, but it was the more prestigious South Course that was scheduled to host the United States Open in 2021. Wade shot seventy eight; Trintignant carded an eighty-three. Wade returned to Los Angeles that night and booked a flight to Reagan International. Trintignant crossed the border into Mexico to meet with Russian officials regarding plans to discredit the Attorney General of the United States, Nathan Bedford Forrest Beale, the erstwhile junior senator from Mississippi.

Before he left for Ensenada, Trintignant told Wade that the new president was a man without principle.

"We'd be in big trouble if he wasn't," he said. "The only problem is Beale. Gaynes is on our side, but he won't put a stop to Beale. He told Bentsen to take care of it and gave him some contacts. Bentsen told me. I'm going to see 'em. I enjoyed the round, Wade. Once we get this matter taken care of, cannabis will be legal in several more states – Arizona, New Mexico, Montana, at least – by the end of 2018. Two years later, a good chunk of the Midwest, and Texas, maybe. It's going to make you a very rich man, Wade. You'll do what it takes to get things done. We don't have many associates as reliable and resourceful as you. The next time we see each other, I'll have something big. Just take care of this little security glitch right now."

"Yes, sir, Pat. I'm thankful for your confidence."

CHAPTER 41

The Incidental Trap

Dad, am in trouble. Need your help. Know yer busy but ... can u come see me asap?

Mickey Statler knew his daughter would not "text" him lightly. She was self-reliant. She had sided with him during the break-up with Vera. Patti, the older daughter, wouldn't speak to him. The shocking encounter in the Triborough hotel room had begun Mickey's change. Guilt overcame him. He had not drawn Marcia into the cannabis trade. She had gone there on her own. She hadn't been blackmailed. She wasn't his fault, not directly, but she was his responsibility. He could absolve himself of specific blame, but Marcia, he felt, was an exposure of his own flawed morals. Mickey should have raised a daughter who would have been immune to such temptations. He wouldn't have minded had Marcia smoked the occasional joint. He'd have preferred better ways for her to work her way through school. As he tried to get up the nerve to call his daughter back, he considered whether or not prostitution would have been better than pushing weed. No. Heroin would have been worse. Painkillers. Cocaine on a bad day. Weed was bad, but whoring was worse.

They had that going for them.

Mickey packed a suitcase and prepared to hit the road. Marcia was back at Hippie Arms with Dylan Wannamacher, who sensed their affair had run its course. She was with him now because her daddy wasn't there, and he was on his way. Milo Hirley was there, too, highly alarmed.

Brynildson Hiers was dead, shot down by the police, allegedly because he fled when they attempted to arrest him. Milo didn't believe it for an instant. Bryne was the sweetest fellow at Triborough. He'd never gotten rich selling weed to the Merry Pranksters. He did it more because he was just a big kid himself, and they were his buddies. Milo regretted complaining about Bryne to Marcia Statler because the only way his murder could have happened – and Milo had no doubt it was murder – had to have been that Marcia complained about Bryne being in her way. Marcia didn't believe she had anything to do with it. She had only mentioned Bryne's name once, to Wade Sanderson, by telephone. He was in L.A. She hadn't said get rid of him. She had just said he was a problem. The notion that he had been murdered by the cops because he was getting in the way of the Consortium – Wade had used that term – was ridiculous. If they had a nobody like Brynildson Hiers killed for no reason other than making complaints that were mildly annoying, why, they'd have to be doing it everywhere.

Like that could be true.

Still, the sparse evidence, shared by a pair of conspirators, was that one had engaged Brynildson Hiers in a small disagreement, mentioned it in passing to the other, and Bryne was, perhaps as a result, dead. Milo wrung his hands and proclaimed that there was no problem, that Bryne had come around and taken his own place in the conspiracy, and everyone was happy until the cops executed Bryne, and, in Milo's mind, there could be no doubt of that. Smoking weed had been fun. Selling it had been fun. Somehow it had gotten more serious than Marcia and Milo could imagine.

Or Dylan. He had nothing to do with Bryne's death. He knew him. He liked him. Dylan hadn't even sold any pot. He had purchased it, though not from Bryne. He had smoked it. He had condoned whatever he didn't want to know that was taking place around him. He didn't have as much blood on his hands, but there was a little. Dylan let Marcia and Milo get emotional. He wondered how he ever let himself get into such a mess. They yelled and cried. Dylan was unsparing to himself. He was just another man who got himself in trouble because he couldn't keep his dick in his pants.

Marcia felt backed in a corner. It wasn't possible that an offhand remark of hers to "an associate" in California had led to his death. Milo wouldn't let it drop. He cried unashamedly and talked repeatedly about how Brynildson Hiers had been a kind, gentle man, one who "never hurt nobody," and now he was dead for no good reason. Bryne hadn't been a pusher. He was a happy-go-lucky man who liked the kids at Enlightened Word, liked smoking with them, and made a little money on the side by selling it. What Milo and Marcia had done was no better and likely worse. Why weren't they dead?

"What'd you think?" Milo asked Marcia. "Kill or be killed?"

Dylan tried to make some sense of the overheated rigamarole. All in all, he was numb and wanted to get number, so he pulled out the bong, still located conveniently underneath the lamp table next to his recliner. While Milo attacked Marcia, and she played defense, Dylan ripped away at some weed. The fragrance drifted into the nostrils of the other two and brought their discussion to a halt.

"Dylan," Milo said, "I've never actually seen you get high before."

"It's the first time in quite a while," he replied. "I just needed some relief from listening to y'all bicker."

"Hallelujah," Marcia said.

"Weed ain't never made nobody murder nobody else," Dylan said.

Wade Sanderson flew from Los Angeles to D.C. via Delta, fidgety and tense with exhilaration. He was a player in the Consortium. He had rid the world of Tripp Fallaw and done so with dispatch. Crime wasn't hard with the cooperation of the cops. He had pursued Tripp with patience and without pity. Vengeance was his, but it wasn't really personal. The world would do without Tripp, and no one would bother much with his disappearance. No one knew he was dead. He was just gone, allegedly wandering somewhere in the wilds of Mexico, where drug dealers and junkies went to hide and die. The man whose cell Tripp had stolen wouldn't miss him. Neither would the bitch who had been Tripp's final one-night stand. She'd likely been pissed off at his disappearance, but she didn't think he was dead. She thought he was just the latest to have screwed her brains out and fled at the specter of commitment. Tripp's family had disowned him. They didn't know where he was. The only person on earth who still cared about Tripp Fallaw was Marcia Statler, and she was who Wade was flying to see. If Marcia got all weepy-eyed and emotional about Tripp's whereabouts, Wade would just have to figure out a cool, calm way to kill her, too. First, though, he would screw Marcia's brains out. He envisioned himself snapping her graceful neck with his bare hands. Imagining it aroused him. He didn't have the cops to cover for him in Virginia, though the local sheriff was on the take. He couldn't do it spontaneously. Another nice, clinical heroin overdose would work best, but Wade had already done that once. Strangulation was too detectable. So was just snapping that neck like a boss. He'd love to shoot somebody, but it was the messiest of all. These people back east – Marcia, her sportswriter dad, the hotshot kid from the private school – had friends, lovers, loved ones. Mickey Statler was somewhat famous. They all were defenseless, but Tripp Fallaw had no defenders. Wade took pride in the realization that he could murder and even fancied himself as having earned that right. He didn't have *carte blanche*. He had to be cool. He couldn't just kill them all. He had to determine whether or not it was necessary for the Consortium. He had to fix the problem if there was one. Many people went through life with quirks buried deep in their brains. With most, it stayed there. In Wade's soul, the banshees had escaped and wanted to play. On the three-hour flight, he never spoke to the businessman sitting next to him in first class. Wade had three gins and tonics with metal blaring through his ear buds. The excitement of the music, and the booze, and an appetite to kill, caused his hair to start sweating. He needed to chill. He removed a zippered portfolio from the pouch behind the seat in front of him. He had a brownie wrapped in wax paper, one that was fortified with relaxing kush. He nibbled it intermittently, consuming half. Still, he couldn't sleep.

Wade's heart was black, bereft of feeling and any semblance of decency.

Milo Hirley missed Brynildson Hiers and mourned his loss, but not as much as Peter Baxter.

Peter had never been prescribed Adderall. He had discovered it. He had wanted to be an overachiever. Adderall made him *over-everything*. It had made him an unbearable bastard who usually got his way with people who just didn't care enough to stop him. Ambition fueled him. He had discovered the stimulant because his sophomore roommate at Enlightened Word had been prescribed it to treat ADHD, Attention deficit/hyperactivity disorder. Peter had persuaded the aptly named Allan Quirk to let him try it. The drug allowed Peter to realize his dreams. He made straight A's, tried out for and won the lead in every drama presentation, played sports, debated, led the National Honor Society and wrote editorials for the online school paper, The Electronic Word. No one liked him. No one cared enough to stop him.

Allan had needed Adderall. Adderall had helped Allan. Peter started stealing Allan's Adderall, at first just to cram all night before tests. Then, over Thanksgiving holidays, Peter discovered that his father took a drug called Allopurinol to combat gout. The tablets looked like Allan's Addies. Lorne Baxter's gout worsened. The pills in his second bottle were shaped differently. They were ovals with recesses on each side. They came from packages of PEZ, a candy whose name was derived from letters in the German word for "peppermint." It took seven packs for Allen to gather enough orange PEZ's to fill his father's prescription bottle. Back at school, Allan Quirk grew more and more morose. On the evening of March 24, 2015, he committed suicide by hanging himself. Allan was only five-foot-four. He had run a rope across the top of the bunk. When he dropped from the side opposite the knot, the jerk of the fall caused the other end of the bunk bed to rise into the air. Allan almost stopped to try again or give up, but he gathered his legs under him and pushed, almost jumped, up. This time the end of the bed held. An astonishingly dumb way to kill himself worked.

Peter found the body. A newly arrived manila envelope sat on Allan's desk. Had he opened it, and taken a dose of the Adderall contained within, he may not have killed himself, but he didn't. Peter took the bottle, put it in his pocket, carefully looked both ways, crept down the hall, and dropped the envelope down the trash chute. He returned to the room, took the bottle with Allopurinol, and hid it in the pocket of his school blazer. Then Peter called nine-one-one.

As a side note, Lorne Baxter's gout got better. As another, the coroner of Triborough County, who was by profession a veterinarian, noticed an absence of uric acid in the body of Allan Quirk, though he failed to mention it in the autopsy. It was suicide, open and shut case.

Peter's next source became a shady character at Triborough College, Tripp Fallaw, whom he found lurking around the frat houses. A political science professor had the last name Baxter. When the frat kids told Peter to get lost, he dropped Dr. Sterling Baxter's name, and they let him be. The fraternities were under constant fire from the administration. No one was going to fuck with a professor's son. Tripp had offered to set up Peter to peddle some weed at Enlightened Word, but, then, Tripp disappeared. His cell phone was disconnected. On Fraternity Row, a Pi Kap told Peter the word was that Tripp had taken off to California, maybe to get away from the local law, because ... wink, wink ... nudge, nudge ... Tripp had been "into everything."

The reliability of the local illegal drug trade Peter found disturbing.

The Merry Pranksters would have nothing to do with Peter. They thought him an insufferable ass. Peter had eavesdropped on them in the football locker room and deciphered their code. He soon figured out they were buying marijuana from Brynildson Hiers. Peter approached Bryne and told him the jig was up unless Bryne could find him Adderall. Bryne said he didn't know how to get it. Peter said he'd better find a way. Bryne did.

Now Bryne was dead, and Peter missed him for purely selfish reasons.

Addies made Peter feel like Superman. Without them, he felt poisoned by Kryptonite. He couldn't stay awake. He fumbled lines at play practice. Teachers asked to see him after class and dressed him down for falling asleep in class. Peter didn't care. He just mumbled something about being a bit under the weather. He said he'd go to the infirmary. When he got back to the room, he went back to sleep. On Thursday, Peter skipped classes altogether and told his roommate, Eli Shouse, to say he was sick. Peter made play practice. Then he walked from the playhouse to Vissage Pizza, where he commanded Mel to fix him an entire pot of coffee. The coffee gave him a bit of a boost, as much from its heat as its stimulative qualities, but it also made his stomach queasy, so Peter ordered a club sandwich, fiddled with his phone, and quaffed more coffee.

Raw emotion turned quietly sorrowful once Dylan, Marcia, and Milo got stoned. Dylan and Milo talked about Ken Kesey's novel *Sometimes a Great Notion*, which Dylan found difficult, undisciplined, and brilliant. Marcia seemed disinterested, though she professed a great love of Beat Generation writers and had, in fact, dubbed Dylan and his friends the Merry Pranksters. They hit Dylan's bong several more times, and the emotion of Bryne Hiers' suspicious, implausible death subsided in Milo's delight at finally getting high with his literary mentor. Marcia didn't try to hide her boredom, but she was grateful Dylan had managed to change the mood from angry to philosophical.

"Shit, man," Dylan said. "Bryne's gone. I can't believe it. It's bullshit, you know?"

When Marcia's cell rang, she couldn't wait to answer it. She walked out in the hall for privacy and returned in a hurry, gathering up her jacket and purse, making sure she didn't leave her cigarettes and saying the call was from an out-of-town friend who wanted to meet her for dinner. Dylan could see in her eyes that the caller wasn't a woman, the purpose wasn't a meal, and the aspiration was sex. Marcia liked to screw, and she didn't like doing it with him as much as she once had. Marcia left, and the literary conversation with Milo petered out soon afterward. He said he had to get back to Enlightened Word. He had basketball practice at seven-thirty because that's what time the next night's game was. It would be his last if they didn't win it. It must not be a strenuous practice, Dylan thought, as Milo left, still high if not stoned.

"Be careful, hotshot," Dylan said.

"I'm good to go," Milo said. "No worries. I got all kinds of time to straighten up."

Marcia met Wade Sanderson at the same bar where she had met Tripp Fallaw. She had been yearning to see him for months. Wade was a winner. Tripp was a loser, a two-bit hustler who'd leave his lover stranded on the other end of the country without a second thought. She couldn't hate him, though. It's just that Wade excited her just as much, and he was all business. He'd take her places. Tonight would be to bed. Of that, she was certain. He made her wait. She drank two beers and stepped outside for a cigarette. When she walked back in, he was there. It looked as if she had made *him* wait. Just as well. It gave her the façade of control.

Wade said he'd been looking forward to some real food ever since he got on the plane and ordered a greasy bacon cheeseburger with fries and cole slaw. He said the people in California tried so hard to be healthy that they'd forgotten what it was like to eat something that tasted good. Marcia said she was tired of greasy burgers and ordered a Caesar salad. She knew the waitress from school, and they chatted briefly. Wade took in everything. Being seen with someone who knew Marcia made it more difficult to kill her, not that he was going to do so. He wanted to kill somebody, but this wasn't Santa Catalina Island, and he couldn't order up a police aircraft to land at some nearby strip and dispose of her body. His job was to evaluate the situation and take the appropriate action, and it wasn't a question of whether or not Marcia was a threat to the Consortium. The question was about her father. He might have gone off the reservation because of the realization Marcia was in the same business he was. He might not have. It might all be a harmless matter. Brynildson Hiers had been a harmless matter. He was dead.

When Wade told her that Brynildson had been murdered by the cops, and it was a gigantic mixup and breakdown, she got chills up and down her spine because she knew she bore some responsibility. She tried to hide the well of emotion. When a pitcher of beer arrived, Wade asked her if she'd like to do a shot, and she said "hell, yes" because booze was a great way to suppress sorrow. She asked him if there was any news on Tripp, and Wade stared right into her eyes and said he didn't know anything. She was more than willing to let it drop. She forgot that her father was almost surely trying to reach her. The phone was set on "vibrate," but it was in the purse, and she didn't want any distractions.

Distraction did not mar the subsequent proceedings. The night became a blur of *déjà vu.* The bar where she had first met Tripp. Wade took her back to the hotel where she had unexpectedly crossed paths with her father. Wade was rough with her. Theirs was a tryst of long-term anticipation. Coitus required little preparation. He banged her unromantically because thoughts of violence fueled his thrusts. He thought impulsively of snapping that slender neck. Imagined it. Seriously considered it. Barely suppressed the murderous instinct growing in his soul. From her perspective, it was exhilarating and dangerous, but she suspected no danger. She thought she gave him all she had to give.

Mickey Statler couldn't get his daughter to answer her cell. He couldn't get her to reply to his texts. He hit the road early in the morning, not knowing where she was in Triborough but just that she was apparently there. Why would she send an urgent text and then not reply?

When it occurred to him that he still had the number of the Enlightened Word football coach in his phone, Mickey pulled off I-85 near Burlington, North Carolina, at a truck stop and remembered that the coach's name was Dylan Wannamacher. When he got no answer, Mickey realized that the coach was undoubtedly teaching class. He left a message and a text.

Mickey was crossing the Virginia line when Dylan called back and said Marcia wasn't at his place at the moment but he was expecting her back later that night. He said Marcia wasn't in any danger, but things were out of sorts, and it was too complicated to explain on the phone. Dylan gave Mickey the Hippie Arms address and said come on over when he got to Triborough.

Peter Baxter, picking at his club sandwich but devouring the coffee, saw Milo Hirley arrive at Vissage Pizza through the window of his booth. It was unlike Milo to be alone after basketball practice. Walt Pegler, Jonny Heinsohn, and Marty Drummond must have been short of money. Milo's acolytes. The Merry Pranksters. Peter felt fortunate. He felt blessed. Why not go straight to the top?

Milo saw Peter when he came in but didn't acknowledge him. Why would he? He barely ever had. Milo Hirley didn't have half Peter's accomplishments, but he got all the attention. He was cool. He was corrupt. He was handsome. He was athletic. Ridiculing Peter came naturally to Milo.

Yet Peter needed him.

He walked over, knowing better than to ask if Milo minded him sitting down. He did. Peter said, "We need to talk," and sat down, anyway.

Milo had his hands on the table. He'd already told Mel Vissage to make him a meatball sub. He didn't say a word, just turned his palms upward in a gesture that said, *Okay, what?*

"I need a favor," Peter said. "I've got to have one."

Milo laughed.

Peter sat down.

"Bryne got me Adderall," he said.

"So?"

"I've got to have it."

"So?" Milo asked again.

"I know you sell weed."

"Prove it."

"It wouldn't be hard, Peter. All I'd really have to do is make the charge."

"Go ahead, Peter, you asshole. I won't say a thing till somebody asks me, and then I'll say you're just a desperate fucking drug addict trying to blackmail somebody into giving you a fix. And you know what? It wouldn't even be a lie. I didn't know what you was on, Peter. I knew you was on something, though."

"'I knew you *were* on something'."

It took Milo a second to realize Peter was disparaging his grammar.

"Sorry my subjects and verbs don't agree, Peter."

"You're selling weed, Milo. Bryne told me he got his from you."

Milo started to speak, but thought better of it and said again, "Prove it. I never took an Adderall. I don't know what it does to you, or I didn't. I'd say, in your case, it must turn a kid into an asshole. Get the fuck away from me."

"You'll be sorry." Peter staggered out.

Mel brought the meatball sub. "Son of a bitch didn't pay me," he said.

"What'd he have?"

"Uh, club sandwich. And a pot of coffee."

"I got it," Milo said.

Beauregard Press Apartments, Number Eight. It must be what he'd heard his daughter refer to as Hippie Arms. Mickey Statler parked on the street nearby. The entrance had no buzzer, no intercom, no security to prevent anyone from entering. The place was charming in a shabby sort of way. Apparently, the ground floor had four apartments, so Dylan Wannamacher probably lived up the flight of stairs. Check. Right above Number Four. He knocked on the oak door.

From inside: "Who is iiiiit?

"Mickey. Mickey Statler."

He heard a ceiling fan switch on. The occupant, presumably Dylan, apparently was moving a few things around. The door opened.

"Sorry," Dylan said. "Had to make a little room for you. I was writing."

A rolling table with a laptop on it was in front of the recliner. Mickey sat on the couches where stacks of papers and books had been shoved to one end.

"Well," Dylan said, "it seems like a long time since the last I saw you. The day after the Lashley game. What can I do for you?"

"I don't know," Mickey said. "Marcia sent me a text saying she was in trouble and needed my help. I haven't been able to get her to answer her phone or reply to a text since. I guess you should know how she is. I don't know whether she's in trouble that's real bad, or whether she's moved on to something else."

Dylan leaned back in the recliner and put his hands on his head.

"I didn't know a lot of this until yesterday," he said. "Marcia and Milo Hirley were here, and Milo was angry at Marcia."

"Milo Hirley. That's the kid who was your quarterback, right?" Mickey asked.

Dylan sighed. "It's sort of difficult, Mickey, for me to talk to you and, I suppose, you to talk to me, without either of us knowing what the other knows."

"Well, that's a fine literary muddle."

"One writer to another," Dylan said.

"Yeah. Different brands."

"Can I get you anything?"

"What you got?" Mickey asked.

"Uh, beer. Diet generic. Uh, peach-flavored tea. Bourbon," Dylan said. "Bong hit."

Mickey laughed. "I'll have some iced tea. I better see what I'm getting into before I decide what I'm getting into."

"Touche. More literary muddle."

Mickey heard the clatter of an ice tray being emptied and the gurgle of it being refilled at the sink and placed back in a freezer. Dylan handed him his tea in a Triborough College plastic cup and sat back down.

"You're a little high," Mickey said, taking a sip.

"I stopped when I was coaching the football team," Dylan said. "Until yesterday."

"What was the occasion?"

"I found out some things I didn't know."

"That Marcia was selling weed?"

"No. I knew that. I didn't know you knew that."

"I found out when I was up here in November," Mickey said. "In the interest of full disclosure, the most surprising moment of my life was when I opened a hotel-room, and the young woman who was there to pick up a briefcase of weed just happened to be my daughter."

"Jesus," Dylan said. "No wonder she's writing a novel."

Mickey told him the whole sordid story, how his job had been eliminated, he'd been busted by the cops in a motel room, set up by the cops and a bartender they'd already set up, and handed a job writing for a web site that was a cover for a nationwide drug distribution scheme that involved the cops, the military, and God knows who else.

When he got through, he said, "I bet you want to call bullshit in the worst way."

"It's quite a story," Dylan said. "Okay. What's going on right now is, and, first, let me say that this is all news to me. I don't sell weed. I haven't bought any from Marcia. I've partaken in what she has provided, but that almost, like, paying a share of the rent. She cooked and bought groceries a lot."

"You and she are no longer … together?"

"I guess we're no longer … involved. We're friends. There was never much commitment. First things, first, though. It seems Milo was selling weed for Marcia. Of this I had no idea. I knew Milo and a few of his friends smoked it. I never had any idea they were getting it from Marcia. She sort of used me to set up a little network of prep-school kids. I thought Milo was getting his weed from a janitor at the school named Brynildson Hiers. Brynildson is dead. Sheriff's deputies shot him in a bust last week. What I gathered from watching Marcia and Milo yell at each other, and Milo crying and almost hyperventilating, is that Bryne complained to Milo about him horning in on his business, and then Milo said something to Marcia about it, and then they all got it settled, and everybody got along, and then Bryne, the sweetest, most gentle fellow you ever knew, was supposedly shot by the cops in self-defense. You're gonna have to follow me closely here. Over Christmas, Milo got busted for weed possession in his hometown – I think it might be Virginia Beach or Chesapeake, somewhere down in the Tidewater region – and Marcia just snapped her fingers and got him off. Great, right? But then Bryne got bumped off in the dead of night, and Milo got it in his head that Marcia just snapped her fingers about that, too."

"Do you think my daughter is actually capable of ordering someone's murder?" Mickey asked.

"She says she isn't. She says she just mentioned it in passing, the same way Milo mentioned it to her. She doesn't think she's responsible, but it could've all been just a mistake."

"I think it might explain a lot of mistakes one reads about in the paper these days," Mickey said. "God help us."

"I sat here, watching them going back and forth, all emotional, just freely exchanging details I had no idea about, well, that's when I decided it was time to smoke weed again. And Milo got high, my student, acting like it was the realization of a lifelong dream. And Marcia got high, and then her phone rang …"

"The one she doesn't answer if it's from me."

"That's the one," Dylan said. "It rang, and she talked to someone, and she got her things and said she had to go, and I haven't heard back from her."

"No idea who it was?"

"If I can read her as well as I think I can, it was someone she was excited to see, I expect, in a sexual way. She perked right up. I went to school and taught today. Got home, and I've been high ever since."

"I think I might try that bong of yours, after all," Mickey said.

An hour later, Mickey walked back down to the car and grabbed his bag. Dylan had invited him to stay the night.

CHAPTER 42

Laying Down the Lawless

Arkady Pankratov had benefited greatly from his machinations within the Russian oligarchy. He was by training a lawyer, though a decade had passed since he had appeared in any courtroom. By title, Pankratov was a banker without fiduciary responsibility. In reality, he was an operative of the Russian president, Yevgeny Borzov. The source of his power was a willingness to work in the shadows. Pankratov made no public appearances. It wasn't he who consorted with the operatives from Martin J. Gaynes' campaign for the presidency of the United States. Pankratov directed it all, and he was only meeting with Patrick Trintignant under the strictest secrecy. The job didn't end with Gaynes' election. The reason for Russia's participation was to install in the United States a regime that would leave Russia alone and accede to her wishes. Russia could not rebuild its empire and restore its power on the world stage without the tacit cooperation of the American government. What had been dramatized in fiction by the British agent James Bond was established through Borzov to Pankratov. He possessed his president's license to kill.

Patrick Trintignant met Pankratov in a resort condominium overlooking the Ensenada port, a popular one for Russian shipping. Pankratov had arrived in Mexico via an intelligence-gathering trawler, but he hadn't had to brave a long sea voyage. He had flown from Vladivostok to San Salvador and then, via small plane, to a remote airstrip on Guadaloupe Island, a hundred miles southwest of Ensenada. A helicopter transported Pankratov to the trawler. What was in practicality an absurd level of secrecy was the normal circumstance of Pankratov's existence. Dozens of Russians deemed dissidents, as well as politicians in the former satellite states of the Soviet Union, had died miserable deaths without so much as knowing the name of the man who had ordered their executions. When Borzov had seen a possibility to get a friend of Russia elected president of the United States, the president had put Pankratov in charge. The Central Intelligence Agency's dossier on Pankratov had never been extensive, but most of its details had been conveniently expunged almost as soon as Gaynes took office. What Trintignant knew of Pankratov had been communicated directly by the new director of the Federal Bureau of Investigation, Edmund Kingsley.

The subject of the discussion was what to do with Nathan Bedford Forrest Beale, who wasn't giving President Gaynes enough cover to suit his purposes and stood in the way of the carefully laid plans of the Consortium. The Kremlin cared little whether Americans wanted to cloud their collective judgment further in a haze of marijuana addiction. It was vitally interested in freeing up the American president's ability to advance his program and the common conspiratorial goals of both Moscow and Washington. Pankratov spoke fluent English. They met alone, although the condo had been outfitted with sophisticated video and sound equipment maintained by the Foreign Intelligence Service of the Russian Federation.

Pankratov dispensed with chitchat and formality. The meeting began merely with each downing the obligatory Russian shots of vodka.

"I am confident, Mr. Trintignant, that you have been briefed, as have I," he said. "Forgive me if I am not adequately prepared, but my understanding is that we are to reach some agreement on just how we can remove the Attorney General from our way. We have mutual interests, your business and my government, though, as fate would have it, they are vastly different."

"Yes," Trintignant responded. "The Consortium wishes to capitalize on the spread of cannabis legalization in the States, and the biggest obstacle is the reactionary beliefs and practices of Nathan Beale. He is a moralistic little man who wraps himself in the Bible and threatens federal interference in the affairs of states that have freely voted for the legalization of cannabis for medicinal or recreational use.”

“Mr. Beale prefers the company of little boys, you know.”

Trintignant thought another shot of vodka might be in order. “I didn’t know that.”

“Mr. Beale visited Saint Petersburg some years ago now, in his first year as one of your senators,” Pankratov said. “We entertained him rather lavishly and catered to his whims. It’s not too hard, when a man is inebriated and drugged, to discern his ‘peccadillos,’ shall we say. We are in position to expose evidence of Mr. Beale’s indiscretions.”

“Very interesting,” Trintignant said.

“The problem with that,” Pankratov said, “is in the uniqueness of your politics. On the one hand, Americans seem influenced by religion to an inordinate degree. On the other, it seems as if hypocrisy is rampant. We have been intrigued by President Gaynes’ ability to surmount his own weaknesses. It seems as if the sinner makes more of a difference than the sin. I will admit to some confusion, not regarding the existence of your country’s hypocrisy, rather, its origins.”

“I believe you have stumbled upon the essence of the Christian religion,” Trintignant opined. “The basis of Christianity is the concept of forgiveness. A sinner may be absolved of his sins by God if he asks forgiveness.”

“Your president doesn’t make use of this.”

“Our president is a special case.”

“It is my belief that merely discrediting Mr. Beale is not enough. Its outcome, based on Russia’s experience, is unreliable. I believe the preferred course is to eliminate the Attorney General completely.” Pankratov observed Trintignant’s reaction. “Perhaps you would like another drink, sir.”

“As you wish,” Trintignant said as if he really didn’t.

“We have two options.”

“Proceed.”

"The first option," Pankratov said, "is rather simple. We eliminate Beale in an aviation accident. You and your associates need not worry. As I believe you know, the best way to implement such a plan is having, as a vital element, the aid of American authorities in covering up any incriminating details. We have discussed confidentially the matter with your director of the FBI, Kingsley, as well as General Armisen of the Joint Chiefs of Staff, with whom you and Mr. Lilley are acquainted."

"Where would this crash – I assume it's a crash, not some midair explosion – take place?" Trintignant asked.

"In the great mountains or the vast, unpopulated desert of your West, but that is not the option I recommend."

"What, then, is your better idea?"

"The versatility of Las Vegas, your country's capital of decadence, is extraordinary, I must admit," Pankratov said. "A week from tomorrow, on the outskirts of town, away from the Strip, one of the hotels is holding a festival of bluegrass and gospel music. The Attorney General is a great fan of bluegrass and gospel music."

"I'd forgotten," Trintignant said. "Nathan Beale plays the fiddle."

"Yes. President Gaynes is sending him to the music festival, which takes place in a state that has recently legalized cannabis for recreational use. It is a sympathetic audience, made up mostly of white, conservative enthusiasts who voted for the president. Beale will address the crowd. Then he will be assassinated, and no one will ever know."

"Why's that?"

"Because, Mr. Trintignant, a trio of armed gunmen, situated in a hotel room high above the festival grounds, will spray the crowd with automatic weapons fire. Amid the disorder, a hidden gunman will shoot Beale with a weapon identical, only semi-automatic, to those being fired from the hotel above. No one will suspect that Beale is anything other than an unwitting victim of the general savagery."

"Innocent people will be killed and injured," Trintignant said.

"True," Pankratov responded, "but no one will bear the expense of losing a plane, or the uncertainty of influencing the investigation. The biggest reason, though, is political. As a result of Russia's revolutionary past, we have many contacts. If Mr. Beale's plane crashes, your country's citizens will consider him a martyr. They may want to honor his memory by advancing Beale's beliefs and policies, but, if we set up a black man, a Muslim, as the assassin, there will be no backlash regarding cannabis. The backlash will be directed at immigrants, terrorists, minorities, the usual objects of President Gaynes' ire."

"A perfect crime." Trintignant made the observation quietly.

They ironed out the details. Pankratov's cool efficiency, not to mention his offhand, pragmatic disregard for innocent lives, intimidated Trintignant. The Consortium would provide a few dependable Americans to work with Russian professionals. Time was short, but Pankratov had everything planned. Trintignant had been presented with what was almost a *fait accompli*. Trintignant acceded to every Russian proposal. Pankratov knew what he was doing, and Trintignant didn't particularly want to be the man who planned a mass murder. The Russians were better at it.

CHAPTER 43

Suspended Adolescence

Mickey Statler slept soundly. He awakened unsure of where he was. He stumbled into the kitchen and found that Dylan Wannamacher had charitably left the coffee pot on. Dylan was off to teach the fine young brats of Enlightened Word. Mickey had nothing to do and no key to lock up Beauregard Press Apartment Number Eight. He placed a cinnamon-and-raisin bagel in the toaster and returned to the guest bedroom, there to find that he'd left his cell on all night and there were no messages from Marcia. He fished the charger out of his backpack and plugged it into an outlet in the living room so that he could hear it beep and ring and vibrate. He got his bagel, smeared it with cream cheese, stirred two packets of Sweet 'n' Low into a Triborough Troopers mug of coffee, and sat down to decide whether to watch a *Columbo* guest-starring George Wendt or a World War II movie with Brian Keith. He opted for the flick, *The McKenzie Break*, and watched without seeing. The phone buzzed. It was a text from Carson Carmine, executive editor of The Ultimate Sporting Life.

Where are you?

Mickey pecked out a reply. *Busy. Call me in 5.*

He needed five. Carmine probably had an assignment, and by assignment, he would mean a sporting event tied to a delivery. As best he knew, Carmine was the only person at TUSL who knew the principal business of the site's owners. What separated "executive editor" from "editor" was Carmine's liaison with the Consortium. It was best not to tell him much.

Mickey quickly checked his email. One from Rashawn Ling had a heading, *I'm free … free falling.*

Uh-oh.

Dear Mickey,

This morning I got canned. Job eliminated. Just like you. Told me today my last day is today. That leaves the News-Free Press with three – three! – in the sports department. I'm too shocked to write more. Call me when you get a chance.

Rashawn

Before Mickey could call Rashawn, Carson Carmine called. He needed Mickey at the Duke-Georgia Tech basketball game in Atlanta. No can do, Mickey told him. Okay. How about a women's game in Columbia, South Carolina?

"Carson, I told you, I've got a serious family problem to deal with," he said. "It might be nothing. It might be really bad. I need the weekend. I've got to have it. I've worked on every holiday I can think of, either sitting on a press row or making whistlestops in a rental car. This ain't a holiday, but I gotta take one."

"All right," Carmine said. "This puts me in a real spot, but a man's got to do what a man's got to do."

"That has never been more true than since I got this job, Carson. Bye."

"Where are you, Mickey?"

"Virginia. It's a commonwealth." *Click.*

Mickey attempted to call Rashawn but couldn't get through. He wasn't the only person who'd gotten a text. Naturally, Mickey did what caring friends did. He sent another text.

For obvious reasons, I can't get a call through. Call ME when you can. – MS

He turned the TV on. The new president, Martin J. Gaynes, was sitting next to the prime minister of Japan, talking about killing health care, arresting immigrants, the "fake media," and not about Japan, whose prime minister seemed, at various times, alarmed, mystified, and amused. Mickey was just alarmed.

So he succumbed. It was something of a vigil he was observing, waiting for his daughter, wishing he could do something about whatever trouble she was in, suspecting it was all an overreaction but not altogether sure. He decided to do something he had never done. He decided to get stoned. He had gotten high. He had gotten drunk. He had never gotten stoned, or baked, or wasted, or whatever the currently fashionable term was. *Turnt. Lit.* Maybe those terms denoted just high. Wherever it was, he was going to go there, thanks to Dylan Wannamacher's paraphernalia and provisions.

Rashawn finally called. He said the job hadn't been eliminated, though he knew they wouldn't hire a replacement. He had been abruptly found guilty of plagiarism, an often shady means of destroying jobs.

"It's perfect by their way of thinking," Mickey said. "Look in handbooks. Everything is phrased so generally. Everybody knows you can't use another's work and steal it, but the big violators are the rags themselves. I used to work for a paper that, out of vanity, didn't want to admit it had been scooped on a story. Reporters would be tacitly instructed to rewrite a wire story and put a byline on it. It became a common practice to begin a story with '*The Clarion* has learned ...' and the translation was '*The Clarion* has learned from the *Silersville Tribune*,' or something, and, then, two years later, the editors have moved on, and that writer, the one who rewrote a story because it wasn't even his own beat, but the paper told him to drop what he was doing and crank something out, is, all of a sudden, being shown the door because some other ambitious, ass-kissing tool of management has been instructed to dig something up so that they can free up another salary, run off another longtime staffer, get rid of the position, or give it to a kid who's not making any money. Any idea what you did to land on the expendable list?"

"None."

"I don't suppose you've been digging into the stuff I told you?"

"No, no, I don't have any contacts. I don't have the time to study it. A nationwide drug conspiracy? Run by cops? I can't even figure out why Starlight High School suspended its quarterback last week."

"Violation of team rules?"

"Yeah."

"Weed. Probably got busted. Probably got busted by a cop not because he had weed on him, but because he wasn't getting it from the cop. Or from the coach. Hell, Rashawn, nothing surprises me. I know too much already."

Rashawn Ling didn't fit the profile of the usual casualty of a newspaper cleaning out its payroll. He was young. He was "diverse." He was the kind of employee who could do no wrong in management's view. Times were changing. The election of Martin J. Gaynes had already made diversity go out of style. It still didn't add up, though, unless forces far beyond the doors of *The News-Free Press* were at work.

"Did you talk to anybody?" Mickey asked.

"Just Myra. I saw her at the Panthers game when the Giants came down. She was on some other assignment, something about the mayor of Charlotte being a fast-rising politico, and she came down to the stadium just to hobnob with old friends from her sports days. We had a conversation, just the two of us, in the dining area of the press box."

"You didn't mention my name."

"Nah," Rashawn said. "I don't usually mention her name to you, either."

"I think I told you that she's right-wing. She works for the right-wing paper," Mickey said.

"We didn't talk long. She pretty much dismissed it as crazy talk," Rashawn said. "She assured me that, if anything that big was going on, she'd have heard about it from one of her colleagues. She asked me if I got it off some zonked-out, pro-weed website."

Mickey laughed. "That's precisely when you should have said, 'No. Even worse. Mickey Statler told me.' That would've set her off. I'm glad you didn't, though. Do me a favor, Rashawn. Keep kind of a low profile for a few days, okay?"

"Mickey? I'm not in any danger, am I?"

"No, not to my knowledge. I'll let you know if my knowledge changes. I gotta go. Is this a new cell?"

"Yeah. Company took up theirs before they showed me the door," Rashawn said. "Got a new account. Same number. Obviously."

"I'll be back in touch," Mickey said. "I got some things to work out myself. Bye."

"Bye." Rashawn sounded a little panicky.

"Oh, Rashawn."

"Yeah."

"Get in touch with Myra. Tell her you appreciate her setting you straight. Come up with another reason to call her. Then just mention it in passing. See you soon, okay?"

"Sure, Mickey. Thanks."

Mickey hung up and sat down. No need to get carried away. Rashawn's firing was strange. So, too, had been his own layoff, but Rashawn hadn't been fired because he was nosing around, looking into a story that had nothing to do with *The News-Free Press* and stretched far beyond the borders of its circulation area. Rashawn would not have mentioned it to the paper's own news desk. They would have laughed at him. He hoped Rashawn's conversation with Myra LeFlore had been as harmless and incidental as Rashawn depicted it.

According to Dylan, Marcia had claimed that her remarks about Brynildson Hiers were harmless and incidental. He was dead. Mickey couldn't form an objective assessment of what was reasonable and what wasn't. The whole matter was conspiratorial. How much so? How far would the Consortium go to protect its security? If Bryne's murder had been a comedy of paranoid errors, as Marcia apparently claimed, everything would be fine as long as everyone stayed cool. If it had been standard operating procedure, then they all – Mickey, Marcia, Dylan, Milo Hirley and the other stoners at Enlightened Word, Rashawn – were in danger. How could one find some balance? How could one settle down and think calmly?

One could get high again.

All day, at Enlightened Word, Dylan Wannamacher found himself preoccupied by the absurdity of it all. The allegedly Merry Pranksters – Milo Hirley, Walt Pegler, Marty Drummond, and Jonny Heinsohn – were in mourning. Peter Baxter, the hyperactive asshole, looked stoned, if, for no other reason, because he wasn't bristling with his usual intensity. Dylan's only worthwhile use of Peter had been as a "go-to guy," meaning that he would always take a stab at answering a question about literature when everyone else in the class was stoned or otherwise inattentive due to lack of sleep or coffee. Peter was often maniacally wrong, but he read the assignments even if he misperceived them.

Peter fell asleep fifteen minutes into Dylan's lecture.

When the bell rang, signifying the end of class, Dylan asked to speak to Peter. When everyone else left, Dylan closed the door.

"What in hell do you think you're doing, coming to this class in that kind of shape?"

"I don't know," Peter said. "There's nothing I could do about it. I didn't want to fall asleep. I tried to stay awake. What do you want me to do? Start slapping myself in the face?"

"When someone falls asleep in my class, I take it as an insult, Peter."

"It wasn't, Mr. Wannamacher. I told you. I could not do anything about it. Maybe I'm coming down with something. I need to go to the infirmary, maybe."

"If you ever feel so sleepy you can't keep up with my lecture, don't come to my class," Dylan said. "Go straight to the infirmary. Go back to sleep. Just don't come to class. Okay?"

"Okay, already." Peter stomped out. Dylan had awakened him and his anger.

Mickey was reading a Dylan Wannamacher short story on Dylan's laptop when he heard Dylan's key in the oaken door of Apartment Eight.

Dylan walked into the kitchen and put away a bag of groceries in the kitchen.

"What you been up to?"

"Oh, a while ago, I watched a huge grouper devour a lobster on the Smithsonian Channel," Mickey said.

"I take it you're stoned."

"Oh, yeah," Mickey said. "Maybe the only time ever. I mean, I've gotten high quite a few times, but this might be the first time I've really been stoned. I just finished reading a short story of yours. I hope you don't mind."

"Oh, yeah. Which one?"

"'Tartar Sauce and Shrimp.'"

"Ah," Dylan said, "that's one I've never had the temerity to submit for publication."

"I liked it."

"You're stoned. I was, well, maybe not stoned, but certainly high when I wrote it."

"So we match," Mickey said. "In more ways than one. Sit down. We've got to talk."

"Should I get high first?"

"I'm thinking yes."

While Dylan packed himself a bowl, Mickey said, "Thanks to my side business, I will be able to generously replenish your stores. I rushed up here to help my daughter with whatever fleeting peril she wrote me about, but there's at least a couple ounces in the trunk of my car. I didn't have a key to get back in if I left to fetch a briefcase in my car. It's actually my briefcase. I keep a quantity in reserve in case something unexpected crops up, and I'd say this was unexpected."

"You better run down there, not because you need to gift me some weed but because, once or twice, a few overzealous local cops have gone on pot-luck expeditions with their weed-sniffing dogs in the parking lot," Dylan said. "It's unlikely, but a man's got to protect himself against bad luck."

"I got a phone number," Mickey said. "One I've never had to use. It's sort of a get-out-of-jail-free card. My instructions are to insist that anyone who arrests me make that phone call. The number must be to a pretty important dude, or an office where important dudes congregate. I think I become some sort of undercover agent, and anyone who hassles me gets told to cease and desist."

"I bet Marcia's got one. I bet she used it to get Milo Hirley off. That's another thing I just heard about in the past two days. Bong hit?"

"Nah, I'm good," Mickey said. "The fog is still there, but it's dissipated to a manageable level. I'm pretty sure I can spell my middle name now."

Mickey sat on the couch. A man's easy chair was his property when he was home.

"I read a short story or two on your laptop," Mickey said. "It occurred to me that we share some common virtues. Vices, too, obviously. We're both observers. You observe real people and depict their attributes in fiction. A sportswriter learns to read people. He learns to tell when they're lying. He learns to see through their bullshit. You know Marcia more than I do. When Vera and I divorced, Marcia was a high school soccer star, president of her school's Fellowship of Christian Athletes and the Beta Club. Then one day, I open a hotel-room door with a silver briefcase full of weed, and she's got a briefcase of cash to swap with me. She's a different person. I don't know what happened. Do you?"

Dylan sighed. "Best I can tell, Mickey, she just went through the disillusionment that happens sometimes when you go off to college, and you're making your own decisions. Marcia told me that one of her soccer teammates tried to seduce her. She sort of freaked at that, quit soccer, got into literature and creative writing, started seeing through the bullshit of life, and, next thing you know, she was hanging out in coffee shops, listening to folk music, smoking cigarettes and then weed, and, you know, one thing led to another, and, pretty soon, she was transferring here to be in the Triborough College writers' program, and I think she decided that a bohemian lifestyle would provide her with the inspiration she needed to be novelist and voice of her generation. I think she wants to revive the Beat Generation."

"I mean, the last thing I want to be is a hypocrite," Mickey said. "I'm not a religious man, but it feels like this is some outlandish way where God is punishing me for all my sins. I got myself blackmailed into selling pot, and there's no way out, and I'm making more money than I ever have, and I was able to shove all the shame into my subconscious right up until my beautiful little girl showed up at my motel door, and the next thing I knew, we were sitting out on the patio of an eighth-floor hotel hotel room, and Marcia was lighting a joint and explaining matter-of-factly that I might as well get used to it because she wasn't going to change. It damned near killed me. She thought it was hilarious."

"It can be read both ways," Dylan said. "Jesus. I'm gonna have a cigarette."

"I think I'm straight enough to be seen in public now," Mickey said. "I'll go get my stash."

Dylan reached in a kitchen drawer and tossed Mickey a set of extra keys. "Don't leave the door cracked," he said. "It's a mite smelly in here. I'll fix more coffee in the meantime."

When Mickey returned, they got high again, and Dylan played his guitar while they each ruminated.

"You know, I don't mind her smoking weed," Mickey said, "and I'm flattered that she wants to be writer, as hopeless a profession as that might be. What concerns me about Marcia is that she's hardened so much. That ought not happen to a girl so young."

"Well, you know, I don't mean to compare myself to you because you're her daddy, and I'm just her, uh, friend, but I've got a little worried, too. She played me like a fiddle. She got me to take her to the Homecoming celebration at Enlightened Word, and I thought it odd that she'd have any desire at all going to that, but I enjoyed showing her off, and the kids loved her, and, come to find out, there was a very good reason for that because she was hooking up my best students with some high-grade, Northern California kush. Now she sort of admits to unwittingly getting the school janitor killed by the crooked sheriff."

"Things are out of hand," Mickey said.

"Today at school, the most alert student I got – not surprisingly, also the biggest asshole – falls asleep in class. Milo, the brightest kid, and the most promising, and a regular gangster on the side, avoids me. Kid's traumatized by Bryne's murder, and I expect he's just about the same as you and me, he's stoned on his ass, and tonight he's gonna play a basketball game in which the winner wins the conference, and I don't like the Dragoons' chances. If Milo Hirley gets high before the game, then Walt Pegler and Marty Drummond and Jonny Heinsohn get high, too, and you've got four of your five starters playing varsity basketball buzzed, and I know what I'm talking about because I had to deal with that issue on the football team. Marcia was apparently hooking them up before Walt's daddy died and I got forced into coaching football. The guy who hooked them up before is dead."

"In a way, we both got forced into this," Mickey said. "Only I'm making more money."

"I don't know what the fuck is going on. I don't know how it happened, where it got started. Shit. It might be Jack Kerouac's fault."

"I'm sticking with God's out to get me."

"Relax, Mickey. God's got too much else to do."

Someone knocked on the door. *Shave and a shoe shine, two bits.*

"Speaking of," Dylan said. "I'm guessing that's Marcia."

He opened the door. Marcia and Wade Sanderson walked in.

"Your dad's here, Marcia."

She ran to him.

"Oh, Daddy, I know you're pissed. I really do need to talk to you. Tomorrow. This is my friend Wade. He lives in L.A. He's known as caddy to the stars," she said. "Wade, my dad's a sportswriter. And, most likely, somebody you ship product to."

Wade looked especially Californian in small-town Virginia. He was a charmer, evidenced in no small part by Marcia being obviously charmed. Mickey could see why Dylan saw him as the death knell of his affair with Marcia. Wade said he had recently caddied for a once-famous golfer in a senior tournament. It was bullshit. The golfer he named wasn't playing the Senior Tour anymore. Marcia was beaming the way women do when they've been diligently screwing for a day and a night. They didn't linger five minutes.

"We can't stay," Marcia explained. "Wade and I are going out with some friends of mine from school."

A likely story.

Mickey was too high to say much. Wade and Marcia left hurriedly. Wade said he was "a huge fan" of Mickey's writing as he was walking out the door.

Weed could be either manic or depressive. For five minutes, neither Mickey nor Dylan said a word. Both hit Dylan's water bong. Finally, Mickey broke the silence.

"Goddamn it," he said. "It ain't like I didn't drive over two hundred miles for a kiss on the cheek."

"What did you think of Wade Sanderson?" Dylan asked.

"I don't like his looks. I don't think he came here all the way from California just to screw my daughter's brains out. I'm worried that she's in danger. I'm worried that we're in danger."

"I'm hoping that we're paranoid," Dylan said.

"I find out this morning that a former co-worker of mine, Rashawn Ling, got fired by my old paper for alleged plagiarism," Mickey said. "There's something wrong with that. Rashawn, as you may have gathered, is half African American and half Chinese. He was a diversity hire. The paper wears him like a medal of honor. Writers get fired for plagiarism because the paper is trying to get rid of them. Everybody knows that plagiarism is wrong, but the bounds of plagiarism are awfully broad. If you write 'so and so said,' and he said it in a press conference and not directly to you, they can call it plagiarism because you didn't write 'in a press conference, so and so said.' It's one of the reasons writers need unions, and there are very few union shops left. The newspaper business is scared shitless, and the response has been to squeeze the product. People don't read the paper because there's nothing in it anymore, and there's nothing in it anymore because people aren't reading. It's a death spiral. The writers die first."

Dylan picked up his guitar and just started idly strumming. "Bummer," he said.

"When I found out I had a daughter who was dealing weed, and she was dealing weed it was my job to furnish, it made me feel worthless in about a half dozen different ways," Mickey said. "I tried to figure out a way to get out. No dice. It's made me prosperous. It's given me a chance to write things that interest me, and it's deadened my soul. I read a novel one time about a man who has open-heart surgery, and, for about a year, he feels like a part of himself died. That's the way I feel right now. I'm worried about Marcia, and I'm worried about Rashawn, and I'm worried about you and me, Dylan. Do you own a gun?"

"Uh-uh. Don't believe in it."

"I got one. A cop named Ronnie Shingler gave it to me. And ammo. I've never fired it. He showed me how, though."

"Marcia has a pistol," Dylan said. "She left it on the dresser in my guest room, where you slept last night. I didn't even touch it."

"You reckon it's here."

"We can check."

They found it in a shoulder belt, hanging in the closet, at the far end, against the wall, hidden by blouses and slacks and cute sundresses.

"It's exactly like the one I got," Mickey said. "Standard issue, I reckon. I wonder if Marcia bought the holster."

He removed the pistol, a Ruger LC9, small, lightweight, and handed it to Dylan.

"This is yours now," he said.

"What happens when Marcia discovers it missing?" Dylan asked.

"Well," her father replied, "she won't shoot us."

They walked back into the den. Dylan sat the handgun on the coffee table. He started strumming the guitar again.

"I had a lot of time to think," Mickey said. "I came up with my own theory about what's wrong with the world and why it's falling apart. Two words?"

"Okay."

"Suspended adolescence."

"I'm with you."

"It explains everything," Mickey said. "You can see it everywhere. You ever look at Facebook. People act like their pets are people. They're as sentimental as an eight-year-old whose pooch gets run over by the mailman. People get offended by everything. A man makes one wrong move, and he's ruined. Politics, and every issue it touches, are consumed in anger. It's kid stuff. Everything has become a sport. Gaynes' voters are like fans of one school who hate the other. Gaynes is the Yankees. Katharine Haymer is the Red Sox. News is fake news. What Gaynes calls fake news is whatever he doesn't like. Smart people are going out of style. Scientists don't matter. What's the woman who works for Gaynes, the one who coined the term 'alternative facts'? Here's what the experts say? Gaynes voter says, 'I don't care. I don't believe it.' Suspended adolescence. I must've thought of a half dozen other examples, but I'm too fucked up to think of 'em now."

Dylan laughed. "It makes me think of the line coach I played for at Triborough. He used to turn around, and squint his eyes, and say, 'Dylan, you make a dadburned good point.' That's you, Mickey. You make a dadburned good point."

"They got any public firing ranges in this town?" Mickey asked.

"I'm satisfied there's at least three or four," Dylan replied. "This is Virginia."

"Let's me and you go figure out how to shoot a gun," Mickey said.

A more unlikely pair never walked into Sharpshooter Inc. Mickey showed Dylan how to load a clip. For fifteen minutes, each learned the art of hitting the side of a barn. Both had hunted as kids. Neither had ever fired a pistol that had anything more than caps in it. They worked up a mild sweat. It straightened them out a bit.

When they returned to the car, Dylan's Honda, he said, "I think I'm gonna mosey on over to Enlightened Word to watch Milo and the Merry Pranksters play."

"The basketball team is the Merry Pranksters?" Mickey asked.

"No, they're just the four badasses I teach. Marcia's who gave them the name, you know, from Ken Kesey, *The Electric Kool-Aid Acid Test*, that Tom Wolfe wrote. Milo, Walt Pegler, Marty Drummond, Jonny Heinsohn. They all four are in my classes. They all four played football, and all four play basketball, and three of the four play baseball. The rest of the time they spend smoking weed. I can drop you back by the apartment if you wish."

"Nah, I got nothing else to do but stew about Marcia. They sell hot dogs at the gym?"

"I hadn't been there but once, but I'm pretty sure. We got time to stop by the local pizza joint first."

"Shit," Mickey said, "let's go."

CHAPTER 44

Not Much of a Game

Under normal circumstances, Dylan Wannamacher would never have gone to an Enlightened Word basketball game at all, though, thanks to Milo Hirley, this was his second one of the month as well as the past five years. Two days earlier, he certainly wouldn't have gone in a state of impairment. He and Mickey were stoned when they got to Vissage Pizza and split a pitcher of beer while wolfing down a Napolitana from Mel's oven. They had no sense of urgency. The girls' teams played at six, followed by the boys at seven-thirty, and Mickey remembered the words of an old coach at what had then been an all-male military academy.

I'd rather watch a man take a shit than a woman play basketball.

"Mind you, those words ain't mine," he said to Dylan. "Those words are many years old, and I doubt old Pursley Ravenel, if he was still alive, would say them now. Well, maybe he would. Pursley was a character. I didn't ever subscribe to it, but it's fair to say that Marcia, when she was a little girl, playing every sport she could find, sort of changed me."

"She wants to be good. She's ambitious. Marcia wants to write a wild-ass novel, so she took a walk on the wild side. Very Beat Generation."

"Did you ever love her?"

"For a while," Dylan said. "Now it's more that she just interests me. Live and let live, I guess."

"Can she write?"

"I haven't read much of it. There's a lot of shock value in it. Overly descriptive, in my estimation. Too many adverbs. She's got guts, though, and that's the most important thing. It's what I lack. I've worked and worked and worked on two novels, but sometimes it's difficult just to say the hell with what people think."

"Why's that?"

"It's the comfort of stability smothering the exhilaration of realizing your dreams," Dylan said, waxing a bit overdramatic in the mental haze. "If they get published, when they get published, they've got to hit it big. Publishing those two means leaving the comfortable obsolescence of Enlightened Word."

"Set in a fictional private school?"

"One of them. It's not that it's true to form. It's not just the names have been changed. It's frank. It's unsparing. It's scandalous. Readers will think it's true even though it isn't."

"You know, this place really is pretty cool," Mickey said, his thoughts sidetracked by the taste of the pizza. "Why is it here?"

"I don't know," Dylan said. "Mel won't say. When he comes back by, maybe I'll ask him for the hundredth time."

"What is the reason we're here again?" Mickey asked.

"I don't know. I'm worried about Milo. He's bright, athletic, canny, street-smart, rebellious, and stoned about half the time, and ..."

"Like John Wayne to Kim Darby in the original *True Grit*. 'By God, he reminds me of me'."

"The line was 'she reminds me of me,' Mickey. You and your daughter."

"That's what made me think of it." Mickey smiled and refilled his mug. "You know, with Gaynes being president, and me making dirty money like it's going out of style, and Marcia doing the same thing because she wants to and not because she's got to, it is quite comforting to be stoned."

"There's this other kid, Peter Baxter, I was telling you about," Dylan said. "He's sort of the anti-Milo. They can't stand each other. Peter is so intense that he's just an irretrievable asshole. Have you ever known anybody who's so pushy that he gets what he wants because he never backs down?"

"Most them were ball coaches. Football coaches are like generals. Basketball coaches are like used-car salesmen."

"Baseball?"

"Baseball coaches, or managers, have an adolescence most suspended of all," Mickey concluded.

"Peter is into everything. He's the lead in every school play. He played football, and he can't do anything right because he's so damned intense."

"Is he the kid who touched off the fight in the game I saw?"

"Of course, he was. Anyway, he's editor of the annual. He's captain of the rifle team. He's in the Young Republicans. Today, in class, Milo was sullen. Bryne's death really got to him. Peter was acting like he was stoned. He fell asleep in class, and when I confronted him about it, he just said there was nothing he could do about it. It was the only thing he showed any spark, any passion about. I've been wondering if, of all people, Peter Baxter is on drugs. I mean, he's like a cokehead, but it's hard to say because, you know, some people are just naturally intense. It's like they have some natural drug coursing through their veins. What I think it might be, and it's just because you hear of kids using it to cram for tests, is Adderall. Whatever it is, he wasn't on it today. Maybe Peter just miscalculated. Kid like him, marijuana would just make him seem normal."

Mickey said, "What worries the shit out of me about Marcia is that she seems like she's gotten so hard, so ruthless. She's my daughter. I want her to be a good person. It's like she's becoming a sociopath. Maybe manic-depressive. She was down in the dumps, texts me that she's in trouble, and wants me to come running. I drop everything, drive up here, and she hasn't got time for anything but a peck on the cheek. It'd piss me off it wasn't my little girl. That'd be a whole letter than the way I feel right now."

"She can be tender, and sweet, and loving," Dylan said, "but I know where you're coming from. I haven't seen that in her in a while. When Milo confronted her about Bryne, she acted like, one, he wasn't dead. Her reaction was what you'd expect if he'd broken his leg in a car wreck, and she was driving the car. Marcia seemed insensitive to the finality of death. It was, like, she just mentioned him in passing, and the people back at, whatever it is, the home office, took it at face value, and, oh, bother, they got him killed. I don't think there's any doubt that the cops murdered him. Whoever told the crook we got for a sheriff, to go get him, it wasn't because of Bryne breaking the law. They assassinated him because they saw him as competition. Or a security risk."

"Well, I hope like hell the sheriff hasn't got Marcia on his wanted list," Mickey said.

"Marcia's got a big advantage."

"What's that?"

"She's white," Dylan said. "That's the good news."

"What's the bad news?"

"I've got a hunch about the person she told there was a problem with Bryne Hiers."

"Wade Sanderson," Mickey said.

They split what was left in the pitcher. Mickey asked Dylan for a rough estimate of the tab. He said a twenty ought to cover it. Mickey left one more as a tip for Mel Vissage.

Wade Sanderson tried to get Marcia Statler to give cocaine a try, but she said weed was just fine. He wasn't tender after a snort. He banged her. It was violence. He presumed she had a taste for it. He had a taste for it. He found it to snap her neck in the heat of passion. It would make her last breath ecstatic. What a way to go. He'd made no arrangements, though, and, besides, he couldn't base his investigation on suspicions and intimations. That was what had caused the misunderstanding regarding Brynildson Hiers. Suppose he determined this little cell had a security problem? They were all in place: Marcia, her father the prominent sportswriter, her mentor the hulking English teacher, and the smart-ass kid who peddled as much product to the prep-school kids as any of

Marcia's frat kids at the college. Mistakes happened. Marcia understood; she could take it. The concerned father, the spurned lover, and the grief-stricken kid were security risks, and these were desperate times.

How could he kill all of them? Set a fire? Perhaps Marcia could be saved. Perhaps Marcia would conspire with him. She understood business. Her mother and father were estranged. The mother had gained custody in the divorce proceedings. Perhaps she held Mickey in scorn. She had thought it funny when they had stumbled into each other in a cannabis exchange. Her father had likely been devastated. He was important, though. He carried a small degree of celebrity about him. The best way to get rid of him was a car wreck or a plane crash. The teacher was physically imposing. It might take more than a bullet to take him down. The kid would be easily intimidated and least risky to ice.

Wade was ahead of himself, coaxed onward by the wondrous immortality that was coursing through his veins.

Quite literally, Marcia was along for the ride. While Wade was pondering her fate, she was considering, through the creative haze of her own high, the merits of masochism. She hurt, but, yes, she hurt so *good*. She was a baby coming along, and he was a rock 'n' roll song.

Through the portal and into the arena strode Mickey Statler and Dylan Wannamacher, a bit the worse for wear. Fortunately, the arena was only half full. Dylan led the sportswriter to a vacant section, down on the end of the court and across the floor from the home side, where the scoring table and two teams were. He didn't want to sit anywhere where anyone could easily smell his breath. Arriving late was functional. Sitting in the fourth row was functional. No one could easily happen by to chat, not with the two teams running up and down the court. Many of the fans recognized Mickey, the writer who had lionized the football team because it was convenient and a weed delivery was nigh.

Eureka! Wannamacher knows the man. So that's why he wrote the story!

The Dragoons trailed, seventeen to nine, a team of vague origin that had "Tigers" stitched across their chests. That narrowed it down to twelve or fifteen in the Commonwealth, not counting middle and elementary schools and YMCA leagues.

Dylan watched closely. The Merry Pranksters were coming around. The sweat was drowning out the impairment. At the tipoff, they had been sluggish, their legs screaming that they were not inclined to exert themselves and their minds replying that it was cool. Sweaty eyes often reddened, but Milo Hirley's were rosy. They'd shed some tears, as well. He passed it around the perimeter, over to Marty Drummond, who tossed it back, and then to Jonny Heinsohn. He passed it back to Marty, who looked inside, but found no prospect, and passed it back to Milo. No shot clock. No hurry. Bob Wasdin screamed from the sideline, something about everybody standing around. Move the ball. Milo tilted his head, trying to hear what the coach was yelling. He dribbled twice, stopped at the three-point line, and swished a trey. Seventeen to twelve. He stole the inbounds pass and laid it in. Seventeen to fourteen. The Tigers called timeout.

Mickey pointed across the court.

"That the Baxter kid you were talking about?"

Dylan looked closely. "Yeah. How could you tell?"

"He looks like hell," Mickey replied.

Peter was wearing a tee shirt, with a silk-screened drawing of Shakespeare on the front, and cargo pants. No one wore cargo pants anymore. Dylan thought he looked five years older than when he'd been sleeping in class, and he'd looked five years older than normal then. Dylan wondered why Peter was even here and remembered the same question could be asked of himself.

Dylan watched the timeout. Wasdin seemed to be insisting that, Milo's two quick baskets notwithstanding, they sucked. Milo sat on the bench, swigged water, and paid little attention. Wasdin must have said he couldn't win the game by himself. Milo yelled something back at him.

"I read lips pretty well," Mickey said.

"Yeah?"

"The Hirley kid said something like, 'oh, yeah, well, somebody else can win it by himself then.' I think the coach just yanked him out of the game."

As the two teams emerged from the huddle, Dylan noticed that Peter Baxter had disappeared from his seat behind the visiting-team bench. The Tigers scored six points in a row. Twenty-three to fourteen. Mickey said, "The Baxter kid's standing in the corner."

Now Peter was standing to their left, near the bathrooms. He must have been taking a leak. He must be waiting for a dead ball before he walked behind the basket back to his seat. Milo ran to the scorer's table to check back in. The Tigers scored again. The buzzer sounded, and Milo trotted back in. He received the inbounds pass and started dribbling up the court. Everything went quiet. Milo crossed the time line and picked up his dribble. Mickey poked Dylan in the ribs.

Peter Baxter had walked out on the court. He was pointing a gun, sideways, the way they did it in the gang movies about young drug dealers, sticking a piece against the forehead of a rival. Peter's apparent target was thirty-five feet away. He pointed the gun at Milo Hirley. His hands were shaking. He stuttered before blurting out the words: "Die, motherfucker!"

Milo did what he did because it wasn't advisable to do nothing. He dove to the floor, flinging the basketball sidearm as he fell, like a baseball infielder, which he also was. Peter must have been on something. Instead of shooting at Milo, he shot the basketball hurtling toward him, and also the trumpet out of the hand of a sophomore in the pep band sitting in the twelfth row behind the Enlightened Word bench. It ricocheted off the cinder-block wall behind the stands and hit the scoreboard, where the Dragoons' score became four instead of fourteen.

Dylan, who couldn't have done it if he'd thought about it, bounded across the lower rows of the stands and pummeled Peter Baxter as if pouncing on a quarterback. He grabbed Peter's left wrist with his right hand, while he pressed his nose into the boy's chest and twisted his body by yanking his left arm around the waist. Mickey followed, though not in a manner that would remind anyone of a football player. The gun slid across the floor. Mickey got it. Two security guards arrived on the scene. An off-duty cop who was friends with Coach Wasdin pulled his Beretta. Virginia was an open-carry commonwealth. That should have come in handy for Peter Baxter, and it should have ended badly for Milo Hirley. The guards dragged Peter away. He was laughing.

"Fucking God must think a lot of you, Milo Hirley, you motherfucker!" he screamed as he grew rapidly winded.

The rest of the game was postponed until a later date. A TV crew interviewed Dylan. It was all on tape, custom-made to lead the eleven o'clock news. Mickey made himself scarce, slipping out through the portal and retreating to the corner of the lobby. Most of the fans had rushed out of the entire gymnasium, and Mickey could see them through the plate-glass windows, milling around. Two of the Tigers' cheerleaders lit cigarettes. Who was going to say anything? The van was on the other side of the building. Everybody seemed to be breathing heavily and shivering in the cold. Mickey thought about bumming a cigarette from one of the cheerleaders, just to add some symmetry to the madness. He waited, though, because Dylan Wannamacher, the hero, was his ride.

Dylan finally found him in the lobby.

"I should've stopped him," he said.

"You did stop him," Mickey said.

"I mean sooner. I knew something was bad wrong with that kid. I knew he wasn't right in class."

"Isn't that why you came?"

"A mere coincidence," Dylan said. "They asked me who you were."

"Me?"

"You were the other guy. The guy from TV asked me what about the other guy. I told him I thought you were a sportswriter. You were probably somewhere, writing the story."

"That may happen eventually," Mickey said. "I bet it pops up in something you write, too."

"Sometimes, if you want to tell the truth, you've got to write fiction," Dylan said, and they walked to the car.

CHAPTER 45

Preventive Measures

"The president is close to Borzov because the Russians played a major role in his being elected," Bentsen Lilley said. "That's simply the way it is."

"Jesus," Patrick Trintignant said. "The Republican Party. Soft on Russia. Who'd believe it?"

"Who'd believe anything that's happened in this country the past two years?"

"So you're saying, Bentsen, that the President of the United States is implicated in a plot to assassinate his own Attorney General?"

"I think the phrase is 'tacit approval'," Lilley said. "Gaynes wanted Beale to protect him from the Russian investigation, but Beale, once it came out that he had also met with the Russians, recused himself, and now there's an investigation, with a special counsel, underway, all because Gaynes insisted upon firing the director of the FBI."

"And replacing him with our friend Edmund Kingsley."

"Yes. A very fortuitous development for our business, but Beale is our enemy. His view of cannabis legalization is archaic. It runs directly against public opinion. Both parties are on the fence, the Democrats less so, but there is a mainstream political advantage, just waiting to be realized, for advocating cannabis, at the very least, for medical use and, according to the surveys, recreational use. We don't need the federal government to act, at least not for now. More and more states will see the potential for revenues in taxing and regulating cannabis. When five to eight more states approve it, then the time for federal approval will be obvious and appropriate. All we need now is for the feds to get out of the way."

"So what do we do when Beale visits?" Trintignant asked.

"We wine him, and we dine him, and we ply him with whatever weaknesses of the flesh he desires, and then we lobby him just to leave it to the states on the basis of states' rights, like the good Republican, the principled conservative, that he purports to be."

"And you think there's a chance in hell he'll go along with that?"

"No," Lilley said, "I do not. If Beale doesn't change his view, he'll pay for it with his life."

"But he can't know that. We can't threaten him."

"No. Kingsley said it was a blind taste test."

"He's giving a speech at the gospel festival," Trintignant said.

"Yes. If he leaves the door open to cannabis, if he just says the feds will yield to the right of states, same policy as the previous administration, he'll live to deliver other speeches."

"And you are willing to leave this entirely up to Pankratov and the Russians?"

"Well, I can't be there," Lilley said, "and you can't be there. No one prominent – not Kingsbury, not Samuelson – can be seen. It's a minor event. A gospel sing in Las Vegas, for chrissakes. Beale's interest is twofold. First, he likes that kind of music. And Nevada legalized cannabis. Beale wants to rail against it. We need somebody there, somebody dependable, somebody who can stop it, if need be, and somebody who can tell Pankratov to go ahead. If need be."

"Pankratov will be there."

"Not publicly visible but there. Who do you know who can represent our interests?"

"I got a man in mind," Trintignant said. "Smart. Dependable. Ruthless. Cool head. He's our best troubleshooter."

"Do I need to know his name?" Lilley asked.

"Probably not."

Dylan Wannamacher and Mickey Statler returned to Hippie Arms at midnight and, fueled by coffee, talked through the night. Dylan dismissed the possibility that Peter Baxter was anything other than a nutcase who had snapped.

"When something like this happens – not that anything like this has ever happened around here – it makes you agonize about what could have been done," Dylan said. "You couldn't engage him. He was intense for its own sake, if that makes sense. You really couldn't tell him anything. He'd stare straight into your eyes, nodding his head, and then it was like he couldn't process a word you said. Peter got away with things because it was just too much trouble to stop him, and you couldn't do it, anyway. He's probably the least likable kid I've ever taught."

"What kind of writer is he?" Mickey asked.

"Self-absorbed. Accusatory in style. Over-long sentences. That's where I succumbed. He'd have a fit if he got an A-minus instead of an A. He deserved no better than a B, and that was with his better work, but I was like everybody else. I'd give an A-minus just to make a point, and he'd raise hell about that."

"Drugs, maybe?"

"I actually suspected that. Certainly not weed. Hell, Peter Baxter could use some weed. I don't know much about it, but I've heard of kids taking Adderalls when they were doing all-nighters before tests. Shit, I don't know. Maybe he ran out, and that was enough to make him go apeshit. Maybe Milo screwed his girlfriend. When I had him in class yesterday, he was out of gas, and that was a first."

"Maybe he found something else to get hopped up on, and it made him want to stroll over to the gym and kill the Hirley kid."

"Thank God he didn't succeed," Dylan said.

Dylan nodded off in his easy chair at five. Noting this, Mickey retired to the twin bed in the guest room. He heard Dylan showering at seven but kept his eyes closed, drifting in and out of sleep and detecting the faint aroma of a daughter who had slept many times in the same bed. He shuddered at the slow-motion memory of Dylan, slamming Peter Baxter to the floor as he somehow managed to concentrate on grasping the wrist and prying the gun loose. Mickey followed Dylan more or less out of instinct, and he scrambled across the floor to secure the black pistol. In the dream reenactment, he saw Marcia and her beau, Wade Sanderson, peeking in from the lobby, exchanging knowing smiles, and slipping out.

Headmaster Nathan Drummond declared "free movement" at Enlightened Word College Preparatory Academy. Classes were canceled. Instructors stopped teaching, and students stopped learning. The faculty and staff became grief counselors, even though no one had been hurt, and only Peter Baxter had been ruined. Dylan Wannamacher had been lionized. One ulterior motive behind the counseling was the need to prepare students for police questioning. Dylan sat in his classroom and talked with a stream of students who wandered by. Most wanted to talk about Dylan's disarming of Peter Baxter. He said he didn't know why he'd done what he had done, only, he guessed, that someone had to do it, and he was just nearby. Dylan knew Milo would eventually show up, and that he'd want to go off somewhere alone, and no one would begrudge them their privacy.

Milo waited until after lunch, and, almost by common, instinctive agreement, they walked down to the little grandstand behind the third-base dugout at the baseball diamond.

"I'm fine," Milo said, "or pretty fine, anyway. When everything went quiet, and I looked up, and I saw Peter Baxter pointing a gun at me, my first thought was, goddamn, what a pussy, and my second thought was, that pussy's gonna shoot me, and that's when I lunged to the ground and just fired the basketball at him. Then I hauled ass on all fours, twisting left and right. But, you know what keeps coming back? That stupid ass shot the basketball! He hit it! If his mind hadn't been completely fucked up, he'd have hit me."

Milo had been looking at the ground. He raised his head. "Why were you even there?"

"I was worried about you," Dylan said. "Bryne's death really got to you. Funny. I came to the gym thinking you were the one about to snap. You know, I was concerned about Peter, too. He fell asleep in class yesterday. Peter. Milo, was he on Adderall?"

"How'd you know?"

"How'd you know?" Dylan asked.

"All right, look, I didn't tell the police any of this. It would have been hard to do without leaving, let's say, a tinge of incrimination. When Bryne got shot, Peter ran out of pills. Somehow, he was getting them from Bryne. I think he bribed him or something, because Bryne wouldn't have sold anybody nothing but weed. Somehow, Bryne managed to get Peter his Adderall, and, when the cops murdered Bryne, Peter, being Peter, didn't care about Bryne's death. He tried to bribe me into figuring out some way to get 'em for him."

"What'd you do?"

"Told him to get fucked," Peter said. "It was the day before yesterday. At Vissage."

"Jesus," Dylan said.

"I just decided to tell the police that I didn't know what he had against me," Milo said. "I couldn't very well tell them he came to me because he knew I sold weed. Next thing you know, they'd be charging me for attempted murder of myself."

"I think you're going to be fine," Dylan said. "You've still got a sense of humor."

"I told the cops we weren't friends, that we didn't particularly care for each other, but that I hadn't ever done anything to him to make him say anything, let alone try to kill me. You know what I'd say is the only mystery?"

"What?"

"What was he on last night? What was it? Adderall? Cocaine? Meth? I couldn't say. I never took any of that," Milo said. "I'm just a stoner. I guess, what? They'll drug-test Peter, right? I guess we'll find out."

"If we need to, I reckon," Dylan said. "Maybe, if Peter takes a plea bargain, it'll never come out. I don't care whether it does or not. What I wanted to make sure is that Peter just snapped, went apeshit, not that it was something staged, you know, to get rid of you the same way they got rid of Bryne. I think that's ridiculous, but I wanted to make sure you did, too."

"Nah," Milo said, "No way. Peter Baxter is about as reliable as an assassin as I am as a Bible scholar."

"Might not be a bad idea to read a little New Testament right now," Dylan said.

"Oh, it's required, Dylan. You know that."

"Call me if you need me, Milo. Come by if you need to. Keep your shit together, best you can, all right?"

"I'm good," he said. "The myriad scars won't come out for years."

Mickey Statler had been worried about Marcia's safety. Then he had rushed to see her, and she'd been elusive and absent. He was still worried. It's just that he'd almost forgotten it. He answered another urgent text from Carson Carmine.

Still occupied. Ttyl.

Mickey finally got around to a shave and shower. Once dressed, he found another text, this one from Marcia, asking him to meet her and Wade at an O'Charley's on Winchester Road. At the same time Dylan and Milo were having their heart-to-heart at Enlightened Word, Mickey, Marcia, and Wade were munching on fried-cheese triangles and looking over menus. They were all starving. Marcia and Wade had slept in, too. They apparently didn't know about the shooting the night before, and Mickey didn't feel inclined to discuss it. The restaurant was almost vacant, the lunch crowd having long departed. Marcia ordered a fried chicken salad. Wade had a bacon cheeseburger. Mickey ordered a club sandwich.

Wade wanted to talk about the Consortium.

"I didn't know there was one," Mickey said. "When Ronnie Shingler, the deputy back in Lovejoy, set me up, he depicted it as a little underground syndicate of the local sheriff's department. The idea was to confiscate all the marijuana and keep it away from the young people there and ship it off to corrupt the minds of kids everywhere else."

Wade laughed. Marcia smiled.

"As time went on, I realized this was a lot bigger," Mickey continued. "As a practical matter, it's been great as a writer. I love just to go places and write columns about whatever it is I can find. I'm making three times as much money. All that worries me is that this gigantic thing, this consortium, you call it, is going to get too big, and it's going to be a big scandal, and I'm going to wind up going to jail. I mean, it's in the back of my mind."

"The fix is in, Daddy. The government's on our side. We got the cover of the cops. It's rigged in our favor," Marcia opined.

"No, no, Mr. Statler, I understand your concerns, but everything's under control," Wade said. "As weed becomes legal in more and more states, we're set up to go legit. This is all about laying the groundwork. I'm not, you know, a big shot in the Consortium or anything, but I'm kind of a troubleshooter. Recently, I've been going to areas where there are problems and getting them fixed."

"So you didn't strictly come here to see Marcia?" Mickey asked.

"No, but I was delighted. I'm from Conover, North Carolina. I've been trying to finagle a trip back east."

"We met when I flew to L.A. with Tripp Fallaw," Marcia said. "He was a golf player here at Triborough. Wade and Tripp were going to hustle these Hollywood celebrities. It didn't really go that well, but Wade and I kept in touch. He hooked me up."

"What happened to, uh, Tripp?"

"Oh, he's, or at least Wade thinks he's in Mexico," Marcia said. "Tripp got himself in trouble. He's sort of a loser."

"It shocked me when I bumped into my daughter," Mickey said, looking at Wade. "I tried to get out. No dice. I'm too good, everybody says."

"You okay with it now?" Wade asked.

"Can't afford not to be."

Wade looked at his cell. "I need to step out," he said. "I've got to take this call."

The food arrived. Marcia's salad came with honey mustard, and she'd ordered blue cheese, so she sent it back. She told her father to go ahead. Wade's burger was getting cold.

"It's all right, Daddy. When I messaged you, I was trying to deal with the Brynildson Hiers thing. My conscience hurt a little, but it was just an accident. A real bad accident, but I didn't say anything about getting rid of Bryne. I just said it was a little problem that I would have to deal with. I never got the chance."

"It's that kind of little miscommunication that is going to bring everything down," Mickey said.

"Everything's gonna be all right," she replied. "Wade says the Gaynes Administration is going to back off on cannabis. The new FBI director is a friend. The president is a friend."

"Presidents tell everybody they're friends. Gaynes isn't exactly trustworthy, in my estimation."

"He's a businessman, Daddy. That's what America is now. It's all down to business."

Wade returned, sat down, and waved to the server, giving him forty bucks, telling him to keep the tip and bring him a box.

"I gotta go," he said. "Something big. I've got to fly to Vegas. You ever been to Vegas, Marcia?"

"No."

"Want to go?"

"I don't know, Wade. There's things I've got to do here," she said, perhaps in some small measure because of her father's presence.

"Suit yourself," Wade said. "I'm going back to the Marriott. If you change your mind, I can work it out. Mickey, can you drop Marcia by later?"

"Yeah," he said.

Wade Sanderson had missed an opportunity, but the machinations going on in Las Vegas were too important to dwell on anything else. Had Marcia gone with him, he might have been able to persuade her to set up her father, even kill him herself. If that didn't work, he could have her killed in a hail of automatic-weapon fire. Or snap that long, petite neck and leave her body lying among the dying pilgrims.

You win some. You lose some. Wade was going to leave Las Vegas as an important man in the Consortium. He would be connected with the Russians. He would change the course of history.

Marcia finally got her fried-chicken salad.

"Don't let him change your mind," Mickey said. "I don't know what this is, but it's dangerous."

"You're right," she said, "but you know already that I like danger. I'm not going, though, because there are things I've got to set right here. I need to patch things up with Dylan, and I need to convince the kids at Enlightened Word that I'm not a murderer, and you and I have some catching up to do."

"I take it you don't know somebody tried to kill Milo Hirley last night."

"What?"

"I was there. Dylan and I went to a basketball game Milo was playing in. In the second quarter, I guess, this kid from the school walked out on the court and pointed a gun at Milo, who was dribbling up the court. Milo dove to the ground and threw the ball at the kid with the gun. He missed. Dylan bounded out of the stands, disarmed the kid, and tackled him. I picked up the gun when it slid across the floor."

"Milo threw the ball at him?" She almost laughed. "Damn."

"Why don't you come back to the apartment, Marcia?"

"You better drop me off at the Marriott, Daddy. I won't let Wade change my mind."

One more night of love, Mickey thought. He still didn't like Wade Sanderson's looks. What could he do but trust her? She was a grown woman, or damned sure thought she was.

CHAPTER 46

Fate in the Air

Marcia Statler fell asleep, at last, in the wee hours, thinking she was going to wind up flying to Las Vegas with Wade Sanderson. He was a hard man to tell no. He was a hard man in general.

Fate intervened. Fate was in the air.

Wade awakened her. She was still rubbing her eyes and clearing the cobwebs, but he said something had come up, and he had to fly first to Colorado and then to Vegas. He couldn't take her on this trip. His was the last seat on a private plane. He said he'd be back as soon possible. He told her to go back to sleep. Just be out by checkout time.

She went back to sleep thinking, *Daddy will be so proud.*

That afternoon, even though it was Sunday, Marcia made a few pot deliveries at the college. She sent a text to Milo Hirley.

Sorry 2 hear bout what happened. R u ok? Lemme know if i can help…

In other words, *it's not the best of timing, but if you need weed, let me know.* Not code. Tact.

Marcia stopped for coffee at Auntie Em's and thought about what she would say to her father and Dylan. She needed to set things straight. Certainly they knew she and Wade were in love. Confessing it was the only justification for avoiding them, particularly her dad, whom she had summoned urgently, and then, when he actually came, spent about half an hour with him in three days, all with Wade at her side.

Not that she was really in love with Wade. She was in lust with him. Just what, exactly, was love? In him, she found animal attraction. He was adventurous. He was bold and unscrupulous. He said weed wasn't illegal. It was extralegal. He said they were going to get rich when that changed, and the transition was all set. Marcia didn't know why Wade was going somewhere in Colorado, and then to Sin City, but she knew it was important, and she sensed he was up to no good.

Mickey was nervous all day. He watched college basketball games while Dylan was doing bong hits and playing his guitar. They barely talked, not because either was irritated at the other, but because they'd been through so much, and talked about it, and mulled it over, until there wasn't much left to say. When Marcia arrived, he smiled for the first time since she'd sent him the emergency text. She looked radiant – probably, it's true, because her charming rogue of a boyfriend had screwed her clear to the brains and out of her mind – but he found simple pleasure in him being gone and her still here. She had *told* him she wasn't going with Wade, but, somehow, he knew there was the element of a lie in why.

Fate was in the air.

Marcia tried to treat Dylan's mild psychic wounds. She hugged him. Said she didn't want them to grow apart.

"No worries," he said. "The reason I'm stoned isn't you. The reason is I'm tired of all the attention. Football coaching. Now everybody I've ever known is trying to get in touch. I wasn't going to get high today. Then I had to call my mother. Christ. The word has gotten all the way to Mississippi of how prep-school English teacher Dylan Wannamacher foiled a student's attempt to shoot a basketball player. Either that, or, 'former college football star Dylan Wannamacher prevented an attempted murder.' They haven't gotten to, 'aging pothead Dylan Wannamacher tackles a would-be murderer' yet."

"There's worse things," Mickey said.

"Potheads prefer privacy," Dylan retorted. "I think it's that 'illegal' thing. Tell me this, Mickey. Did you scramble out of that gym because you didn't want people to notice you on purpose? You can't really tell from the video that it's you."

"I just handed the gun to the cop, and got out of there. I don't know. Maybe I thought there might be somebody else with a gun. Maybe I thought a cop might start firing. I don't know. It was so fast. I just didn't want to hang around."

"You haven't even talked to the cops?"

"No. They must have forgot about me," Mickey said. "Owing to Marcia and me's little side business, I tend to err on the side of caution."

"Me, too," Dylan said. "As I was just saying."

"Milo Hirley's still alive," Mickey said. "Peter Baxter's probably going to get the treatment he needs. Don't let yourself get eat up with modern problems. We're safe. Those two kids are, too."

"My hero." Marcia feigned swooning.

"Well," Dylan said, "the fucking *Today Show* wants me to drive to D.C. in the morning and be on. I told them I had to teach. 'Fine. We'll send a crew.' A literary agent, probably one who has rejected me, sent me an email about a book deal. I don't want *that* book deal. I don't want to write about two troubled kids at a basketball game."

"That's the type of book I would write," Mickey said.

"Have at it," Dylan said.

"Let's just stop," Marcia said. "Let's have happy thoughts. Let's get high. Me and my daddy and my favorite, most admirable friend."

Whom I'm never going to fuck anymore, Dylan thought. Admirable. *Al Gore is admirable.*

"I'm there," Dylan said. "You two go ahead. I'll have another rip when we have some sort of stoner symmetry."

They talked about literature, and writing, and fiction versus non-fiction, and first versus third person, and Dylan's view that the Gaynes Administration was becoming just like Borzov's regime in Russia, and that was a kleptocracy, or government by thieves, and Marcia's view that kleptocracy was just a word, and if that's what worked, it wasn't necessarily a bad thing.

"That's the most intelligent defense of the Gaynes Administration I've ever heard," Dylan said.

"He's been president, what? A month, already," Mickey said.

At dusk, they went to O'Charley's in Mickey's spacious rental car, and this time they all had steaks. Mickey decided it was time to get back to the beat, and he sent a text to Carson Carmine, who instructed him to drive to Hickory, North Carolina to pick up a briefcase full of cannabis on Monday, and then drive over to Winston-Salem, where Mickey could make the transaction before the basketball game between Clemson and Wake Forest.

Life seemed to be getting back to regular abnormal.

CHAPTER 47

Little Deceptions

Nathan Bedford Forrest Beale, recently appointed Attorney General of the United States, formerly junior Senator from the State of Mississippi, was not an imposing man. He was courtly and effeminate in a Southern sort of way. His wife, Marjorie, was six inches taller and lorded over him in personal and family matters. He called her "Mama" and made a show of attending to her every need. She accompanied him on the flight to Denver in Bentsen Lilley's corporate jet. Two aides and a four-man security detail boarded with Beale. The last to board were three representatives of the Consortium: Wade Sanderson, Stedman Andersen, and Angelique Blount. They were unacquainted but had been well briefed. Wade was Patrick Trintignant's troubleshooter and the only one of the three who drew a direct livelihood from the Consortium. Stedman's salary originated in a conservative think tank but his job was to analyze government policy and curry favor for the legalization effort. He moved in Libertarian circles and, under the cover of conservatism, distributed money to politicians who would vote pro-weed when the time came for legislation that really mattered. He and Beale barely knew each other. As a senator, Beale had been celebrated and reviled for his obstinacy regarding drug reform. Angelique was an organizer and systems analyst who allegedly worked for the corporation, Choice Tobacco, that Lilley headed. She organized cannabis distribution for the Consortium.

Nathan and Marjorie Beale loved Jesus, first and foremost, but Nathan also asked forgiveness each night for his love of bourbon, cigars, and a few other private peccadilloes. Marjorie was fond of wine. They grew more animated as the flight progressed. The Attorney General took a liking to Wade because half a decade in Southern California had not altogether diluted his North Carolina mountain twang. Beale's dialect was thick and deficient in enunciation. He attended *chuhch*, read the *Bobble*, played *gahf*, and enjoyed a *seegah*. The ones Angelique brought him were Cuban. *Veh fahn, veh fahn.*

Wade had been conservatized suitably for the trip by having his beard shaved and his locks shorn. He wore a navy suit, light-blue dress shirt, and a red-and-navy striped tie, with an American flag lapel pin for good measure. Stedman, more accustomed to such attire, wore a white shirt and solid red tie. The suit was almost identical. Angelique wore a bright blue pantsuit that seemed a bit out of place on an African American. Wade was attracted to her. She seemed lively for an organizer of delivery schedules. The cabin of the jet was organized in four groupings of seating areas, each with facing rows of two comfortable, reclining seats and a table. Wade sat next to Stedman, facing the back. Angelique sat across from them. To the left rear, staggered next to a small kitchen, sat two security agents. Ahead and to the left were the Beales and their aides. On the other side of a meeting table, straight ahead, were the other two government bodyguards.

Over Kentucky, Stedman nodded off. He undoubtedly needed the rest, but Wade wanted to make the best impression. He wanted to be alert and *impressive*. When the flight attendant came by for a drink order, Wade ordered black coffee in a good-sized mug. Angelique ordered Diet Coke. The Attorney General, his wife, and his aides all felt comfortable enough to party. Beale drank bourbon and "spring water." Marjorie sipped wine that cost a fortune. His acolytes drank what Beale drank and roughly at the same rate. Once Wade grew weary of observing everyone – the agents drank bottled water – he took out his phone and found a text from Angelique, though she was sitting across from him.

Psst.

He looked up. She nodded. He texted back.

What brings u on this trip?

4 now, kissing cracker ass … got conferences at lilley's place in rockies. U?

Goin w/ beale 2 vegas. 'No sin' city 4 me.

Lol. Who u work 4?

Trintignant.

Ooh. Know any other Russians?

Huh?

Stedman's one.

No shit?

Trust me. Watch him.

Didn't know Russians slept.

He isn't.

"We are prepared," Trintignant said. "Beale ditched his wife, who has a speaking engagement with the Republican Women's Club of Denver and a tour of the city's homes and gardens. The Attorney General and Marjorie will spend the night at the home of Congressman Wes Outland, and then he'll fly up with Angelique Blount, Wade Sanderson, and Stedman Andersen. Afterwards, Wade – he's the young man I was telling you about – will fly to Vegas to assist in preparations for Beale's arrival there."

"Wink, wink," Bentsen Lilley said. "No one would ever suspect Andersen of being Russian."

"Iznetsikov. Yuri Iznetsikov. A thoroughly dangerous man. How long have you been affiliated with the Russians, Bentsen?"

"Oh, ever since our business went sour in the States. Tobacco still flourishes in most of Europe, Asia, Africa, South America. When we came under legal assault by our own government, we had to go where we weren't … embattled. I haven't found a whole lot of communism in Russian and Chinese money. It was the seed money for the Consortium. The Russians are the tie that binds. We have a relationship. The President has a relationship. Neither Gaynes nor Pankratov is trustworthy. There is no loyalty, no honor. Only mutual self-interest. It's the only way to do business."

"It all boils down to self-interest," Trintignant said.

"Among the more misused words in the English language is 'strategy.' The key to a successful operation is tactics, not strategy," Lilley noted. "Conditions change. Strategy is tenuous. What matters is adjusting the tactics on the fly in a cohesive way, responding to unforeseen opportunity. Beale has become a liability to Gaynes. He recused himself from a Congressional investigation, brought on in no small part by his own perjury in front of the Senate Judiciary Committee. Now the President needs protection that Beale is unable or unwilling to give. He has become expendable, and, in death, he provides Gaynes with an opportunity to divert attention away from his own vulnerabilities. If the Attorney General is an apparent casualty of a mass killing, perpetrated by a black, Muslim militant on an audience of white Christians, it will boost the approval rating of a president already embattled after a month in office."

"Bentsen, all that really concerns me is the unintended ramifications. The country is tense. Violence is rising. The alt-right will go crazy. We could see pitched battles of blacks and whites in the cities. Flames. Looting."

"The President will have to deal with that. If this creates a monster, he will have to slay it."

"What if Beale becomes a martyr of cannabis prohibition? What if this hurts our cause?"

"*Que sera, sera,*" Lilley said. "Whatever will be, will be."

"It was better in the original Doris Day," Trintignant said.

CHAPTER 48

Survivors So Far

Dylan Wannamacher didn't sell weed. He enjoyed it. One advantage of his tepid affair with Marcia Statler was that cannabis was plentiful and didn't cost him much, if anything. Mickey Statler was a reluctant conspirator, no more infatuated with illegal business than Dylan. They had grown close, acquaintances of fate, journalism, and Marcia, similarly resigned to some sort of impending disaster they could do nothing to avoid. The budding presidency of Martin J. Gaynes would have left them feeling numb and hopeless, anyway, only not so close and personal. Most of the country suffered in a general way. Some even realized it. Dylan had a macro and a micro. He had spent close to twenty years trying to mind his own business and lurk in life's background.

Twenty years of apathy, down the tubes.

Most of Dylan's thoughts, as he sat in the twilight darkness of Hippie Arms Number Eight with only the flicker of around-the-clock news casting light across the room, were of Milo Hirley, a young man of great promise and risk. The other three Merry Pranksters would turn out all right. They'd go off to college, choke on the freedom for a while, learn some hard lessons, and find their way to a wife, two kids, and a home in the country. Milo would either surpass them all or sink into oblivion. He didn't have their breeding. He hadn't been sent to Enlightened Word as a legacy. He'd been sent there because his hustler dad and depressed mom couldn't figure out anything else to do with him. He was bright, insightful, and gallant, but, also, cynical, corrupt, and exploitative. What drew Dylan to Milo, and vice-versa, was that each was the other's greatest project. Each saw in the other a bit of his own imperfection. They read each other. When Dylan observed Milo, he felt a kinship with his own younger self. He felt occasionally as if he were his own father.

Naturally, as Dylan was thinking about Milo, Milo called.

"Hey, Dylan, mind if I come over?"

"Where are you?"

"On the way."

"Well," Dylan said, "I guess it's settled."

Dylan didn't relish the visit, but Milo breezed in, unexpectedly buoyant.

"I'm back," he announced. "I have rallied the troops."

"Fellow Pranksters in the car?"

"No," Milo said. "My forces are all internal."

"You are remarkably resilient, Milo Hirley. You have every right to milk what has recently happened to you for all it's worth. You may find out, one day in the distant future, that it is, coincidentally, the right thing to do."

"Who says I haven't? I rule the school, man. Nobody tells me shit. I can't remember if it was you who told me, Dylan. If you could go through a natural disaster, and be guaranteed you wouldn't even get a scratch, it would be, like, the ultimate amusement park."

"It's obsolete," Dylan said. "You get that from technology. Virtual-reality games."

"Weed."

"Acid, maybe. Mushrooms. I can't say. Weed is as far as I've ever been down the road that escapes reality."

"Another thing we have in common, Coach."

"Praise God that forever it thus be so," Dylan said.

"Guess where I been?"

"Where?"

"Triborough. Coach wants me to play basketball," Milo said.

"And?"

"I told them they needed a shooter, not somebody who gets shot at."

"Charlie the Tuna," Dylan said.

"Huh?"

"Never mind. It's a dated reference. Old commercial."

"I'm fairly excited," Milo said.

"Any other offers?"

"Couple letters. It's amazing how getting shot at can increase one's exposure."

"Do you think it will work to go to school at home?"

"Duh," Milo said. "Enlightened Word ain't home."

"Hell of a point."

"You know, Milo, playing ball at the collegiate level means you get drug-tested."

"Aw, I'm not worried about that. Where there's a will, there's a way. Besides, the discipline required to play sports will be good for me."

"The discipline of being clean for scheduled drug tests?"

"You gotta walk before you can run," Milo said, "and who wants to run? Besides, you made it through all right. I know you smoked weed when you were playing football."

"When I was playing football, there weren't any drug tests. The wanton recklessness of my generation is responsible for the loss of privacy in yours."

"You bastard." Milo laughed.

"You know, I've been teaching at Enlightened Word for eighteen years," Dylan said. "Until you came along, I managed to keep a professional distance from my students. I must be starting to lose my wits. I must be middle-age crazy."

"Tapping that young woman made you start thinking you was a kid again. She's bad, man. Bad ass."

"That's true," Dylan responded. "I already knew that most men let women rule their whole life. They're in denial at the time. They don't even realize it, but everything they do is to get laid, basically. Why did I play ball? Why did I teach myself to play guitar? Why did I introduce myself to this hot co-ed, and why did I wind up getting high with her, and falling in love with her …"

"Get laid, man. Makes the world go around. Where is Marcia?"

"I don't know. She hasn't spent the night here for several days."

"I saw her," Milo said.

"What?"

"She met me and tried to explain to me again how Bryne's death was just an awful accident, a breakdown in communications. She said she specifically told … whoever the boss was, that Wade guy, I guess … that she would take care of it. Plus, I guess she heard about me getting shot at, and, you know, I guess she wanted to check on me. Make sure I wasn't losing my shit or something."

"When?" Dylan asked.

"Last night. After practice."

"She leave anything with you?"

"Yeah. … It wasn't, you know, as scheming as all that. I think, genuinely, she wanted to make things right. I think she cares. A little."

"I thought she just wanted to see what campus life at Enlightened Word was like," Dylan said. "I never dreamed she was setting up a distribution network."

"We weren't exactly blameless," Milo said.

"Few people ever are."

CHAPTER 49

Just a Hunch

Rashawn Ling was fifteen minutes late to the barbecue joint in Lexington, North Carolina. Mickey Statler nibbled on hush puppies, reading *USA Today*, and a story caught his eye. When Rashawn arrived, Mickey ordered a minced platter – Yankees called it "pulled pork" – and Rashawn decided on a salad. A barbecue salad, which meant his minced barbecue was scattered atop lettuce, tomato and slices of boiled egg, slathered with blue cheese dressing. Mickey considered such a concoction sacrilegious, but who was he to judge another man's palate?

Mickey folded up the paper. "You found anyone willing to publish a story about a nationwide weed conspiracy?" he asked.

"I sent out some queries. Respectable web sites. A few magazines. All quite reputable," Rashawn replied.

"I hope you were careful. Don't forget, most people would consider The Ultimate Sporting Life respectable."

Rashawn smiled. "I'm careful. I don't want to get shot or nothing."

"It might not be a bad idea to set out on a wing and a prayer, write a story, and submit it. You can go out there on my dime. An idea just occurred to me, going through this rag. There's quite a coincidence I discovered."

"Oh?"

"Mr. Gaynes' celebrated Attorney General, one Nathan Bedford Forrest Beale, is flying to Las Vegas to attend, get this, a gospel music festival."

"In Vegas."

"In Vegas," Mickey said. "The honorable Mr. Beale is going to give a speech. Nevada recently voted to legalize cannabis. My guess is he's going to rail against the evils of deadly marijuana and announce that the government isn't going to respect the states' rights to legalize it."

"I thought everybody like Beale – he's from Mississippi, right? – believes in states' rights," Rashawn said.

"Where it suits their purposes, they do."

"So what's that got to do with the conspiracy? Where's the coincidence?"

"My daughter is seeing a young man who works for the Consortium," Mickey said. "I don't trust him as far as I could kick him. I don't like his looks. I wrote a column on the ballgame in Winston-Salem last night. Before that, I was in Virginia. Marcia sent me a text saying she was in trouble and needed some help. I lit out for Triborough, told the site I'd be out of circulation for a few days, got up there, and I barely saw her. She was shacked up at the Marriott with this kid, name's Wade Sanderson. Me and my friend Dylan Wannamacher ..."

"He's the English teacher turned football coach."

"Yeah."

"I read that story."

"Well," Mickey said, "what I didn't put in the story is that Dylan and Marcia were seeing each other. He's a frustrated novelist. She fancies herself a budding novelist. Anyway, Marcia goes from acting like her life's in danger to acting like nothing's wrong as soon as this Wade shows up. It appears he's some kind of troubleshooter for the Consortium. It could be that I'm part of the trouble he was shooting."

"Did you think you were in danger, Mickey?"

"I didn't mind it a bit when he lit out, all of a sudden, for Colorado."

Rashawn hadn't touched his barbecue salad. He took a swallow of his sweet tea. He stared at Mickey, waiting for the rest of the story.

"Beale is going to Colorado first, staying a few days. Marcia didn't go with Sanderson, but I know her, and I think she wanted to, but he told her, no, he didn't want to get her involved with whatever business it was he had to take care of. I don't know whether he told her or not – maybe she got it somewhere else – but Dylan says she found out Sanderson was going from Colorado to Vegas, too. I'm headed back to Triborough, but I've got a feeling Marcia is going to fly to Vegas herself. I think she's in love with this guy. She falls in love a lot."

"So why don't you go?" Rashawn asked.

"I'm known," Mickey said. "Apparently they're suspicious that I might spill the beans, and, of course, they're right. I'm worried that all this is out of control, that something big's gonna happen, and I think it might happen in Vegas. I'm going back to see if I can find Marcia and talk her out of going. I'll pay your way to Vegas. It might be good for you to see a gospel sing. Might get you right with Jesus."

"It might be that all this really is a coincidence."

"But, if not, you might get yourself a story that'll put Lovejoy in your rear-view mirror from now own."

"I don't know," Rashawn said.

"You ain't got nothing to do. It's not just a coincidence. It's fate. If you hadn't been late meeting me, I wouldn't have read *USA Today*, and I wouldn't know about Beale going first to Colorado and then to Nevada, and about how strange it seems for this holy-roller, Ten Commandments-recitin' Attorney General hobnobbin' around a couple weed-legal states."

"You'll be wasting your money."

"What? You don't like Vegas? It'll be fun, Rashawn. You might make your fortune there, one way or another. I don't believe I'd use nothing but cash money, if I was you."

"You a regular gangster."

"Growing more and more reluctant," Mickey said. "Let me show you something. Look out the window. You see that fellow wearing the Chapel Hill cap?"

"Yeah."

"That's my rental car. He's unlatching the trunk. All right. Now he's putting a silver briefcase in the trunk. Taking one out just like it. The one he's taking out has twenty-four one-ounce bags of weed. The one he's leaving has five thousand dollars in it."

"Goddamn, Mickey."

"That guy's an off-duty cop."

"I hope he remembers to lock the doors," Rashawn said.

"Have you noticed, Rashawn, that I called you from a different number?"

"Yeah."

"Save it. I've got a business cell I keep turned off most of the time. You don't still have your work phone, do you? I mean, you answered the same number."

"J.D. told me it was paid for till the end of the month," Rashawn said.

"Get a new one now. New number."

"Why? What are you getting at?"

"Well," Mickey said, "I been thinking. It's possible that you got let go at the *News-Free Press* because you were poking around into the Consortium."

"I haven't told anybody."

"You told Myra LeFlore."

"I know you hate her, Mickey, but that's batshit crazy."

"I think she's in with them. I don't know it, but I've got a hunch. You getting your job eliminated for no good reason … I'm just putting two and two together."

"Don't you get me killed, Mickey Statler."

"You don't need to get out there till Friday. That gives you most of three days to screw around between now and then. Get the new cell. Get back in touch with me before you leave. Keep in touch when you get there. … Hey, you got a middle name?"

"Yeah."

"What is it?"

"Smitherman."

"Shit, Rashawn, you might be the quintessential American. Rashawn Smitherman Ling. Middle name on your driver's license?"

"Yeah. Why?"

"Buy the plane ticket as Smitherman Ling. Tell the lady at check-in you go by 'Smitty'."

Mickey paid the bill, and they went outside. Mickey told him to get in the car for a minute. Mickey reached in the console and counted out ten hundred-dollar bills.

"Five hundred dollars for air fare, hotel, and rental car. Five hundred more for spending money. Air fare to Vegas is cheap. Cheap rooms are available when you get there. Bring back what you don't use. You get lucky at the blackjack tables, and we'll split the profit."

"I don't know what I'm looking for," Rashawn said.

"Me, neither," Mickey replied. "You're a pro. Just observe. Talk to people at the music festival."

"I'll probably be quite the novelty item."

"That's right," Mickey said. "Everybody will want to talk to you. Don't wear a beret."

CHAPTER 50

All Reasonable Alternatives

Bentsen Lilley was a decisive man. Once he made a plan, he stuck to it, and, in its mission, the Consortium was close to success. Unfortunately, the Attorney General of the United States stood almost alone in its path. If Nathan Beale wouldn't get out of the way, he must be eliminated. Business was business. Lilley was past the point of morality.

Patrick Trintignant feared disaster. The death of a prominent politician would inevitably arouse a hornet's nest of inquiry. Such a nest was already swarming at the arbitrary behavior of the erratic new president, Martin Gaynes. Trintignant thought Lilley overestimated the protection provided by their partners in law enforcement. Edmund Kingsley had been appointed director of the Federal Bureau of Investigation. Garlin Samuelson had been instrumental in building a network of friendly officers through the National Confederation of Law Enforcement Officers. Samuelson joked that crooked cops were invariably smarter than honest ones. As a general rule, and with few exceptions, the idealism melted away in what few had ever had it. Most looked the other way. The ones who butted heads with the system didn't last very long.

Beale's fate was in the hands of Trintignant, the Consortium's image maker and propaganda minister. Trintignant's intention was to turn him. Beale had many reasons to oppose cannabis legalization. He used religion as his foundation, but his Senate post had been a receptacle for funds from two sources, the prescription drug industry and the producers of alcoholic beverages. Both stood to lose if cannabis were legalized nationally, whether for medicinal or recreational use. The battle was half won. Half the states allowed prescription use in various forms. Eight states had passed full legalization. More were on the way. National polls reflected a majority of Americans who favored it, but national polls also revealed a vast consensus of citizens favoring modest gun regulation. Opinion was nothing compared with money. Beale got money from the National Rifle Association, too, but he had gotten rich off drugs and booze.

Trintignant could save Beale from death, but clearly it would take more than friendly persuasion. Lilley was past the point of caring. He had grown weary of fucking around with Nathan Beale. He had been willing to go forward with a plan to kill off Beale in a plane crash. The Russian, Arkady Pankratov, had provided a workable plan but advised against it. As coldhearted as Lilley was, he had a sense of humor. The notion of having the drunken, bisexual attorney general assassinated by a native-born, African-American terrorist at a gospel music festival wasn't just delightfully absurd. It set the perfect tone. Gaynes' far-right base would rise against the left. People on both extremes were already marching in the streets of America. Soon they would be fighting, and it would give Gaynes a justification for cementing his control and demonizing his opponents. Lilley thought it perfect. Trintignant thought it madness. Lilley didn't dissent. Madness appealed to him, too.

Thus did Beale's surreptitious visit to the compound in the Rockies transpire. The small party – Beale, his aides, his security detail, Angelique Blunt – was en route. Stedman (Not His Real Name) Andersen and Trintignant's fixer, Wade Sanderson, were orchestrating the mayhem in Las Vegas. With Lilley's blessing, Trintignant had prepared to serve the Attorney General's every need. The university sent a delegation of its president's blue-ribbon interns, all male, chosen for their wholesome good looks and disarming lack of masculinity.

The Attorney General arrived with a certain woozy courtliness intact. He had enjoyed several of his signature bourbons and "spring water" en route, first in a motorcade to the Denver airport and then on Lilley's plane. They all congregated in Lilley's foyer, where everyone exchanged pleasantries, raised toasts to the republic's health, and Lilley himself proclaimed, "Long live the President!"

"Hear! Hear!" Beale added. "While the godless Democrats spread their scurrilous lies, Mr. Gaynes … remains!"

"Long may it thus be so!" Trintignant added.

They dined on beef Stroganoff and oysters Wellington and Welsh rarebit, exotic and exotically named. The wine included 2007 Gaja Barbarescu, 2008 Didier Dagueneau Silex, 2005 Bodegas Roda Cirsion, and 2008 Spottswoode Cabernet Sauvignon. Dessert was Quetschentaart, a plum tart native to Luxembourg. A quartet from the university played chamber music.

Trintignant schmoozed with Beale's aides down at one end of the table. The security detail congregated socially at the other end. The safety of the Attorney General was obvious at Lilley's Rocky Mountain fortress. Lilley's own wait staff prepared the food expertly with the supervision of a chef who came with Trintignant from San Francisco. The apple-cheeked lads from the university assisted with the service. Trintignant had allowed as how no one would be bothered if the interns sampled some of the booze in the privacy of the kitchen. The scattering of the personnel gave Lilley private access to Beale.

"My, oh, my, Bentsen, what Mama wouldn't give to be here," Beale said. "I believe it best that I do not tell her about this fine wine. I'm gon' say we had a picnic with fried chicken and pimento-cheese sandwiches. And Dr. Pepper over ice."

"Nathan, I know you to be a man who appreciates fine food and beverage, good music, and Jesus," Lilley replied. "The Savior wasn't available, but I trust he is watching."

"Oh, yes, I assure you he is," Beale replied. "There's no hiding from Christ. I'll ask His forgiveness this very night at bedtime, but I know He wouldn't begrudge me these earthly pleasures."

"That's the greatest virtue of Christianity. Forgiveness."

"Are you a godly man, Bentsen?"

"I'm like you, Nathan. Yes, I'm a godly man, but I spend a lot of time asking for forgiveness."

Beale sipped his wine. "Bentsen, just what have you to do with what I'll ask forgiveness for tonight?"

"You have excellent grammar for a Southerner."

"You have an excellent knack for changing the subject," Beale said. "You've got me wined and dined. I expect you had a reason."

"I have some business affairs, Nathan. One of my associates, the young black woman you met, Angelique Blunt, is meeting with Garlin Samuelson for the remainder of the afternoon, at least, as soon as he gets here. I assume you know Garlin."

"Oh, yes. NCLEO. He knows more about effective law enforcement than anyone in the country."

"My associate, Patrick Trintignant, has a presentation for you and your associates in the Justice Department. Patrick is producing a film. I believe it's named, uh, Righteous Cop. That's one of the working titles. I think you'd like it. It's sort of a throwback to those law-and-order dramas of the seventies. *Dirty Harry. Magnum Force.* A tough guy fighting the radicals on one side and the liberals in the media and government on the other. Now that you're the Attorney General and Gaynes is the president, we're going to need men like Patrick, a movie producer, a conservative news purveyor, to grab the public's attention, lest the radicals of today plunge us back into disorder."

"Is Mr. Trintignant looking for investors?"

"No, nothing like that. I believe there might be some issues regarding the cooperation of the federal government," Lilley said. "Holding down the expenses, things like that. I think he's close to lining up the funding. He's hired Norman Hardie to direct. Norman's one of the few quality directors who ain't lefty. Patrick wants to make an Oscar-quality film. He's got a script written, he's got a commitment from Bill Dimond and Victoria Wetteland to star, but they've got to get started within a certain time frame while the two of them, and several more in lesser roles, don't have other commitments."

"That sounds wonderful, Bentsen. You let me know. The new Secretary of the Interior is a good friend. If the timing is right, we're gonna free up a lot of public land for oil and mining exploration. We might be able to let Trintignant use it before the privatization is finalized."

"The story is about a manhunt, so that could well work," Lilley said. "Have you had enough wine? I've got the best bourbon you ever tasted waiting on you."

"My judgment might be a little clouded already."

"This bourbon is from Utah. It's distilled by wayward Mormons. It has the effect of giving a man clarity at the same time he is allegedly impaired."

"You're getting me drunk so I'll nod my head at everything you want."

"Good bourbon makes the world go 'round," Lilley said. "We wanted you to enjoy 'a working vacation,' what with all you and the president are going through in Washington."

Beale didn't mention the charges of campaign collusion between Gaynes and the Russian intelligence apparatus. He didn't mention that he had lied under oath in front of a Senate committee. He apparently didn't realize one of the men who had been on the plane with him from Washington was himself a Russian operative. Stedman Andersen and Wade Sanderson were en route to Las Vegas now, where they would, with Arkady Pankratov, painstakingly prepare for a clean, quick assassination of Nathan Beale. Beale didn't know the reason he was at Lilley's mountain compound was to give him one last chance to save himself. He would never know if he didn't change his mind. All it took was for him to leave things be. All he had to do was nothing.

A pity.

Garlin Samuelson arrived, which ended the schmoozing. The agents assigned to protect Beale occupied themselves making sure the property was secure, a routine task since the ranch was five miles away from any other human occupancy, and the presence of the Attorney General wasn't widely known. Only local media covered the Denver visit and followed Marjorie Beale's honorary duties. She said her husband was getting needed rest at a spa, which he needed to overcome the rigors of the long hours he had been keeping while resetting policy and hiring personnel at the Department of Justice. The media didn't buy it, but they figured he was ducking questions about his plans for dealing with marijuana legalization in states such as Colorado, where it had been in place for several years.

Samuelson and Angelique Blunt joined Lilley in his vast office while Trintignant took the Attorney General and two of his aides, the more senior, to a conference room decorated with oil paintings of Herbert Hoover, Robert Taft, Barry Goldwater, Ronald Reagan, George H.W. Bush, and, of course, Martin J. Gaynes. Beale asked how Trintignant had managed to procure such an impressive portrait of the new president only a month into his term.

"The other paintings Bentsen purchased. They were all painted in sittings. The Hoover portrait is from 1925, while Coolidge was president. President Gaynes' portrait was done from a photograph of him at his seaside estate in Scotland," Trintignant said.

"It's an impressive piece," Beale said.

"Between you and me, Bentsen considers it a bit garish. He told me he planned to have it moved to the Choice Tobacco headquarters in Raleigh, once he secures a better portrait for here."

They sat down. The interns arrived with trays of drinks.

"What do you think of the Mormon bourbon?" Trintignant asked.

"It may be the best I've ever tasted," Beale said. "Of course, my tastes may be a mite pedestrian by the standards of you and Bentsen. My standard libation is Jack Daniel's Old Number Seven."

"I've got another surprise for you, Mr. Attorney General."

"Call me Nathan. Please."

"Nathan, I, like you, enjoy a good cigar, and I've come across the best tobacco blend that exists on the face of the earth," Trintignant proclaimed.

"I hope it's not Cuban, Patrick. I'd hate to let that get out, particularly the since the President has no plans to open up further recognition of Havana, unlike his predecessor."

"No. It's a bit of a secret. During the years when its government had a close relationship with Castro and the Soviets, tobacco cultivation was introduced in what is informally known as the Island of Spice. I don't know if there's a connection between land that produces the world's best nutmeg, ginger, and cinnamon, not to mention exceptional cocoa, and tobacco, but whether it's by the richness of the soil or the skill of Cuban advisors, it's really unique, sir."

"You're talking about Grenada," Beale said.

"Very perceptive, Nathan. Most of the tobacco there is a wild variety used strictly by the locals, but once I discovered this blend, I had some of it shipped to Florida and hand rolled by Tampa craftsman. Only a few boxes exist," Trintignant said. "If you like it, I'll get a box shipped to you in Washington."

It was all a lie. Trintignant snapped electronically to summon another intern, who brought a wooden, hand-carved box and placed it on the long Brazilian rosewood table. The "tobacco" had been expertly blended from rich Cuban and robust Northern Californian. The Emerald Triangle produced high-grade cannabis, not tobacco. Indica, ground thoroughly, mixed nicely with tobacco, providing hints of orange and purple amid the brown of the tobacco. A careful pothead might notice and rejoice. Beale was not such a man.

One of the aides, Gerald Behr, looked to be in his fifties. The other, Clauson Downey, was in his mid thirties, Trintignant guessed. They both seemed humorless enough. Beale and Behr retrieved cigar cutters from their pockets. An intern assisted Downey.

Beale puffed thoughtfully. "This is really wonderful, Patrick. It has such a rich aroma."

"Let me tell you what's truly remarkable about this tobacco," Trintignant replied. "It goes beautifully with the bourbon. I've never had even the slightest hangover the morning after smoking these cigars with the accompaniment of the bourbon. I think there's a little magic in the bourbon and the cigars both."

Trintignant asked the interns to afford them some privacy in their discussions. They left two bottles of bourbon and an ice box, cleaned up the cutting from the cigars and placed them on a tray. Only the four of them had any suspicion that these were not ordinary cigars. In the kitchen, one remarked that the aroma of these cigars reminded him of weed. Another said he had the same thought.

"Why don't we grind these cuttings and roll one up?" he asked.

"I don't know. We better not."

"I think I got some papers in my overnight bag."

"Let's wait until dark. Maybe we can slip outside."

"Shit. They can smoke it. Why can't we? This is Colorado, man. Know what I'm saying?"

Back in the conference room, Trintignant and the three representatives of the Justice Department discussed environmental policy, or lack thereof, but they also talked about the lack of morality in American life, and the gross unfairness of all the regulations that were squeezing the life out of American industrial prosperity. Beale railed at the unfairness of all the Hollywood types whose insults of the new president he deemed treasonous. Pretty soon Behr broke the ice and rambled a bit about how Democrats were really communists in disguise. Downey said he couldn't wait for President Gaynes to attack North Korea and "settle that matter once and for all."

"Gentlemen," Trintignant said, "let's get down to the matter at hand. Nathan, what would you consider to be the reasonable bounds of states' rights?"

"I think, Patrick, that the intention of the Founding Fathers was to provide the states with the right to govern in the interests of their own citizenry as much as possible when there is no overriding, practical reason for federal control. I believe the states should maintain control of their own schools, set the standards for education and regulation, and even reserve many of those decisions for the people at the county and local level. Reversing a century's growth of power at the federal level is going to be the top priority at Justice."

Beale's drawl thickened with his impairment. Communists became "commonists." Democrats became godless Democrats and then fucking Democrats. He said he didn't know whether or not he could truly send the defeated Democratic nominee for president, Katharine Franklin, to prison, but that was the President's wish, and Downey was going to lead an investigation into her alleged misdeeds while in the Senate and serving as vice president under Gaynes' predecessor, Fabian Carmichael.

Behr laughed. "You know, he's black," he said.

"By God, we'll never let another nigger in the White House if I can do anything to stop it," Beale said. "Forgive my fucking French."

"In Jesus's name we pray," Downey said. "Amen."

"Amen. May the Lord forgive me," Beale added.

"Why should not the states be charged with the regulation and control of marijuana?" Trintignant asked.

Beale squinted first and then gave Trintignant a stare through bloodshot eyes.

"It's the same reason the country cannot allow the people of this country to murder little babies, Patrick. Morality cannot be a matter of choice."

"With respect, Nathan, seventy-six percent of the people in this country favor legalization of marijuana in some capacity, and that's from a Gallup poll. According to CBS, sixty-one percent favor legalization for recreational use. Government policy lags far behind public opinion. Legalizing marijuana, and taxing the shit out of it, is the best and easiest solution for budgetary problems at the state level and deficit spending at the national level. It's wildly popular here in Colorado. What's more, gentlemen, it is no more of a public health problem than alcohol consumption, and it is far less than smoking."

Beale, Behr, and Downey had not a clue that they were, in fact, proving Trintignant's point as they sat there.

"I will not be a party in allowing public policy to turn generations of young people into drug-crazed zombies," Beale said with as much passion as he could muster.

"That's the point that no one realizes," Trintignant replied. "You know why kids smoke pot? They can get it. The people they buy it from, they don't ask for an I.D. When I was a young man, kids smoked pot then, but it was legal to buy beer at eighteen. Now the legal drinking age is twenty-one. It's hard to get alcohol. They can buy marijuana as easily as they can snap their fingers."

"What's your skin in this game, Patrick?"

"Nathan, for fifty years the federal government you want to get out of people's lives has been gradually running tobacco out of business. Bentsen has been investing a lot of money in legal marijuana. He brought me, and dozens of others, prominent men, good Republicans, big donors, and we have used our efforts, with discretion, and positions ourselves to be a leader in a legal marijuana industry that has already reaped benefits in a number of states. We can corner the market, and we can assure that the industry will be responsible. If you'd just look at the example of Colorado, and Washington State, and Oregon, and California, and, now, Alaska and Nevada and Maine and Massachusetts, you'd see, or will see, that legalizing marijuana will keep it away from kids, specifically meaning, those who are under the age of twenty-one, just like alcohol."

"I don't believe the facts bear that out," Beale said, exhaling a plume of smoke.

Trintignant wasn't straight. He had difficulty keeping a straight face. He smiled endearingly without going full Harvey Korman on the old *Carol Burnett Show.*

"Patrick, this is not something that is generally known or that I generally prefer to share," Beale said, "but my only son, Beau …"

Trintignant bet it was short for Beauregard.

"… has experienced struggles with illegal drugs, and he tells me it all began when he and some of his buddies experimented with deadly marijuana."

"Nathan, I'm not gonna sit here and argue with you. My own son has been named president, or whatever it is, of the Pepperdine Law Review, and he uses marijuana responsibly. It's no more of an entry-level drug than alcohol, or cigarettes, for that matter, or … cigars … but the thing is, Nathan, Bentsen and I, and our associates, aren't asking you to do a thing different from the way it is now. If you start using the might of the federal government to impose its will on what the states have lawfully and responsibly done, you're going to unleash a protest from these kids, and, by the way, a whole lot of adults, that's going to make the marches and protests by women, blacks, immigrants, Latinos, Muslims, what have you, look like tea parties, goddamn it. We can make it worth your time, and it's gonna help the President get re-elected, too. You have no idea how behind the curve you are. What's more, the President is not against it. He told Bentsen that he wouldn't have a problem if cannabis was legal in all fifty states, but he said it didn't mean enough to him to have a fight with you over it. We set this little parley up with his approval, Nathan. You're really all alone on this."

Beale sighed. He leaned back in his seat and smiled.

"I'll sleep on it," he said. "We'll talk, Gerald and Clauson and me, on the plane to Vegas tomorrow. I'll see what Mama says. I'll pray about it."

"That's all I ask, Nathan. Forget it even came up. Let's enjoy ourselves. Let's celebrate what we agree on."

When darkness fell, they all returned to the great room for a lavish dinner of cured filet mignons, baked potatoes, steamed asparagus, and cheesecake for dessert. The chamber music was replaced by an acoustic folk quartet that played every gospel song it knew. Beale got up, borrowed a fiddle from the musicians, and played a passable version of "Turkey in the Straw."

Trintignant quietly said to Lilley that he thought he'd made some progress. After the interns from the university got through cleaning up the tables, they slipped outside and split the joint one had rolled. Four young men sharing a spliff that wasn't even wholly made of cannabis wasn't enough to get stoned, but they had been hitting the high-dollar bourbon, too. All but one went to bed with a nice, rosy buzz. Beale retired to the guest bedroom and put on silk pajamas and a bathrobe. He figured out how to page the kitchen.

"Excuse me, but would one of you fine young men come up here to my bedroom? I'm in need of some assistance," Beale said. "See if you can find a couple of those cigars Mr. Trintignant brought here and a fresh bottle of bourbon. I'm gonna have a little nip and a smoke before I retire."

CHAPTER 51

Back at the Arms

"You know, Milo, you staying here instead of being in the dorm is going to cause a problem," Dylan Wannamacher said. "I don't mind, but people love to talk."

"So … are you worried that word might get around that I've been known to smoke weed, and you might be considered guilty by association."

"I was more thinking they might infer we were gay lovers, and I'm a pedophile."

"I hadn't thought about that," Milo Hirley said.

"The weed issue is pertinent. It could ruin me, cost me my job, and all that good stuff, but the fundamental difference is that there's some truth in it, and I am not, in fact, gay," Dylan said. "You put me in a bad spot, Milo. I'm not supposed to be a bad influence."

"You're not, Dylan. I was into pot before I knew you smoked."

"Yeah, but I let Marcia get involved, and she got you involved in selling weed, and, whether I meant to or not, I was an accomplice. I know better. Besides, I really do worry that it's bad for you when you're a kid. I think being an athlete means it's less damaging because you're active and in good shape and all that, but it probably affects your attitude and your belief system."

"The fuck's 'at mean?"

"It means you call bullshit on things that aren't bullshit," Dylan said.

"Cite one example."

"Uh, just now. When you said 'the fuck's 'at mean.'"

"Okay."

They sat in silence for a while. The Houston Rockets were playing the Boston Celtics on TV. Neither paid much attention.

"I tried to go see Peter," Milo said.

"Oh, yeah?"

"They wouldn't let me see him. It was some legal reason. I'll have to testify against him in court, maybe, if the D.A. decides he's sane enough to go to jail," Milo said. "I reckon I'll have to do something, regardless. You, too. Maybe they'll send him to the funny farm."

"Why'd you want to talk to him?" Dylan asked.

"I wanted to know why he shot at the basketball and not me."

"What do you think?"

"I don't know," Milo replied. "Most likely, it's on account of he's nuts. And he's a pussy. Always has been."

The timing was inadvertently fortuitous. On the very day that Milo moved back to his Enlightened Word dorm room, Mickey Statler showed up at Hippie Arms.

"Uh, Mickey," Dylan said. "Come in. Off the road for a day or two?"

"I'm scheduled to write a basketball feature in Richmond, Kentucky, next Wednesday," Mickey said. He pulled his rolling suitcase in, wearing a backpack with his laptop and carrying an aluminum briefcase.

"No news from Marcia," Dylan said, anticipating the question. "Milo Hirley said he saw her earlier in the week."

"Delivery?" Mickey glanced at the briefcase.

"That's the likely reason. Sit down."

"I stopped in Roanoke for a burger and bought a copy of *USA Today*," Mickey said. "I've got some, uh, deep, dark suspicions on things going on in the country."

"Things are just crazy, man. The people who support Gaynes rationalize away anything the son of a bitch does," Dylan said. "Who knew the far right would go soft on Russia? When you talk to people who say they support the president, invariably they say one of two things. Either he tells it like it is, or he cares about their problems. This from a man who can't go a paragraph without telling a lie. What he doesn't lie about, he exaggerates. Man, it makes you realize how Mussolini came to power."

"Or Hitler."

"I mentioned Mussolini because I don't think Gaynes is as smart as Hitler," Dylan said.

"Pursuant to those thoughts, he's not hard to figure out. Whatever he accuses anyone else of doing, from spreading fake news, to secret emails, to claiming his campaign didn't collude with the Russians, Gaynes is doing himself," Mickey said. "He's constantly stirring up shit to draw the attention away from the latest disclosures. Gaynes has been raising hell ever since his attorney general, Nathan Beale, recused himself from the Russia investigation. Now, all of a sudden, he keeps tweeting all these warm praises of Beale, whereas, until yesterday, he was talking about firing him. When I read that, it sent chills down my spine."

"Why?"

"Well, this, uh, Wade Sanderson fellow, the one who got my daughter into this mess, went to Colorado and told Marcia he was going from there to Las Vegas. Nathan Beale flew to Colorado at the same time, and now he's in Vegas. It's the same time. I'm scared something's going to happen to Beale."

"As conspiracy theories go," Dylan said, "that's a damned good one."

"I'm scared to death Marcia is either out there or headed that way."

"You're going out there, aren't you?"

"Unless I can find her here," Mickey said.

CHAPTER 52

Entrapment

Nathan Beale never felt better than on Friday morning as he and his entourage prepared to return to Denver, pick up Marjorie, and fly on to Las Vegas for the National Gospel Sing on the grounds of the Bonneville Junction Hotel and Casino. By noon of the following day, Bentsen Lilley, Patrick Trintignant, and Angelique Blunt would be out of the country, in Ottawa to discuss Canada's impending legalization of recreational marijuana with representatives of Parliament.

Never let it be said of Trintignant that he didn't give Beale every opportunity to change his mind and, in so doing, save his own life. The Attorney General had one last chance.

Trintignant had made his pitch to Beale, and he was gracious as Beale boarded Lilley's corporate jet.

"It goes to show what the virtues of good bourbon are, Patrick," Beale said. "I was a bit concerned that I had overindulged last night, but I never felt better than when I awakened on this glorious morning."

"I wouldn't overlook the cigars, Nathan," Trintignant replied. "Those Grenadian cigars are a marvel. Their curative qualities are undeniable. For some reason, that particular blend, whether by mystery or science, lengthens a man's life, not shortens it."

"For God's sake, Patrick, don't ever let the scientists get their hands on it. I have come to believe that all they tell us is what we do not need to know."

"Sure enough. It's been a pleasure to get to know you, sir. I've made my pitch regarding cannabis. I won't bother you with it anymore. I hope you will consider the points I made, but, as a gentleman, I will live with your conclusions and respect your view."

"Duly noted," Beale said at the foot of the boarding stairs. "While I tend to disagree with you, you have made some points, particularly in regard to states' rights, that I will study most diligently."

On the short flight to Denver, Beale, his two aides, and the four-man security detail enjoyed coffee and danishes. The attendant informed them that there would be no need to leave the plane once they landed. Mrs. Beale would be joining them on the tarmac. She also said that the plane had developed some plumbing problem that would be repaired in Denver, but should the Attorney General or his aides need to relieve themselves, they should use plastic containers that had been provided.

Beale gave Gerald Behr the contact information of one of the bright young men from the university and told Behr he would make an exemplary summer intern in the Office of the Attorney General. Clausen Downey remarked that coffee had never tasted better than on this lovely flight across the Rockies. When the plane landed, Beale remarked to the attendant that coffee flowed right through him, and he needed an opportunity to use the facilities before the workmen came to clear the toilets.

"Let me show you the light trick," Arkady Pankratov said to Wade Sanderson as the two stood in front of the stage that had been constructed on land adjacent to the Bonneville Junction Hotel and Casino southeast of the Las Vegas Strip.

Beneath the stage was a control center, reputedly a command post for security and crowd control. Centered at its front was an opening and a counter sat at just below the height of an average man's chest.

"Yuri," Pankratov said, "step forward."

Yuri Iznetsikov was a naturalized American citizen better known as Stedman Andersen. His cover was the Libertarian think tank known as Americans for Youthful Normalcy, which reflected not the age of its membership but an alleged vision of the country in its early years, when the experiment in democracy had minded its own business without bothering with world affairs. A.Y.N. stood for Ayn, as in Ayn Rand, the novelist whose works had included *The Fountainhead and Atlas Shrugged,* which, in turn, expressed the tenets of objectivism. Rand had been a great critic of Soviet communism and had left her native Russia for the United States in 1925. Now A.Y.N. was a front for the advance of the Russian Federation's political interests and a retreat by the U.S. from meddling in world affairs.

Andersen, or Iznetzikov, stepped forward in the opening and raised an automatic rifle, anchoring it with his left elbow and pointing sighting it outward across the green lawn where Pankratov and Sanderson stood.

"Now, Yuri, flip the switch," Pankratov said.

Andersen disappeared. The opening went black.

"It's actually a rather advanced screen, using light technology," Pankratov said. "The Attorney General will preface the concert with remarks from the podium. Then he will be seated … there."

Pankratov turned around and pointed to a red folding chair in a roped-off seating area bordering the lawn.

"With the playing of your national anthem, Beale will stand, and at the end of the second line, 'by the dawn's early light,' an African American Muslim from Detroit, Yousseff Cameroon, formerly Reggie Lennart, will begin strafing the crowd from the eighth-floor, corner room of the Bonneville Junction. Once the firing commences, the assassin will fire a single kill shot to the head of Nathan Beale. Then he will calmly place the weapon in a briefcase, walk calmly to an SUV marked with the insignia of the Clark County Sheriff's Department and leave for a private landing strip between here and Lake Mead, where a Lear Jet awaits."

"This is a done deal?" Wade asked. "I mean, no turning back?"

"Mr. Beale will have a chance to save himself if his remarks do not include, as expected, a condemnation of the legal cannabis movement and an announcement that the U.S. federal government will ignore the wishes of the states, Nevada being one of them, and enforce federal restrictions. Coming to Las Vegas, in a state which has recently passed a law allowing recreational consumption of cannabis, and establishing a federal policy of defiance and eradication, to an audience of Christian evangelicals, is the purpose of the Attorney's attendance," Pankratov stated. "Our associate, Mr. Trintignant, has made the case for a state's right to set its own policies to Mr. Beale in Colorado. If the Attorney General chooses to revise his remarks, his life will be spared. All of this, by the way, is being conducted with the tacit approval of President Martin Jerald Gaynes."

"Damn," Wade said. "If the assassination is canceled, everything else is, too?"

"No, of course not," Pankratov replied. "The random shooting will go off, as planned. All the shots will be fired at the portion of the crowd closest to the shooting point. It will be all over in no more than fifteen seconds. The shooter will die because two men accompanying him will kill him. They are law-enforcement officers who will quickly change into S.W.A.T. gear. Like you, Mr. Sanderson, they are associates in the Consortium."

"Why would you go ahead with the killing of innocent people?"

"Because Gaynes is already unpopular just a month into his term," Pankratov said. "Because the killer in the hotel is a legitimate Muslim extremist. Because tragedy committed by a black radical against white Christians will increase racial tensions, and that will enhance the president's position politically. It won't be a large crowd, no more than a thousand, probably closer to five hundred. Casualties? Five deaths, maybe. Twenty wounded."

"What if this Cameroon fellow crosses you? What if he tries to shoot Beale?" Wade asked.

"He will die sooner. It's all quite well planned, I can assure you. We have some experience in matters such as these, Mr. Sanderson."

"Andersen is the shooter? I mean, he's Yuri to you, right? The shooter of Beale."

"No, Yuri will be in the Attorney General's party," Pankratov said.

"Then who is the assassin?"

"The assassin, Mr. Sanderson, is you."

"The President had some nice things to say about you this morning, Nathan. Have you talked to him?"

Nathan and Marjorie Beale had dined at a Ruth's Chris in Denver and were preparing for bed at a Westin adjoining Denver International Airport. The flight to Las Vegas would embark early the following morning.

"No, Mama, President Gaynes played golf today," Beale said. "He's a hard man to figure. He has a rather unenlightened view of how the judiciary operates. He considers the job of the Attorney General to be protecting his interests. I had to recuse myself from the Russian investigation. In our conversations, he insists that I should have told him ahead of time that I could not participate in it. My honor has already been tarnished when it came out that I had met with the Russians during the campaign. If he said I was doing a good job, it was only for appearances, I expect."

"That man has no honor," she said. "I have noticed his tendency to destroy everyone and everything he touches. I don't think he's going to serve out his term."

"Don't say that, Mama."

"It's true," she said. "If they impeach him, Sammy Hopewell will succeed him as president, but he'll be ruined, too, by the time the 2020 election rolls around. Nathan, this marijuana enforcement program will endear you to Gaynes' base. The next President of the United States will be Nathan Bedford Forrest Beale. You watch. You know how right I usually am on political matters."

"President Gaynes is ambivalent about marijuana, Mama. He doesn't like to talk about it, but he said I'm in charge of the Justice Department, and he won't stop me if that's what I think is right to do, but I get the impression that he thinks I should back away from it, at least for a while. He just won't come out and say it."

"That's because he knows what will happen, Nathan. You'll be more popular with the base than he is."

"If that's the case, he'll claim it was his idea," Beale said.

CHAPTER 53

Old School

Mickey Statler showed up at Hippie Arms with a quart of Tanqueray No. 10, two bottles of tonic water, and a fistful of limes.

"Enough of these controlled substances," he said. "Let's me and you get high the old-fashioned way. I trust you like gin."

"My experience with booze is that it's worth a lot more drowning sorrow than commemorating success," Dylan Wannamacher replied. "Sit down, Mickey. But first, mix me a stiff one. I haven't gotten drunk in quite a while."

"I like the way you think."

The sportswriter and the would-be novelist sat in silence for a while, sipping gin and tonics and watching twenty-four-hour news.

"Martin J. Gaynes," Mickey said. "President Twitter."

"Never been another one like him," Dylan said. "When he gets through with the Constitution, there won't be anything left."

"Ever been to Vegas?"

"Not yet."

"Go with me?"

"Don't you think it's futile?" Dylan asked.

"Do you not think my daughter is worth saving?"

"Yes," Dylan replied. "I mean no. 'Do you not think?' I do think Marcia is worth saving. I just think it's quite possible that she can take care of herself better than either one of us can. I admire her. She took advantage of my suspended adolescence. Humored me, I guess you could say."

"She can weave a tale," Mickey said. "She can turn a phrase. I reckon she got some of that from you, and I reckon she got some of that from me. You know, I've got two people I've got to find in Vegas. I'm fucked. The only thing I did wrong was let a good-looking bartender trap me to get her own ass out of trouble. That little spark, that little … indiscretion … it put me in the tank with a single, crooked, two-bit cop, and, next thing you know, I'm a slave to a fucking nationwide drug conspiracy. You know, Marcia could get out. You aren't even in it. But this fire, this fucking prairie fire, is gonna blow up something big, and I'm gonna be the ashes nobody notices. I can't get out. I might as well save somebody else. Marcia is my kid. Love, Dylan, is unconditional. She gets that because my blood flows through her veins. Respect? People, even my kid, have to earn that. The world's history is crafted in equal parts tangible and intangible. The best thing about writing sports is that, if you fuck things up royally, it doesn't lead to the end of the world. Now I've managed to stumble my way into even that. In my bones, I know that something is going to happen to Nathan Beale in Las Vegas. Either he's going to knuckle under and push disaster down the road a ways, or he's gonna show some backbone that I don't believe he's got, and the whole goddamned country's gonna disappear like Hiroshima in 1945. Gaynes is gonna ruin the country because all he cares about is himself. Everybody he touches is ruined. He hasn't actually killed anybody, to my knowledge. He's in cahoots with the Russians, who got him elected, and now somebody is going down, and I think that somebody might be your fellow Mississipian, Beale. I know this doesn't make sense to anybody but me, but I've learned to read people. If there's a rumor out there, and nobody will deny it, it's true, and the truth is never more evident than when being vehemently denied. Shit, I can't articulate it. I wouldn't blame you if you thought I was as crazy as Gaynes is. It doesn't make much difference whether you go with me or not. You're looking at me right now like I'm Don Quixote, and you don't have any interest in being Sancho Panza. That's cool. I'd never hold it against you.

For right now, though, let's have another drink. Either I'll make even less sense, or I'll start making more."

"Who's the other one?"

"What?"

"The other one in Vegas you've got to save. Or find in Vegas."

"Oh," Mickey said. "Rashawn Ling."

"Who?"

"He's my ex-colleague at the *News-Free Press*. He got laid off recently. I told him about the Consortium. I told him to go to Vegas, told him something big was gonna happen there. Rashawn, and Marcia, and Wade fucking Sanderson, and I, and, I hope, you, are going to be the last people on earth anybody would expect to find at the National Gospel Sing, but I'd bet my last dollar we're all gonna be there. I've fucked up everything in my whole life in the past eight months, and all I want to do now is save the country, and freedom, and the fucking pursuit of happiness."

"Might as well," Dylan said. "You know, the more I think about it, weed ought to be legal, and gin and tonic ought to be against the law. I'm ashamed to admit that I'm starting to think you make sense."

"Rashawn's a sharp kid, but he's not as experienced as I am. I've been thinking about him, too, and about how he lost his job for no good reason. He's young. He ain't making enough money to be expendable. They get rid of him, they can't save money by hiring a kid out of college for one third his salary. He's already that kid. I've sent him into a trap. I got a hunch he went to someone he thinks is his friend, and she's ratted him out. I gotta get him and Marcia both out of there."

"Can we get a flight?"

"There's always plenty of seats available to Vegas," Mickey replied.

The buzzer on the door rang.

"Hey, Dylan, you in there? It's me." They heard the voice of Milo Hirley.

"You might need three seats," Dylan said. He got up and let Milo in.

"Season's over," Milo said. "Oh, hey, Mr. Statler. Dylan, he's cool, right?"

"I know you blaze, son," Mickey said, "but do you drink?"

"I ain't against it."

"It's time you developed a taste for gin and tonic," Dylan said. "Sit down."

"Well, shit," Milo said, and did so. "We got beat in the first round of the playoffs. I missed a shot at the buzzer that would've won it."

"I figured you'd be out with the rest of the Merry Pranksters," Dylan said.

"I couldn't take it, man. Walt and Marty were crying and shit. I'm just numb. I told them I just wanted to be alone. They might be looking for me. They probably think I'm busy committing suicide or something."

"You're resilient," Mickey volunteered. "Ain't no jump shot rimmin' out gonna faze a kid who's been shot at."

"Oh, yeah," Milo said. "You were there. What's the occasion?"

"Mickey and I are flying to Las Vegas in the morning," Dylan said. "Mickey here thinks his daughter, Marcia, needs to be rescued from her boyfriend, and that something really bad is going to happen at a gospel sing, and we're the only people who can stop it?"

"Way cool," Milo said. "Okay, I am, like, a little high. Can I go?"

Dylan laughed. "Who knows, Mickey? Maybe Milo's athletic ability would come in handy."

"Here, son," Mickey said. "Don't drink too fast. Just sip it. We got all night."

CHAPTER 54

Viva Las Vegas

Nathan Beale awakened his once-lovely wife, the former Marjorie Mandeville, with breakfast in bed: bacon and country ham, eggs over-medium, grits, biscuits with jelly, sweet rolls, freshly squeezed orange juice, and a pot of coffee. Their penthouse suite on the Strip opened to the north with a view of downtown and the towering Stratosphere. He told her to enjoy herself while he met with a local Congressman for breakfast downstairs. It was a lie. He was headed to a meeting, all right, but it was the young man, Stedman Andersen, who had accompanied them on the plane from Washington to Denver. If he'd told Marjorie he was meeting with a mere lobbyist, she would have deemed it beneath him and demanded that he enjoy his repast with her.

Andersen had looked familiar. Beale had dealt with many lobbyists during his career in the Senate. AYN was familiar to Beale, but he had never received any specific benefit. He had often joked privately that libertarians were mainly "conservatives who smoked pot." They espoused a certain conservative purity that Beale found restrictive. The lobbyists with whom Beale was friendly were the ones whose money had showed up prominently in his campaigns. He wasn't sure if they had ever spoken before exchanging pleasantries two days earlier. Beale had paid more attention to Angelique Blunt because she was a black woman, making her something of a novelty in Republican circles, and to Wade Sanderson, who had seemed out of place because Beale had seen in him a certain roguish charm. He was southern in speech, though Beale had been surprised to learn he was living in Southern California.

Beale was meeting with Andersen because President Gaynes wanted him to do so. That was all Gerald Behr had said. Beale was anxious to get back in Gaynes' good graces. He enjoyed being Attorney General. He knew he'd never be president, his wife's aspirations to the contrary. No matter how conservative the country got, it wasn't going to elect a Mississippian.

Two security agents accompanied the Attorney General to the outskirts of the city, passing Nellis Air Force on the right and arriving, in their armored sport-utility vehicle, at an industrial park adjacent to Las Vegas Motor Speedway. They entered a presently unoccupied building that had once housed an Indy-car racing team. The agents posted themselves at two entrances to a small theater where Andersen was waiting.

"It is my understanding, Mr. Andersen, that you work for AYN, the libertarian organization," Beale said. "I'm getting old, I fear, but I am vaguely aware of having met you at some point. When we were on the plane to Denver together, I kept trying to place you in my mind."

"We met in Saint Petersburg, Mr. Beale."

"Ah, now I remember. The Saint Petersburg Conference on World Affairs, was it?" Beale asked.

Однажды я феллатед тебя.

The intent was to make Beale aware that he was Russian. The translation was, *I once fellated you.*

"It was sixteen years ago," Andersen said. "I was twenty-one. I don't think we exchanged names, Mr. Beale, but my name then was Yuri Iznetsikov."

Beale was speechless. Stedman, *nee* Yuri, pressed the advantage, by handing Beale a lab analysis.

"This came from the urine sample you provided on the tarmac of Denver International Airport," Anderson, nee Iznetsikov, said. "You tested positive for marijuana, Mr. Beale."

Beale's face, previously white, reddened.

"Now, see here, you're dealing with the Attorney General of the United States!"

"The cigars, Mr. Beale. Mr. Trintignant tells me you enjoyed them immensely."

"Why, you son of a bitch, Andersen, or Iznet … whatever it is, I shall defend myself vigorously against this scurrilous slander!"

"Hahaha! Go right ahead, Mr. Beale. As Americans are fond of saying, it's a free country. I'm not done, though."

He picked up some sort of remote-control apparatus. The lights dimmed, and the screen became illuminated.

"The sound will be muted, lest it draw the attention of your security agents outside," Andersen said.

What followed was a sequence of video clips showing Beale and a young man engaging in sexual acts of which the Attorney General did not publicly approve.

"I was drugged," Beale said.

"Willingly so," replied Andersen.

"I will not be blackmailed."

"It is your choice, Mr. Beale. I don't want to release these through Wikileaks to widespread circulation," Andersen said, "but I think you know all too well how these matters work. President Gaynes has benefited famously from my country's efforts in his behalf. I've no particular desire to make these an issue of public debate here in our … free country."

Beale rode back to the Strip without saying a word.

Mickey Statler sat in a window seat on a 10:15 a.m. American flight out of Philadelphia. Dylan Wannamacher and Milo Hirley were twelve rows back, Dylan on the aisle and Milo next to him. Dylan explained that the time change would mean they'd land at McCarran International Airport in Las Vegas at roughly the same time they departed Philly. All three slept for most of the flight, but in the interest of secrecy, Dylan and Milo exchanged text messages even while sitting next to each other. It was the first time Milo had ever flown. Even on the aisle, Dylan felt terribly cramped. His knees ached. Milo had a headache, and his innards were in full rebellion. He remarked that gin and tonic ought to be against the law, and he was of the opinion it was definitely a buzz inferior to weed in every way. That's when Dylan suggested that texting might be better in the interest of discretion and decorum. The woman in the window seat asked the attendant if she could move to another seat but was dismayed to learn there was no other seat.

A dozen rows ahead, Mickey Statler contemplated. He counted out the months in his mind. In a span of eight such units, he had probably distributed enough cannabis to rank in "the mythical Associated Press Top Twenty-Five." It had not been by choice, but, by necessity, breaking the law had made him prosperous for the first time in a decade, perhaps, depending on the measure, ever. Now, he was spending a ridiculous amount of money to do something about it. What? He didn't know.

Oh, Marcia was in Vegas, all right. She didn't know for sure why Wade Sanderson was there, but she suspected he was up to no good. She knew he was doing something important, and she knew it was bad, and that it was something that would make him more important than he already was with the Consortium. Wade had an animal magnetism about him, and he had transferred it to her in bed. He was rough and passionate. Dylan Wannamacher had been gentle. She didn't want gentle anymore. She wanted her brains screwed out. He wasn't the easygoing caddy she had met in L.A. He was a man who would do what it took. She saw his evil edge and was mesmerized by it. She didn't know what he was doing, but she knew the Attorney General, the distasteful Nathan Beale, was in town, and it didn't bother her that he was giving a speech, undoubtedly one that was a threat to her chosen line of work, and it was Wade's line of work, too, and she was going to something called the National Gospel Sing because she knew it was where she would find him, and she wanted to see him in action. She couldn't wait to see what was in store because she figured Wade was part of some plot to humiliate the holier-than-thou proponent of keeping cannabis illegal and underground. Beale was in the way, and the place to stop his crusade against sin was the city known as Sin City.

Naturally, Marcia wasn't going to any gospel sing sober. Nevada had voted to legalize weed, but it wasn't legal yet. She'd smuggled a little weed in her luggage, but she smoked it all on the little balcony outside her hotel room, where she had spent her first evening in town with a bottle of wine and a pack of Marlboro Lights. She got high on the rest of it the next morning, then walked downstairs and ate breakfast in the hotel lobby. She went to the casino and played blackjack, winning a hundred dollars' worth of beginner's luck. A young man who claimed to be a law student tried to pick her up. He said he attended the William S. Boyd School of Law at the University of Nevada at Las Vegas. She asked him if he had any weed, and he said he knew where he could get some. One wouldn't expect a young man who went to law school in Las Vegas to be a sober, sensitive type. He said he would meet her in a half hour at the entrance. They left the casino before noon. He drove a Mercedes SUV, and the smell of it indicated to her that he was married and had a kid.

But she needed a buzz. She needed something that would make the absurdity of gospel music palatable. She needed to mingle with all the god-fearing pilgrims, here in the country's most renowned den of iniquity, and make absurd comments that they would take at face value. If this lawyer cadet would get her high, she'd scare him with the same brand of weirdness. It would be fun.

They drove to what Marcia had never considered in pondering a visit to Las Vegas. A natural area. Twenty miles west was Red Rock National Conservation Area, where visitors could hike, picnic, view plant and animal life, and with a modest amount of discretion, smoke weed. The law student's name was Jared Canavan, a native of New Bedford, Massachusetts, who had enrolled in law school after graduating from Roger Williams University in Bristol, Rhode Island. He told her he had majored in historic preservation, which she considered so dubious that it might actually be true. To his credit, he said he had never heard of Triborough College, either. Once they got high, Marcia set her sights on ditching him. The weed made her inventive. She was losing touch with time. It occurred to her that she needed to be at the National Gospel Sing early so that she could find her man, the budding tycoon of bud, Wade Sanderson.

She let Jared kiss her, leaning across the console of the SUV, then, when he said they could go back to "my place," Marcia grew quiet as he drove out of Red Rock.

"Anything wrong, honey?" he asked.

"Oh, no," she said. "I'll be all right."

A small box of Kleenexes were in a compartment at the front of console.

"Oh, good," she said, and grabbed one. She willed herself to cry. It wasn't like her eyes weren't red, already. She daubed them and smeared a bit of makeup to her eyes, thus creating tears.

"Oh, baby, don't cry." Jared apparently was either dumb or crass. He couldn't remember her name. Maybe it was the weed. She thought about returning the favor by referring to him as "Sparky."

"Oh, it's silly. I'm going to hell."

"What? You got me to go find some weed, and now you're worried about going to hell?"

"I bet you're Catholic," Marcia said.

"Duh. My last name is Canavan."

"So?"

"It's Irish."

"You can do anything. All you have to do is go to confession, and all is forgiven."

"You don't know anything about my faith."

"And you don't know anything about mine," she said. "I'm Pentecostal."

Marcia was making it up as she went along and doing it beautifully. "We're always torn between good and evil."

Crazy bitch. He almost said it aloud.

"You've got to take me to the Bonneville Junction Hotel and Casino," Marcia said.

"Christ, honey. It's on the other side of town."

"No, seriously. I've got to perform."

"What?"

"I'm in a gospel singing group, Jared," she said. "My family is performing as part of the National Gospel Sing."

"Seriously."

"I'm not kidding." She sang the chorus of "Let Us Have a Little Talk with Jesus." "See?"

Jared Canavan was exasperated.

"You've got a wife and baby, Jared. What? They're out of town, right?"

"No."

"The baby seat in the back is the giveaway, stupid," Marcia said. "Do you mind if I have a cigarette?"

"I don't allow anyone to smoke in my wheels," he said.

"I knew it. What's her name? Your wife. I bet it's Melissa."

"Genevieve," he said.

"Same difference. Now take me to the fucking gospel sing."

Jared didn't say another word, but he took her to the Bonneville Junction.

Marcia was pleased with herself. She couldn't wait to tell Wade all about it.

CHAPTER 55

Plain English

What wasn't generally known about Yevgeny Borzov, president of the Russian Federation, was that he spoke perfect English. Surprising no one, the president of the United States, Martin Gaynes, spoke not a word of Russian. In public appearances, Borzov always used a translator. He spoke to his trusting ally, Gaynes, in plain English, by phone from the Kremlin.

"Martin, I wanted to inform you of the Russian Federation's impending military action," Borzov said.

"I assume, Yevgeny, that you are referring to a peace-keeping effort in Syria," Gaynes said.

"No."

Gaynes paused for a few moments, waiting for Borzov to expound.

"Martin, my Army is conducting military exercises near the border with northern Finland," Borzov said. "I assume you are aware of this."

"Yes." Gaynes had no idea. He rarely read the international reports or listened attentively when his advisers briefed him in meetings.

"These exercises are a precursor to an expedition into Finnish territory. You have announced publicly that the United States is unwilling to provide further military protection to NATO unless the major European powers compensate the U.S. equitably," Borzov said. "NATO will not intervene without the participation of your military forces."

"You are invading Finland?" Gaynes asked. "Why would you consider such a move?"

"Finland was once a part of Russia, Martin. For many years, following the end of World War II, our country and Finland enjoyed a cordial and cooperative relationship. In recent years, the Finnish government has grown increasingly hostile toward Russia."

"I can't very well stand still to a Russian invasion of a fellow NATO member."

"As you know, Martin, Finland is a member of the European Union but not a member of NATO."

"Oh, yes, of course I knew that." Of course, Gaynes didn't.

Borzov was intent on rebuilding the old Soviet Union. In fact, he was intent on expanding it.

"The centerpiece of the new cooperative relationship between our countries is that each of us will respect the political interests of the other," he said. "It was the whole point of our requested assistance in your election to the presidency. I expect your government to respect the policies of my administration. In fact, Martin, I demand it."

"Yevgeny, for God's sakes, we've never discussed an expansion of Russia into Finland. Down south, you have interests in taking over Ukraine, establishing formal control of … Crimea." Gaynes was feverishly going through papers and using his cell phone to access Wikipedia. "But Finland? Finland! You can't invade Finland!"

"I intend to, Martin. I am just giving you the courtesy of advance knowledge," Borzov replied. "You are adept at distractions. I suggest that you pick a fight with Finland and the EU. I'm sure you can come up with something."

"How much time have I got?" Gaynes asked.

"Two weeks," Borzov said. "I will be back in touch. I hope you have a good day. Goodbye."

"Yevgeny. Wait."

It was too late. The president of the Russian Federation had hung up on him.

Gaynes could make little sense of the Wikipedia information regarding Finland. It was scheduled to assume full membership in NATO in 2025. That must be what angered Borzov. Gaynes summoned his Chief of Staff, former general Duke Teasdale, and told him to find information on American trade with Finland. Gaynes had picked a fight with Canada over milk policy, of all things. Surely he could raise a ruckus over Finland. He thought about picking a fight with the Finnish prime minister but decided to get someone else to call him when he realized he could not possibly pronounce the fellow's last name. Gaynes gazed at a map. Russia must be invading Lapland, the northern region. He thought northern Finland looked like a man, facing east, with a small dog on its head.

Some kind of spaniel.

Nathan Beale felt as if courage did him no good. He wanted to stand up strong and take action to correct the den of iniquity that America had become. He had seen the promise of Gaynes, seen how this corrupt billionaire could somehow raise the hopes of the out-of-work coal miner, how he could placate a desperate man without any intention of helping him out. Beale had thrown in with Gaynes, stupidly believing he could control him. Since the miraculous victory, Gaynes had treated Beale like a child, demanding that he do whatever was necessary to keep the imperial president in power. Beale had seen the Department of Justice as his platform to transform America. When word got out that the Russians had actively worked to rig the election, Beale had lied for Gaynes and insisted there had been no collusion with the Russians and that he had never ever heard of any such relationship even though he himself had attended meetings to discuss how the Russians could derail the candidacy of Katharine Franklin. Once that lie had been revealed, Beale had recused himself from the investigation, which, in turn, had led to the appointment of a special counsel.

Gaynes had been in office a month. A month! The president expected absolute loyalty, though Gaynes had shown no such loyalty to those around him. He ruined everyone he touched in order to save himself. Beale found himself caught in some infernal form of purgatory, paralyzed by the man for whom he had gone to work. If he could not reinstitute the so-called War on Drugs, just what way was there for him to distinguish himself? For Beale, putting down the growing spread of legalized cannabis was a holy war. He wouldn't listen to reason. It was personal. His only son, Beau, was a drug addict. It had taken all the power Beale could exercise – as a prosecutor, a federal judge, a senator – to keep his son's indiscretions out of the public's knowledge. When Beau had been fifteen years old, Marjorie had found a small bag of marijuana in the boy's jacket. They sent him off to military school and private clinics, but it didn't matter where they sent him. The boy had been busted numerous times, though, thankfully, never in a place where his father could not save him. He'd used it all: cocaine, heroin, LSD, painkillers, anything to get high. Beale and Marjorie blamed it all on weed, "the gateway drug," though, in Beau's case, it hadn't really been true. They boy had sniffed airplane glue before he was out of grade school, been kicked off his junior-high football team for smoking cigarettes, and nearly drowned after dropping acid on the beaches of Gulfport. Beale's envisioned world was one that would protect his son from himself. His father didn't have the time.

Now, even that dream was gone. It was Gaynes who had insisted that he go first to Colorado and then to Nevada. Beale had seen it as a crusade into the den of the sinful, and it had proven to be so. They had trapped him, though, by wining, dining, drugging, and servicing his secret sexual indiscretions. Beale should have been strong. He had no one but himself to blame, but he had also been set up by Bentsen Lilley, Patrick Trintignant, and the Russians, and the president, his president, the man he served, had let it happen.

It had happened before, though. Nathan Beale was no stranger to adversity. He would prevail yet. Not today, though. Not today.

Almost no one knew Arkady Pankratov was in Las Vegas. Edmund Kingsley, the Director of the Federal Bureau of Investigation, knew that Pankratov was the personal representative of Yevgeny Borzov. Stedman Andersen knew. Two FBI agents, charged to pose as Yousseff Cameroon's accomplices, met with the Russian on the morning of Nathan Beale's appearance. Then Pankratov arrived secretly at the entrance to the control center beneath the stage that had been designed and constructed to his specifications. Andersen, whom Pankratov knew as Yuri Iznetsikov, briefed him and introduced him to the assassin, Wade Sanderson. The window at the front had been opened, its electronic shroud activated hours ahead of time. To outward appearances, there existed no window at all. Pankratov knew Sanderson's background. Iznetsikov assured him that the Consortium's troubleshooter had the requisite cool ruthlessness needed to execute the plan and, by extension, Gaynes' attorney general. Borzov felt his puppet, Gaynes, lacked the proper resolve. Gaynes had let this happen, but Borzov doubted the American president believed the Russians, not to mention Lilley, Trintignant, Kingsley, and Sanderson, would actually go through with it. Borzov thought it time to make Russian resolve abundantly clear. An act of terrorism would make Gaynes understand the folly of standing in front of Russia's expansionist intentions. Americans couldn't seem to understand how terror in Las Vegas could lead to conquest in Fennoscandia. Randomly killing a dozen or so of President Gaynes' most loyal partisans would have the result of enhancing his sagging popularity by demonizing his opponents, and, at the same time, let Gaynes know that the Russian Federation didn't play. Iznetsikov did not believe Beale would have to be assassinated. They were merely prepared to do so.

The legal gambling age in Las Vegas was twenty-one, which should have made it a bummer for Milo Hirley, who had recently turned eighteen and mistakenly thought he might enjoy some time at the tables. He could enter the Bonneville Junction casino with the adult of accompaniment Mickey Statler, who had grown to like him for his roguish ways. One would think being the host of the National Gospel Sing would limit the casino's business. One would be wrong. The Christians were not an experienced crowd. They tended to play the slots instead of the tables. Perhaps they thought Christ Jesus might find it easier to affect the operation of an electronic device than to save the soul of a dealer of cards. Or perhaps they pulled the handles and mashed the buttons because … they just did.

Mickey, who had flown to Vegas for no good reason other than to keep his daughter out of trouble, seemed relaxed for a man with moral qualms. Milo sat next to him. Once they were inside, no one seemed interested in hassling Milo, so, with a bit of advice from Mickey, Milo started playing the quarter slots.

"Milo, my boy, it's possible to clear a little money playing the slots," Mickey said, "but it's all a matter of keeping yourself under control. All these bells and whistles cloud a man's judgment. What pays for all the glitter is a single fact. Most gamblers tend to play till they lose. If they've got a lick of sense, there's going to be a time when they're ahead, but you hear these other machines going off, and you see other people winning, and it clouds your judgment. Let's say you're a hundred bucks ahead. Here's what the voice inside you says: 'Shit, I didn't come to Vegas for no hundred bucks.' So you keep going, and most people, no matter how far they get ahead, keep playing till they lose it. Understand?"

"Yes, sir."

"Good," Mickey said, "'cause it's a heap easier said than done. You gotta let it come to you. That's why I'm sitting here. I could comb the streets of Vegas, looking for Marcia, but I know she's gonna be wherever Wade Sanderson is, and Wade Sanderson is gonna be here, or in that big desert lot outside. If I know Marcia, she'll drift in, a while before it starts, and she'll probably be either drunk or stoned because she won't be able to put up with the atmosphere of a bunch of hicks listening to gospel music straight, and she'll appreciate the irony of it all. Her being stoned, she'll probably blend right in, and she'll masquerade as a devout Christian, just to amuse herself."

"That's why she's so cool," Milo said.

"I'm worried she's gonna get herself killed," Mickey said, "but that's my girl. She scares me to death but at least I know her. 'Cause I raised her, and she's got my blood in her, and that's true for better or worse. It could be that I'm not a bit different from all these pilgrims, come to Sin City to testify to Jesus. Look around you, Milo. They've succumbed to the fatted calf. That's what they'll ask forgiveness for tomorrow. Hey, where's Dylan?"

"I think he's up in the room. Probably reading a book, or writing a little, I'm guessing."

Mickey looked at his watch. "It's getting time to go over to the concert grounds and see what the Honorable Nathan Beale is going to say. I'm fairly sure Marcia will show up, either with her hotshot boyfriend or looking for him. Go get Dylan. I'll cash in my slips and meet you out front. I haven't got a clue what's gonna happen, but I'm fairly sure something is."

Dylan Wannamacher had a visitor. Rashawn Ling knocked on the door, looking for Mickey Statler.

"Come in," Dylan said. "I'm guessing your name is Rashawn Ling."

"That's right."

"I'm Dylan. Mickey and I have become pretty close over the past few months," Dylan said. "I teach English at Enlightened Word, a prep school in Virginia. I got to know Mickey when I was filling in as the football coach."

Rashawn sat on the couch. "I know a little bit about you, too," he said.

"I expect Mickey will be here directly," Dylan said. "I'm guessing he's in the casino, just killing time and trying to get himself settled down before we go over to the big gospel sing. One of my students, Milo Hirley, came out with us. Mickey's trying to find his daughter and keep her out of trouble."

"Marcia," Rashawn said. "I've never met her."

"Oh, she's quite a pistol."

"So I've heard. I've been trying to get hold of Mickey. I guess he's gotten himself a different cell. Me, too. He told me I'd better stop using the number I had. I guess he did, too. That left us mutually exclusive of each other," Rashawn said, smiling. "I finally found him by asking if he was registered here."

"I reckon it's a deal where everybody knows that everybody else is going to be at the most unlikely place that all of us would congregate," Dylan said. "I'm a hippie writer. Mickey's a reluctant weed delivery boy. Milo's a little hellion, smart as a whip but high as a kite most of the time. Marcia's a devious, ambitious little tart, and I don't think her father would object to that description, and we're all here to watch the sanctimonious Attorney General of the United States rail against the very corruption that we all represent. Fucked-up world."

"And Mickey's funding the whole sordid, hilarious expedition with his ill-gotten gains," Rashawn said.

"Yep," Dylan said. "I don't know why in hell I'm trying to write fiction. Truth is stranger by a country mile."

"I've got a gig," Rashawn said, "but it's not the one Mickey sent me to find. I sold a story about Nathan Beale's crusade against legalized pot to what I guess you'd say is a counterculture magazine."

"Oh? Which one?"

"Cannabis Countdown."

"I read it online," Dylan said.

"I don't even smoke it," Rashawn said. "Pay's pretty good, though. This is gonna be a cover story."

"Keep your eyes open. Might get a good bit more, if Mickey's right."

They heard a knock on the door. "That's probably Mickey right there," Dylan said.

It was Milo.

"Mickey says meet him at the casino main entrance," Milo said. "Who's this?"

"This is Rashawn Ling, a sportswriter friend of Mickey's," Dylan said. "He's in on the whole deal, Milo."

"I think we might have time, you know …"

"Nah," Dylan said. "I ain't got none. Get a beer out of the fridge. Shotgun it. That'll give you a little buzz."

"That works, I reckon," Milo said.

CHAPTER 56

A Hasty Retreat

The music that started it out wasn't gospel.

As the gates opened, a military band started playing patriotic songs. John Philip Souza. "The Marine Hymn." "Anchors Aweigh." "The U.S. Field Artillery March" (which Mickey Statler knew as the North Carolina State University fight song). "The U.S. Air Force" (Off We Go into the Wild, Blue Yonder). The members must have come from all the services. When a decent crowd had filed in, Nathan Beale would give his speech. Only a few would understand its significance.

Mickey Statler and Rashawn Ling went one way, Dylan Wannamacher and Milo Hirley another.

Two black SUVs arrived, five minutes apart. One backed into a gated pathway, enclosed by a tarpaulin-enclosed canopy. Most figured Beale was in it, but the Attorney General was in the other, which entered through another gate and parked along one side of the stage. Yuri Iznetsikov, also known as Stedman Andersen, and Wade Sanderson got out of the first and made their way to the area beneath the stage. Nathan and Marjorie Beale, the Attorney General's associates Gerald Behr and Clausen Downey, and the security detail proceeded to the edge of the stage, where Beale talked with several of the event's organizers.

Mickey was untroubled by Rashawn's inability to come up with evidence regarding the Consortium's existence or conspiracy with the authorities. He told Rashawn not to be apologetic. Mickey said he only cared about the safety of his daughter and that he looked forward to reading Rashawn's irreverent story in *Cannabis Countdown*.

"Give me some advance notice when it's published." Mickey smiled. "I've not been a voracious reader of that particular rag. I probably should have been."

"What do you think?" Rashawn asked.

"What? You mean, what Beale will say?"

"Yeah. You think he'll use this captive audience to reinstitute the War on Drugs?"

"I doubt it," Mickey said. "I don't know, but if I was a betting man, I'd say Beale will turn on a states' rights dime. It's all about money with politicians in general, but it's the only thing that matters with Republicans. I doubt that's what Beale was planning to do when he set up this trip to Vegas. He thought of it is as venturing into the den of the lion, and standing up for old-fashioned family values, but the Consortium's probably bought him off. They might have done it through Gaynes, but I bet they've done it. He'll probably give a speech about how weed is evil, but he'll concede the right of the voters to choose for themselves. He'll take the easy way out. I've been thinking about it. I'd be shocked if that isn't what happens."

Fifty yards away, Dylan was alone, leaning against one of the cyclone fences that bordered the viewing area. Green vinyl prevented those outside from seeing the performances. Dylan scanned the crowd of gospel fans, there to enjoy a who's who of the country's great old-time gospel groups. The men wore blue jeans and plaid flannel shirts with pearl snaps, as did some of the women, but some wore gingham dresses, checked in red, blue, and green with white. His mind took him back to the square dances of his rural Mississippi roots. Milo was mingling with a few kids of his age, the ones who had been unable to prevent their parents from dragging them along on their pilgrimages. They had managed to wander off from their parents, secretly looking for a chance to sneak outside and sneak cigarettes, or, perhaps, find a place outside where they could pass a joint around safely. Not even the National Gospel Sing was completely safe from the weed menace. It was Milo who spotted the arrival of Marcia Statler to the grounds first. He excused himself from his new friends and trotted back to where Dylan stood.

"There's Marcia," he said. "Let's go see her."

Milo pointed her out to Dylan. She looked stoned, which he expected.

"No," Dylan said. "Mickey will see her. Let's me and you go back to the casino. I need a drink."

"Me, too," Milo said.

"The bar in the casino's got to be dead. This is the worst day of the year for business," Dylan said. "Just act like you know what you're doing. You got any kind of fake I.D.?"

"Nah," Milo said. "That's the whole purpose of smoking weed. Don't need one."

"Just let me do the talking, and follow my lead. If they ask for an I.D., just show 'em the one you got."

They left and walked a hundred yards back to the casino, where a bar was located adjacent to the entrance. It was almost empty. Not everyone staying at Bonneville Junction was a holy roller. A half dozen or so were drinking at the bar. Dylan and Milo slipped into a booth, chosen because it was a safe distance from the door. Dylan told the waiter that Milo, his son, was in school at UNLV, and that he'd come to see him on his twenty-first birthday. Dylan slipped the young man a twenty, and Milo winked as he flashed his Virginia driver's license. He ordered giant margaritas for the boy's big day. And a platter of chipotle-chicken quesadillas.

Mickey was preoccupied by his discussion of politics with Rashawn. Sanderson happened to be scanning the crowd with Iznetsikov's binoculars from behind the electronic cloak. He immediately felt a flash of anger, muttering to himself, "I told that bitch to stay away."

"What?" Iznetsikov asked.

"Nothing," Wade said. "There's just something I've got to deal with. Won't take five minutes. I'll be right back."

Wade ran through the canopy and past the SUV before Iznetsikov could tell him no. He flashed his credentials badge at the entrance to the

V.I.P. area and was conspicuous due to his all-black attire and sunglasses. He ran within ten yards of Mickey and Rashawn. Mickey turned his head and glanced at but didn't recognize him, thanks, no doubt, to the shades. He was almost there when Marcia recognized him.

"Wade, darling," she said. "You know I had to come."

Wade grabbed her by the arm and drug her through the gate, then around to the back of the ticket booth and into a space of about five feet between its back door and the cyclone fence.

"I fucking told you to stay home," he said, grabbing on the shoulders, close to the neck. Then he lifted one hand and slapped her across the face.

"If you don't get the fuck away from her, and I mean now, I will kill you, Marcia. I will fucking kill you dead!"

Her eyes welled up, but the sight did not soften his tone.

"I just wanted to be with you on your big day!"

"No, you fucking don't," Wade said. "I'm gonna let you in a little secret. Tripp Fallaw is dead, Marcia. The reason I know that is that I killed him. His body was dumped from an airplane into the waters off the coast of Baja California. I can fucking do the same thing to you, and I will unless you get your ass back to the airport and on a plane back to Virginia. If you don't, I won't have to kill you because a bunch of people are going to be killed in about an hour right here on these grounds. Do you understand me? Can you tell that I'm serious?"

That she could see in his eyes. They were dead. They were cold. They were ruthless.

"Now I gotta go," Wade said. "If I need you dead, all I gotta do is snap my fucking fingers. Now get the fuck out. This didn't happen. Understand?"

"Yeah," she said. "I just gotta get my jacket. It's on the ground where I was standing."

Who cares about the fucking jacket? Wade thought. He had no time to argue.

"I'll be backstage in two minutes," Wade said. "Don't you be inside these goddamned fences when I get there."

The second time Wade ran past Mickey and Rashawn, Mickey recognized him.

"See where that guy in black goes," he said to Rashawn. "I'm gonna see if I can find Marcia."

Mickey saw her walking hurriedly through the gate. Marcia's face was white as a sheet.

"Marcia!" he yelled. It didn't occur to her to reflect any surprise.

"Daddy, we gotta get out of here. We gotta get out of here now!" She put on her jacket and started running back toward the exit. He followed her. She outdistanced him, but Mickey kept her in sight until she stopped and nervously lit a cigarette.

"Where's your car?" Marcia's ability to regain her breath was hindered by sucking furiously on a Marlboro Light.

"Hold your horses, Marcia. Dylan and Milo came out here with me. I got to round them up."

"Wade said he was going to kill me if I didn't get out of here," she said. "Trust me, Daddy. You should have seen the look in his eyes. He was serious. He told me he killed Tripp."

"Who the hell's Wade?"

"He was a guy I met at Triborough. I flew out to Los Angeles with him," Marcia said. "We haven't got time to talk about it. That's how I met Wade."

"Do you have a cell with you?" Mickey asked. He pulled his room key out of his pocket and repeated the Bonneville Junction's number from the paper sleeve that contained the plastic strip. "Ask for Room 837."

Marcia placed the cigarette between her lips and hurriedly dialed. The front desk rang the room. No answer.

"No one's home," she said.

"Quick, let's go in the casino. They must be there," Mickey said. "They were in the concert grounds last I saw them."

"We gotta go."

"We can't very well leave them in Las Vegas," Mickey said. "I brought them out here with me to look for you. Never mind that it became obvious that all we could really do was let you come to us. It was kinda one of them 'all for one and one for all' deals. I'll go one way, and you go the other, and we'll meet back at the entrance."

By chance, as they headed down the broad avenue of concrete that led inside, Mickey glanced through the windows of the bar and happened to see Dylan and Milo sitting in a booth.

"Hang on," he said. "There they are."

"Thank God," Marcia said.

Mickey slid in next to Milo, and Dylan moved over to make room for Marcia.

"I never drank much liquor until last night," Milo said, drawing on a straw from a margarita the size of a Big Gulp from a Seven-Eleven. "It's pretty fuckin' good. Marcia, I don't suppose you've got some weed on you."

She frowned.

"Marcia says we've got to get out of town before Wade Sanderson kills her," Mickey said. "I'm pretty sure she's not kidding."

"It's not just that," she blurted. "Wade says a bunch of people are about to get killed."

"Fuck," Dillon said and turned to Mickey. "You said you had a feeling something was going to happen to Nathan Beale."

"I didn't think it was a bomb, or, maybe, a mass shooting," Mickey said. "Shh. Be quiet a second."

They could hear the military band faintly, playing "The Battle Hymn of the Republic."

"Beale's gonna speak once they're through," Mickey said.

"Let's fuckin' book, man," Milo said. "I've had enough of being shot at. Know what I'm saying?"

"Don't you think we ought to tell somebody?" Dylan asked.

"We don't know for sure the cops ain't in on it," Mickey said. "Marcia and I will go get the car. Dylan, you and Milo go get your shit out of the room. I'll pull up to the front desk. Don't even fuck with checking out. Just leave the key cards in the room. They'll know we're gone."

Marcia and Mickey found the rental car in the parking lot. They pulled up to the front of the hotel.

"Shit," Mickey said.

"What?"

"Wait for Dylan and Milo in the lobby,' he said. "I'll be right back."

"What?" she asked a second time.

"Rashawn's at the concert."

"Who's Rashawn?" she asked.

"He's an ex-colleague of mine," he said. "He's on assignment. There's no time to explain. I'll leave the car parked here. Just get them in the car. Here. Take the keys. I gotta go get him. It's my fault he's in this predicament. I'll explain later."

Mickey found Rashawn standing near the front of the crowd.

"Beale's gonna be at that reviewing stand," Rashawn said, pointing to a roped-off area directly in front of the stage.

"Come with me," Mickey said.

"What's up?" Rashawn asked.

"There's going to be some kind of attack. I don't know. A bomb. A shooter. Who knows? I've got to get you out of harm's way."

"Are you crazy?"

"Maybe, but I don't want you killed at my expense."

"Mickey," Rashawn said, "I'm a journalist. I'm on assignment. I've got a story to write. Don't matter what story it is."

Mickey stared at him. He could see he wasn't going to get Rashawn to leave.

"Then get away from where Beale's gonna be," Mickey said, thinking it through hurriedly. "Go to the back of the grounds. Up against the fence. Near the exit. I'm taking my daughter to the airport. Let me know you're all right. Send me an email from your phone. I can access it through Marcia's phone. Be careful. Be safe."

As Mickey walked back through the gate, the band stopped playing. He heard a man walk up to the microphone stand on stage and identify himself as the chairman of the Nevada Republican Party. He said the Attorney General of the United States, the Honorable Nathan Beale, would be addressing the crowd in a few minutes.

McCarran International Airport was a twenty-minute drive. Marcia lit another cigarette and cracked the passenger-side window. Milo asked if he could bum one from the back seat. He said he'd kill for a joint, but a cigarette would have to do. No one else had anything to say. Milo's fear was subsiding. He could feel the margaritas again. When they got to the airport, they found a flight to Reagan with four empty seats, but they'd have to wait three hours. By the time they'd checked their bags, gone through security, and arrived at the gate, Nathan Beale was winding down his speech. The monitors were showing it live. The crawl across the bottom of the screen read: *Breaking News -- Attorney General Beale expected to announce federal intervention against weed-legal states.*

CHAPTER 57

When the Whip Comes Down

Nathan Beale was twice as afraid of wife Marjorie as President Martin Gaynes. Marjorie was smarter than Gaynes, just as ambitious, and twice as smart. She wasn't going to like it when he abandoned his plan to use federal law enforcement to close down the marijuana dispensaries of Colorado, Washington, Oregon, and California, and the plans being made in Nevada, Alaska, Maine, Massachusetts, and the District of Columbia. The prepared text he had planned to deliver to the conservative fans of gospel music was useless to him now. He would have to go off the cuff, and he planned to let his wife's expectations down easily. He knew well the talking points he was about to abandon.

Beale prayed, for he had much for which to ask the Lord's forgiveness. He hated himself for his indiscretions, and he knew he had only himself to blame. He had succumbed to the temptations of drink, smoke, and the flesh. Beale knew that now he would have to sacrifice what he considered his virtuous principles. He told the Lord that he was unworthy of forgiveness but had to ask for it, anyway. The Lord did not reply. The Lord, he knew, was angry. The Lord, he knew, was powerful. He was weak, but he bared his soul as diligently as he could. Finally, Beale pronounced himself ready to speak, and the junior senator of Nevada, his former colleague, delivered a glowing introduction he did not deserve.

"I wish I could say," Beale began, "that I came here, to Las Vegas, for the same reason you folks did. I have loved gospel music since my earliest memory, when my mother and father brought me to gospel sings in my native Mississippi – in Jackson, and Starkville, and Tupelo – to rejoice in the Lord and the music that praises Him. I remember the Florida Boys, and the Hinsons, and the Cathedrals, and many were the nights I fell asleep, in prayer to my Jesus, listening to that sacred music.

"But what I came here for today was a testimony of a far different kind," he continued. "I chose the National Gospel Sing as a platform to speak out against the moral decline of our country, and I chose this particular place because this city, Las Vegas, is noted as something of a center of vice, iniquity, and sin. I believe folks call this Sin City, and you folks have come here just like me, partly to hear the music you love, but also partly to cleanse this glittering place of its sinful underside."

Beale was at home with the gospel crowd, which interspersed his remarks with individually inspired shouts of "Amen," and "Praise Jesus," and "Yes, Hallelujah, I know it's so!" He paused, and they responded with applause.

Beneath his feet, Wade Sanderson's trigger finger grew itchy. He was going to do it. He was going to send Nathan Beale to meet his Maker. Wade didn't believe in Jesus or the Devil, but if they existed, Beale and he were headed in different directions. Wade reveled in this. He was excited, too much so. Separated only by wooden flooring stood he and his antithesis. Wade needed something to make the raging adrenaline subside. He had a small vaporizer that held a cartridge of cannabis extract. The vapor he exhaled subsided quickly and without odor. Yuri Iznetsikov watched Wade closely. Wade asked "Stedman" if he'd care to partake. The faux libertarian declined.

"Don't worry, comrade," Wade said. "It won't make me stoned. It will only make me calm and merciless."

Iznetsikov nodded and kept on observing. The Americans had so many ways to impair themselves. In Russia, vodka had always been enough.

While the Attorney General continued to describe Las Vegas as a thinly disguised Sodom with an order of Gomorrah on the side, Mickey and Marcia Statler, Dylan Wannamacher, and Milo Hirley arrived at McCarran International Airport. The speech was being televised live on the monitors at the gate, though the screen was muted and would have been anyway in the din of slot machines good for relieving visitors of what money they had left from their gambling adventures. While the others read the text of Nathan Beale's words from the closed captioning, Milo, bored and drunk, played the slots in spite of Mickey's advice that he had never seen anyone actually win on them at the airport.

Two security agents sat near Marjorie Beale. The other two stood on either side of the stage while the Attorney General continued to ramble. No one expected any trouble. Beale was in his element. The African-American agent, Ted Wallis, noted via radio to his colleague, Ron Tippit, that he could find only one "brother" in the audience.

"Would you like to go interrogate him?" Tippit said. "If we're going to 'profile' somebody, I'd prefer it be you."

"He appears to be wearing some sort of credentials," Wallis replied. "I believe if I was him, I'd display them prominently, too. He's standing by himself, taking notes, against the fence, at the back, taking notes."

"Most of the press is on one side of the reviewing stand," Tippit said. "I bet he's working for some alternative magazine or website. When Beale gets through, we'll accompany him to his seat. You slip away and check him out."

"He won't be hard to find," Wallis replied. "This is a strange scene. The music seems too Southern white gospel. Why in the world would there be a market for that in the West?"

"Outside the big cities, it's mostly white out here."

"What do you figure the crowd size is, Ron?"

"Oh, two thousand, tops. I don't think there's much to worry about. The Clark County Sheriff's Department is out in force."

"Is there anybody on duty in the hotel?" Wallis asked.

"It's all covered. It came up in the meeting this morning. Half dozen officers, I think."

Two of those Clark County officers were in a corner room of the twelfth floor, posing as Youseff Cameroon's accomplices. Ostensibly, they were to join him in spraying the crowd with the AR-15s, equipped with bump stocks, they had been provided by Arkady Pankratov. As the lead shooter, Cameroon's rifle was mounted on a tripod. The officers would allow him to fire off twelve to fifteen rounds, then, while he was distracted, execute him. Then they would retrieve SWAT uniforms from their zip-up bags and take credit for stopping the killer before he did more damage. The sheriff, a close personal friend of Garlin Samuelson, was in on it. Samuelson was president of the National Confederation of Law Enforcement Officers and a board member of the Consortium.

"Marijuana is a dangerous, insidious drug that is robbing our young people of their morals, their religious convictions, and their work ethics," Beale said. "We are constantly assaulted by liberals who rationalize it all away by saying it's not that bad. Well, let me tell you what is bad. Marijuana is a gateway drug that leads the youth of our country down a primrose path to hard drugs like cocaine, and opioids, and hallucinogens. When President Martin Gaynes offered me the opportunity to lead the Department of Justice, I told him my first act would be to reform our nation's War on Drugs in a way that works. I don't believe in giving up on that which is righteous, just because we haven't managed to succeed yet. I don't believe in turning criminals loose from our prisons, and I don't believe in failing to enforce the laws of our country as long as those federal laws are on the books. I don't believe you give up. I believe you continue to seek a path that works, and such a path cannot be anchored in weakness and appeasement. Appeasement didn't work in putting a stop to the Nazis before the Second World War, and it won't work in putting a stop to the heartbreaking epidemic of drug abuse in America now."

Beale paused to hear the applause, none more fervent than from his beloved Marjorie, smiling for any cameras that might drift her way while the good people, the predominantly white people, who still kept the country going, were cheering Nathan. Beale waited a long time, enjoying the cheers, until, finally, he raised his arms and said, "Please … you're too kind" because he knew it was time to disappoint them and, more importantly, Marjorie.

For five more minutes, Beale discussed the marijuana menace with lines he had used since he was a member of the House of Representatives in the late 1970s. At the McCarran gate, Dylan Wannamacher grew irritated at Beale for citing one "fact" after another that wasn't. Across the "crawl" of the CNN feed ran the message:

Breaking News – Attorney General Nathan Beale Calls for Resumption of Nation's Controversial War on Drugs …

Marcia remained something of a wreck. She went to Barney's Lounge, a designated smoking area, where she could order a beer and chain-smoke Marlboro Lights. A man next to her noticed she was crying and tried to console her. She told him to fuck off and put her sunglasses on.

The news crawl was wrong about the breaking news.

"The problem," Beale told the crowd, "is that enforcing the federal law in states like this one, where the people, in their infinite ignorance, have voted to legalize marijuana for recreational use. For my entire career in public life, I have believed in states' rights and home rule. I have taken great pride in being a principled conservative, and, as much as I detest the legality of marijuana, I must respect the wishes of the people of Nevada, as well as California, Colorado, Washington State, Oregon, Alaska, and, back east, Maine and Massachusetts. Unfortunately, while the Constitution does not mention it, I'm afraid that one of the rights retained by our citizenry is the right to stupidity. I believe in a state's right to adapt its rules to its own collective morality. It is with great reluctance that I have decided to respect the right of Nevada and other sovereign states to determine its own policies, with regard to the people's will, in regard to marijuana legalization."

No applause greeted Beale's pause. The crowd went silent, all except for Marjorie's audible gasp and a single kid on the fringe of the audience, who blurted out "all right," and, likely, his father, who threatened to whip his young ass.

At the airport, the crawl changed.

Breaking News – Beale Surprisingly Announces that Feds Will NOT Enforce Federal Marijuana Prohibition …

"I'll be damned," Mickey Statler said to Dylan. "I was right, after all. The Consortium did get to him. You can't fight those people."

"You seem disappointed," Dylan replied.

"I don't know what I think. I'm pro-weed and anti-corruption. What Beale just said is probably gonna keep me corrupt."

"Maybe when it's legal back east."

"You're lucky," Mickey said. "You aren't a slave. Maybe Marcia's not a slave. She got in this of her own free will. Me? I might have been better off if that deputy down in Lovejoy had just let me rot in jail."

"One never knows," Dylan, who couldn't think of anything else, said.

Under the stage, Wade Sanderson, who had been squinting through the scope of his own AR-15, just semi-automatic, and putting the crosshairs on Marjorie Beale, and her two security agents, and the junior senator from Nevada, looked at Yuri Iznetsikov, and said, "So it's off, right?"

"I assume that to be the case," he said in his best Midwestern Stedman Andersen.

"So, why not get to packin' to go ahead and get the hell out of here?"

"I must await word from a comrade."

"Pankratov."

"Yes," Iznetsikov said. "He is in contact with President Borzov."

"I fuckin' want to plug Beale," Wade said. "The faggoty son of a bitch."

"Yes," Iznetsikov replied. "That he is."

"What about the other thing?"

"You mean, the mass shooting?"

"No," Wade said. "The Cuban Missile Crisis. Of course, the mass shooting."

"My suspicion is that it will go on as planned," Iznetsikov said. "There is a political motive. The whole point is that a Muslim Negro, murdering a dozen white Christians, will foment racial strife and benefit President Gaynes' popularity rating."

"I do kind of admire the way you Russians think," Wade said, "but if it's still on, isn't that all the more reason for us to get the fuck out of here while the getting's good?"

"Perhaps," the Russian said. "It is not for me to say. I can only say that your safety is assured."

Beale, who had been remarkably cogent for a man speaking largely off the cuff, started to grovel a bit now, speaking directly to Marjorie's scornful eyes. It hadn't been completely extemporaneous. He was using a teleprompter, but the speech had been written to announce the Justice Department's agents moving in on what states had declared to be legal activities. Beale had just departed from the script to change the message. He said the same harsh things about marijuana use. He announced a massive funding program that existed only in his own head. He said the Justice Department would announce a $500 million program – it sounded less wasteful than a billion – to discourage the spread of marijuana legalization. He said the President would recruit Republican candidates who would pledge to get legalization repealed in states like Nevada.

The big news was what Beale hadn't announced. The 24-hour news networks started muting his remarks and talking about how he had apparently succumbed to Republican strategists who felt the party should embrace marijuana's growing acceptance.

Then they left altogether and switched to a new round of news breaking at the White House.

Martin Gaynes had decided he had taken as much from the Russians as he was going to. He was, after all, the president of the most powerful country in the world. Yevgeny Borzov didn't own him. Borzov had merely assisted him. The Russians couldn't just go in and invade Finland. Finland had white people.

Gaynes had decided he wasn't going to let the Russians take the world by surprise. He had decided to expose them.

"This morning," Gaynes said from the Rose Garden, "I was informed by our military intelligence apparatus that the Russian Federation is massing troops along the northern and eastern border of Finland with the clear intention of invading that sovereign nation. I have instructed the Secretary of Defense, in conjunction with the Joint Chiefs of Staff, and, in particular, with the Commander, United States Fleet Forces Command, to begin moving American forces, particularly the Navy and Air Force, into position to combat this serious Russian threat. We will provide further information as it become more available."

The president had said nothing about cooperation from European allies, NATO, the British, the Germans, or the French, nothing. He ignored questions. He would have been more specific had he merely said, *Welcome to World War III,* but he strode back into the White House, and so did all the spokespersons, the Cabinet officials, and the military representatives who had been standing behind him.

Ten million Americans said "holy shit" all at once.

In Las Vegas, Arkady Pankratov received word from President Yevgeny Borzov that the assassination of the Honorable Nathan Bedford Forrest Beale was on.

The schedule of the National Gospel Sing had drifted long. Everything had dragged on longer than expected. The military band had played twice as long. Beale had spoken twice as long. Piped-in music played for an hour while the crowd waited for the show to begin. The original plan had been for the shooting to begin during the playing of the national anthem. It had to wait while Beale bided his time before being accompanied to the reviewing stand, dreading the confrontation with his wife. Pankratov briefed Borzov via a secure cell connection with the Kremlin. Yevgeny Borzov had to be briefed about his American counterpart's remarks. Borzov had miscalculated Martin Gaynes. He hadn't expected Gaynes to cross him. They had agreed that the United States would not interfere with Russian expansion. Finland was a gut check that Borzov hadn't expected Gaynes to pass. Pankratov tried to convince Borzov that going through with the assassination of Beale served no strategic purpose. Borzov said he didn't care. The Americans would pay. Beale would die. The anthem was over, and the first act was preparing to take the stage. Mickey and Marcia Statler, Dylan Wannamacher, and Milo Hirley boarded their flight. It took off for Washington.

Wade Sanderson prepared for the kill. Pankratov briefed Cameroon's accomplices. The Muslim killer was growing antsy. Now the plan was to fire into the crowd at the end of the first gospel song. The opening act was a 72-year-old Navajo singer from Arizona. He was backed by a house band that had been recruited to back the early acts. The band required a short sound check.

Pankratov knew everything about the mission was senseless. It was no longer in Russia's interest to prop up the double-crossing Martin Gaynes. Nathan Beale was no longer an impediment to the Consortium's plans to corner the cannabis market. It was all taking place because Yevgeny Borzov was angry, and he wanted to embarrass Gaynes and teach the United States a lesson. Pankratov could not belabor his points. He could not afford to lose favor with Borzov. Pankratov was angry, too.

Nathan Beale was disgraced in the eyes of his audience. Hardly anyone clapped when he finished his speech. He wanted to leave, but he couldn't bring himself to budge. He sat on the stand as the Native American prepared to perform. He watched Marjorie, seething, out of the corner of his eyes. She said nothing. She was trembling. The vein on her forehead was pulsating.

Finally, Beale's wife of twenty-three years, his partner in life and guru in politics, turned to him, and said, "Nathan Beale, you will rot in hell for that."

Beale knew she'd have him shot if she could.

In the corner room on the twelfth floor, Levander Suber said quietly to Yousseff Cameroon, "It's almost time. Are you gonna do this or not?"

Suber pulled a pistol from a shoulder holster. Cameroon got the message.

"Oh, yeah, I'm ready to kill me some white motherfuckers."

Suber nodded to his partner in Las Vegas law enforcement and corruption. Suber and Darnell Cowlings were old hands at eliminating the Consortium's competition. This was their first involvement with Russians. The money was good. It was already in the bank.

The two officers grabbed their rifles.

"The first song's starting," Cowlings said. He wore earbuds. "I'm listening to the concert feed. As soon as this guy, this Indian singer, sings his first chorus, I'll tell you to proceed. Levander will break the panel. It's glass. You get in position. When I tell you, start firing. We'll both join you in approximately ten seconds. Aim at somebody at the back of the crowd. Doesn't matter who. Kill him. Then hold down the trigger and begin strafing the crowd. They'll be dead before they know what hit 'em."

"I want to shoot that fuckin' whitey politician," Cameroon said. "That's who I want to aim at."

"No," Suber said. "He's the inside job. A few seconds after we start firing, a pro, hidden in what's basically a concealed turret, will fire one shot at Beale's head as soon as he rises at the commotion we start. That rifle is trained on him right now. As soon as he stands, he's a dead man. Got it?"

"Yeah," Cameroon said. "I got it."

Pankratov slipped into the door that led to Wade Sanderson's post. He informed Iznetsikov to make sure the Escalade was ready for departure and the area secure.

"As soon as everything is ready, when you hear the first pops of the shooting, calmly walk back in here, and assist Mister Sanderson and me," Pankratov said. "I'll take it from here."

Iznetsikov left.

"Mister Sanderson, have you ever visited Russia?"

"I've never been out of the country, except once to Vancouver," Wade said.

"That is about to change. We'll let things cool off for a while. You'll live like a king in Vladivostok. In due time, we'll smuggle you back into the U.S.A. You can be a valuable operative."

"Cool," Wade said. "I mean, yes, sir, Comrade."

Pankratov smiled.

The Navajo singer sang the last verse in his tribal tongue. Suber prepared the shooting path. He took the butt of the rifle and pounded the glass. Glass fell to the pavement below. An alarm should have gone off. It had been deactivated. No one would have time to notice, and if anyone did, it would be too late to do anything. Cameroon affixed the rifle to a bipod and crouched. He looked through the scope. He focused in on a black man. He certainly wasn't going to shoot a brother. He swung the AR-15 to the left. A man in a straw hat, wearing a checked flannel shirt beneath a sleeveless down jacket. Cameroon wanted to make sure he killed the first one.

The song ended. Cowling said "go." Cameroon pulled the trigger and killed the man in the flannel. Then he held the trigger down as people started to scatter. Suber picked up his rifle. It just took a shot to snuff Cameroon. The last round Cameroon fired killed Rashawn Ling, who was running toward the exit and serpentined right into it. Suber and Cowling changed into their SWAT jackets.

At the first sound, Wade trained his scope on Beale. The first shot sounded like a firecracker, exploding in the distance. Then it sounded as if popcorn was popping. Beale stood up. Wade pulled the trigger. It was a powerful weapon. The Attorney General's head exploded. Ron Tippit kneeled over Beale's body. Two agents attempted to lead Marjorie Beale to safety. Ted Wallis radioed for medical assistance as he looked at the carnage of Beale's face. It was colorful but not pretty.

Wade should have quickly backed away from the shrouded opening. He should have calmly disassembled the rifle and placed it in its case, as he had been trained. He felt sexual arousal and lingered on the bloody corpse, noting that the federal agent kneeling over him had been on the plane with him from D.C. to Denver. He was oblivious to Pankratov, who stood calmly at his side.

Arkady Pankratov, the liaison of Russian president Yevgeny Borzov, raised the pistol to which he just attached a suppressor, and shot Wade Sanderson, who now thought himself an agent of the Russian Federation, in the temple. Pankratov spoke in Russian.

"Извините. Дальнейшее использование для вас не существует."

Sorry. No further use for you exists.

CHAPTER 58

Nothing Matters

The country dutifully mourned the violent death of Nathan Beale, who earned respect he had never earned in life. He was buried in his native Pascagoula, where grateful citizens raised funds to erect a memorial. If Yevgeny Borzov had intended to quiet the international tension and soften American calls for war, it worked. He claimed the Russian Army was merely conducting routine exercises, and Martin Gaynes, who knew better, did not dispute him.

Rashawn Ling had been one of eight concert attendees killed in the brief hail of gunfire from the twelfth floor of the Bonneville Junction Hotel. Beale's murder was officially the result of a collaboration between Wade Sanderson, described as a marijuana legalization activist, and Yousseff Cameroon, also known as Reggie Lennart, a militant Muslim from Detroit. Mickey Statler got in his car and drove to Anderson, Indiana, where Rashawn found his final resting place to the sorrow of his father, a pediatrician, and his mother, a middle-school teacher. Mickey tried to comfort them at the funeral home, and they told him they were grateful he came all that way. Mainly, though, he kept a low profile and spent two nights in a Super 8, where he mainly grieved and tried to forgive himself for putting Rashawn in a place to die. On the road, Mickey called on the numbness he had cultivated in a life marred by a failure to realize his ambitions. He had repeatedly aspired to greatness and learned to live with being merely above average. He'd botched a career, a marriage, and the raising of at least one daughter. As he'd said many times, he was depressed, not clinically, but for a damned good reason. He tried not to think because it required the admission of repeated failure. What little he concluded was that no system could work effectively if all outcomes were fixed. When he left Indiana, he took his time going to a week-long assignment writing about baseball spring training. No one gave him any delivery assignments because, whether forever or just a time, the Consortium was inactive, its leadership lying low, waiting for any heat to settle down. Mickey didn't know if it would call on him again. He didn't ask Carson Carmine when they talked about the spring training assignment. Carson didn't say anything. Mickey didn't care. He did a competent job writing about the Atlanta Braves, the New York Yankees, the Pittsburgh Pirates, and the Boston Red Sox, because he was a pro, and he could repress his sorrow by doing his job. He ignored his text messages, other than from the website, and didn't answer his phone. Everyone knew Rashawn had been his friend. They understood the sorrow but had no concept of its depth.

No one knew how Sanderson and Cameroon had gotten together. No one investigating it could get anyone to talk, certainly not Edmund Kingsley, the director of the Federal Bureau of Investigation, and Oscar Leggatt, sheriff of Clark County and close, personal friend of Garlin Samuelson, former police chief of Houston, Texas, and president of the National Confederation of Law Enforcement Officers. Mickey knew he ought to be comforted that the fix was in because, if a massive investigation were conducted diligently, the great conspiracy might find its way all the way down to him and his daughter. Marcia was back in Triborough somewhere. He hoped she was working on that novel she had been allegedly writing. Dylan was teaching American literature and had agreed to continue coaching the Enlightened Word Fighting Dragoons. The Merry Pranksters started to dissolve as Milo Hirley, Walt Pegler, Marty Drummond, and Jonny Heinsohn prepared for graduation and college.

For weeks, all of them held it in. Mickey and Dylan were accustomed to the numbness. Marcia acquired the knack. Milo discovered it existed. Everyone around them knew they had changed.

Don't ask. Don't tell. It had been a cliché related to the quiet acceptance of gays in the military. It applied to everything else. Mind your own business. Don't expect anything to work. Lose the idealism. No system has anything to do with what they tell you it is. *Don't ask. Don't tell.* You'll survive. You'll be fine right up until you die and go to hell.

It was late April when Mickey and Marcia finally got back together. They both sensed it was time. Marcia called him and said she'd meet him wherever he wanted. Mickey suggested Kings Mountain National Military Park, near the border of North and South Carolina. He had taken her there when she was in grade school.

"How about a baseball game?" she suggested. "You always said it was the only sport that was relaxing. You said it was the best place in the world to talk. It was where you become friends for nine innings with someone you'll never see again. I remember."

"How about a minor-league game? Next Tuesday night. No postgame fireworks. Shitty crowd. Won't be many people there. We'll sit down the line and pick out seats where there's nobody around," Mickey said. "Let me check a few schedules and see who's home. I'll call you back."

Mickey found a home game in Hickory, North Carolina, home of the Crawdads. He called her back.

"That'll work," she said. "You can buy me some peanuts and cracker jacks."

"I'll meet you out front," he said. "Game starts at 7:05. How about quarter till?"

"Deal," she said.

They bought general-admission tickets and sat down at a location a brief survey revealed was ten rows and ten yards from any other fans.

"It's a rivalry," Mickey said. "Kannapolis Intimidators."

"That's a strange name," Marcia responded

"Most minor-league teams have strange names. Intimidators honors Dale Earnhardt. His hometown was Kannapolis."

"Oh."

A breaking ball made a lefthanded Crawdad look bad. He check his swing but made solid contact, and the ball popped high in the air down the left-field line, far from being in play. It landed two aisles over and bounced on the concrete. Mickey reached out and caught it with his left hand. A passel of little boys came running down the steps. Mickey tossed the ball to a black kid he estimated to be the one who wanted it the most. For some reason, this seemed to stimulate conversation.

"How you making it?" he asked Marcia.

"I didn't do much of anything for three or four days," she said. "Finally, I guess I kind of buried myself in writing."

"Me, too. Writing is good therapy for sorrow."

"I sent some samples out," she said. "I think I may have an agent."

"I had an agent once," Mickey said. "I never made much money, so he made a whole lot less off me. He only handled non-fiction, said he couldn't make money because everybody wanted to write novels. Then he died, and, from then on, I just dealt with publishers on my own."

"You look like hell," she said. "I do, too. I've been living mainly on coffee and cigarettes."

"I can't get over Rashawn's loss," Mickey said. "I'm the reason he was there. I tried to get him to look into the Consortium. He couldn't find anything, but he got a gig writing about Nathan Beale at the National Gospel Sing, railing against the legalization of weed. He was writing for something called *Cannabis Countdown.* That's what he was telling me the last time I saw him. He was a good kid. He would've gone as far as anybody can go in journalism nowadays. I can't say for sure, but I was probably the reason he got laid off at *The News-Free Press,* too. I'll never know, but he was trying to find somebody who would talk about the Consortium. Somebody probably heard about it and got him canned. I've got an idea about who it was. That's probably bullshit, too. It's just me trying to lessen my own guilt."

"How come you cared?" Marcia asked. "You were making good money. Writing good stories."

"I was worried about you."

"Then I guess I've got some of your friend's blood on my hands, too."

"How about you? How about Wade Sanderson?"

"From the second he said he killed Tripp Fallaw, I didn't care about him anymore," Marcia admitted. "In retrospect, what I liked about Wade was power. I knew he was a shitty person, and I guess we made a decent match. You never knew Tripp."

"All I knew about Sanderson was that he was an asshole and a thug," Mickey said. "The fact that you seemed to … love him … I figured that was my fault, too. I should've raised you right."

"Tripp was a loser," she said. "Flunked out of school. A hustler. The first time I met him, he was passing out something called parlay cards. Gambling, I reckon. But he was cute, and he was caring, and he was fun."

Between innings, they became aware of fans staring at them. They looked up. They were on the video board.

"Probably got us pegged as father and daughter," Mickey said. "We're supposed to kiss each other."

"Let's do it like I'm your mistress," she said.

Mickey leaned over. Marcia fell back. He kissed her on the lips. She waved her arms like a damsel in distress.

"That what they expected?" she asked.

"No. That was better."

Hickory scored several runs in the third inning. Kannapolis changed pitchers at least twice. The Crawdads scored six times, but Mickey and Marcia weren't paying much attention. They just noticed that the home side of the scoreboard had a six on it when the inning was over.

"Has anybody called you?" Mickey asked. "I mean about the shootings."

"No," she said. "Why would they? Nobody knew any of us was there."

"I guarantee there were surveillance cameras that showed you talking to Sanderson and then me talking to you."

"I should have known that."

"I figure nobody wants to know," Mickey said. "It's obvious everybody was bought and paid for. Local cops. The Consortium bought 'em all is my guess. Probably even Beale's security detail. The Secret Service would have inspected the place, known something about the post under the stage where Sanderson fired the shot that killed Beale. The SWAT team that took out the shooter in the hotel. That was too fast. Shit, I'm a sportswriter, and I could figure that out. I'm not sure about the security detail. They might have just let their guard down. Who'd have thought Nathan Beale would be assassinated at an all-white concert of Southern gospel?"

"Eight innocent people dead," Marcia replied. "One of them was the only black man there."

"One Secret Service agent was black. I expect it was just an accident, though," Mickey said. "The man shooting from the hotel was black. Ain't no way he singled out Rashawn. Rashawn just took off running and got killed when, whatever his name is, Yousseff Cameroon, was spraying the crowd."

Mickey choked up.

"I killed him as much as that dude did."

"Rites of passage, Daddy."

"What?"

"Rites of passage," Marcia said. "I took a walk on the wild side. I made it. We both made it. You got forced into it. I just loved getting stoned, and running off to L.A. on some wild adventure, like Tripp and me, and Wade Sanderson, were Kerouac and Neal Cassady, and maybe I was Joan Haverty, Jack's wife, but I fancied myself as more significant than her because, mostly, she just kept him drunk and drugged up, but, anyway, it seems incredibly stupid now."

"I reckon rites of passage always are," Mickey said.

THE END

AUTHOR'S ACKNOWLEDGEMENTS

What a tangled web I've weaved.

It occurred to me that *Don't Ask, Don't Tell* applies to more than gays in the military. That was the original germ of thought.

I watched numerous stories about innocent people being shot by police, and thought, what if they aren't all accidents? That led me to the notion of a vast conspiracy.

I watched the country change.

I wrote a general outline of a novel I wanted to write, started writing, and strayed far from the original premise.

I sat it aside and wrote two other novels.

I shaved about twenty percent of what I had.

I wrote an entirely new ending and wrangled with finding sense in the conglomeration that emerged.

Now I like it. It's ready. It's hardly the final word. Your evaluation is the one that matters.

Jim McLaurin, who could be a modern Mark Twain if he so desired, gave it the benefit of his editing prowess. He is, at this moment, the only human being I know personally who knows what's in it. The others are nameless and didn't want to publish it.

The people with whom I interact regularly play a role they hardly realize. Scenes in this book began in overheard conversations, lyrics from songs, snippets of novels, scenes from movies, plays from ballgames, and conversations with people I like and people I don't.

Monte Dutton

March 27, 2018

ABOUT THE AUTHOR

Monte Dutton is a resident of Clinton, South Carolina, and a graduate of Furman University. This is his eighth published work of fiction and fifteenth book. He is a free-lance journalist, amateur musician, and prolific blogger. He writes because he loves it, and it is most of what he knows how to do.

www.ingramcontent.com/pod-product-compliance
Lightning Source LLC
Chambersburg PA
CBHW070237200726
48293CB00005B/1661